Deborah Henry is a natural storyteller and she is far more. Her novel *The Whipping Club* is a compelling read, but it also seriously explores the terrible ways the world—as a society, as individuals—often fails its children. Most importantly, her book offers a searingly lovely vision of how wrongs can be made right. Deborah Henry is a splendid young novelist who deserves a wide audience.

— **Robert Olen Butler,** Pulitzer Prize-winning author of *A Good Scent from a Strange Mountain*

An intimate, assured first novel, the story of Marian McKeever and her child hidden by cruelty and custom. It rings with the authenticity of shame and courage. You can put it down but you will not forget it.

—**Jacquelyn Mitchard,** bestselling author of *The Deep End of the Ocean,* named by *USA Today* as one of the ten most influential books of the past 25 years

Deborah Henry's debut novel is a wonderful portrait of a world seldom depicted in fiction, that of a small Jewish enclave in 20th-century Ireland. Echoing Joyce's *Ulysses,* the novel nonetheless creates its own compelling vision, peopled by vivid characters and compelling voices. With near pitch-perfect dialogue, the story's long-buried secrets compel the reader forward in a way that is both intriguing and heart-wrenching. A new and exciting voice in fiction.

—**Michael White,** bestselling author of *Soul Catcher* and *Beautiful Assassin*

A hauntingly beautiful literary landscape. Henry writes with great passion, deep vulnerability and sharpest prose about perils and plights, joy and triumph. Commanding a winsome literary voice, Henry would go far to tell many a tale. And she should.

—**Da Chen,** bestselling author of *Colors of the Mountain* and *Sounds of the River*

Harrowing, haunting, and brilliantly written, Henry's stunner of a novel is about secrets, so-called sins, and the way even the deepest scars can begin to heal. So breathtakingly good it seems burned into your heart.

—**Caroline Leavitt,** *New York Times* bestselling author of *Pictures of You*

Set in 1960's Ireland, a family drama that unflinchingly confronts prejudice and violence in Catholic orphanages, in the ghettoized Jewish community, and in Northern Irish Troubles. The world's madness plays out in Marian and Ben's family. Through their secrets and lies come redemption and hope. Deborah Henry is a novelist who is fearless in her gaze and compassionate in her heart. This book is on fire.

—**Martine Bellen,** author of *The Vulnerability of Order*

Gripped me from the beginning. Henry beautifully evokes the terrifying journey in and out of church-run systems in a heart wrenching and lyrical manner. She creates a frighteningly authentic world of authority gone mad and the long term effects of abuse. Her provocative novel is very timely in today's Ireland which still suffers from the ghosts of those whose lives were destroyed, yet the book transcends and gives us the hope of the human spirit. Henry has a great future ahead of her. A beautiful writer and a stunning debut.

—**Alan Cooke,** Irish filmmaker and writer, winner of a 2009 Emmy for *Home*

Exquisitely written, unflinching and spare. Deborah Henry is a gifted storyteller. The steely realism of her prose, her fiercely drawn characters and startling plot twists make *The Whipping Club* one of those rare novels that linger in the mind long after the last page is turned.

—**Dawn Tripp,** Bestselling author of *Game of Secrets*

A story of survival, redemption, and the courage that is born of love. One of my favorite reads of the decade!

—**Susan Henderson,** author of *Up From the Blue*

THE WHIPPING CLUB

A NOVEL

DEBORAH HENRY

ts T. S. Poetry Press • New York

T. S. Poetry Press
Ossining, New York
Tspoetry.com

Cover image by Will Amato. willamato.com
Author photo, copyright Marion Ettlinger.

ISBN 978-0-9845531-8-1

Library of Congress Cataloging-in-Publication Data:
Henry, Deborah
        [Fiction.]
        The Whipping Club/Deborah Henry
        ISBN 978-0-9845531-8-1
        Library of Congress Control Number: 2012933293

The author and publisher wish to express their grateful acknowledgment
to the following publications, which first featured portions of this work:
The Smoking Poet, The Copperfield Review, and *The Litchfield Literary Review.*

for Brian
and our beloved Catherine, John & Sara

PART I

1 ~ 1957

MARIAN spent the morning in Dr. O'Connell's office. The room was frigid and she wore nothing but a threadbare gown. She did not look at him as he examined her but stared at the low chair in the corner. It was yellowed with wear, the kind of chair used in the classrooms at the Zion school where she taught. It seemed out of place here.

"I'm ringing your uncle," said Dr. O'Connell. "Nurse Dwyer will take you to my office when you're clothed."

Once Marian was ready, the nurse escorted her to Dr. O'Connell's office. A small diamond ring winked on the nurse's finger. The girl had a soft look, and Marian could see why she'd been asked to marry so young. She felt a strange kinship with this girl now, as if she wanted to share with her that they were travelling on similar paths. But then a surge of heat ran through her. She pushed high above her guilt, then returned to the nagging fear again. The Catholic self-loathing. She was a degenerate to have done the misdeed. She'd been taught better, hadn't she, but she had been unable to control her desires for Ben. No, she wasn't like her because the young nurse was a lady and ladies waited. The girl closed the door behind them and invited Marian to sit down while she herself remained standing, hovering by the door. It was then Marian realized the nurse wasn't there for comfort, but to keep her from running.

Marian gazed out the window. The broad avenue bustled with men carrying umbrellas, youngsters lugging school bags, and she would have given anything to be at home getting ready for work. She felt a sudden longing for her father. She needed his arms around her now, his smoky neck pressed against her nose, the comforting smell of his woodbines filling her up inside. He was a small, sturdy man with a big voice, and she could hear him telling her that the hard times would pass away, and she should rise above the inbred and useless shame, the way he used to whenever she'd gotten herself into trouble with the nuns. But this trouble was different and there was no rising above it. It was inside her and it was growing. Why hadn't she done something before this?

The door opened and her uncle, Father Brennan, entered. He thanked the nurse for her time as she scurried away. With a deep breath, he ran one hand through his thick hair and sat down. As good looking as Spencer Tracy, he could have played the part of a priest in the pictures, she'd told him after his first Mass at Loreto College Church last year. But he was acting no role then, nor now, and she knew she should not count on a familial smile to help her get through this conversation.

"Hello, dear." He gave her a grimace; his presence held no warmth.

"I'm sorry, Father," she said.

"Well, you're not married, Marian."

"I have a plan in place, though."

"Does the boy know the state he's put you in?"

"I didn't know until a few minutes ago."

"That's best, anyway. No need to involve more people into this mess. He's a Catholic?"

"No."

"No," Father Brennan said, nodding.

Marian pressed down her skirt. "I should ring Ben," she said.

"What, child?"

"I should ring Ben Ellis, the father."

"Ellis? Ellis," he repeated, and then paused. "I'm surprised he's not here, Marian."

"He loves me, Father."

"He loves *you*?" Her uncle sat back in his chair.

Marian looked down at her black boots, anger rising inside her. "I know he loves me. We're getting married. I'm meeting his parents tonight."

"Oh, you are? So when is this wedding, Marian?"

She looked hard at him. "Whenever we decide, Father."

"Listen, girl. Don't you be bold with me. I'm trying to help you. And your mother. She's never to know about this, you hear?"

Marian straightened in her chair.

"What you don't seem to understand, is that there is no *whenever you decide* anymore. You tossed that option long ago."

She'd known girls who had left quietly for London to see a doctor on their own and rid themselves of their trouble. The vision of their humiliation horrified her.

"You'll be ruined in Dublin if anyone finds out. There are only two options left." He lit a cigarette. "You can go to this boy right now, and tell him that you're pregnant. If he marries you immediately, and we don't know how this Johnny will react, you can have this child and start a life."

He took a long drag and blew the smoke upward. "I know this sounds rosy, but let me tell you, he'll resent you. And he'll resent the baby, as well. Further, whatever love's between you will be lost."

She could feel the drumming of blood in her chest.

"Because sometimes love is not enough, Marian. That's the truth."

"You don't know us, Father."

"Ah! But I do, Marian. I've seen it over and over. You think this baby will bind you together, but it won't. It'll burden you. I don't want to scare you, Marian, but I want you to fully understand your predicament."

"We'll withstand this, Father," she said, still growing hot as he spoke.

"This is not just an obstacle, Marian. It's a person you're going to have. Do you have any idea of the cost involved to raise a child? For God's sake, Marian, you're little more than a child yourself. How are you going to manage a job when you're getting up in the wee hours, night after night, sacrificing for this infant? Think straight. And what about this boy? What does he do for work?"

She was about to tell him but he waved her off with his hand.

"It doesn't matter. Whatever he does for a living, he'll lose his standing. Would he be needing a night job to make ends meet? Would you put him through that? These are tough times, Marian, look around you. Would you live with his parents? Ah, that's right! You're meeting them for the first time tonight." He shook his head.

"Marian, let me tell you about option two. I have a place in mind," said Father Brennan.

He leaned in close and when he spoke his voice was conspiratorial. It was the muted tone she remembered him using with her when she was a child and he sneaked her candy cigarettes.

"It's a gorgeous spot down the country. Great Oaks line the driveway. It's only available to the best families, Marian. I took it upon myself to call before I came over and these nuns—very kind nuns—have a bed available. They've agreed to hold the bed for one week as a favor to me."

"You're talking about giving it away?" A yet untried instinct drove her hand to the flat of her stomach.

"I'm talking about giving you a chance at happiness, Marian. If you really do love this man, you'll think this through. If you go to that man of yours, tell him your situation and he agrees to marry you immediately, you won't have my confidence but you'll have my blessing, you know that," he said. He stamped out the cigarette butt.

"Or option two," he continued, "and the far better decision. Let him marry you on his own terms, Marian. Trust me, dear, he'll thank you and you'll thank me someday, too. If you choose this, you don't mention the pregnancy. You never tell him. Instead, you come to me this Sunday and I'll bring you down to the lovely place."

She'd heard about those hideaways where the girls give up their babies and whisperings around Dublin about the wicked girls who had stained the world. Marian remembered the derogatory remarks about her friend Ceci, who mysteriously left secondary school and was never the same after that. She'd told Marian about the smell of watery oatmeal and about the iron bars in vertical rows, the invasive silence punctuated by the ping of knitting needles.

"One week to get married to this young man, or all the time you need to give him and yourself a proper start, are we clear?" he said.

"Yes, Father, we're clear. You have one week to marry us."

He gave her a sad smile. *He's just a lonely, old man,* she thought. *He might even be a virgin.* She pictured his evenings spent reading under that one lousy lamp in that small, one-room sublet. He would never understand what he'd never had.

Patting the back of her neck with a dampened paper towel hours later, Marian saw Principal Rosenberg on the school playground, making another assessment of the less experienced members of his staff.

"Come on, everyone. The bell's ringing," Marian said, ducking them into their classroom. She made her way down the school hall, taking a deep, calming breath of potter's clay in the air. The children put on their caps and coats, and soon came the parade of mothers chatting up and down Bloomfield Avenue as they collected their children.

Marian pretended to grade English papers after hours in the privacy of her classroom, and then studied Ben through the side window of the Zion School, his leg fidgety, his left hand tapping the school's black iron gate with his newspaper. She sighed in exhaustion, all too aware of his deliberate tardiness; tired, too, of all the elusive tactics the couple now employed to halt the spreading of more gossip. Slick auburn hair, strips of sideburns an inch and a half below his ears, a *Think Yiddish Dress British* red button pinned to his lapel, a paisley tie. Sure Ben Ellis was different. *An rud is annamh is iontach,* Marian thought. What is strange is wonderful.

"I spent the entire afternoon running to the ladies to hairspray my hair and look," she said, meeting him by the gate. "Your parents expect a serious schoolteacher and they're going to get a hot bird instead."

"Hotter than Maureen O'Hara. You look perfect," he said, casting a look at her as they continued together along the Zion School perimeter, blue hydrangeas still in bloom lining the red brick walk.

I'm not perfect, is what she thought. She paused. "Do you need me to be perfect?" She lingered in the inviting smell of his peppery aftershave.

"We have thirty minutes before sundown," he said. He took her hand and they walked to the left, down Bloomfield Avenue and on to the South Circular Road, their steps quick and bold, a faint autumnal chill in the air.

They had only five blocks left to walk when Marian started to panic. She had strolled through Little Jerusalem twice before, but never at sunset, never on the Sabbath, and now everything felt teeming and ancient and threatening in its foreignness. Across the street, ladies in dark kerchiefs huddled around a bucket of thrashing mackerel. Men in black hats dragged lines of children by the wrist down the pavement. The Hebrew letters in storefronts and candlelit windows made her think of shattered tombstones, graveyards filled with crows.

She clung firmly to Ben.

"We're almost there," he said.

She tried to smile. Three girls chattering in Yiddish glanced as they passed by and she wondered if they were talking about her: the pale goy clutching one of theirs. But he wasn't theirs, and she forced herself to remember this; Ben was more hers than anyone's.

"Let's grab a raisin babka from Erlich's," he said. "Tatte loves them." Ben opened the storefront door and the sour smell of pickled herring made Marian nauseous. She told him she'd wait outside.

"Are you okay?" he said.

She gave him a quick kiss. "I'm grand."

He walked into the store and entered the frenetic line. Marian looked around her at the crowds. Everyone seemed to be rushing, trying to get home before dark. One after another, men tossed their newspapers in the trash. A woman carrying sweet cakes bumped against her and hurried off. She felt like an obstruction standing immobile on the street corner, strangely invisible yet scrutinized. She turned toward Ben and watched him thumb through his wallet, noticed his clumsy mess of hair, the way the thin, brass arms of his eyeglasses hugged his temples. He drew close to the cash register. The lining of his pocket hung against his coat after he retrieved his wallet, and Marian felt an impulse to reach across the store and tuck it back in place. He turned to check on her, and when he spotted her on the curb he gave her a wink.

Thank you, Ben, she thought, looking through her own reflection in the glass. *Please.*

Marian and Ben crossed Lennox Street in silence and made their final left to Portobello Road, a cobblestone street with stucco homes, moisture eating away their paint.

"We're here," Ben whispered. Clematis vines drooped from a trellis against the side of the house, and it occurred to Marian that the plant was dying from a lack of attention.

Ben gave her an embarrassed smile. "None of the Ellises plant seeds well," he said.

She touched her belly, imagining the cells forming inside her to create another living being, another person, who was theirs. *Tell him,* she thought. *Tell him right now and forget Father Brennan's selfish offer.* They could run off, be married in London. It was their life. For a moment, all her angst about meeting Ben's parents seemed trivial. She must tell him about the baby, they should decide together what to do. But now Ben was opening the door.

She squeezed his hand as they entered his parents' foyer, the house warm with the garlic smell from the cholent she'd heard schoolchildren talk about at Zion. She felt her nervousness returning and reminded herself that she had been invited to this Sabbath dinner.

Low heels tapped across the ceiling.

"They must be getting ready," Ben said. "Come and sit in the living room," he said, and handed her the bakery box. Yarmulke caps lay in a glass bowl on the coffee table.

"Are you all right, then? I've told Tatte all about us. It's the Mammy we'll be telling tonight. And I'm sure Mammy will love you, too. Just a case of the frayed nerves, you have."

There was some truth to this prognosis. Sabbath dinner with his parents would be difficult under any circumstance. She recalled his frayed nerves the one time she'd brought him to her empty home. He'd sat in the kitchen, gazing at the wooden crucifix hanging on the wall. *Judaism, Catholicism, and Marianism,* he'd joked—that was his trinity. *Especially Marianism,* he added quietly, pulling her closer until they kissed. Her eyes fixed on the crucifix.

"I'll just be a moment," he said, and he walked through the foyer, went into the toilet and closed the door.

She sat on the couch with her hands folded around the gift box in her lap and looked around. The dining room was set for four. A white lace tablecloth and silver platters adorned the table. They'd gone to great efforts to create an elegant impression, she thought, and sunk her black shoes into the maroon living room carpet. Family pictures stood on every side table: Ben graduating from Trinity College; a rabbi's arm around Ben's shoulder at his *Bar Mitzvah*; Ben as a little cowboy with holsters. She wondered if their baby would be a boy, if it would look like him.

If her ma knew where she was, she would be livid. Marian stood erect, raw blisters rubbed against the heels of her stiff new shoes. *It is strange how life turns out,* she thought. Growing up there wasn't a Jew around her, and here she was, in a Jewish home, about to marry Ben. She stood stock still, staring into the foyer, wishing she could stop the sweat from dripping down the underarms of her new dress. Marian heard the toilet flush and Ben walked towards her into the living room. They surveyed the dining room, a platter of chopped liver and unleavened bread on the table, candles ready to be lit. She would try a little, even though she knew the breadsticks tasted like dog biscuits, worse than the Host.

"We are here!" Ben called up the stairs. He took Marian's hand. "Mammy! Tatte!"

Mr. Ellis tiptoed down the staircase, like a pirouetting bear. Marian could see the blueprint of Ben's face in his father's.

"Excuse us," Mr. Ellis said. "We're off form at the moment."

"Why don't you rest a bit longer," Mrs. Ellis said as she came downstairs. Mr. Ellis didn't budge. She gave Marian a polite smile. She was a delicate, slightly hunched woman; her posture reminded Marian of a cursive C. She wore an evergreen knit suit with a circular emerald pin on her lapel. The sharp violet and musk smells from Old Yardley perfume overwhelmed the living room as the matron entered.

"We are delighted to meet any friend of Benjamin's," Mr. Ellis said to Marian. He clapped Ben on the back and placed a black velvet yarmulke on Ben's head.

"Friends?" Mrs. Ellis let out a hard laugh. "Since when do friends hold hands?"

"Come, Marian. We'll eat. We're all friends," Mr. Ellis said. "You'll call us Sam and Beva, won't you?" he said.

Marian approached Beva and held out their gift. The woman took the bakery box, said thank you, but added something about Sam being on a strict diet. From the kitchen came Beva's maid with a tray of glasses filled with white wine.

"That was Patsy," Ben explained as Beva and the maid returned to the kitchen. "She's the *Shabbos goy*. She shuts off the electric lights, puts out the fire when it gets dark."

"She looks like she could be my cousin," Marian whispered before Beva returned and instructed them to stand behind their chairs.

"Benjamin, would you like to start the prayers?" Beva said.

Ben nodded in silence and bowed his head, his eyes shut. Marian watched him almost sing the prayers, oscillating slightly, and she was intrigued and desirous of his belief in something that she could never grasp. Beva and Sam listened, their heads bent, and all of this comforted her somehow. Catholics knelt and the Jews stood, yet it occurred to Marian that the two groups were more similar than different in their devotion.

"*L'chayim!* Cheers." Ben raised his glass as he finished.

"*Gut Shabbos,*" Beva said. She kissed her son.

Marian sipped her wine. "Sweet," she said.

"It's kosher. I'm afraid you'll have to live with the *matzoh*, too," Beva said, passing the unleavened bread. "I made salmon, Marian. Is that okay with you?"

"That's grand," Marian said. "Catholics eat fish every Friday. It's the standard."

"So, fish was the right choice. You see, Benjamin? We're not the only ones with religious duties. Catholics have rules coming out of their ears."

"Oh, there are rules. So many of them," Marian agreed. She recalled privately her own litany of the Saints: *Pray for us. Pay for us.
There's a better way for us. Give us a cuss, your mouth is puss.* How she'd
giggle as a girl with her friends, chanting this until the nuns marched
over and twisted their little ears.

"Every religion follows rules," Beva said. "Am I right, Sam? What else
holds people together?"

Sam shrugged and gave a warm smile to Marian.

"Tradition," Beva said. "You go to church; we go to synagogue.
We keep a kosher home. We have different plates for different times.
I bet you didn't know that, Marian."

Marian smiled and pretended that Ben hadn't told her about the
meat and dairy dishes. Between Ben and her students, she knew
more than Beva realized. A black radio sat silent on a plastic tablecloth, and Marian wished Beva would turn on a little music but
guessed there would be no music after sundown.

"*Mazel tov* to Da Valera on getting those desperate families visas
into Ireland, Benjamin," Beva said. "I read your commentary. *Mazel.*"

"They tried for ten, but five families were better than none."

"Don't you forget that," she said, pointing a finger at him. "If you
read one book this year, read *The World of Sholom Aleichem.* Beautifully done about Jewish *shtetls* in Russia. I don't know if Benjamin
told you, Marian, but we're all refugees from Eastern Europe. All of us
were thrown out of somewhere. It was either leave or have my father
and brothers waste their lives suffering as nobodies in the Tsar's Army."

Beva passed the salmon.

"What did it matter? They wouldn't let them out. Maybe because
I was a girl, and I was fair, only I got out."

"Beva, don't get yourself–"

"No. She should know this. I wrote lots of letters to everyone, and
to the Minister of Justice. I was desperate to get all of them visas.
I was told no." Beva lowered her voice. "My mother died. My father
died over there. And still, they wouldn't let my brothers enter Ireland. They were killed like animals during the *Shoah.*"

"I'm so sorry," Marian said, and she meant it, but she heard something accusatory in Beva's tone.

"My two smart brothers, in Lithuania," she said, pointing at Marian. "From then on, no one stops my family."

"Mammy, nobody's going to hurt you anymore." Ben looked worried. No, compassionate. It was what drove him to become a journalist. It was funny, Marian loved the same things in Ben that his mother did. She wanted to say this to Beva, to create a bridge between them, but she sensed too much in the way.

"The war's over," Sam broke in, potato bits in his teeth. "The Irish didn't kill your relatives."

"The Irish didn't do anything at all. Let's face facts," Beva retorted.

"Listen, the Irish have been very good to the Jews. They've no trouble here in Dublin. Enough talk about the war," Sam said. "If you have to talk about something, talk about the salmon. It's divine."

"It is lovely," Marian said.

"Brain food. Lithuanian Jews have a thirst for education, am I right, Benjamin?"

"There were two scholarships given by the Department of Education the year Marian was leaving Secondary School. Only two. Marian received one of them," Ben bragged.

"You must be very proud, Marian," Beva said, passing platters.

"She was the smartest girl in her form," Ben continued.

"Ben." Marian rolled her eyes.

"The first one in her family to graduate college. The first one to become a schoolteacher."

"A twist of fate," Beva said and laughed. "God knows she hasn't been inside a temple, has no idea what the Jews are about, and yet gets hired at the Zion School."

Marian felt the shrill sound of tin whistles racing through her.

"But I'm sure she's a good Catholic and understands the profound implications of her religion, am I right, Marian?"

"No, not really," Marian said, and took a sip of her wine. She made a point to meet Beva's stare.

"Forget religion. Did Benjamin tell you he got a raise?" Sam said.

"Tatte, I was saving that. I was going to tell you later tonight," Ben said, taking Marian's hand. "We're going to make it, Marian."

"Don't tell me you two talk in the *we* and *next year we'll do this or that!*" Beva said.

Ben dropped his fork and stood. Positioned behind Marian's chair, he spoke.

"I have an announcement," he said. "Mammy and Tatte. Marian and I are in love, as you might quite rightly have figured out. We want to be married."

Silence from the yenta at last.

Beva stared at her son and then at Marian. Marian stared right back at her. "Benjamin, who do you think you're inviting to such a wedding?"

Nobody answered. Marian rose now, standing close to Ben.

"Where would you do it?" his mother asked, coming closer, clutching his arm for balance.

"A civil ceremony. Nice and quiet," he said. Ben looked at Marian, and she nodded her approval. Father Brennan's words came back at her, but he was wrong. Ben was enough, and she was enough, and they were more than enough together. She would tell Ben later tonight about their baby, and they would more than manage.

"No canopy? No breaking of a glass? I'm sorry, it's not a real wedding without the *chuppa*," Beva said.

"How about I'll break a glass here, right now?" Ben said.

"Don't be smart."

"When would you do this, Marian?" Sam asked.

"Very soon."

"I was thinking in May," Ben agreed.

"May?" Marian said.

"I've found this house. I think I'll be able to put a down payment on it by mid-April. I have a raise now. That's my surprise."

He looked worried as if he could sense her disappointment.

"That okay?" he asked into her ear.

"We can talk about that later, Ben." Marian turned to Beva. "Please try to accept it. I know it's hard."

"She knows it's hard," Beva said. "I wanted our son, our only child, to marry a Jewish girl. Is that hard to understand?"

"You know mixed marriages are difficult," Sam said, looking from her to Ben.

"Well, of course, they are," Beva said.

"No doubt you'll come across some hard times," Sam said to them.

"And where will you live?" Beva said. "You can't stay in this district. You'll be stared at."

"I was thinking of Donnybrook," Ben said, giving Marian's hand a squeeze.

"Full of *goyim,*" Sam said.

"It's a mixed neighborhood, Tatte."

"And what about the *kinder*? Did you think of them? Your children will suffer. Neither Jew nor Christian. They won't belong. You have a lot of *chutzpah*, Marian," Beva said.

"Excuse me?" Marian said.

"A lot of nerve."

"And your son, Mrs. Ellis. What has he got?"

"He's the big savior. Had to do his part to raise educational standards for the Zion School children. And boom, there you are, like out of a Doris Day movie." The woman threw her arms in the air as she walked into the living room, stared out the bay window.

"Mammy, let me ask you this" Ben said. "Did you marry Tatte for love?"

"Of course," Beva said.

"Remember how you felt, being in love?"

"Not often," Beva said.

"Can't you try to understand?" Ben said.

"I'm sorry. It's very different."

"You know, Mammy. I dream every night of receiving yours and Tatte's blessing. You're robbing me of that."

"And I'm being robbed of a good son. And Jewish grandchildren."

"It's a new world, Beva," Sam said, rising slowly. "They're freer in their thinking than we were."

"Hogwash," Beva said. "I'm calling Sylvie Rosenblatt tomorrow. Her daughter's in love with him, she told me. They'd make a good *shiddach*. They'd be a great match. Talk to him, Sam, before it's too late. Tell him that a *shiksa* colleen–"

"*Schweig!*" Sam followed after her into the foyer.

"Mammy!" Ben raised his voice, holding tight to Marian's hand.

Beva turned. "Let me just ask the two of you. Do you think Marian's mother wants–"

"I'm going," Marian decided, reaching for her handbag.

"If she goes, I go," Ben said. "Mammy, apologize. Look what you've done."

"What I've done? What have I done? You're the one who brought her here!"

"Shut it!" Tatte shouted, holding the sides of his head. He gripped the staircase, then leaned on Ben's shoulder.

"Sam!" Mrs. Ellis leaned over her husband; his eyelids were opening and shutting, and she began slapping his flabby cheeks. "Benjamin, call Dr. Eisen."

"No doctors. Marian, get me a glass of water, would you," Sam said.

Marian turned back to the dining room, grabbed a glass of wine from the table, and hurried to the foyer washroom to dump it and return with water.

"Listen, you're a smart girl. I'm trying to save you both from a lot of pain. The two of you, it'll never work."

Marian looked past Beva, watched Mr. Ellis.

I don't have to listen to this a second longer, Marian decided, and fumbled the glass onto the foyer table. "Ben, take care of your da," she said. "And ring me later."

"Wait. I'll be right with you," Ben said, as he helped his father shuffle to the living room couch.

She left the house and came out onto the street. The cold air from the canal washed over her, a relief from the heat in that house.

What had she been thinking, waltzing over there, hoping for their approval? Had she really deluded herself into thinking that teaching at the Jewish Day School would be enough for his parents to accept her? And what about Ben assuring her that they would love her? In the bay window Ben tried to comfort his parents. Marian wanted to protect him from the pain they were causing him. There was something about the exhausted look in his eyes, something she couldn't pinpoint, something simple and complex; she loved this essence of him. But a complex relationship is one thing. Complications are another, Father Brennan would say.

Ben rushed outside.

"I wish you had warned me about her, Ben."

"I had no idea this would happen. Tatte told me he'd handle everything. Marian, I'm sorry."

"I'm sorry, too," she said. "Your da's splendid."

He was perspiring, and she reached out and wiped his forehead. She felt dizzy and confused, but one thing was certain. Ben loved her, and she loved him. She could see the excruciating love he had for her; it was right there on his troubled face.

"I'm going home," she said.

He looked across the narrow street and wiped the back of his neck. Neighbors peered at them from doorways; small children in upstairs windows made funny faces at them.

"I can walk home alone tonight," Marian said. "You help your da now."

Through the bay window she watched his mother give Tatte a sip of water.

"I'm going with you," Ben said.

"I know you are, but not now, Ben. Go and straighten out your parents. Please."

Marian looked down at her swollen ankles. "Not so perfect now, huh?" she said.

"I've loved you from the start, Marian. Don't worry about them," he said. His parents were going at it still, just audible from where they stood. "My mother's all talk, but she'll come around."

"You promise me you'll marry me, and you'll love me and no one else, so help you God?" Marian said.

He grinned at her in that shy way of his. "I promise."

"I've been wanting to tell you something, Ben."

"Yeah?"

She put her hands in his pockets, and he drew her close.

"I'm going away with my uncle, Father Brennan. You've heard me talk about him."

"Sure. The priest."

"Right." The fabric of his shirt felt soft against her skin and she leaned into him.

"What do you mean by it, Marian?" Ben asked.

Marian bit her lip. "Ring me later. We can talk about it then."

"But where are you going?"

"It's a rest I'm going for. A lovely rest."

She laid her head on his shoulder. She would do the right thing, she thought. She'd not force him into it; she'd not rush him. They weren't ready to take on anymore than what they had. They'd all be better off, even him; she had decided now that it was a him. In her mind, she placed their baby somewhere far away from here, far from this street corner, far from the winding streets of Little Jerusalem, from Dublin, from the western mountains, far away from Ireland all together. She imagined him somewhere full of light and warmth where he would have a better life. This would be her gift. Someday he'd thank her for it. She slipped out of Ben's arms and walked toward home.

Yarmulke caps rested with the Easter eggs in a cut crystal bowl, fabric swatches beside painted curios. Marian rearranged the assortment and then dusted the photograph on the mantelpiece of Johanna as a toddler, petite and smooth-skinned, a bow in her silky hair, a golliwog doll in her arms. In the phone cradled to Marian's ear the school principal admonished the girl. Marian agreed to Mr. Hinckley's request for an afternoon conference and hung up the phone with an audible sigh. She brushed the image of her daughter's face. This was only her daughter's third year and already she had been called in twice on account of her antics. Why was Jo acting out? Marian listened to the *tap, tap, rap* of her pumps against their oak floor as she shouldered the swinging door into the kitchen. Through the bay window, the wisteria cascaded over the iron railings enclosing their backyard. She took a moment to admire the effect; she had interlaced the waif-like vines back in the first week at their new home. So much had changed since marrying Ben Ellis in 1957. For the better— though she wondered if anything would ever shake the graying veil over Dublin.

"*Póg mo thóin,*" she spoke aloud. "Kiss my ass." She slapped her butt at an imagined Principal Hinckley and folded her dust rag into a perfect square. *Nothing will be perfect. Not for me. Not for anyone. Not ever.*

Marian swiped the Loreto Church of Christ Mass cards her ma had taped to the fridge and put them in the junk drawer. She took a cigarette from Ben's Players pack and went to smoke it underneath the white trellis in the garden. She stared at the frozen spot where an extravaganza of zucchini and tomato plants, scallions and parsley, might grow later in the year. For a few moments, she felt something dead inside her, something vague and untouchable, and she stared out into the garden without really seeing. Everybody has problems. She wasn't the only one. Hidden inside the red and brick homes, behind the perfectly painted doors, there were problems. She looked at the weighty rose climbers drooping over the gates of a brownstone across the way. She noticed the thorns. The vegetables were lovely, too, but underneath the soil there were grubs mixed in with the roots.

Ben had asked her last night to redouble her efforts toward Johanna. "God, what?" she'd said. *Johanna asks too many questions. She talks too much.* She didn't remember talking as much at ten years old. She was exhausted from her daughter. Was she alone in this, too? Her own ma came to mind. As a child, Marian believed her ma would have preferred a more ladylike daughter, someone quieter. She stamped out the butt and threw it in the garden trash bin before reentering the house. Maybe she and Johanna were more similar than she realized. Letting out another sigh, she weaved back into the foyer, touched the blue violas she'd pinned to a white beret and slanted it over her yellow-gold curls, courtesy of Miss Clairol, shimmer blonde #33. She loved these blonde colors much better than her natural Orphan Annie look.

You can't keep the McKeever in you down, Da would have told her. *Sure, you're a regular Marian McKeever, better looking than any Marilyn Monroe,* he might have said.

She slipped on her cotton gloves as she started down the four steps of their Georgian townhouse. She noticed a threesome of young mothers from the neighborhood talking codswallop by the news-agent on the corner. Their necks craned when they saw her like the unfashionable ostriches they were. Ostriches without any pretty feathers. They had gray woolen coats and identical black nursemaid shoes. All holy Joes, they feigned busyness as she drew nearer, ending their blather abruptly, casually crossing the street. They'd probably been talking shite about her and Ben, and she knew the lawdy-daws would all be relieved to see them both leave town. She would be happier, too. But the more she felt the sting of their rejection, the angrier she became and the more she resolved to stay put. She was happy and happily married for over ten years, and a mother as well. She was just like the women she chatted with in Dolan's greengrocers, the ones who seemed so casually confident about everything.

She had her father, God rest him, to thank for her inner strength. He'd be proud of her today. From the beginning, he made sure she went to the best schools. Somehow he talked her way into Loreto College, with the big back garden and grass courts and the respect the nuns offered middle-class graduates of the institution. The National School right next door would not do for his girl. And whenever the nuns complained about "Marian's boldness," he'd not flog her. Rather, he whipped the nuns with his tongue, and took her by the hand, out for a day at Sheridan's pub, where he drank Guinness and she ate gobstoppers all afternoon. They laughed and told his mates about the grievous expression on a nun's face when he praised his clever Marian. She had a right to question and receive a decent answer from a teacher. She wasn't bold, she was brilliant, he told the nuns; he reminded them who was paying their salary. He took her in his arms, told her that the hard times would pass away. He held her there in the pub, the rest of the world be damned. He struggled, she knew, driving that taxi, not drinking as much as he would have liked, to give her the new dress and the new books to keep up with the middle-class kids on her street.

When they called Marian to come down to the bar and identify her da, she was twenty, just two years from graduating from University College. Why did he have to go and die before seeing her graduate from college, she wanted to know. She'd always have the picture in her head of Da lying outside of Murray's bar, in the alley across from the busy intersection of Parnell and O'Connell Streets, there on the North Side. Thrown out of his taxi into the alley by hooligans, a typically brutal brawl, the guards had said. Hard to control bar fights from getting out of hand, they said, and dismissed the case. He owed some money, his mates whispered to her. The hooligans bullied him, beat him with sticks to his skull. She felt the dried blood, sticky in his hair, and she lay there beside him, rubbing his head, helping him into a calm sleep.

Down the block, Marian admired Mrs. Parker's home, her toddlers playing hide-and-seek in their yard. There was nothing more
enjoyable than a cigarette and a saunter in this neighborhood. The
only thing missing in this pristine setting was perhaps a bit more ca-
maraderie. She had some friends, mothers of Johanna's school chums.
Though if she were honest, they were little more than acquaintances.
Nothing went deeper than ordinary talk about their children's lives.
The only one who ever dropped in on her unannounced was her own
mother. But this was not a drop-in-on-someone neighborhood, like
she was used to. She pretended not to peer into Mrs. Parker's back
garden, fighting an urge to tiptoe across the lawn and sneak a peek
into the flower beds hidden behind the wall. No time to look now,
anyway. Ben promised he would meet her at the school for the
appointment with Principal Hinckley, and Marian didn't want Ben, who
would no doubt be swayed by the principal, to arrive before she did.

Marian passed through the gothic-style railings around the
grounds perimeter of the Muckross Park House School, centuries-
old weeping willows wearing their vines like Victorian gowns. A large
statue of Saint Michael stared down at her from an archway. She
climbed the intimidating front stairs and braced herself.

Stepping into Mr. Hinckley's office, she was again amazed that
such a dramatic space—the highest of ceilings, crown moldings of
naked cherubs, floor to ceiling windows that cried out for dark velvet, a never-used mosaic fireplace—remained a cold, drab setting.
Everybody had problems beneath the surface but this man seemed to
create problems for himself. Getting his gander up over the antics of
a couple of kids in the schoolyard. She'd like to tell him off.

She moved closer to Hinckley's desk and received only a cough from
the geezer. Some things never changed. Not even the Beatles would be
able to shake the dust off this place. There was always some crotchety
grouch behind a desk. A nun, a priest, an ordinary man, it didn't matter
where you went to school in dreary Dublin. She was tired of all the dirty
whites on the school walls, wanted to paint his office a delicious cranberry and watch the light play off the high ceiling.

"Received a call from Miss Harpin saying Johanna is stuck in the principal's office." Marian raised her eyebrows at Mr. Hinckley. "What seems the trouble this time?"

"Have a seat, Mrs. Ellis."

"I'm fine standing."

Johanna slouched in a leather chair, her shins streaked with dirt, her brown knit knee socks round her ankles. The bow that sat prettily in her mahogany hair this morning now dangling from the pocket of her jumper. She sat up, but kept her head down, dark lashes fanning sea-green eyes. Full of dance and trouble, she hid nothing with those eyes. The sullen maroon skirt and striped tie of her uniform did not suit her. A handful of teachers had already remarked that she was "extremely playful," as if that was a bad thing. Johanna's exuberance, what Marian would call charisma, had been a challenge early on. She couldn't walk, couldn't even crawl into a room quietly. She would never go unnoticed.

"It seems there's been an incident," Hinckley began, his fingers entwined, his beefy thumbs tapping together as if to music.

What'd she do, put a frog down your pants or something?

"The suspense is killing me," Marian said and turned toward Ben, who just then hurried into the room, his hair a mop-top. Bulging from his suit pocket was a journalist's handkerchief, what Marian called his crumpled white pad of paper.

"Mr. Ellis." Hinckley nodded and continued, "It seems Johanna has been caught calling a couple of the other boys and girls in third class very bad names."

"What!" Marian exclaimed. She put her hands to her mouth in mock horror.

Ben squeezed Marian's arm. "Johanna?"

"Only after I'd been called names, Da."

"Let me see your palms, Jo, dear," Marian said.

Johanna stared at her hands as Marian turned them over. Short red streaks engraved her palms.

"I was a first year teacher myself, and I don't believe in hitting."

"Now there was no harm done, Mrs. Ellis. You can see that plainly," Hinckley said. "A tap to the palm is all any of them receive here." The principal coughed.

"If she called them names, you can be sure there's a reason. Tell us what happened, Jo?"

"Jimmy Barker called me a slimy Jew lover, and then some kids told me and Anne-Marie that Catholics were gik."

"Who did?" Hinckley clenched his chubby hands.

"Jimmy Barker did, sir," Jo repeated. "And Libby Higgins started them yelling gik at me."

Marian looked to Ben now. "We were told Muckross avoided this nastiness."

She took Johanna out of the chair and fixed her bow back into her shoulder-length hair.

"Sure, there are at least two versions to every story," Ben began, making light of the situation, even trying to assist Mr. Hinckley now. "And what did you call them, Johanna?" Ben pressed his daughter. Marian widened her eyes, and Ben swallowed and turned away from her incredulous look.

"Proddies," Jo said, her eyes peeking at Hinckley's reaction, a Protestant man, born and raised.

"And?" Mr. Hinckley said, a squint in his heavy-lidded eyes.

"That's all," Jo said, but Marian suspected she was fibbing. She'd only called them ugly proddies this time, perhaps. (Last time she'd confessed to saying they had pooly coming out of their mouths. She'd kicked Jimmy three times, too, with her Mary Janes, though only after he had thrown dirt at her and told her slimy Jews killed the Lord.)

"Are you sure that's all?" Ben asked.

Johanna nodded.

"Ah, you owe Mr. Hinckley here, and those children, an apology," Ben said.

"I don't see Jimmy Barker or the others in here," Marian said.

"Jimmy Barker and Libby Higgins have been duly reprimanded,

Mrs. Ellis," Hinckley said. "They've already been picked up by their parents."

"Let's not have any more incidents with the pointer, shall we?" Marian said.

"Mrs. Ellis," Hinckley said, uncrossing his hands. "This is an open, well sought-after school."

"Come on, Marian," Ben said, taking her by the arm. "It's not worth it," he whispered. "What do you say, Johanna?"

"I'm sorry. Thank you for teaching me the right way, Mr. Hinckley." Marian squeezed Jo's waist and led her down the hall.

"Why did you interrupt me?" Marian scolded Ben as they stepped out into the sun.

"You have to know when to pick your battles," he said.

"Sometimes you have to give someone like him a taste of his own medicine, Ben. You have to fight when it comes to your kids. Do you not feel it in your blood?"

Johanna walked out in front of them, managing to buckle her leather satchel as she looked back at the school building.

"Hold up, Jo," Ben called, and Johanna stopped.

"What really happened today?" he asked when he and Marian caught up.

"Da, today my teacher asked me if I was Jewish."

Ben looked at Marian. They had prepared their answer long ago. "I'm Jewish. Ma is Catholic. And people say you are what your mother is, so you're Catholic. Technically. If someone asks. But really you're a blend of me and your ma."

"There's another Jewish kid in my class. And her sister's a sixth year," Jo announced.

"What's their last name?" Ben asked.

"I don't know. I think her name is Hedda Bernstein."

"There are a few Jewish families in Donnybrook. We should invite them over," Ben suggested. Marian gave him a vague nod. Both of them knew full well any invitation would likely be refused.

"Stay on the pavement," Marian called as Johanna skipped ahead.

Their daughter had the agility of a much older girl but only average maturity, and the combination was troublesome. "Sure, she's quick as a whip," Ben recently bragged while they played in the expanse of their front yard. "Can throw the ball, and'll be coming with Da to the tennis courts soon."

Marian sighed. The start of another afternoon, shaky from Jo's mischief. But she reminded herself the Convent school would have given Jo a licking she'd remember.

Ben kissed her cheek, took her gloved hand. The air was gentle this April. It was warm and lovely walking along Mount Eden Road, the cherry blossoms in bloom, and the soft wind on their faces.

"I also told Libby that she's fat, even though she's a rail," Jo called out.

"You did?" Ben said, a perturbed surprise in his voice.

"Gran told me Protestants don't eat as good as Catholics, 'cause they're stingy."

"Well, Gran is wrong," Marian said, thinking about her mother, always venting in one way or another against Marian's marriage to Ben.

"Our little Johanna has a lot of *chutzpah*," Marian said.

"Sure, she's got *chutzpah* from you," Ben replied.

"From me?" Marian laughed.

"From you," Ben said. "Just ask Bubbe," he added without thinking, and he looked immediately sorry.

"*Chutzpah?*" Johanna shouted, apparently liking the feel of the word in her mouth. "I thought *chutzpah* was a Jewish thing."

"You can be Catholic and have *chutzpah*," Ben told her. "You can be anybody. And children should be seen and not heard. Go on ahead now, but slowly."

Marian studied Ben in his embarrassment, the way he scrunched up his nose, the way he shuffled along, a cigarette hanging from his soft wide mouth, the way his squinting eyes talked to hers. She reminded herself that he'd been full of *chutzpah*, too—at the start. She took his arm as Johanna hopscotched ahead on their quiet street of red and brown brick homes, the smell of lilacs beckoning as she admired the plants lounging beside private iron gates.

"You look like one of them stewardesses," Ben muttered. He lit another cigarette and gave her the look.

"You're no Humphrey Bogart," she said, tossing back her blonde wavy head.

"You're better than Bacall, baby," he said and she laughed.

They approached their neighbor Mrs. O'Rourke, with her stingy, strict face, and Marian thought what a pity she is so tight, her brown hair cut short above her heart-shaped face. And she's no Twiggy, either, not in those drab clothes. "A bit Mary Hick, she is," Marian whispered into his ear.

"Shh," Ben whispered back. "I know a few things."

Mrs. O'Rourke turned toward them, and they all nodded their unspoken hello.

"Mr. O'Rourke missed work again, poor man," Marian said when she was sure they were out of earshot. "And Mrs. O'Rourke never looks happy. She's completely fixed in her ways: nine o'clock Mass every morning, the grocers on Tuesdays, the fish market on Fridays, His Drunken Highness on Saturday afternoons. Even their lovely twins don't seem to brighten her pinched face."

"Marian, I heard yelling a few weeks ago and went outside to see them sitting on their stoop. Mr. O'Rourke explained that his first wife died in childbirth in Cork, giving birth to Anna and Rona. Nine years ago, he was alone until your Mary Hick," he whispered, "Barbara Koliknova, his first wife's sister, left Poland. Sacrificed her own future to raise the girls."

"I didn't know," Marian said. It occurred to her that the woman was too sad to smile.

"Always give people the benefit of the doubt," Ben said.

"Thank you, Mr. Reporter." Marian rolled her eyes.

"Ma?" Johanna took her hand.

"Yes, love?"

"Can you come pick me up the next time alone?" Jo pulled her down close and whispered, "Promise next time can be between us?"

"Hopefully there won't be a next time, okay?"

Marian eked out a smile as Jo tiptoed towards Anna and Rona, and then the three girls raced into the O'Rourke's backyard.

Ben touched Marian's waist, and then moved his hand lower on her hip as they stood on the front steps to their glossy blue door and watched Mrs. O'Rourke pick up her garden shears and go inside. Marian took a cigarette from Ben's shirt pocket as they ducked into the house and leaned against the oak-stained door closing it behind them.

Ben pressed his body close in to hers and lit her cigarette. She exhaled as he loosened the white sash around her rayon shirtdress and let it fall to the floor. Moving with him to the drawing room beyond the front hall she quickly extinguished the fag, and together they walked clumsily, arms entwined, up the wide oak stairs. Resting against the stair-landing window, they kissed and kissed and then kissed some more. Marian glanced out the small window to see Mrs. O'Rourke cleaning her kitchen before they fled up the rest of the stairs to their bedroom. Through their open window they could hear the music of the girls' high, pretty voices. Marian kicked a copy of *Ulysses* under the bed and out of the way.

"Your ma'd have your head for that smut," he said.

"That's why it's kept under the bed," she said, falling onto the patchwork eiderdown.

"Ah," he said. "We'll have to keep the smut from the kids as well." He looked through the window, making sure Johanna was still outside in their neighbor's yard. "Another child would be welcome, no?" he said and held her. She looked away, not willing to talk about that again right now.

They made love quickly, before he had the buttons of her dress undone, though Marian sensed that Johanna's nearness was just the excuse for its brevity. Once, she had asked Ben if he thought she was a disappointment. Of course not, he had said, ever the one in the dark.

She breathed in the lilac scent from the fresh cuttings on their consignment sale bureau, and Ben lit a cigarette. Cool air flowed in as she lay there, and with it the earthy smell of newly-turned soil. She pulled herself together knowing she had to make something for dinner, not having had the time to make it to the market because of the day's detour. She considered Ben during his office hours, having coffee with someone or other and she suddenly resented him his busy workday away from all the boredom. But there was something more there, too. Oddly, it was the inner calm he exuded that annoyed her more than anything else. He was too focused for a wandering mind like hers, which always led to some level of discontent. She picked up his notepad from the nightstand, read something scribbled about lung cancer and its possible connection to cigarette smoking, and turned to gaze at the pale chipped ceiling.

"How's my favorite journalist?" she said after a moment.

He squinted at her, and she smiled. *Stay afloat, my Ben,* she wanted to say with that smile. He would move on, keep trying to fix the world, while she lay there struggling, and now she felt the old undertow dragging her down. *Don't let me pull you down,* she thought, getting up to wash her face before heading back downstairs to start the evening meal.

3

As nice as it was to walk, it was equally nice Ben decided to take the bus more often and leave Marian with the car. Brand new last year, it did attract attention. She had Mrs. Brady over for lunch in the spring, and a few of the other neighbors along, too. It occurred to Marian that they were all quite jovial and that maybe her perceptions were off. Some in the neighborhood might have seen her as the unfriendly one. Maybe we reflect who we are in others, after all they had accepted her invitation. On the way into the house, everyone had *oohed* and *aahed* and patted the swanky lime-green Ford Cortina with the black top in the same way that they used to *ooh* and *aah* and pat their babies' heads.

This afternoon, the geeky mothers from the neighborhood were having coffee at an outside table at Furlong's and pretended not to notice her when she drove past on the way to Johanna's school. They didn't return Marian's waving hand. She drove on wondering why they were so insular. Never enough chitchat for these boring women. Nothing better to do than gossip. Well, with the good ones come the bad apples; she shrugged them off and turned up "I Want to Hold Your Hand" on the radio as she waited for Johanna in the pickup zone at Muckross School.

Although she enjoyed the car, she looked forward to next fall when Johanna would walk back and forth to school with her chums. It was a godsend when Jo finally loped over to the car and got in, too exhausted from her day for much else. *Join the crowd,* Marian wanted to say. *Not easy trying to fit in, is it? Not easy trying our best. That never changes,* she would tell her, when she was older.

"I'm hungry," Johanna said as if exhaling her last breath, practically horizontal across the passenger seat.

"There's a meatloaf, and I'll give you twopence for a flake bar." Marian lowered the music and kissed Johanna on the forehead, looked into her daughter's vivacious eyes. Jo let out a smile. Funny how children need that attentive look so they know that they are being heard. It was the devoted smile she used when she kissed her daughter goodnight. Those were the times Johanna would tell her something private, something that was bothering her. It was always after reading to her but before lights out, when she would sit on Jo's bed and massage her lanky shoulders, that Johanna would open up.

She rummaged through her purse for the coin and placed it in her hand.

"Why don't we have a holy water font by the front door? Anne-Marie does. Gran does," Jo said.

"Because I don't like plastic holy water fonts. You can bless yourself at church," Marian answered, pulling out of the school's driveway.

"But when are we going to church? Anne-Marie says she goes every Saturday to confession. The whole parish does, she said, except for us. Her ma told her we're lapsted."

"Lapsed. And we're nothing of the kind. You want to go to confession every Saturday? I'll take you to confession. We'll go to the eleven. Father Riordan's in charge and he's decent. Says mass like a speed reader," she said. "Under twelve minutes from beginning to end."

"Da should come with us again," Jo said.

"I think he should wait a bit."

Marian remembered Father Riordan's face on that Sunday when she'd brought Ben and all three of them had talked in the rectory after Mass. Ben had said that he'd been curious about the Apostle's Creed. He'd seriously wanted to know, where in the Holy Land was Pointus Pilate. He was fascinated because he had never heard that town mentioned as a destination in Israel. Father Riordan had excused himself, and Marian had laughed until she'd cried, giving Ben a look as if he should burn up. He was a Roman governor, not a place, Marian had explained on the way home, and Ben had been mortified by his ignorance. Such a *kappore*. A faux pas, he explained when Marian's face became puzzled. She gave him a playful shove.

"Anne-Marie said she can't come to my birthday party," Jo continued. Marian wondered if the two points—going to church and to birthday parties—were related.

"So you'll invite someone else," Marian said and began the slow search for a parking spot close to their brownstone. "Go on. Put on your Mickey Mouse Club cap."

Johanna jumped around with her black ears on. "Bubbe said that she would introduce me to Jewish kids from her neighborhood. She told me being half-Jewish is better than nothing."

Ever since Ben started taking Jo to see his mother, all Marian heard was Bubbe said this and Bubbe said that. *Bubbe said a lot of things she shouldn't have,* Marian wanted to say but she kept the McKeever in her down. "No matter who comes to your party, you'll get lots of presents."

"I don't care about presents, Ma. I've got my cap, and that's all I want. Margaret's ma says there's lots of kids without all what we have and being grateful just to have a Ma who'll–"

"You get lots of attention, Jo. You know that," Marian said, opening her eyes wide at her.

It was then that Marian noticed a peculiar woman wearing a nurse's hat and white shoes, prowling around like a rabid rodent, entering their front gate. Marian pressed the brake, thrusting Jo against the back-seat cushion. The clumsy trespasser hit the door-knocker once, leaning forward to peer through the bay window. The strange-looking person's head moved in small jerks.

"Who is that?" Jo asked.

Marian backed up.

"No parking, Jo. We'll have to go round again," she said, reversing carefully to the corner and then making the swift right.

"There is someone at our door, Ma. God, don't you ever listen to me?" Jo said. "Look."

Marian glanced and then made the turn, parked on a side street and sat in the car rummaging intently through her handbag for a minute or two before turning off the engine. Johanna huffed out of the car.

"Get back here, girl," Marian hissed. "Take your book satchel, my friend, before you skeddadle. And your dirty runners."

Marian got out of the car and looked around the corner, thankful that the strange woman had run off. She hurried to get to the letterbox before Jo could grab at the note stuck inside. Marian smashed the envelope into her coat pocket.

"Who was it, Ma?" Jo asked again as she trudged up the stairs to the front door.

"Oh, nobody," she said. "Nobody important. Go on in, Johanna. Go upstairs and wash up before you start your homework."

Marian walked mechanically into the kitchen, opened the refrigerator and took out the string beans, placed them on the cutting board, began chopping off the ends. She listened to Jo thump upstairs and a whirlwind of anxiety blew through her. She filled the large pot with water and garlic cloves, watched the skinny beans twirling around. She had been a bad girl with unbridled thoughts and actions. She had not been able to control her desires and now she was paying. They would all pay, and she felt real fear course through her body. Had she really thought she could keep her secret forever? Maybe she could, still, maybe she could make this incident go away. She took the horrible crumpled paper from her overcoat and stuffed it into her apron, wiped the counters clean with ammonia spray before she would continue her cooking. Her mouth felt dry, and she took a glass of water from the tap. She meandered into the dining room and studied Johanna who was memorizing her Latin verbs. She was suddenly aware of her daughter's preciousness, the fragility of her thin young limbs. Everything in the dining room seemed fragile, too. The curvy legs of the wooden dining table, the hand-painted vase on the end table in the adjoining drawing room ready to crash into bits by a mere brush past it. The peony plates looked woozy behind the glass of the bureau; the second-hand oak bureau itself looked weary as if it might collapse. Johanna's forefinger and thumb squeezed her thin yellow pencil with an intensity that suggested that it, too, might break.

Why was Nurse barging back into her life after all these years? Marian believed she had wiped clean that part of her life a long time ago. Swept up the young Marian and thrown her away like a dirty, unwanted rag, never to be thought about again. How dare Nurse violate her family's right to privacy. From what she'd glimpsed of the poor creature, nothing much had changed for her. She recognized the erratic movement of Nurse's muddy eyes, eyes that had frightened her then and frightened her now again. Was this visit simply a cry for help from a pitiful person? Whatever had prompted such unbalanced behavior, she couldn't let Nurse in. Nurse had to remain in the past.

Marian smoothed back Jo's dark hair, gathered it in a proper ponytail and out of her eyes. She left her alone to do her lessons, walked through the swinging white door and into the kitchen. No need to dredge up the sins of her youth; she had moved on, she told herself. Still, she found herself unraveling the note.

Marian, I have information. Something you need to know about the boy. Do not tell Sister Paulinas I came by. Can be reached there – Castleboro Mother Baby Home. Nurse

The front door slammed and Marian threw the piece of paper in the trash bin, digging underneath the coffee grinds, her stomach rumbling. She washed up under a stream of water and then got busy scrubbing the dirt off the potatoes. She opened the oven and heat rolled over her body, little demons raced around her chest. Ben walked into the kitchen, his trench coat dripping. He gave her a wink, and immense gratitude that Ben loved her sprang through her clouding mood.

"*Níl aon leigheas ar an ngrá ach pósadh*," her da used to tell her. "The only cure for love is marriage." She would pass that one along tonight if she could muster up any humor.

Marian smiled and then hugged him. Ben's face brightened as he surveyed the kitchen and all her fitful cooking. There was nothing

Marian wanted except for a cigarette in the garden. She urged herself to focus hard on the present. "How was your day?" She asked and immediately wished she hadn't spoken. He looked through her, put his hand on her shoulder.

"Wet," he said, and Marian forced a faux frown his way and turned back to the washing.

Ben hung his coat to drip-dry on the far kitchen door, called something to Johanna and left for the dining room. Marian put the large mixing bowl underneath the hem of his trench coat to catch the droplets of rain and listened to the drip in the quiet of the kitchen, remembering the soft flip of a Bible page turned by some bored girl, a Nat King Cole number playing so low on the Victrola that it had sounded like a musical version of the mush they'd eaten in the refectory.

Marian stood straight and still now, listening to Johanna and Ben's familiar banter. Their voices were everything she had ever wanted to hear and she scrubbed the soiled earth from the potatoes she had forgotten to bake. Whatever it was that Nurse thought was important, it wasn't worth allowing the past to spread like syphilis onto Johanna and Ben. Nurse could never come back. Sister Paulinas shall never come back. None of them from the underworld would corrupt her and her family now. Marian felt an inescapable heat rise in her stomach. There would be punishing repercussions for Nurse, she must know that, if anyone were to find out that she'd paid them a visit. She stirred the beans around in the boiling pot, wondering how she could squash Nurse from ever being so bold again.

"And how was *your* day?" Ben said, opening up the refrigerator.

"Oh." She laughed. "What did you say?" She wondered if she should tell Father Brennan about Nurse's resurrection. Even *he* would be angry. She remembered his blank face that belied his horror at being mixed up with her mistake in the first place.

It would all be sorted out, Marian decided. She opened the oven, realizing at once she'd failed to marinate the meatloaf. The grainy beef looked like a mound of crumbling leather stuck to the bottom of the burnt glass casserole. Marian turned off the stove, defeated, and watched the limp beans dead in the water. She couldn't move from where she leaned against the kitchen counter. She was worried sick about Johanna; she could never know anything about her mother's past. She couldn't imagine a young girl's reaction to news like that. She figured the boy was almost eleven-and-a-half, having been born on the twenty-second of November. She'd asked Nurse to look after him, yes, she remembered that. She had wanted to do the right thing by him, always, that had been true.

"Eh-hem, Ma." Jo stared hard at her. "I'm starving, Ma. And Da is too."

"Johanna, you scared me. How long have you been standing there?"

Marian shook her head as Ben walked in the kitchen, told Jo to clear her books off the table, and then set it for dinner.

Marian tried to breathe, tried to stop the numbing sensation inside her.

"Oh, for God's sake," she said, taking the blackened meat out of the oven, smoke everywhere. The raw potatoes wobbled as Marian put them back in the veggie drawer, one of the spuds falling to the black-and-white linoleum floor.

Ben tried to help, but she pushed him away.

"What's the matter with you?" He seemed worried. "Are you okay, Marian?"

"I'm *grand*," she said, a bit exaggerated. "Let's just make do tonight. I'm a bit distracted at the moment, that's all. It happens to the best of us every now and again, doesn't it?"

The two of them, her beautiful Ben and Johanna, sat smiling up at her, quiet and confused. *Is he sick?* Marian worried, as she dutifully served her deflated family. *Is he dead? Had he been asking so many questions about his roots that his parents in America felt compelled to answer and now he's come here to meet me?* She should never have befriended the half-wit Nurse. It dawned on her that Nurse could return to her home at any time and divulge her shameful secrets. She would have to protect Johanna from such an incident. There was no telling what further damage Nurse could do.

4

"Wearing your signature style today?" Marian said, pushing her hand through Ben's wavy hair and then loosening his thin, red tie.

Ben kissed her on her soft mouth. Marian smiled, one that cracked open her face, the shell of her façade fading. It was a rare moment when she allowed herself to beam like this. He kissed her again, harder this time. Was he hoping the kiss would cement in her mind this moment of real joy between them? She couldn't bear that horrifying look of his, when his voice would fall into that remote tone, as if he were dreaming a different life. She fluffed up the blue-striped hankie decorating his pocket, and he grabbed her tight around the waist as if to stop their distance. She had always been sensitive to Ben's inner workings, and now, he felt like a stack of antique dishes in her arms. Were they meat or dairy dishes?

She noticed he looked tired, too. Exhausted even. Or was it guilt?

"Want to walk me to the bus stop, have a coffee?" he asked, but then he laughed.

Talk to me; we don't talk enough. Why don't I just say it? Do we not talk enough because you're talking to someone else?

"Ben." She closed her eyes, then let out one of her sarcastic sounding chuckles.

He was right, of course, standing there in her robe with the little flowers all over it, her hair a poofy mess, a basket of laundry in her arms, it was an impossible idea, going for coffee. She should be dressed, is what he was thinking.

Ben picked up a children's book and gave her a stern look.

"Even though she's ten, Johanna still loves kid books, not teacher books," she said. "We read storybooks together."

"I think she's ready for more than Peter and Jane books, don't you?"

"I know. You were reading the *Torah* at seven." Marian dropped her shoulders and sighed.

"Never mind. You're doing a bang-up job, honey."

"Yeah, well. You're going to have to try harder to pitch in," Marian said, rolling her eyes upward toward Johanna's bedroom. "Not just with your reporting, and the typewriter clacking to all hours. You'll have to be hands on," she said, finally putting down her load.

"You're going to have to show me just how hands on you mean," he whispered and reached under her robe.

"Go on with you." She chuckled at him again, and pulled his hands away. *Why doesn't he know I detest this forced affection?*

"Ah, you can have the car today," he said then, grabbing his coat. "I have an interview downtown. Easier to take the bus," he added, giving her another kiss as he opened the front door.

Marian gave him a perplexed frown like she always did the few times he mentioned downtown, which they both knew was his way of saying Little Jerusalem. She wondered how he could hold on to so much anger for so long. She wondered about her own mother's ire and wanted to say aloud: *Enough is enough already!* the way Beva had that horrid night she'd kicked Marian out of their *Yiddishkeit* neighborhood. *Must be a thing he'd learned from his mother,* she guessed, *to remain poised in cat fights.* She couldn't figure it out at all.

"At any rate, I'll be home regular time," he said as he opened the front gate. "Give Jo a big kiss for me."

"As if there's a regular time," Marian said and gave him her prim smile, which made her uneasy because it didn't feel right. It wasn't authentic and was always followed by his trancelike look. They both knew she wasn't priggish or prudish or straight-laced at all. Why did she want to convey that she *was?* Just last week, she'd let out an unnecessary burst of anger at the television's constant replaying of the angelus bells instead of her American game show. And she went on and on about it. And yet, in those moments, he felt she was most alive, didn't he?

"Don't be late," she called out. "Please. I'll be making the cholent for us."

He grinned at her, and she met his eyes. "I'll most definitely come home early for that," he said, and he walked toward the Leeson Street bus stop.

Marian's stew. It wasn't cholent, but it was good.

"Eat," Beva had commanded everyone, throwing some mush on Ben's plate.

"I made chopped liver for him. He loves it." Beva smiled broadly at Marian, putting her arm around Ben as he spread some of the liver on a stick of *matzoh*.

"You'd have to *shlep* yourself over to Gold's to get it, and then push your way into the store during Passover, forget it. It's better home-made. Who wants a little more gefilte fish? Marian?" She walked towards her with the platter of molded fish.

"Not for me, thank you."

"Try a *biselah*," and Beva shoved a tiny portion onto Marian's plate. "Benjamin used to come home with homemade honey-dipped apples from his teacher for *Rosh Hashanah,* fruit baskets for *Sukkoth,* the teacher would have a menorah lighting, et cetera, et cetera."

"I know how to light a menorah," Marian said dryly.

"Ah," Beva said pointing in the air. "But do you know why?"

"Of course I know about the victory of the Maccabees. I know about all the holidays, including Passover . . ."

Beva threw her hands ups. "I'm sure you're a very good Catholic and understand the profound implications of your Easter, am I right, Marian?"

"No, not really. I'm still trying to put the pieces together."

Beva looked at her, dumbfounded. "How was the liver, Benjamin?"

"Delish."

Marian removed Ben's empty plate from him.

"Let Benjamin do that. He knows where to put them. But come. You can help carry. The salmon's ready."

Beva rose and took the plates Marian had been clearing away from her. Ben gave her a look that meant *hold on, it's almost over.*

Marian waved goodbye, and then went into the kitchen, sipped her tea. Somehow Beva convinced Ben he was needed at home that night, which was understandable. She wished things were different, that she had been there helping them out, too, but she couldn't; Beva made it all too clear that she was not welcome. "Marian," Mrs. Ellis had said, coming out the door, her arms wrapped around her petite waist, as if to keep her from collapse. "I'm sorry, but do you think my husband would be lying on the floor if Benjamin hadn't invited you over? Think about it. I know you're a smart girl. Does this seem right to you? You and my son?"

She glanced through the bay window at Ben, holding his dazed father's head in his hands. Ben's father was staring at the ceiling, his yalmulke pushed to the back of his scalp baring a balding crown.

"Yes, Mrs. Ellis. I think this is right. Me and Ben."

Ben had placed the white cap and *talith* on his father, washed and dressed in white linen, after Samuel Ellis was taken to the mortuary. Earth from Israel was sprinkled three times over his body; the Gabbai covered him in a second sheet, and closed the plain, wooden coffin. His mother threw three shovelfuls of earth onto the coffin, and they remained standing there until the grave was filled. Once home, Marian pictured him lighting a cigarette, his right leg shaking underneath the dining room table. How gruesome was it for him to see the hall mirror covered in black? That first week, he never left the house, never shaved, never bathed. *Did he think about her,* and guilt attacked her again. *Hadn't she heard the news at the Zion School and up and down Clanbrassil Street? Is that what underlined his anger?* She thought this often, but after the Mammy's contempt, who could have blamed her for staying away?

"Do you think I caused your father's heart attack, Ben?" Marian whispered one evening after Ben mentioned that Beva was a walking bone, that her black dress hung on her as if she was a wooden hanger.

"No," he answered quietly. Beva did not speak of Marian since the funeral, she was sure, but did Ben bring up Marian's name to Beva? Beva must have thought Tatte's death finally rid him of the inappropriate girlfriend, the derelict schoolteacher. But that was not so.

Marian picked at a scone and then went up to her room, perused her closet. As she selected her brown woolen tunic dress with the patent leather black belt, she remembered dressing in the predawn the day she'd left Dublin for Castleboro, wrestling with all the layering: the oversized bra, the tight blouse, the bulky knit sweater. Slowly, she slipped one leg and then the other into her black nylon stockings, chose her black pumps, recalled her scratchy skirt as she'd grappled with it, left the button undone under her sweater. She felt strangely removed, even now, and found herself eerily going through the motions of getting dressed as if she were watching a film about somebody else's life.

Ben said his appointment today with the principal of the Zion School would be brief. An interview with the notable alum, the journalist, to recognize his great achievement. They should be interviewing her, the notable, and to her knowledge, the only Catholic schoolteacher, but no. And then, at noon, he looked forward again to *Pesach* at his old synagogue. But this year, not alone, he'd mentioned, rather offhandedly. His buddy Jerry from the old days who had married Marcia Golden would join him. He had bumped into Marcia and her little sister Penny, too, on one of his recent lunches at Morton's Restaurant. Did he think Penny was as pretty as she was in high school? Marian had seen his yearbook. Short girl with flowing hair, thick and straight down her back, a headband framing her face. Penny reminded Ben of a pixie doll, no doubt. He'd taken her to the senior prom. Were they all giggling about that? Were they all having lunch after *Shul*? How many years had it been that they'd had lunch at Morton's? Fifteen? She wondered if he still felt the same way he did back then. Was he tempted? Now that he was married, nothing would happen. He would refuse her if she flirted, Marian was sure. She pictured his hand lingering on her knee and then moving along her smooth thigh, and she stopped this silly thought.

Was he aware in upper school how bad a crush these girls had had on him? Why were children so secretive about their crushes?

He'd told her he'd lost his virginity to "what's-her-name", who he couldn't even stand to see after that one time. Did he wish he'd done it with Penny Golden? Or Marcia? Did he wonder if his marriage to Marian had noticeably altered him? Did he wonder what it would be like married and living in his old neighborhood? Did he feel different inside now? He was a husband and the father of a child, and she was sure he didn't exude the lightheartedness that he once did. Penny wasn't married yet. It was clear to Marian that if Ben wasn't, pixie Penny would be on the top of his list to ask on a date. Attraction is not something that human beings can hide.

By now, Ben would have approached the Rathgar Road and jumped off the bus. *We're all just animals.* He would be breathing in the smell of the hot bialys and bagels steaming in the bakeries. It had been way too long since he'd had an onion bialy with smoked salmon and cream cheese and raw onion and she was sure he'd invite Jerry and *Marcia* to lunch after service. Did he hope others would be there, too? Marian was pretty sure others would be. For a few seconds, she pictured Ben slow dancing with one of those girls. She put the thought out of her mind, feeling strange that she would fantasize such a thing, and then she pictured him dancing with her. Perhaps they would dance tonight. Ben would turn on the record player after dinner, and the three of them would dance. For now, though, he would eat until he couldn't eat anymore. He was ravenous. He was starving, yes, but for what?

Being alert to his wife's moods, Ben must think that there was no need to upset her by describing his innocent romps around his old neighborhood, no need to bring up ancient wounds. (He shouldn't have mentioned it this morning, then.) And he did not need to tell her about Penny certainly. There was something between them, but as long as he didn't follow through, and she knew he would not, why mention it? But might he have begun to follow through already, she wondered. Wasn't he getting in too deep, this being his second visit in only one month? And if he was honest, seeing Marcia and Penny wasn't just a spontaneous visit with friends. Jesus, Ben probably daydreamed about Penny sometimes, maybe more often than some-times. He thought about these "friends" in a way he shouldn't. He had better cut it out.

Marriage was certainly not easy, she considered. True, she was so unpredictable. One minute alive and smiling, and lots of other minutes dead to the world, a haunted mask hanging on her face. Ben could never predict what frame of mind she would be in when he got home. More often than not, though, it was not the sexual mood she was in last night. What was up with women and their moods? he jokingly said. On more than one occasion. He'd even asked Jerry, but Jerry only offered a sheepish grin. His wife was the same. The honey-moon was long over, and Jerry and Marcia didn't even have a kid yet. He would walk past his old, cobblestone street soon. His mother would probably be waiting for him. Was Ben lying? Was this, in truth, the *third* Friday in a month that he'd made his way to syna-gogue following this route? The loneliness for the familiar smells, the jokes, the people, all of it, was eating him up inside. As it was, he'd brought Jo to meet his mother twice already, and she would soon blurt this out, no doubt. Johanna saw Marian's Ma at least once a month. Why should she be denied her other grandmother? "Where is my other Gran? Why doesn't my other Gran come over?" Johanna asked incessantly before the visits to Little Jeru-salem had begun.

Women, Ben concluded recently, would have to get over it. He'd be the one to lead the way, he added. "You and Mammy might actu-ally like each other now," he said. "Who could know?"

If Marian had been a Jew, it would certainly have been easier, yes. She could hear the Jewish community arguing with him, but *better*? He had fallen for Marian the second he'd seen her on the Zion School playground, of all places. It had been a hazy September af-ternoon and he'd remarked to some of the older students about the redhead teaching in this Jewish institution. Marian had retorted that it seems some of us haven't learned that we don't judge the book by the cover, and the kids had said she was hot under the collar when

she'd made her hasty retreat. From that moment on, he knew she was
the one. Love is like that. It felt like a strange familiarity, as if they'd
waited their whole lives for this chance encounter, as if they'd somehow met before. He had made his choice in love, so what woman
could be better than her? What child could be better than Johanna?
No, there was no one better, even on her bad days, he joked. Still, she
felt a private unhappiness. She wished things had gone slower, that
their delirious love hadn't got out of whack.

If he passed the Hatch Street Nursery where he was born, no
doubt he thought of Tatte and Johanna. Marian pictured his *maidelah* walking hand-in-hand with him, up and down the bustling
streets, just like he'd done with his own father. She felt the deep
melancholy of missing someone. A flash of embarrassment went
through her as she remembered that Ben had once spied her cradling
a doll in her arms, listening to some old fogie tune of her da's, and
he'd gone upstairs without a word. With their ambiguous start, she'd
lost so much more than he had, really. Her miserable guess was that
she was living in a state of heartbreak more often than she let on.

"Marian, you look *benkshaft* these days," Ben said last week.
Johanna was a handful since she'd learned sports, which she somehow
couldn't keep outside. Always the basketball bouncing in the kitchen
or those damn tennis balls underneath Marian's feet. That one was so
fast that it was hard for either of them to keep up. In private, this was
surely a source of pride for him; he'd been an athlete once, too. But for
her, Jo's headstrong ways were taxing. She went to the emergency room
twice in four months from the bangs Johanna had taken on the playing fields. She needed some quiet time away from the noise of raising
a child. She decided that as soon as he got home, she would suggest
that he take her dancing or to the cinema, or to sit up very late at the
Green Tureen on Harcourt Street. She remembered when they first
dated, he took her to the Shelbourne for high tea. He wiped her mouth
decorously, incapable of suppressing a genuine smile, the clotted cream
she lopped onto her scone an obvious treat. He touched her buttery
cheek then, and she smiled and leaned over, and they kissed.

He'd be walking up Bloomfield Avenue by now, crowds of *Yiddishkeit* everywhere bellowing on the hectic street, the smell of smoked fish rising like a vapory veil over the neighborhood. A world unto itself. He'd be glancing into the busy store windows, the boot maker, Freedman's Grocery, and Betty Fine's Drapery. He'd stroll past handsome brownstones, gold Stars of David visible on window ledges, apple trees lining vegetable gardens, beefsteak red tomatoes in baskets on front stoops. Ben would look at girls covered by their dark coats coming out of Barron's, bags of coconut macaroons under their arms, their youthful faces peeping out from their scarves. He would make his way toward the canal, the smell of sour fish from the bins and the atrocious smells coming from the canal would bring back boyhood memories of stick ball in short pants until the street lamps came on.

From a distance, Marian imagined that he would see his "delicate" mother yakking to someone in front of the house, her hands still doing a lot of the talking. Nothing that ingrained could have changed, and, yet, things were not the same. Marian had admitted last night that she became furious when she remembered that as a girl she'd allowed others to think for her. She wouldn't allow Johanna to make the same mistakes she'd made, and she would not allow her to be afraid of Mr. Hinckley. But Ben had no worries about Johanna sticking up for herself, that she would was obvious. All these talkative, strong women in his life had a lot in common, he said. *Ben, though, I am different.* She fluctuated between listless and forceful. Even though they were all mysterious to him, especially her, after ten years with his little family, Ben said that he felt life was pretty good. Johanna should not be denied her family. Johanna should have both her grandmothers. No one's parent should be left behind, he said. He would not be the type of man who would walk away from his beloved family, *she knew this.* She imagined Ben bending down now to kiss his mother hello.

5

The drive down to Castleboro Mother Baby Home wasn't as long as it seemed that first time, when Marian rode in the backseat. What she remembered was the scorching silence. This time she had the radio on low, but she turned it off as she sat in the parking lot. She watched the fog bleed over everything and listened to the moans of the motionless cows. She could not bring herself to look at the buildings and gazed far beyond into the verdant farm pastures with their bungalows and haystacks and bales of straw like the shredded wheat cereal Jo might have for breakfast back home. Finally Marian looked over at the Motherhouse, an imposing pewter residence with double stone doors, a slot letterbox used by the nuns to peek at anyone who used the cast iron door knocker. Statues of religious figures stood beside each door, one a saintly-looking woman with eyes rolled back too far in her head, the other a depiction of Mary Magdalene, a black serpent entwined in her bare feet. Marian pictured the Reverend Mother, with watery eyes, her cheeks like plums embossed into her plump face, sitting by the electric fire, and she remembered the feeling of being tricked, remembered feeling something was very wrong when Nurse had led her away just minutes after her formal admittance.

Beyond the Mother Baby Home across the gravel driveway, a couple of depleted girls, clad in scant sweaters, sweeping pebbles off the road in the wind and drizzle. It looked worse than before when she'd been so young and indifferent to outer appearances. All that lack of caution was gone. She watched Sister Paulinas enter the van and drive away down the back road. She had given the woman a nickname during her residency, Sister Penis. Marian could tell that Sister was still a willowy nun. Her narrow face peeked through the car window, with the beauty mark on her high drawn cheekbone, which led to arresting eyes. She hadn't changed much. Marian had counted on Sister Penis's schedule to be just as it was back then, when she'd leave

Nurse in charge of leading the pregnant outcasts to chapel. Every
Tuesday meant penance, arms outstretched, without moving, for a
quarter of an hour for their lewd sins. She watched from a distance
the women in their worn smocks, mantillas on their heads, enter the
little cathedral after the nuns, about thirty of them, who would kneel
on the far left side of the chapel, the girls on the right. She listened
to the women singing, sweet as children, and studied through the
pale light the two ash trees at the chapel's entrance, emaciated now,
no more downy leaves gracing them.

The fog settled into her bones. She thought about Ben making a
pot of coffee right about now, just before rousing Johanna, or would
he take her absence as an opportunity to have his coffee in little
Jerusalem. She blocked the thought. The shock of Nurse's reentry
had demanded that petty issues about her life in Donnybrook take
on an inconsequential value. What had seemed important had dis-
solved, and Marian was transported back into her overwhelming
past. It was as if Johanna and Ben were eons away from her. She had
to hold on to her resolve and the secrets she held to protect Ben and
Jo. She opened the car door and stepped onto the gravel, wanting to
quiet its crunch, like skeletons underneath her shoes.

She veered to the right; every sound she made was too loud for
her. As she skirted past the ancient stone Motherhouse with all its
cold magnificence, she peered at the stained glass windows and then
walked past the stone pillars toward the Mother Baby Home. Closer
now, it looked run down. A concrete slab, it had the feel of a sanatorium, and she could almost hear imaginary shrieks and screams in
the locked birthing rooms. She did see real, shadowy figures by the
barred windows in the toilets looking down at her, smoke coming
from a crack in one window winding and waving like a thin sheet in
the air, a desperate SOS call for help. A familiar and uncomfortable
heat rose within her. Feeling like an inmate again, she began to lose
her composure and wished she could stop the bones beneath her,
and stop herself from shaking. They couldn't lock her up again. She
was having trouble swallowing, her throat contracting like a muscu-

lar cave; she might choke. But she walked to the front door with its slanting eaves and rows of narrow windows with black iron bars. She decided instead to enter through the side door of the maternity ward. She looked out at the yard, with its three dry evergreen trees, some scattered scrub brush, and a row of unkempt bushes surrounded by an old barbwire fence. She pictured her hard shoe pressing down on noticeable dips in the wire, and she wondered why no one really tried to escape. Here it was so easy to get in. But how many miles would they have gotten before the officers returned them? And where on earth were they to go? How true it was that there was no escape, even if no one knew. *I know, even if I pretend I've forgotten the place.* Beyond the fence to the gray horizon were more patchwork fields, meandering and imprecise. She wondered if anyone from afar could see her shameful silhouette. Out in the fields she saw girls spreading fertilizer, and further to the far left, the old silos and creaky farm outhouses, the smell of manure and the raspy churl of crows sickening her again.

At this hour, with Sister Paulinas gone and having rid herself of her charges, Nurse would be having tea in the refectory. Marian made her way toward the front staircase. Two white-clad nuns were whispering down the dark hall that led to the entrance offices where the new girls were signed in. Three bulging girls on the staircase stopped and stared at Marian as she walked upstairs. She bent her head down in concentration, wondering if Sister Paulinas, or anyone who treated the downtrodden so cruelly, could be heard by God. Sister Penis used to tell her she did not appreciate her stubborn, sneaky face, and Marian would just shake her head and walk away. Yes, she was stubborn and came to judge the nuns, remembering the hate she had felt as a small girl, hating the smack of the ruler for the "shifty" look on her face, or for being "vain." She glanced at the large bodies now in their tattered blue smocks with their hungry glares. These girls with hollow eyes frightened her. Everything seemed even baser and rougher than she remembered. The haze of her younger years had protected her with its numbing fog.

She continued down the frigid hall. There was the smell of mansion polish in the air and two girls shuffled along on the second story, rags tied to their raw feet. She wanted to shake them, stop them from turning into ghosts, stop the shuffling sounds that made everything eerie. It would be hard to run back to the front gates from up here. She felt trapped in the middle of this haunted place.

Marian stalled outside the barren dormitory-style room for a moment, noticing the linoleum floor polished to a heavy shine, and the two long rows of iron beds made with creased, white sheets and pillows, lumpy, green coverlets on top. Except for a large oak crucifix on one of the whitewashed walls, there was no ornamentation, no individual mark of who slept here, no night tables, no pictures, no flowers. No personal effects of any kind near or under the beds.

"Take off your clothes," Nurse instructed, those eleven years ago, scurrying into the room after Marian.

"Excuse me?" A younger, different Marian held tight to her leather satchel. Nurse tilted her head forward, staring with unblinking eyes. She reminded Marian of an old, fat skunk.

Nurse was dressed in the same blue uniform Marian was given but with a white nurse's hat pinned to her gray-streaked brown hair. The woman folded the oversized green tweed suit Marian had bought at Brown Harris, and which she planned to discard when she left this place. *Soon,* Marian thought as Nurse clicked her suitcase shut. Observing Nurse's fidgety gestures, Marian couldn't help but wonder how long this strange creature had been in this hellhole.

"This is a far cry from the convent parlor. Pack of lies," Marian said.

"All the girls are greeted at the convent, and then you're over here until they place your child, or until your two years run out," Nurse told her.

"Two years? Nothing could keep me in this place for two years."

"Sister Paulinas will discuss all that. I'll keep that bracelet for you," Nurse said.

Marian hesitantly opened the gold clasp of the one piece of jewelry she owned, a present she'd received from her parents for her confirmation twelve years ago. She looked at Nurse's clumsy, outstretched hand and then into her face, a couple of coarse black hairs underneath her chin.

"Everything will be returned to you when you leave. No shoes in the hall." Nurse placed her own brown leather flats with all the other pairs of shoes arranged in neat rows by the dormitory door. "No making marks on the floor," she added.

Marian looked at her unprotected feet and followed Nurse through the chilly hallway and down the stairs to the offices. Marian was horrified to see her Uncle Stephen, or rather, for the past two years, Father Brennan, her ma's brother, standing in the doorway of Sister Paulinas' office.

Humiliation welled inside of her.

Sister Paulinas sighed loudly as Marian entered the office.

"Father Brennan brought you here at your request."

"Yes," she answered, though she felt she'd been coerced.

Sister Paulinas pushed some papers forward across her desk. "She'll have to sign these consenting documents before you go, Father."

Marian took the pen from Sister Paulinas, and began to read the admissions form. Father Brennan cleared his throat, impatient to be on his way. She hastily signed her name.

"Father?" Marian blurted.

"Be a good girl for the Sisters, now. Good-bye, Marian," he intoned and left.

She nodded, keeping her head down.

"So you're a schoolteacher, are you?" Sister Paulinas said.

"That's right."

Sister sighed.

Shame coursed through Marian's bones at the thought of all the sacrifices her parents had made for her to become a teacher. She recalled the years of schooling, the high scores on her Leaving Certificate, her proud father.

"Date of birth is November 1, 1933."

"Yes."

"All Saints' Day. Twenty-three years old, and let's hope we can save you from a life of continued blemish." Sister Paulinas stared down at her desk, shuffling some papers.

"Did Father Brennan mention anything about a headage fee?" Marian couldn't speak, tried to swallow.

"If you have one hundred pounds for the headage fee, your baby can be found a home right away, as long as it's born healthy."

"I don't have one hundred pounds, Sister, but I've ten pounds with me. I'm sure I can get the rest. Contact Father Brennan, if you would."

"Father Brennan notes that you come from a respectable background. We'll see what can be done. In the meantime, in here you're not to use your own name. None of the girls do. You'll be known as Francie. Don't forget that name, and don't be sharing your past with the other girls." She turned her gaze. "Take Francie to the others," Sister ordered and settled back down to her work.

Nurse had been waiting at the door with Marian's belongings and bowed when Sister Paulinas acknowledged her. "Come with me," Nurse dictated, placing Marian's suitcase near the office files.

"I'll be needing my books and my Pond's vanishing cream, then," Marian said.

Sister Paulinas looked hot, her face squeezed into her wimple.

"Schoolteachers, washerwomen—all here for the same reason, are you not? Consider yourself lucky you've been sent to us to look after you, when no one else will have you. The cheek of some of you girls—novels and vanity creams! Read the Bible. Keep your nose clean. Honor the code of silence here, and use your time to pray for God's mercy. Go on, now. I haven't all day to mind you. Go on to the day room and knit that baby of yours a day dress."

Marian followed Nurse back upstairs. "Father Brennan has made a mistake. He said these nuns were kind," Marian muttered as they eased past a girl furiously scrubbing the floor.

"You'll settle in," Nurse said. She placed a piece of carbolic soap on her nightstand. "That's your bed," Nurse continued, pointing to one topped with a pile of folded sheets and a blanket.

Everything had happened in no time. The car waiting outside to zip her away, she had little chance to change her mind. She remembered trying to think fast how best to get word to Ben right away.

"There's a record player in the day room," Nurse said. "Occasionally, the girls are allowed a song in the evening. No talking here, though," she said. "No radio, no newspapers, no horsing around, no visitors, no post."

"No post?" Marian said.

"You'll manage. You're not the first been through this."

Marian thought of Nurse's words of encouragement eleven years ago and wondered if she *had* survived it, or if some of the most integral parts of her had died. She looked down at the rows of shoes and then walked over to the small window at the end of the long, narrow room. She studied the scraggly barbwire, and she felt herself growing faint. She heard voices, and to the far right, she watched two police officers patrolling the grounds, a long set of keys dangling from one of their belts. She recognized one of the men and remembered Nurse would dawdle by that window often, looking goofy, as if she believed she was a looker. She turned and made her way down the frigid hall. She drifted past the empty nurses' quarters and turned into the refectory. A waiflike selvvy gaped at her, two inches of black roots and then stringy blonde hair hung to her chin. Marian slid into a metal chair, pulled it close and forced herself to look into Nurse's possum-like face.

"Listen," Marian said. "I know this is your break and we don't have much time."

Nurse rattled her teacup.

"You shouldn't have come," Marian said.

Nurse put her head down.

"How is Sister Paulinas treating you?" Marian said.

"It's too much work. Too much, I think. It's been a bad Easter."

"Did you do something wrong," Marian said, "coming to see me?"

"No, no," Nurse said, and then stared into her bowl of pandy before taking a bite.

Marian wanted to get to the reason for her visit before Nurse lost herself in her food. "Tell me straight out. We don't have time to fool around, Nurse. What state in America have you placed him?" she said loudly, glad for the jerk reaction she'd hoped for.

Nurse put down her spoon and her hands went to her lap.

"What's the matter, Nurse? Cat got your tongue?"

Nurse looked down still.

"At least I had the likes of you, Nurse. What would I have done without you? At least I know Adrian's in America." She picked up the knife on the table and studied it before turning to Nurse, the blade raised in the air.

Nurse shook her head in little quivers.

"Best to keep him away from an Irish couple, I think you said, too, Nurse."

"I don't remember very well." Nurse rubbed her fists into her eyes.

"You don't remember, Nurse?" Marian said, open eyes staring at her, running her forefinger up and down the knife.

"I don't remember much. I do remember a nig-nog years ago."

Marian looked into Nurse's uneasy eyes as the woman spoke. Nurse lowered her head, her graying roots giving her the look of a woman in her sixties, yet she couldn't have been more than forty-five. "A nigger boy who ended up in an insane asylum up north. No one could control him. And I knew that should never happen to our Adrian."

"You knew that should never happen to *our* Adrian, did you? I don't trust Sister Paulinas, do you, Nurse? I ought to have checked all the sanatoriums in the country."

"You might do well checking the orphanages," Nurse blurted.

"Orphanages?" Marian allowed the word to pass onto her tongue.

"I know a lot more than people think," Nurse said defensively.

"What state in America have you placed Adrian, and that'll be the end to it," Marian pressed. She was sweating now. "Sure, Sister Paulinas keeps us down, Nurse. Scares the wits off all of us, but I'm not

afraid anymore, and neither should you be. What orphanage?"
Marian insisted. "I need to know. He may die. I just found it out.
He has some terrible genetic disease inherited from his da."

"Deficient genes, I remember Sister Paulinas said, would be likely
with the mixed blood. People don't understand. I know more than
they think." Nurse wiped her mouth with her napkin. "I'd been let
out of Silverbridge to spend a weekend with a host family. I was only
fifteen," she said. "I had a baby, too," she admitted.

Marian said nothing.

"The McGuire's, a lovely family. I didn't know what I was doing,"
she rattled on. "The son liked me, and I liked him."

"I'm sure that boy did love you," Marian said, worrying about
nothing but Adrian. "Can we find your man?" Marian offered.

"All these years later." Nurse giggled. "Men can't help loving the
next girl if the first isn't available. You must know that."

Marian got up abruptly. "You had a baby yourself, you told me."

"A little girl. Beth her name was."

"I know a place in London. I'll do anything to help you find her."
Nurse was drenched in sweat.

"Okay, Nurse. You have my address and you can use it if you need
me. But I've come all this way. You know where Adrian is and you're
not telling me. I'll go to Father Brennan—that I can tell you. I'm
sorry, but a friend is a friend. I'd tell you where Beth was, if I knew.
Is Adrian in an orphanage in America?"

"You can check orphanages here," Nurse uttered.

"Orphanages here?"

"I couldn't tell you. No, no—I had no choice but to do what
I could do. They brought him back, the farmer family, but I took
care of him for you. No, no—he was the only baby in the place
getting bits of sausage from my pocket. His cheeks puffed out
from all the extra food I stole for him. I read to him, too, until
Sister Paulinas said he was too old for me to be carrying on like
I was."

Marian took a long sip of water, tried to calm herself.

"I'll be locked up if Sister Paulinas knew I told you." Marian put her hand slowly on the table as if trying not to frighten away a stray cat.

"Where? Just tell me. I won't have you locked up if you tell me. Tell me which orphanage."

Nurse retrieved a tattered note from her wallet and placed it on the table. "You could try Silverbridge for a start."

"Silverbridge..."

"Same orphanage I grew up in. No, no—I visit him when I drop off babies. I dropped him in there myself. But now he's having rows. Some of the teasers took him from his cot and locked him in the boiler room with the rats overnight, then beat him in front of everyone for wetting his pants. I was there the one day he had his wet knickers on his head and the boys were all chanting, 'He thought he was a sailor of the sea, but he was a sailor of the pee!' No, no—I couldn't bear it. He's not looking well."

She could tell Nurse was about to speak more and Marian furtively put her finger to her lips.

"You had no right coming to Donnybrook."

"No post here."

"Stop listening to Sister Paulinas for everything. If you had mailed that letter, my husband would have come to save me and Adrian."

Nurse looked down.

When Nurse and Sister Paulinas had arrived in the nursery, all those years ago, Sister Penis barked at Marian to come over to them.

"What age children do you teach?" Sister Penis asked.

"Kindergarten and first year."

"At the Zion School?"

"Yes."

"Isn't that for Jewish children?"

"Sure, for the most part."

"And have you made many friends amongst the Jews?"

"Not really," she said, looking away.

"No?"

Marian shook her head. "I just hope to keep my job."

Silence from Sister.

"Sister?"

"What is it now, Francie?"

"May I hold Adrian?"

"Who's Adrian? Oh." She peered into the cubicle as Claudette was burping him. "This is our first Jew-boy," she said, turning to face her. Marian flushed, her blood pumping hard.

"He's been baptized already," Sister continued, staring at her. "I did it myself."

"Thank you, Sister," Marian managed.

"I'm scarlet for you. You're ashamed aren't you?"

"Yes, Sister. Of my sins. But not of this child," she added, taking him from Claudette. "His father has inquired about conversion, Sister." All she could think of was her baby's safety, and she would have said anything.

Sister made the sign of the cross over Adrian. "Good for him. We pray for the perfidious Jews."

Marian had lowered her eyes.

"Do you recognize this?" Sister Penis pulled the letter from her pocket.

Marian glanced at Nurse, who averted her eyes.

"He seems quite the man with quite a journalism career in front of him. Do you really think he wants the likes of you? Are you trying to create a scandal for the poor fellow?"

Marian looked at her letter in Sister's hand but kept her mouth shut as Sister left the nursery.

Nurse kept her head down still. Marian had always known Nurse felt remorse about the letter incident; she had to imagine there was something decent about her.

"I pray for him—no, no. It fell out of my pocket."

"I have to get back to my family," Marian said.

Nurse pressed down her uniform. "I thought you'd want to know he's in trouble. I was helping you, I thought."

"No. I don't want your help."

"The farmer family returned him," Nurse said. "Sister Paulinas said he had a face on him that would turn milk sour. Said we'd take care of him, better than some nests, better than those Protestant orphanages which would ruin him."

"Okay, Nurse," Marian said. "You told me he was in America," Marian repeated.

"No, no—Sister Paulinas said no. 'Americans come all the way over here to avoid colored genes. How could we give them this one, this Jew?' she said."

"But you told me . . ."

"I told you what I hoped would be. You kept asking. You wanted to hear that," Nurse said.

Marian gazed at a young girl hovering by the industrial sinks and felt faint. She hit the hard floor. First there was the wet, cool towel behind her neck and then her forehead. Then the close smell of Nurse's putrid breath above.

"Are you all right, then?" the girl whispered.

"I'm okay, now. Thanks," Marian said, taking a sip of the sugary tea she was given. She managed to get up. Everything in the room, particularly the girl's voice grew strangely amplified and uncomfortable.

"I should go," Marian said.

"I'll see you out," Nurse said, and walked next to Marian as she groped the wood plank staircase.

"I gave him up. It was the right thing to do," Marian said to Nurse as they stood for a moment outside the Home. "An orphanage right in Dublin? All these years?" Marian said.

"I've done my job," Nurse said, looking over at a group of girls waiting in two lines by the side door for Nurse. "No, no—I have to do my job here."

"Tell me again the name of the orphanage."

"Silverbridge. Sister Agnes took custody of him years ago, and he's not one of her special pets, I'm afraid. No, no—he begged me to find you," Nurse said and scurried toward the side door. She had the girls line up in single file. As Nurse turned to leave, Marian looked at her anxious face, her sincerity hard to ignore. Nurse blushed as she waved goodbye to Marian in front of the inmates, and then stood there shooting prideful glances at the girls like a young child and waited for Marian to wave back.

Marian put her hand in the air, an anger and disgust for herself and for Nurse gyrating inside her. Whatever desperate friendship they had shared had curdled long ago. Still, as wrong as it was for Nurse to have opened the wound, it was not lost on Marian that without Nurse, she would have spent her life wondering. Marian walked back to her car. It had been that bad in there. She would have done anything to survive, and her desperation mortified her. She would have stooped much lower than she did to get out of there. If she had really cared about her newborn, why hadn't she gone to the Reverend Mother and gotten Father Brennan involved to guarantee Adrian a decent home in America?

She slammed the car door, sped away from her ugly girlhood mistakes. She felt unrefined and clouded again. How could she have depended so heavily on Nurse? She felt she had been a stupid girl, a sheep; no wonder Sister Paulinas had so much power in there. She flipped on the radio, lit a cigarette and rolled down the window, the smell of fresh rain and manure everywhere. Dogs pranced after old men carting wheelbarrows through the fields as she drove through the near-deserted country roads.

By dusk she was back in Donnybrook. Marian shut off the car engine and sat there, looking from across the street at their brownstone. Although at times as punishment for her sins she forced herself to remember, she never shared her unspeakable shame with anyone. But now that the facts had come into stark relief she could no longer keep from Ben the secret of Adrian's birth eleven years ago. *And, oh God. Johanna.*

6

Once Marian left, she never gave second thought if Nurse was as slow as she appeared. Nurse watched Officer Dolan glance at her and then look toward the shed, and she dawdled a bit longer inside before she left for her refectory duties. The hell with them, these girls, draining her morning, noon and night, Nurse thought. She often lay awake, her strained eyes closed, listening to staccato sobs that echoed through the dark halls. Well she needed a break from their pain, and the shed was her break, so to speak. She made it her business this spring to enter the shed in full sight of Officer Dolan. She swept the place out, made it useful for storing more than kindling and a rusty wheelbarrow. Perhaps hooks could be nailed in, a place to keep an umbrella or two, a few mackintoshes, muddy boots could be left to dry. Odd what a crush will do to you, odd the extra energy it brings. And now he's seen her with Marian, too, and knows there's a lot more to her than this job.

After the girls said their prayers, they rushed like animals into their chairs, grabbing at the crusty bread she left in the small room off the refectory. She trusted Marian, knew she needed the information about Adrian and felt good all over seeing her again. Yes, she felt an unaccustomed happiness remembering Francie's hugs so long ago. Perhaps Francie could still be her friend. "Not Francie, you mentaller," she whispered to herself. *That is Marian. She's out of this place and her name is never Francie anymore. Your real name is not Nurse. Get that through you, you mentaller.*

Nurse sat on her cot and thought to the future now. She would have more connection to the outside. Marian, that one had been determined to get out of here as quickly as she could. She would never forget that about her. No, no—she was a good one. Nurse would have to think hard about Marian telling her not to be afraid to send a letter out of there. She carefully wrote a little note and pressed it inside a thin diary she kept hidden. She touched the photo of her baby daughter Beth pasted inside the diary's back flap. Twenty years old, she'd be now.

She took out her little penknife and methodically cut the inside of one thigh, just enough so that she could feel. Watching the thin line of blood kept her vital, cleared the sadness from her mind.

She reminded herself that she must remain a help, not a hindrance, if she hoped to stay in good stead with Sister Paulinas. She won a better fate than many. Room and board. A roof over her head. And a respectable job, Sister Paulinas told her. She must remain good and quiet at Castleboro, or be returned to the Magdalene laundry.

She cut herself again. Blood was good; blood made babies.

Nurse watched the small dot become bloated before she dabbed her thigh to stop the blood from getting on her sheets. To keep the blood off the sheets must have been why Sister Paulinas had pushed Marian forward onto the chromium commode, so shiny Nurse could see any anal swelling as the girl progressed toward birth.

"I need to lie down," Marian said.

"You need nothing of the sort. This is the fastest way for the baby to come down," Sister told her.

"Oh, God, please," Marian said.

"It's a little late to be asking God for anything," she retorted.

This manner of child delivery, a recent demand from Sister Paulinas, was unfamiliar to Nurse, and she worried the baby would drown in urine and amniotic fluid on the bottom of the commode.

"Put a blanket around her. I'm going to the convent. See that she doesn't disturb the new mothers with her whining. And keep her on the commode."

"Yes, Sister." Nurse wrapped a blanket around Marian's shoulders. But as the head was crowning, Nurse moved her to the bed. The final push, and then the cry. A six-pound baby boy was born.

"Blood is good. Blood makes babies," Nurse said as she wiped off the child.

Marian fell back, as Nurse continued to clean him up.

Sister Paulinas arrived later, examined Marian, and then placed some cotton swabs in her knickers.

"She'd do with a stitching," Nurse recommended.

"She'll be fine. I'm assigning her to nursery duty. She'll mind the toddlers and come back up here to the newborns every four hours to express her milk." Sister took the baby boy, inspected him, and handed him back to Nurse.

"I'll be in the office."

Nurse placed Marian's baby gently in her arms, whispering that she'd bring some hot sweet tea, and wiped her forehead with a washcloth.

"Thank you, Nurse," Marian said, clutching her hand.

"Ava," Nurse mumbled.

"Ava," Marian repeated. "A lovely name."

Nurse smiled her awkward smile and tried not to laugh.

"His name is Adrian."

Nurse looked into the infant's red, grumpy face, his tiny fist in his mouth.

"He's bald." Nurse began to laugh, but Marian interrupted her.

"Did you...did you mail my letter?"

"I'm hoping to soon."

"Please." Marian squeezed her hand again. "I don't know how I would manage without you. Thanks for being here," Marian whispered. "My da would have loved this little man," she said. "And my fiancé, Ben Ellis, will love him, too."

Nurse smiled, told her Ben Ellis was a nice name, though Sister Paulinas already told her that he graduated from Trinity. Even Nurse knew they didn't allow Catholics at that school. And a Catholic would be damned to Hell if they ever set foot on that university. Sister Paulinas ranted that Ellis was no Catholic, certainly, and that he lived amongst them.

"You can rest assured he'll be well looked after," Nurse said to play along. Marian seemed so hopeful with that bright smile of hers.

"Will you make certain?" Marian said. "Will you help him get to a good place in America, Nurse?"

"Only the ones who go fast get to America. And Sister Paulinas likes you, being educated and all and from a good family."

"Leave us alone for awhile, would you?" Marian asked.

Nurse nodded and had left Marian sitting in the bed, rocking Adrian.

Now Nurse looked at the picture of Beth she had, and then wiped off the little bit of blood resting on her thigh. She'd bathe the babies early tonight, get everything in order. There was so much excitement to this day and she wondered if there would be more tonight. She washed up and combed her hair back, put her nurse's cap on, studied her face in the glass. For the past year, she'd had the sense that Officer Dolan was watching her and she was starting to get the nerve to look back at him on a regular basis. It thrilled her that last week he had actually smiled at her before she'd blushed and turned away. It seemed she would always have a way with the men wherever she went, whatever her circumstances, she thought, and smoothed down her uniform, readied herself for her nighttime duties.

Much later in the evening, Nurse returned to the shed, wondering if Officer Dolan's curiosity about her twilight activities would finally arouse him. After lights out she heard muted footsteps, his black shoes buried in soft moss, and without a word, he entered, shutting the door behind him. They looked at each other for a minute before Nurse found her tongue and said, "I'll be going now. I was just finishing up the cleaning of the shed."

"You've taken to fixing up after hours?"

"The mess does my head in," she answered. "It needs doing."

As she moved past him he held out his thick arm, and she stopped. It was then that he kissed her on the cheek, moved to her mouth with the finesse of an awkward teenager, and she responded to his advances. He smelled of smoke and Brut, and she was touched, never before noticing his appreciation for aftershave.

"Go on now," he nodded toward the door. "Wouldn't want to get you into trouble," he said.

"No, no," she said as she quietly left the shed, going back out into the crisp night air, back into her small room. She sat there on her cot, impressed by the gentlemanly quality he possessed, certain of his concern for her well-being.

7

Marian returned to Inchicore and the Silverbridge Orphanage with a compulsion, hoping to spot her son. She noticed a boy, around four years old, who looked as if he was a recent arrival, standing in the middle of the dirt lot staring at the older boys playing cards on the side wall. Two teenage girls were sitting together on the steps that led to the main building, each with a box of shoes by their feet to be shined. Small children in scratchy knickers twirled on an old roundabout. A thick concrete wall surrounded their playground, closing them off from the schoolchildren down the road who walked by in their proper uniforms for outings at Mulvin's Sweet Shop without so much as a glance at the orphanage kids.

For days after her visit with Nurse at Castleboro, Marian said very little. It was as if she'd been flung down a hole and she was lost in that foggy place and couldn't clear her head.

"I'm going to bed early," she told Ben and Johanna many evenings now. "I must have come down with something," she said as she cleared the dinner plates. Leftovers and a can of Heinz beans again was all that she could muster. "I'll take a cold tablet, get to bed early," she repeated and excused herself.

Why had Nurse kept Adrian a secret from me for so long?

As time shoved on and pushed her life into the busyness of the present, Marian had thought very little about Adrian, hadn't cared to interfere in *his* pleasant life, either. It was enough to have known that he was living in America, and she had been secretly proud, too, that she had provided a child with such a life. She had moved on, or so she thought. Wasn't that right? No. It wasn't. *I know that isn't true, come on.* It had never been true. Something had been missing, something she liked to pretend coincided with the death of her father but had never been that alone. What about that first year, peeking into other people's prams in the hopes of seeing a glimpse of him? And throughout their marriage, there had been her secret comparisons between

Adrian and Jo as infants, and worse, the secret anger that she must
pretend Jo was her first.

On her fourth visit to the orphanage, Marian was sure she saw him
in a rowdy group of boys of all sizes and shapes, pushing and shoving each other, poking a fat one in the stomach. They seemed completely disinterested in a bunch of girls gathered nearby giving them
a giggle or two. A stout nun named Sister Agnes tapped the butts of
little boys and girls with a stick to keep them in line. In the yard, the
one with the freckles who kept shouting that he was going to climb
the wall like a hairyman was jumping, trying to hold on to the wall,
and then falling to the concrete floor. Sister Agnes noticed him, too.
He would be still until she turned her back, at which point he would
imitate her, his legs spread apart like a drunken cowboy. The one with
the freckles—she could feel it, knew for sure that this gawky pread-
olescent with the broad shoulders, his eyes red with exhaustion, was
Adrian. She saw her father in him, knew that her da would have gotten him the hell out of there, knew that he would have been loved by
her da. She was falling in love with her son as well. She waited there
until recess was over and watched without seeming to, she hoped.
He was entertaining her with his silliness, and she felt—no, saw—
something unmistakably familiar in his expressions.

Finally, Marian decided to enter the front hallway of this house of
horrors to look for Sister Agnes.

"Can I help you?" Sister Agnes said as Marian glanced at some
teenagers hanging off the stair landing on the second floor making
grotesque gestures behind Sister's back.

"No," Marian said. "Well, I guess, yes, you can actually. I'm looking for someone."

"Yes?" Sister Agnes said, folding her arms across her chest.

"Actually, I've been told that my son, whom I'd given up for adoption to America, is here in Dublin. I'm his mother."

"You're his mother but you don't know where he is?" Sister Agnes
said. "Do you know his name?" Sister Agnes said in what Marian
perceived to be a mocking tone.

"His name is Adrian Ellis."

"Ah," she said, flicking a tick off the sleeve of her robe. "Our dear Adrian Ellis. Yes, he's one of mine. A bit of a Devil, too," Sister Agnes said.

8

Marian took solace in the garden as the light began to fade. Her favorite time of day, this period between light and dark, the twilight hour. She listened to the American tune "Lola" faintly coming from the O'Rourke's open kitchen door. Marian gazed across the way and watched the girls helping Mrs. O'Rourke pin sheets to her clothesline.

"Can we go out with the ball and play with Margaret?" Jo suddenly asked Mrs. O'Rourke, noticing her friend from the neighborhood sauntering by.

Mrs. O'Rourke didn't seem to hear her. Someone (must be O'Rourke home yet again) turned the record player on to Roy Orbison's hit, "Only the Lonely." Marian listened as Mr. O'Rourke sang out from the kitchen.

"I don't like this music," Jo said to Anna. "My ma listens to this every day. Can we change it?"

I do not listen to music, period, it seems. Why say that, Jo? Marian thought about her son, brought up in a Dublin orphanage—raised so different from Jo—and yet, there was a similarity. A spunk, a spark (if Adrian's mimicking Sister Agnes in the playground was any indication). They both seemed to be rabble-rousers. No doubt in their kids' genes on both sides. *No one tells you anything, or warns you except by way of joking, about the pre-adolescent years,* Marian thought. Jo was right; she was like a bag of cats.

"How about Chubby Checker?" Rona said, putting on one she knew Johanna loved.

"Come on, girls, let's see how handy we are with our feet," Mr. O'Rourke said, coming out of the kitchen as Johanna skedaddled toward the front of their house with their red dodge ball. "Let's do the twist."

"You mean the mashed potato, Mr. O'Rourke!" Jo called out, running down the street after Margaret.

"All right, then. Let's do the mashed potato," he said. As he began to dance, he looked around for her but she was gone.

Jo kept running, bouncing her ball, calling to Margaret. The ball came loose as Margaret stopped and waved, and Jo ran to retrieve it from the road, waving at her friend as she went. It was then that Marian heard the sound of a motorcar screech to a halt. Marian ran from the garden and saw Johanna lying on the road. She shouted to Mr. O'Rourke to shut off the music and call an ambulance.

Mrs. O'Rourke stood by her front door, aghast, as neighbors gathered around the street.

"What in God's name?" Marian gasped, running over. "Get a washcloth," she shouted to Mrs. O'Rourke who seemed frozen by her door.

"It's okay," Marian said, now by Johanna's side. "Not a big gash at all." Relief. Only a bloody chin, nothing more. Marian looked to her neighbors who had gathered around them. She rose as the ambulance arrived and watched over Jo as the medics cleaned her wound. She was not in need of more than one stitch, thank God. By the time the medics had finished, Jo looked dazed and what Marian observed enraged her. Mrs. O'Rourke had not budged from her front yard and was now receiving comfort from the neighbors who migrated to her stoop. *Do my neighbors see me as a mother with a rambunctious imp or as a bad mother who lets her daughter stay out too late?*

"I thought I told you to stay on the pavement," Marian said to Jo as she sat up.

"Da said I can play kickball in the street—"

"Before dark, Johanna!"

"I was just getting the ball, Ma."

Marian marched over to Mrs. O'Rourke's gate. "Just want to protect the kids, right?" she said. "Who gives you the right to decide my daughter can play outside after dark, in the street, no less?"

"I didn't know she took the ball," Mrs. O'Rourke said.

Marian hated the cublike gentleness in her voice. She returned to the street.

"Is she all right, then?" Mrs. Brady called out.

"She's fine," Marian said. She helped Jo limp into the house. Marian looked to Mrs. O'Rourke for a better apology but received only a blank stare. She shook her head and left, dragging her body into the kitchen to put on the kettle. She was up to ninety, though, bursting with anger as she walked Jo up the stairs and saw the same group of women still on Mrs. O'Rourke's stoop, smoking and whispering. "Why were they all there," she muttered.

"I would not be surprised if Mrs. O'Rourke enjoys making waves. People have private issues, Jo," she said and her tone sounded like a harsh reprimand. "Make sure other people leave our family alone."

Marian opened Johanna's door. "Up to your room without supper, you. You could have been killed. You're not a baby anymore, Jo. I can't watch you day and night, like an infant."

Marian shook her head at her but also felt a surge of guilt.

"You'll not have any cocoa later, either. Not a thing. And *stay* in your room," Marian said and shut Johanna's door.

9

A night with Johanna safe in her room was exactly what Marian needed. From the cabinet, she retrieved the Black and White Label and waited for Ben. Huge audible sighs were her forte, she thought as she turned off the kettle and breathed out her anxiety. She gave herself a good pour of the whiskey, took a long, warm swallow, and poured another shot.

Marian could make out Ben on the far corner of their street, his briefcase covering his head, slowing past Furlong's Sandwich Shop, gazing in the window at a solo customer who might be eating his favorite dish—sauce and meatballs—probably wondering what Marian was making for supper tonight. She had no time or inclination. How could she have his dinner on her mind today? This wasn't your ordinary, busy, family shenanigans. Marian wasn't sure about what to do or what to say. The two of them should get away, they both knew. And then there's Jo on top of it. Always. He suggested trips abroad but he hadn't followed through. Did he think that she was pregnant? He was so understanding about her odd, quiet, confused self. Or was it indifference? He truly is an eejit, Marian thought. She was not tired or nauseated, the way she'd been stomach sick with Jo. She was demoralized. Maybe Ben's aloofness was a sign that he had fallen out of love with her; was that the underlying problem?

She watched him pull up the sides of his collar and walk with his head down, tapping his newspaper against the iron railings that lined the front yards of their street. Passover just past and he was still feeling cold all the time. Another Passover without a real family celebration, without Tatte, *olev hasholem*—peace be on him. They would have to pay more attention to their marriage. She could feel herself drifting away. He quickened his pace, counting the steps to their home.

She turned off the telly. Ben would have already talked with Mr. Darby about the troubles in the North and another fit of violence that occurred that afternoon. Three Protestant males were beaten to a pulp during a Catholic civil rights demonstration. Years ago, he tried to get his article approved on a history teacher and his young pupil running away together but was flatly refused. Recently he decided to take a different tack, hoping his elevated status at the paper would protect him, but printing a commentary about violence in the national schools, without Darby's go-ahead, infuriated his boss. Darby told him he was thick as shite for this latest publishing stunt. He spent most of yesterday being yelled at by crusty Mr. Darby and arrived home deeply perturbed. He had been clandestinely researching for months. "Ridding the schools of abusive teachers," was the caption. Five bishops called the paper. What in God's name had he been thinking, Mr. Darby shouted, writing an article about physical abuse in schools taught by our holy Christian Brothers! Ben argued with him against censorship all afternoon. Columnists were paid for their opinion and read because of the controversy, he insisted, but it was a no-go. Mr. Darby said he'd rather gargle with rusty razor blades than listen to the reactions of the clergy to Ben's scandalous prose. Ben was ordered to write a personal apology, including the statement that by causing insult to so many he'd alienated his audience. Mr. Darby wrote a public recantation as well. Both would appear on the front page in tomorrow's *Irish Times*. Their conversation ended with Darby putting Ben on probation. No more elevated status.

After closing the front door behind him, Ben walked past their oddly silent foyer and switched on the living room lamp. The only sound heard was the soft ticking of the clock on the mantel. Not knowing how to react to the quiet, he called out as he walked into the kitchen. "No kisses tonight?"

There was Marian, a bottle of Black and White Label in one hand, two glasses on the counter.

"Did you wait for the bus in the sprinkle, sans umbrella, with the other shmeels?"

"*Schlemeils,* Marian. Hey, slow down on the whiskey," he said, coming over to kiss her.

"I'm ashamed," she said. "How can you stand me?"

"It's not easy," he said with a smile, then asked, "What's happened? For God's sake, I'm worried sick about you, Marian."

"I'm making you miserable, aren't I?"

"Ah, you are."

"I'm sorry. I'm sorry altogether. That's what I told Father Brennan, too."

"This is the last of it, Marian. No more hiding from me."

"How have you been able to work with me so—"

"I write better when I'm miserable," he tried to joke.

Inside, she was bracing herself.

"What is it you're trying to tell me, Marian?"

"I went somewhere, long ago."

He stared hard at her.

"It won't happen again. I went back for information," she said, louder.

"Shh, it's okay. Talk softly, but talk," he said, though he looked petrified.

"Have you given Johanna dinner?" he asked.

She shook her head no.

"Ben, I'm a bad mother," she said. She noticed her words were slurring.

He touched her cheek with the back of his hand, as if feeling her temperature.

"The Northern troubles percolating on the telly all day, you've had enough unrest tonight," she said.

"No worries," he said. "Let's get through this."

"We'll talk tomorrow," she said.

"Have your drink. We're getting this out tonight."

She shut her eyes, then opened them, smiled at him, then frowned. He lit a cigarette.

"Rhododendron bushes in red, pink and white, I think," Marian said, looking out the window, her eyes wet and burning. She took the fag, inhaled deeply, and then passed it back to him.

"I'm going to make us the poshest garden in all Donnybrook," Marian said. "Loaded with color. Geraniums and mums. Daffodils and roses and lilacs. The lot."

"Oh, you are, are you? You are such a person?" Ben teased, and took his drink. "Such a grand gardener."

"No, I suppose, no." That concerned look of his returned. "I have dreadful, shameful memories, Ben. Memories I shouldn't share with anyone, and they keep drifting into my head. They make me feel less than a person."

Ben moved close to her. "You'll plant bright red roses and yellow daffodils. And you'll wear a red fedora while you garden," he said. "And you're no such thing. You're far from dreadful. There's nothing you could tell me that could make me love you any less."

"I've seen pictures of red fedoras and convertibles on the newsstands, fashionable American women in Marilyn McKeever red lipstick," she whispered.

"Yeah?" he said, squinting at her playfully, their entwining bodies resting against the counter.

She began to tear up and he held her, sniffed as if he smelled something unfamiliar. Where had she been today? And yet he leaned closer, played with her hair. He loved her. She knew this. She always knew this. Long before he undressed her. Long before he said the words.

"I'm listening," he said.

"Well, it just seems that God's not really part of the plan and that some of those married to God must have henpecked Him to death," she said.

He smiled to encourage her. She was about to make a point.

"Have I committed adultery? Have you committed adultery, Ben?" she asked and then chuckled.

"Of course not, Marian—Jesus!"

"Have I murdered anyone? Did I not ask God for forgiveness a zillion times, and didn't God so love the world that he sent His only begotten Son to save humankind? Didn't Mary Magdalene wash

Jesus' feet, and though she was a prostitute, didn't He forgive her? Doesn't God have the power to forgive all?"

"You need to talk. Talk," he said. "I'm after an explanation of some sort."

"You better sit down, Ben. Here, next to me." She walked into the dining room and pulled two chairs together.

He brought the Black and White and the two tumblers with him.

"Ben, I've kept something from you for years."

Ben refreshed their drinks.

"I'm ashamed. And I'm terrified, actually, that you're going to go mad when you hear what I have to say."

"Marian, enough! Shutting me out is worse. I'm ready to tear my hair out."

"Okay, Ben. Do you remember the night we met your parents?" she said.

He sipped his drink, gave her a sarcastic look.

"Well, I told you I was going on holiday with Father Brennan," she said. Blood heaved through her. The moment she hoped would never come was here. "I wasn't on holiday. I went to a hellish place, Ben. Ben—I had a baby, and they took him. Sixteen days after he was born."

She forced herself a brief look in his direction. Ben stared into his glass, tapping the side of his tumbler. *I have blindsided him on an ordinary day. Will we ever be the same? Not likely, from the look on his face.*

"I hoped to never hear that," he said hoarsely, taking her hand. "I thought we both buried it forever, but secrets have a curious way about them."

"You thought *what?*"

"Okay. It's clear as day still." He paused. "Me, tapping the steering wheel driving to Westmeath. I'd been screaming bloody hell for over seven weeks, and been to hell and back trying to find you, yeah. Robert Thompson? He straightened me out. I told him everything about our marriage plans and about your sudden disappearance.

He asked if we had had relations. I felt an eejit. Your stonewalling priest of an uncle was involved. By then, I knew that much, that he sent you to a Mother Baby Home."

Thompson, Ben's confidante at the *Times* and the only witness at their wedding, told him County Wicklow was a good start, so he went there first and found two Mother Baby Homes, but neither of them had a clue who Marian McKeever might be. He drove south to Waterford and Cork and on to Kerry, and saw more than a few Mother Baby Homes littered throughout southern and western Ireland before he found Castleboro Mother Baby Home, and he was damn sorry that he lost so much time.

Am I hearing right? Marian straightened in her chair but to no avail. She entered that place of disbelief she'd entered when her da died. The world altered forever.

"I had to tell Mr. Darby I'd be back in a few weeks. He was livid, especially that I missed the Soviet satellite Sputnik over Dublin for the second time in a month."

He missed seeing the Sputnik over Dublin? Oh poor, dear Ben. Poor Mr. Darby and the newspaper. "What are you saying, Ben?"

"I'm saying I was there at Castleboro."

Marian felt shock, complete disbelief.

Two nuns, not getting any younger, were having tea."

Am I hearing jokes now?

"They peered at me. I slammed the car door, grabbed my Kodak camera," (a perk for his promotion to features reporter at the *Irish Times,* one that he bragged about, even now).

She pictured a pencil tucked behind his ear. Disrespectful. Wonder if he took off his hat.

"I explained that I was here to get you. The nuns gave a queer look before the Reverend Mother ushered a Sister P-something and me into a room off the parlor. 'What is your relation to this person?' they asked. I knew I'd found you." He took a sip of his drink. "I told them your name, that you were sent by Father Brennan to deliver a baby, and that I would take you home when you're ready. Very calm. I had them."

She got up and got a glass of water from the tap. Ben waited.

"They spent a good deal of time questioning me." He looked around the dining room, scrunching up his nose, as if sniffing a memory of musty incense in the air. "Look, Your Eminence, I said. I'm not leaving until I see her."

"Your Eminence?" Marian couldn't contain a burst of shocking laughter, which both she and Ben (from his distressed look) found odd. It *was* odd, but then Marian might also be near hysterics.

"Sister-something whispered something to the Reverend Mother and then went on a diatribe about men not permitted to see their girls. They're to be hidden from society until they have their babies and resume their normal lives. They said even if 'Miss McKeever' were there, they wouldn't allow a visit, for reasons of confidentiality. But regardless, they all of a sudden didn't know any Miss McKeever. Sometimes they said the girls protect themselves, by not using their real names, so they couldn't be absolutely certain."

Ben reached for his hat and stood to make his point. "'I'm a journalist, Sisters, and if you don't give me what I need—a visit with Marian and more definitive information—I promise you I will be back with the press. Tomorrow,'" Ben continued, and Marian began to feel numb. She moved in her chair "They left for a while. I grabbed my camera when they came back, too quickly in my opinion, to have done a proper search for you."

He really was there.

"Again, Sister P said that there was no one here by that name, but she thought she knew who you were. Bizarre. She said you didn't have the proper 'headage' fee to leave, that without that fee, you'd be staying there for as long as it takes to find him a foster home."

Hadn't that bitch ever contacted Father Brennan about me?

"'Did you just say *him*?' I said. Marian, I was devastated." Ben glared at her. "You're from a respectable Irish *Catholic* family is all they would tell me. Is she a red-head with freckles? I asked. 'There are some freckles to this one,' Sister P said. I'll never forget that line. Like she was talking about a cow." Ben shook his head. "She said the boy has taken on your genes so I should leave. They had work to do."

Ben shook his head again. "A healthy baby boy and I should leave! I was ready to pop one of them. I demanded to see you. There was no way I was leaving either of you there," he said. "Sisters, I'll take them both with me today. I pushed out my chair, stood, held my camera to my eye. You should have seen the alarmed faces."

He wants to see an alarmed face? Does he see mine?

"The nun took out a letter, waved it like a surrender flag. Written by you. 'It is Miss McKeever's wishes that this child be protected from the disgrace attached to her present circumstances. These girls are like tin cans rattling down the street, Mr. Ellis. They're weak,' she added. 'If you mention the baby, well, her mental state will deteriorate further. She just wouldn't be able to live with others knowing.'"

He stopped, sipped his drink. "You could leave as soon as they found a proper Catholic family. There was one hundred pounds involved. The letter confirmed you didn't want your baby, she told me. They're a bit like spoofers, aren't they?" Ben concluded.

"Are you making light?"

"Of course not! I was shouting at this point, asking for real confirmation that these weren't more lies, confirmation that you didn't want your baby."

Marian felt something engulfing her, something hot and raging pounding her temples.

"Go on," Marian said with deliberate calm.

"'Ah, okay,' I said, bluffing. 'Ah, well, *I'm* sure Marian would want to see me, and I must see her immediately,' and I ran. They yelled some crap after me about your need for privacy."

Marian could picture Sister Penis in a tizzy.

"I kept snapping photos as I ran across the drive. 'Call the guards!' They ran, screaming, 'Get him and that camera.' Officers pushed my face into the dirt, handcuffed me, confiscated my camera. I swore at Sister P, and she huffed off to the maternity ward." Ben looked straight at her now. "Didn't you ever wonder where that state-of-the-art camera went?"

Marian didn't answer.

"There was some crazy, scary-looking nurse helper in a state herself who slammed the maternity door. I took a good look around on the way out. All doors and windows were clamped shut; a *No Entry* sign was posted in the fields. My only thought was you, and I told the guards I'd pay whatever it cost to bring you out of that terrible place. Marian, they took the money. I waited days. They told me to go home or they'd lock me up in Mountjoy. My biggest question to this day, Marian. Why didn't you tell me?"

He was angry? "I couldn't tell you," she said. She gazed into the bowl of nuts on the table before managing to look at him. "It was Father Brennan's idea. But after that night—"

"Enough, Marian," he began, "I'm not buying blaming my parents."

"That day I found out I was pregnant, I was going to tell you. I wanted to. Instead, I went down to Wexford and I had our son. The nuns gave him to an American family who could properly take care of him. That's what I thought. I thought it was the right thing to do," she said.

Ben looked intently into her drained face. "I thought it was the right thing to do, too," he said. He hesitated, took a deep breath. "I'm the one who paid the money to get you out, remember." His face turned pale, even more so than it already was. His lower lip was trembling. "They said without the fee, you'd be stuck in there and he'd go to a foster family. It was the only way he'd find a decent home."

Marian whirled her hand out of his, stood up unsteadily, and staggered across the room.

"Listen, you have to understand," Ben said, rising from his chair.

"No, I don't."

"Understand that I was only doing—"

"Understand that you've been lying? All these years, you kept that from me? Did you know even more about him all along, you bastard? Did you know where he ended up?" She yelled.

"Listen, you. Don't you dare raise your voice at me! I kept it a secret, just like you. I was trying to fecking protect you. They told me you wanted to pretend it never happened. The nuns said if I mentioned anything about it, you might go mad and I believed them. Why wouldn't I have? You didn't tell me, ever, which is the real shocker."

Marian felt enraged, hated him.

"Ben, I would have stayed in there the rest of my life. A nightmare, yes, but once I had my baby I didn't want to leave. I could have had two years with him there." She began to sob in short bursts.

He looked stunned and hurt. "And then what? Tell me, where would those nuns place him? The guards told me the lucky ones go to America, but it costs. I wanted the best for him, too. I wanted what you wanted. It was ours, Marian. Not just yours."

"*It* has a name." He could see her body was quivering and tried to wrap his arms around her, massage her shoulders, but she refused his help. "I named him Adrian. I was going to name him after you, but I remembered Jews don't do that."

"Why *did* you disappear like that, Marian?"

"Your budding career would have been over before it–"

"That's not what I asked," Ben said.

"What about you?" She screamed. "You're the one who let me down. There, I've finally said it, loud and clear." She tightened the wide lavender belt of her flare skirt.

He almost coughed up his drink with that. "Me?"

"I was worrying more about ruining your career at the *Irish Times* than the future of my own son, imagine that. And your goddamn mother that night was killing you. I didn't want to overtax you," she said, incredulous. She wouldn't recognize that girl now.

She got up abruptly and walked upstairs to check on Johanna. She seemed asleep and she was glad about that. She looked down at her slight face, remembered the day Jo was born in Rotunda Hospital. A private room with a young nurse attending to their every need. Ben had spent most of that first week painting the nursery pink and outfitting her white crib with pink tea rose sheets, a pink blanket and a clockwork bear, some plastic dolls. He'd bought a rocking chair and a porcelain doll as well. How happy they had been. But maybe that wasn't the truth. Maybe she hadn't really been happy. Just lying. Maybe he had been doing the same. She headed back downstairs, holding the mahogany handrail to lighten the clatter of her shoes.

"You should have told me," he said, back in the dining room. "You knew. I didn't."

"You should learn to make faster decisions, Mr. Journalist," she said, snapping her fingers.

He sat back down, poured both of them another whiskey. She kept standing, drumming the table.

"Marian, I never stopped thinking about you the whole time you were away."

There was silence.

"I needed you, right then," she said quietly.

"I ran to the maternity ward and met that half-wit, too. I ran about the ward, trying to locate an authority. She scuttled right up to me, ran out a door, brought in that patrolling officer who handcuffed me and took me down to the Garda station, all the while I was calling your name."

"You must have been whispering."

"Oh, for fuck's sake! The officers said that you girls just want to get the hell out. I could believe it. I saw some sights up close, Marian. Desperate faces of clammy, pregnant girls about to fall into huge baskets of hospital sheets and towels they were hauling somewhere. What a photograph this would make in the *Times:* 'A medieval maternity ward.' They told me not to ever bring it up, either, if you didn't. Finally, I paid," Ben said.

"So you've said."

"Are you blaming me?"

"Let me ask you this. You're a journalist, and you believed that I was going on vacation with my uncle the priest?"

"Marian, I–"

"And you're calling Nurse a nut?" She picked up the bowl of cashews and threw them at him. He leapt from his seat and grabbed the bowl away from her.

"Where is the child, Marian?"

Marian glared at him.

"Johanna said the visitor was peculiar," Ben said.

"Nurse. And apparently you've met. He's eleven-and-a-half, and he lives in Inchicore. In an orphanage. The nuns never sent him to America like they told me, but put him in a hellhole in Dublin," she said perfunctorily. Ben looked horrified. As well he should.

"I've been going there. It's hideous. Nurse has been seeing him all along. He's not faring well at all. He's being bullied."

"My God."

"I was so busy with Johanna, I suppose. I just buried it," she mumbled, leaning against the wall. She began to cry, and he tried to hold her again but she shoved him away.

"You know, you're always off in la-la land, Ben, thinking you're helping the world. Helping others starts at home."

"I'm not going to put up with Pollyanna shit from you, Marian. They gave me proof, all right? You put it in writing that you wanted to get out of that jail. Tell the truth for once. They showed me your letter. Proof you wanted out."

He could see she was ashamed, but also, he couldn't believe he'd been snowed and his actions were the cause of so much suffering. She knew he was ashamed as well.

"Now what?" he said. "God, those fucking black-robed people."

"Don't be talking shite about things you know nothing about! I don't allow anti-Semitism, and I won't have the other, Ben. It was my fault. No one else's."

"Damn Catholics. You're eating yourselves alive."

"Don't be damning the Catholics, either. Damn those sinister nuns, though," Marian muttered. "I wanted us to take Adrian home together," she said.

"They never would have allowed it," he said.

Marian looked away. She wondered if he was thinking what she was thinking: If only he had gotten there before she had the baby, could he have saved her and their son? He should have gotten there sooner. He should have hounded Father Brennan until the priest fessed up instead of driving around Ireland on hunches.

"We can't hurt Johanna," Ben said.

"It's all too much to think about," Marian said.

"No more lies, Marian. If there's anything else we're hiding, we should tell each other now."

"That's the only thing I've ever kept from you. And you from me, Ben? Is that it?"

He nodded.

"Are you sure?"

"Yes, I'm sure, Marian."

"I want you to know I waited for a donkey's years in that hellatious doctor's office, thinking about you and wondering how I would tell you. I should have told you before we got to your parents. I know that much now. One misstep and look at all the consequences. I wanted everything to happen in the right order, stupid girl that I was: the meeting of your parents, the dreaded meeting of my mother, more *craic* wandering the streets of Little Jerusalem and all over Dublin in the evenings after work, more Gaelic lessons for you, more Hebrew lessons for me, the marriage proposal. Please, I imagined your face transforming into something joyous when I told you about the pregnancy. You wouldn't leave me, I reminded myself as we walked to your parents' house that night, but you never gave me the time to get the words out."

He nodded, took a sip of his drink and waited for her to continue.

"We could have left for England immediately, could have married there and come back home to live," she said. "No one would have been privy to the order of things."

Ben took another sip, and Marian thought about her first year schoolchildren and all the questions they would have had watching her belly grow.

"I haven't been the same, Ben. I'm a derelict to have damaged myself. You must see that. I've never stopped thinking about him." She shook her head. "And I've been so alone."

"I thought you wanted to move on. I didn't want you to suffer anymore."

She didn't look at him but nodded in his direction.

"We've abandoned him," she said into the air, and then gave him a steely look.

"We'll figure something out, I promise."

She sat down, rested her head on the tabletop.

"Who's he like?"

"He's like me," she said, lifting her head. "He looks like me."

"Marian, I wish we'd talked."

"I wish we'd waited," she said and gave him one of her hard looks. "You've told me you can't bear living without me. Well, I can't cope knowing that Adrian is in Dublin right near us, living in poverty, being beaten," she said.

Ben got up, draining his drink.

"Look in on Johanna," he said and left the house. Up and down the streets, he would berate himself for his suppressions. He'd recall with shame a newspaper article that he wrote, just after Johanna was born, it was March of 1958, about abuse in industrial schools. He began it immediately after reading a column in which Gay Byrne discussed the misuse of fists as a school tool. He said he admired Mr. Byrne for his piece, and Ben—a new father and, admittedly now, a father who lost a son to the orphanage system, a scary thought— he was passionate about the subject. Had he often worried about his newborn son's placement? Once more, crappy Mr. Darby refused to print his take on the matter. Too scandalous, he said. Bollocks. He hadn't shared with Marian the myriad story ideas that Mr. Darby recently shot down, but Marian knew he was he on probation for more than writing about the violence in the Catholic schools. He worried more and more over the bills, even their recent splurge on new gardening tools added up, he said. He didn't want to worry her but his inheritance, generous as it was after selling Tatte's picture frame gallery, would not last forever. He told her how much he missed visiting regularly with his mother, how he wished they could all move on, that he prayed Marian would be the big-hearted one and make the telephone call to Bubbe, who was all alone and becoming increasingly frail.

When he returned from his walk, he sat in the living room alone until Marian came down the stairs in her beige bathrobe, a faint smell of Dippity Do gel in her hair. He looked calmer, and she came over to sit with him on the couch.

"Well, at least he's ours," he whispered. Was he *also* thinking what a mess the boy must be? Probably not good for Johanna, his *maidelah*—but voiced none of his doubts.

"We'll use everything we've got, all your connections down at the *Times*. And we'll get him home," Marian said.

"We'll do everything we can," Ben agreed, though being on probation was a huge worry. He would have to make amends to his boss somehow.

10

Downstairs, Marian could hear Jo crack her bedroom door ajar to listen to her parents talk and whisper on the couch. How long had she been listening?

"Children should be unseen and should listen!" Jo shouted from her room, startling Marian.

"How long do you think she's been listening to us?" Marian whispered to Ben.

Jo came down the stairs and stared at them, still in her school uniform. She had her door ajar long enough so that her heart leapt with all the murmurings about a long lost big brother, that the odd-looking lady knew exactly where he was, that she'd brought him to the secret hiding place herself, and a Mulvin's Sweet Shop was on the way. He toughened up over the years, rest assured, Nurse told Marian, and Marian told Ben that she was seeing purple. A ward of the state, Nurse had put it. He was raised less than one hour away. Less than one hour away, Marian repeated over and over, each time getting Johanna more and more excited. The girl had big ears.

"The place is awful. The orphans spit at each other!" Jo yelled with anger and excitement mixed together in her little body.

"Johanna, you shouldn't be eavesdropping on your parents," Marian said in a low voice. "You've disobeyed me again. I asked you to stay in your room."

"Stupid," Jo said, looking at Ben as she stood by the front door, playing with the doorknob. "Ma's been doing a lot of oddities lately, but no more so than tonight."

"Johanna! Up to your room. How dare you talk like that about your mother," Ben said, somewhat surprising Marian.

"And now, of course," Jo said, somewhat mocking him, "Da, you'll chime right in!" Then, no dummy herself, she marched upstairs and closed her door.

Marian told Ben with her finger to keep mum. Ben nodded, put his head in his hands. He must have realized, too, that Jo was not done with them yet.

They listened to her door creak open, waited for her to descend. Jo cocked her head halfway down the stairs.

"Children pick up on stuff, even very young children. The parents think they're fooling them, but they're not. Don't you know I know something's up?" she asked.

Marian and Ben looked at each other.

"I didn't come up the Liffey on a bicycle, ya know. Silly and stupid," Jo said. "Annoying as a bag of cats, too. Whatever it is, I ought not to be sitting in my room. I ought to be told, too. I'm not a baby, for God's sake! If I'm old enough to walk to school, I'm old enough to know!" she screamed.

Marian sent her immediately back to her room.

Ben got up and held onto the stair railing. Jo appeared at the top of the stairs again.

"All right, spit it out. Spit it out!" Jo seemed to be begging now as she came down the stairs and stood on the bottom step, staring quizzically at her father.

Marian and Ben looked at one another and then at their daughter, dumbfounded looks on their faces. Marian walked over to the two of them, staring at each other like a cat and mouse, Jo ready to pounce.

"What you heard is correct, Johanna," Marian said. "You have a brother. We're going to be filling you in on the details all along the way, love."

"*Tanzhe, tanzhe vevyeke*," whispered Ben as he put his arm around a droopy Jo. "Dance, dance, little squirrel. Up to your room." He wrapped her blanket around her slender shoulders as he trudged upstairs with her like a sack and plunked their daughter onto her bed. But Johanna soon came back downstairs, shook her head at them and then ran up the stairs and whacked her door shut.

Marian and Ben looked at each other and trudged upstairs.

"We're all going to bed now. Good night, Johanna."

"Good night," Jo answered.

They listened by Jo's door and heard her quietly climb out of her window. They watched her clutch the drainpipe, and then climb over the tricky spears and axes railing that adorned the fence which separated her house from the twins'—no doubt to spread the word. Marian saw the kitchen light on and crept down the stairs and out the front door, stooped by the fence to listen. Jo sat at the O'Rourke's kitchen table enjoying milk and bread pudding and sharing with the girls and their mother the news of a secret older brother. Marian stood on the ledge and peeked into their kitchen window. Upon hearing of a lost child, Mrs. O'Rourke turned scarlet, the little veins on her face deepened making her white cheeks look even more like radishes. Her evident discomfort prompted Johanna to thank her for the snack and change the subject.

11

Ever since Jo had told her classmates that she had a brother some-where, that's all the boys and girls wanted to talk about.

"My ma says your ma's mixed up in the head," Jeannie Johnson chided Jo one afternoon, when Mrs. Crowe the monitor had gone off the playground. Johanna could feel her blood churning up inside her as her body prepped for a battle against the bull of bulls. She could feel the kids forming a circle and then she heard, "Don't let her sit on you, Jo!"

"She's a lying whore," Jo told Jeannie. She added, "You fat pig!" inciting a burst of laugher from her friends before she spat at the ground and readied herself for an attack from a girl-woman twice her size.

"Don't let her sit on you!" someone shouted again.

"I won't." She raised her dukes. "You know, your ma's a lying whore, Jeannie. Your last name's Jelly, too. Not Johnson. You're a right bastard," Jo said, listening to the cheering noises and watching Jeannie's shoulders hunch round her large frame, ready to pounce.

The crowd roared when Jeannie launched her attack. Jo felt like running, this mound of blubber could kill her if she got hold of her, got her to the ground. But Jo reminded herself she was an athlete and a lot quicker than this dimwit. She sprinted around her, poking close to her stomach, antagonizing the furious bull.

"Jeannie Jelly! Jeannie Jelly!" Jo got the crowd to chant. Victory, thank the Lord, was speedy. Somehow Jo reached over and grabbed Jeannie's thick ponytail knot and—thank the Lord again—long ponytail, and keeping her distance, dragged her down and around in circles until she looked like a hunchback or some kind of wild beast, her hands reaching out above her head.

When Jeannie managed to grab hold of Jo's arm, Jo's hand squeezed tight she didn't know how she had the good luck—and snatched at Jeannie's shirt. In an attempt to get away, Jo raised the

shirt. The buttons flew off, and then a huge hush came over the playground, as if they'd all inhaled together.

Everyone stared at Jeannie's ginormous, old-fashioned brassiere,
the likes of which no one in this class had ever needed or seen up
close on a person before, and never on a classmate. Jeannie Jelly, in
what must have been some sort of panic, stood still, and allowed the
crowd a moment of viewing before she stalked off red and white in
speckled patches of her skin. *No doubt a memory this bull of a girl-
woman will never forget,* Jo thought, still shell-shocked herself from
the bird's eye view of a brassiere that was almost as large as a girdle,
and the sudden triumph, the startled joy from the entertainment she
had by some means provided on the faces of her mates.

Mr. Hinckley's brow furrowed when she told him, too, and his
mouth got squishy, lines going everywhere, and she knew instantly
that she said too much to him. She tried her best to have the tears
boil up and, miracle of miracles, it worked, leading to yet another
pleasant surprise when Marian came to retrieve her. Mr. Hinckley
told Marian that there had been a dislocation but it was minor and
already resolved. Marian gazed at his foggy face. She had bigger
things on her mind. She thanked him with a sincerity she never before felt. Marian repeated on the way home that we shouldn't brag
about Adrian, but she wasn't harsh. She just said to her that it was
time that Jo outgrew the stage when you tell the teacher, the stranger,
anybody everything, and asked her if she told the O'Rourkes yet.
Johanna looked up at her mother, the way she did when she wanted
something. This time she wanted forgiveness. Marian knew soon
there would be talk up and down the street, if there wasn't already.

Jo was helping Marian clean out the attic when the full extent of
Jo's talking became clear. She couldn't wait to show her much-antic-
ipated new playmate the stuffed toy chest with the gun holsters and
the cowboy hats, the clown costumes, and all the circus attire that
surrounded her and her mother. She convinced Ben to buy the whole
lot. "We must get some things that boys like, too. I don't want any
dolls for myself," Jo said, "but I do think the circus games would be

fun for me, Da." All the kids wanted to meet him, wanted to come over and use the new games, and Jo kept them updated on any over-heard progress to get her brother into their house.

So much Johanna didn't know, but one thing she did: Things were changing. And there was a part of her that was excited that soon her parents would tell her more about her brother, but Marian worried that there was a part of her that no longer trusted either of them. When they came down from the attic, Johanna noticed the photo-graph of her was no longer in its place on the mantelpiece. She stomped into her pink bedroom, sat on her high bed, and poked the hard buttoned nose of her stuffed Toto. She wondered why her mother was not including her, wondered if she herself could have anything to do with Adrian's fate. Marian told her, again, that was ridiculous, as she did last week when Jo asked; she was not even born yet. She didn't want to upset her ma, so she didn't tell her until now about the nun who visited her school and asked her some questions. At first, when Sister Agnes asked Johanna about her prayer life, she said she prayed that her parents would stop fighting over Adrian, and Sister Agnes prayed with her. But her puffy eyes stretched wide open when Johanna asked her if it were true that some people thought Catholics were damned. Jo knew that she went too far, and said she must have misunderstood her father.

PART II

12

Adrian Ellis was fairly good with numbers, for a boy of eleven years, as proved by his skill in maths class at Silverbridge Orphanage. Late last night he taught his friend Peter Twombly how to multiply by tens. The outside teacher, Mr. Callahan, was the kindest man he'd ever known, and beside the large pictures of the Joyful, Glorious and Sorrowful Mysteries of the Rosary, he posted a bright ten times table on the wall and gave out navy blue sticky stars when the class correctly recited their tables. His friend Peter hadn't the benefit of the outside teacher. Peter wasn't a real orphan, but Sister Agnes called him one anyway. Although his mother visited twice each year, she couldn't pay anything so she wasn't like a real mother, and he had no other visits from relatives. Real orphans were treated far worse than the children who had regular, paying visitors. Sister Agnes told them that it costs to raise the spawn of whores and that orphans had nothing to add to what the State provided for their upkeep. Peter's ma was visiting today, this June morning, and taking Adrian with them. Adrian was over the moon.

He couldn't wait to get out and breathe in the smells from the Inchicore sandwich shop and try to read a book and—ah, just everything!

Adrian fought the weakness he felt from lack of sleep, though. He was sick to his stomach from the slop he'd eaten for supper, and ran to the toilet with the smelly flood rushing down his legs. He tried to do a job of cleaning himself, but failed miserably. Wanting a bit of comfort, he meandered into St. Peter's Dormitory, where the babies lived, to watch Sister Adela on duty feeding them. Approaching her with mouth wide open, she pushed a spoon filled with goody into his mouth, then put a finger to her lips silently telling him to keep his pie hole shut. He reached out and hugged Sister Adela. It was the sweetest food he ever tasted, milk-soaked bread with sugar. She held him close to her. And kissed him on his head.

"When I grow up, I know for sure I'll be wanting to marry you," he said.

"Oh, for the love of God, when will you learn? You can't be marrying me," she said, wiping his cheek. Sister Adela and the orphan Rosemary, who had entered the room to help put the babies to bed, exchanged mocking glances, but he didn't mind as he was concentrating on the tingling feeling radiating from his head, the exact spot where Sister Adela's hand was resting.

"I'm already married to God," she added softly. He felt the tingles going up his head as she spoke, and he could have lingered there for hours.

"You'll just have to marry Rosemary," she said.

Rosemary blushed and laughed at what must have been the thought of marrying in general.

"He's a bit young for me," she said, "but he'll find himself a proper girl. He's as wide as a gate." Rosemary flashed a smile at him, and he fell under a trance of happiness.

"Here you go, Adrian. Clean up fast and then be off with the others," Sister Adela said, handing him some strips of newspaper. Sister Adela was the only one who called the orphans by their names. And why were they all called orphans anyway, he wondered. Many of the children had destitute parents who placed them there to insure three square meals and an education for a nominal boarding fee, Rosemary once told him.

He watched a young orphan girl, one of Sister Adela's helpers, slap a baby hard across its face to shock him out of crying. It made Adrian want to run over and punch her. Who did she think she was? She'd been little once herself, probably in this very room. The girl, he realized, was not much older than himself. She stood on a stool to reach into the infant's cot, and was more than likely, deathly afraid of a severe punishment if the baby in her care kept wailing. The nursery girls on duty were not the ones the nuns favored. They always put the detested ones with the babies, giving them no time at all—night or day—to play. Up all night they were, most of the time, with no way to stop their workload.

Sister Agnes thumped in and throttled him for being out of his dorm. Adrian was almost as tall as Sister Thunder Thighs and he loved that, wanted to compare heights with her all the time. He stood back from her now; she was in a mood.

"Sister Adela, what is Four Seventy-Six doing here?" Sister Agnes asked.

He hated watching Sister Adela become nervous. Her sweetness gone, she stared down at the wood floor.

"You know the boys are not to be in here with you."

"I'm sorry, Sister Agnes. He just needed a wipe," Rosemary interrupted. "Come with me," she said, and led him away. Sister's anger went through him, though, and he felt pee running down his leg, making a tapping noise as it hit the linoleum on the way down the hall. Rosemary cleaned up the stench quickly as he hurried away to the dormitory. He lay down on his cot, listening to the blessed brown radio discuss weather on a shelf across the room. Rosemary came in and sat beside him, wiped his face with a clean, cool towel, smiled and shook her head at him, ruffled up the top of his head.

"Meteorologists have argued that tornadoes don't happen in the British Isles. Thus, damage of this sort is attributed to a freak gust. Strong winds prevail out over the Atlantic and the Irish Sea, with speeds in the range of one hundred-twenty knots, and that, mixed with the rains forecast for..."

Rosemary's beauty and the weatherman held Adrian's attention.

"Wind gusts from the south-southwest with low visibility in the north around Mizenhead...severe convective storm on its way..."

"Now, are you all right, then?"

He stared up at Rosemary, prettier than any rose, with her black curly hair and large brown eyes. What he'd told Peter was wrong; she was even cuter than Betty Boop.

She hung his wash bag from the end of his iron bed.

"I'm sorry, Rosemary. Please forgive me."

"Ah, go on. I'm here for you, you know that," she said quietly. "You're grand. Peter's ma rang up, Adrian. She's unable to make it today, so you'll have to be content with the likes of me," she said smiling, her two front teeth slightly curled. "I'll keep you company, young man," she added as a comfort.

"Have you a fellow, Rosemary?" She giggled and blushed, and he knew, of course. She must.

"Thank you, God, for your mercy," he whispered, his hands clasped together.

"Are you praying to God for me?" she asked him.

"Yeah."

Her pretty face lit up, her dimples laughed out at the world.

"You'll be all right, then."

She leaned down and kissed him on the forehead and left.

Marian and Ben secured Mr. Greene, a solicitor from Parks, Greene and Sons, Limited. To no avail, Marian spoke with Judge Moran at the Four Courts to gain custody of Adrian. In 1960, Sister Agnes, Headmistress of Silverbridge, had become Adrian's legal guardian, Mr. Green reminded them, as if they didn't know. Institutionalized, marginalized, Marian thought with bitterness. Although it was not easy to face, Marian knew they would have to come to grips with the fact that Sister Agnes would determine Adrian's future. Still, Marian could not understand how a wanted child, their biological son, could be forced to remain someplace cold and unwelcoming, when their own warm home beckoned. No matter how loudly and often Mr. Greene spoke in her ear, Marian did not hear, could not be convinced of his drivel.

Mr. Greene advised them that Ben was throwing away his money trying to get custody of Adrian. Marian implored Mr. Greene to talk with Judge Moran, that Adrian's case is unique and should not require the input of the Silverbridge Orphanage Headmistress.

"You know the adoption laws, we've gone over it," he said.

"Any overruling by a judge is a pie in the sky dream," said Marian.

"I'm afraid it would be impossible. The final consent order is irrevocable." He waffled on and on about it.

"What about bringing this to the High Court?" Marian asked. She looked to Ben who did not return the look. He seemed only to hear Mr. Greene.

"I've rethought it, and the passage of time, I'm sorry, would defeat us. Your child has, according to law, assimilated into a new environment, and would not be awarded a subsequent adoption order."

"How can you be so sure? We're his parents. We want to adopt him." She spoke slowly in low tones. "He's in an orphanage, Mr. Greene, for God's sake. He has not assimilated; no doubt he would like nothing more than to be with his proper family. He's suffering in there. The law should not apply to children who have not been properly adopted, certainly."

"We'd have to employ a barrister for any court hearings, but I wouldn't recommend going that course."

"Why not?"

"Let's listen, Marian," Ben admonished her. Marian felt a tidal wave of anger.

"In the end, the process would be long and fruitless," Mr. Greene advised. "You would be wiser to convince Sister Agnes to relinquish her rights to your son; that would be the better way."

"Laws can be changed," Marian said.

"To change the law for minors, particularly orphans, will not—"

"Our son is not an *orphan*. Neither are half the kids in there. The Irish Constitution is all for preserving the family, first and foremost."

"Yes, but according to law, you abandoned your child. He was left in the care of the Sisters of Benevolence. There is no law stating that you automatically get him back on your slightest whim just because you have since married and had another child."

"My slightest whim?"

"It'll all be for the good, Marian," Ben said, placing a hand on her arm. "Isn't that right, Mr. Greene?"

"'Tis."

"I've had a meeting with Sister Agnes on your behalf," Mr. Greene continued. "The whole family needs adjusting, that's all."

"Johanna's to be considered as well," Ben agreed.

Marian flashed Ben another look. His mild contempt of the system was diametrically opposed to her rage. He was letting her down, again.

"I didn't relinquish my rights to him. I don't even remember signing that supposed legal paper."

"You did. That's your signature and there was a public notary that signed as well."

Marian studied the papers. Memory vague, but still, there were two documents: one admitting her into Castleboro Mother Baby

Home, the other, the release papers, placing Adrian in the care of the Sisters of Benevolence. She studied the signatures.

"Wait," she said. "These are not the same signatures. Look at this, Ben," she said. "This is mine, but this, I never signed this!" She passed the papers to Mr. Greene, Ben standing and leaning over the table.

"I don't know. That would be hard to prove."

"They look nothing alike," she said.

"We can raise the issue, but there will be claims that your signature differed because you were not yourself after the birth: tired, upset, et cetera. There's really no way of proving whose signatures these are."

Marian hadn't been able to recall signing release papers before Adrian was taken away in a black car. She couldn't remember walking past the guards and out those iron gates. She had a hazy remembrance of meandering down O'Connell Street some time that week. She'd bought Ma a scarf at Marks & Spencer, from England, supposedly, and herself a simple blue suit, leaving the maternity green tweed outfit Nurse had folded into her suitcase when she first arrived, in the fitting room.

"I've something else," Marian said now. "I thought I'd wait and show it to Mr. Greene as well, Ben" she said, pulling the tattered letter Nurse had left for her, the identical letter both she and Adrian had received at the orphanage. "'Dear Adrian,' it reads, 'I gave you to the nuns as I couldn't raise you. Be good for the nuns now. Pray for them every day, Ma.'" Marian searched their faces. Ben read the letter, looked at the solicitor for an explanation.

"That's a form letter, probably given to all the kids, as a comfort."

"A comfort?" Marian said.

"I don't know. Perhaps it's better than what they might imagine in their little heads," Mr. Greene said.

"Most of the children, I would imagine, would be too ashamed to show anyone such a letter, and might go into adulthood believing something appalling like this," she countered, feeling herself losing her temper. "This is an outrage. I never gave him up!" She stood up. "He was ripped from my arms. I was told nothing. Nothing!

Dress him in this. He's leaving in the morning. Just like that!" she said, and snapped her fingers. "They took him from me. I wanted him." She was now crying.

"We should leave," said Ben, rising from his chair.

"It's best to cry," she shouted at him. "Something has to be done." Ben's arm went around her as she fell back into her seat.

"Where in these documents is Adrian's birth certificate, Mr. Greene?"

"I don't know that they would have formally produced such a document."

"You mean no title, no record of his birth, not even a baptismal certificate?" Marian asked.

"The baptismal certificate. I believe that's usually left to the adopting parents in a Catholic church of their choice before obtaining a passport and leaving the country."

She recalled an American couple, in her childhood parish, Father Riordan baptizing their child, handing them their baptismal document to sign, the couple beaming over their three-month-old little girl as if over a miraculous gift. Mary Elizabeth Cooper was to be her name; the couple couldn't thank the Irish enough for their generosity. "So the child is born untitled according to this policy," she said. "The original name changed. If ever the child should want to search, there would be scant records, tampered records, or no record."

"Look, I'll ring up Mr. Toole, a barrister, for his opinion, see if he can get a court date, but I'm advising now. I wouldn't do anything you might think would annoy Sister Agnes, because the truth is, I'm afraid, it's going to be all up to her. I can guarantee you Judge Moran will side with her, and you should know that."

"Perhaps you're right, I'm sure you're right," she said in a daze, and apologized for the outburst. They'd work with Sister Agnes before they took legal action against anyone or any institution, she said, feeling frustrated that she had to genuflect to lawyers and clergy to get her own son back, yet grateful for the unique circumstances which had led to her reuniting with Adrian—grateful in the oddest way to Nurse.

Father Brennan, she thought, revving her heart like a Ford engine. He had surprised her recently when he told her he was trying to see the world more openly. Recently he'd borrowed Ben's copy of *The Screwtape Letters* by C.S. Lewis, and they had in-depth discussions about personal faith. Rather than a solicitor, Father Brennan might convince Sister Agnes to let Adrian come home. Mr. Greene's advice had been spot on. She would forget her uncle's part in the past. She would make an effort to befriend Father Brennan.

14

"I will get the job of Reverend Mother," Sister Paulinas professed in the privacy of her office, just before twilight hour, a time she reserved for personal dreams. "I am the Reverend Mother." And then she bowed her head, peeked into a dainty mirror, and practiced her serene smile. Hidden beneath an array of prayer books was *Psycho-Cybernetics,* by Maxwell Maltz, a book she found unattended on a train seat eight weeks ago and confiscated, a book she found fascinating and shameful. In the twenty-six years since she'd been received by ballot into the order of the Sisters of Benevolence, the vow of obedience struck her as the most challenging. Inquisitive by nature, her greatest joy as a child had been the hours spent reading books with her father. The memory of the scent of his tobacco still brought comfort. More than once she succumbed to purchasing a packet of unfiltered Old Golds and lit them behind the farm buildings just to be reminded of his smell. Behind closed doors, she read and reread this psychology book, imagining the possibilities that life might offer. Her one major indulgence.

That and the dainty mirror. And the occasional cigarette. The Reverend Mother, now seventy-one, was in failing health, and Sister Paulinas daydreamed in this office and around the convent grounds of a second ballot establishing her as the next Reverend Mother.

Sister Paulinas heard the vibration of Nurse's heavy, thudding feet. A timid knock and Sister slammed her desk drawer shut as Nurse peeked through the door. Sister ushered her into her office with a brisk, exasperated wave of a hand. She knew how to keep Nurse in her place. It was sad, the Sister sighed, but necessary for Nurse's own good that this constant balance be maintained.

Sister Paulinas once again sat flabbergasted in her wooden swivel chair, looking at paperwork on her desk. It had been less than one week earlier that the Reverend Mother informed her that on the Saturday coming Nurse would escort Adrian Ellis, along with Sister

Agnes, and Father Brennan, from the orphanage to Donnybrook to meet Mr. and Mrs. Benjamin Ellis, Adrian's biological parents. Sister Agnes did not want to cause undue stress for him or any of the other children for that matter, the nun had told Judge Moran, who was still in charge of this case down at the courts.

"Happy endings do not begin with witless indiscretions, Nurse," Sister Paulinas said now, exhaling a long, tired breath. Nurse stood in her office and nodded, her nurse's hat already removed from her ragged hair. "You look ready. Are you off, then?" Sister Paulinas wished Nurse would stop fidgeting and said so. The halfwit reminded her of a squirrel. She added, "You might want to go to your room and fix up your hair."

"Yes, I'll be off, then."

For a moment, Sister Paulinas remembered Nurse's dear sister Anne, God rest her, who had been her supervisor when she was only an acolyte and so alone out here in the countryside. She'd felt responsible for Nurse after Sister Anne's debilitating pneumonia and subsequent death. It was Sister Paulinas who found a home nearby in County Westmeath for little Beth, Nurse's bastard child. And what a blessing Beth's adopted family had been for her, sending her off to Dublin to earn a college degree, bless their hearts. She made the sign of the cross and prayed that these occasional visits to deliver babies to the orphanage did not make Nurse pine for her daughter.

"But you're a crafty one after all, are you not? A lucky one at any rate, with another day off on your hands."

"They think Adrian might become their–"

"I know what they think, Nurse, thank you," she retorted. "You mind yourself, girl, and don't miss your train," she said, handing her enough shillings for her fare.

"Yes, Sister Paulinas."

"You are aware that telling the Ellis family the whereabouts of their out-of-wedlock child was against the rules?"

Nurse lowered her head.

"You had no right to involve yourself in a past inmate's life," Sister Paulinas scolded. "You had no business sharing information with her, you realize that now."

Nurse shook her head.

"Are you a dumb ox?"

"Yes, Sister."

"Pray for all the Ellises now, every day, Nurse."

"I will, Sister."

"I'm not to be toyed with."

"No."

"Further, you do realize if there should be any sort of repercussions from this, you will pay the price?"

"Yes."

"You will be asked to leave. And where you shall be taken, I wouldn't think you would want to return. Or worse. Do you understand?"

"Yes, Sister."

"I don't want to hear any more about this. This is your last visit to the orphanage and to the Ellis residence. Go on, now." Sister couldn't stand the possum any longer.

Nurse curtsied and waited for Sister Paulinas to shoo her away before she hurried off.

15

Everything seemed perfect.

Marian surveyed the table, rearranged a set of peony and leaf dessert plates, teacups and saucers, and took the matching tea tray from the cupboard. Linen tea cloths were laid out. Platters of scones and clotted cream and raspberry tarts looked lovely. The kettle was steaming.

Everything seemed perfect if you didn't count the undercurrent of nerves flying about the room like late summer moths batting against screen doors. Like a calculating housecat, Johanna sat on her father's knee, eyeing her mother's marmalade sandwiches. Ben looked out the bay window; an overzealous bounce of his knee belied his composed face. Even their garden, just beginning its new season of life, budding green flowers peeking out from tomato stalks, was tentative in its infancy.

Tentative yet hopeful, Marian thought. These feelings were to be expected. How would Adrian react to all this. Marian walked to the love seat and placed a firm hand on Ben's shoulder.

"You look perfect," he said absently.

"Ben, don't say that."

Why did he try to say what he thought she wanted to hear? Why the desire to please her with platitudes? He hid behind the passive expression on his face. Didn't he know that she'd been robbed of the girlish belief that anything was perfect?

"You look motherly?" he said. "Better?"

She looked at him and let out a nervous chuckle. Somehow, a mystery to her, Marian suffered piques from Ben, and yet, the core of her love seemed to remain intact.

"Better," she said and walked toward the gilded hall mirror, courtesy of Tatte's picture frame shop, and smelled the day-old lilac blooms on the foyer table, their heavy fragrance filling the stained oak entry, and she scolded herself silently for having arranged her flowers too early. She cleared off the fallen blossoms, brushed them into an ashtray.

"You're too old for that," Marian said, rousing Johanna off Ben's knee. Marian looked into Ben's glassy eyes. A spring cold reddened his nose. He looked miserable, and she knew he suffered inside as she did. *Suffer in silence.* Oh, how she hated that old adage growing up, and still did. All the stifling repression had to end. She thought of a recent news story about a single, pregnant, Dublin-born woman who had decided to keep her baby. Her sister was moving in and would help her.

"Johanna, dear, I think you should stay in the background when he first arrives," she said. Johanna slid up against the armchair. "Only until he gets a bit used to the place." *We wouldn't want to make him jealous of you,* Marian was thinking.

Ben wiped his eyeglasses and abruptly rose and Johanna walked dutifully upstairs. "Go and read in your room awhile, Jo," he said.

"Nothing's ever going to be perfect," Marian reminded him.

"You don't have to keep fecking reminding me," Ben said, the curse thrown in for heft. He hurled the newspaper in her direction right after that, with another curse, but she ignored him and walked into the kitchen.

"I've asked Father Brennan to take charge," he called after her.

"That's grand," she answered, coming back in. He was picking up disheveled pages, and she picked up a section and rapped him on the head.

"Oh, for goodness sake, come on down now, love," Marian said, spotting Johanna on the landing. "Or go into your room for a bit longer. Unless you want to do a bit of vacuuming," she added, turning on the Hoover for one last go around.

After Jo had told Mr. Hinckley and Sister Agnes about her brother's homecoming, her classmates' wide-as-a-kite eyes stared at her when she returned to class, waiting for more of the explanation. Even as she rejoiced inside, when the class fell silent, she felt for the first time her parent's shame and wished she hadn't shared with her principal. Marian heard Johanna opening her window and calling to Anna and Rona.

"Sure, we should have gone to England rather than sneaking about like nincompoops, behaving like children ourselves," Marian said. "Stop your leg shaking when we sit for tea," she added, hoping Sister Agnes would find them and their home in good form. Ben rubbed his temples, lit a cigarette.

"Everything's going to be set right now," she said to him, but he just stared out the window.

16

The cast-iron gate creaked. Footsteps could be heard coming up the walk. Father Brennan's signature three quick taps of the lion-mask knocker, and Marian took off her apron, gave Ben and Jo a nod, and Jo raced to answer the door.

Adrian.

The child she had never forgotten stood there, in between Father Brennan and Nurse, and to Father Brennan's left, the short and strapping Sister Agnes, but they could all disappear into thin air. Except for him. The yearning had never diminished. All these years, all she had ever wanted was to see him again in the flesh, and dreamed that he would be returned to her and their home where he would be safe and happy.

Marian crouched down so that she could gaze into his eyes. She desperately wanted him to feel her love for him. She wanted him to know that she was sorry, wanted to tell him that she hoped they could make up for lost time. *All this time.* Still, she could have never found him. How many times had she secretly daydreamed about him since he was ripped from her life? How her da would have wanted him, too! She must remain calm in front of the fat Sister. He was a big boy, a beautiful boy. He had the map of a McKeever on his face. She reached toward him and brought him into her arms. She felt her body shaking, the heat of shame scouring her.

Ben ushered the others into the living room and she wiped her eyes. A timid smile passed over Adrian's hesitant, perfect face; freckles like wet sand reached across his wide bridge and cheeks.

"Go in, go in," she said to Nurse who stood there gawking at them.

"Leave us for a minute," Marian insisted.

Alone with him in the entryway, she felt his scrawny shoulders underneath an itchy brown jumper, then ran her hand over his blond head, his hair trimmed nearly to the scalp. She could no longer contain her emotions and let out a sob. She hugged him again, and he put his arms around her, too. She wanted to stay there with him, their arms growing tighter around each other. She smelled nit cream and whispered to him that she had never stopped thinking about him. Not for a moment had she had a day's happiness without him. He began to cry now, and she moved them closer to the front door, out of view of everyone's peering eyes.

Ben came back into the hall looking helpless, turned on the teardrop fanlight and retreated to the living room.

"Remarkable your resemblance to your granda," Marian whispered to Adrian, and then she softly wiped his cheeks. A shadow of fright crossed his face. *Why?* Adrian didn't budge from the arched doorway. *He's feeling out of place.*

"You can trust me, Adrian. I love you. I never wanted to give you up, and I never will again," she whispered in his ear. "I'll protect you from those grownups in there," she said, slanting her head toward the living room. She took his hand and smiled broadly at him. He smiled back, breathed deeply and took a step. He couldn't seem to take the smile off his miraculous face now. He kept breathing in deeply and grinning, too. He could smell something delicious roasting in the oven, cinnamon and apples. He could smell the love in their home. He could literally smell it. He glanced around the foyer and up the wood stairs. He was in the home that he'd seen in adverts pasted on storefront windows. Ben came toward them. Adrian wished his da would kiss him, but Ben just reached for his hand to shake it, and then suddenly sneezed. He stood smiling down at his son, one hand in his trouser pocket, and then wiped his nose, trying too hard to appear casual and familiar. Finally, Marian led Adrian into the living room. She noticed Johanna holding the doorknob, twirling her ebony braid, her mischievous smirk masking her momentary bashfulness.

Adrian's eyes seemed awash with the scene before him, and Marian was thrilled by his young boy's hand in hers. The adults observed as he concentrated on various objects around the room. Marian followed his gaze, realizing anew the luxury of her living room: the acanthus leaves plasterwork molding, the Siena yellow marble mantelpiece with the gold-plated mirror atop, a gilded clock, their wedding present to themselves, the statue of Justice on the stand in the far corner of the room holding her scales and sword.

She led him through the swinging door into the cinnamon smells of the kitchen. Johanna followed behind them, cream crackers in her hands. They walked out through the back door and through the white painted trellis. Several camellias were waking after a cold spring; the purple flowers of clematis had sprouted. Marian pointed to the spot where cucumbers would grow gigantic later that summer.

"Why don't you two have something to eat in the other room while I check on the meal?"

Adrian and Johanna left together, and Marian sneaked back into the kitchen where she put a wet rag to the nape of her neck and took a minute to collect herself. If the summer went well, Sister Agnes said she would consider releasing him, and the courts would stamp the transition complete. Marian peeked through the swing door.

Nurse looked almost normal sitting on the sofa with Sister Agnes. Johanna and Adrian cut pieces of cheddar, their eyes darting around the room every few moments, the way fawns do in open fields. The week before, standing in Judge Moran's private chambers, Ben had agreed with Sister Agnes that an institutionalized child would need an adjustment period. Seeing firsthand this intimate liaison between the Church and the State burned Marian up inside. She ranted at Ben that John McGahern's second book, *The Dark,* was banned and the author sacked from his teaching position because he addressed emerging adolescent sexuality as well as sexual abuse. The whole world was changing but Ireland was still in the Dark Ages. That day in front of Judge Moran, fed up and frustrated, she had spoken harshly to Ben and had felt the judge become as thick as a stone slab before her. Now she watched Father Brennan with Ben and was astonished at how close the two were becoming. Father's growing respect for Ben revealed a congenial side to him. Still, he seemed to be a conflicted man.

Any attempt at relaxation caused him worry and he would retreat back to his old rulebook style.

If anyone was to blame for Adrian's misery it was Father Brennan. After they met last week with Sister Agnes, Ben mentioned he'd gone to talk with Father Brennan, who had admonished Ben for not fully considering the affect Adrian's presence would have on his family. Marian glanced at Father Brennan now. Whatever progress had been made, he seemed as tight as ever today. Her uncle seemed to be watching Adrian and Jo like a hawk now. She opened her high lace collar, pushed the back kitchen door open a bit more with her foot and let the fresh air cool her.

Marian was still flushed when she returned to the living room. Things were going well. Adrian and Johanna were chatting and she could tell by Johanna's natural ease and her attempts to make Adrian comfortable, that the children could sense the ties that bound them. Marian knew intuitively, too, that it would be a mistake to fuss over Adrian, that she shouldn't hover, but rather tread lightly, even though she wanted to scream with madness that her children were both here. Finally, in the same room. For all their different upbringing, both were needy, she thought, in the same way, funny enough. They just wanted their parents. They just wanted to be loved.

As the children moved toward the stairs, Sister Agnes called to them. Johanna ran to her and Adrian followed slowly behind. Marian wanted to stop him, pick him up, hide him, and she moved closer but held herself in check, pretended to be busy by the dining table slicing some currant cakes.

"Pray for your brother, that he gets on with the family," Sister Agnes said. She had told Marian about Adrian's misconduct, that he undermined her, called her as sick as a small hospital, and had once encouraged the other boys to climb over the orphanage wall and run like hairymen. She stated that there were other incidents, though nothing serious, and Marian shrugged them off immediately.

"Of course he will get on, Sister Agnes," Johanna said, loud and clear. This time, Marian was grateful Jo talked so much. "We're going to play with all the toys my parents bought that are in the attic. Wait now, 'til you see the holsters and silver guns. We can play cowboys and Indians," Johanna said.

Our parents, she should have said. Adrian listened but seemed to be eyeing the soda bread and cheese. *He was hungry. He's starved, for Heaven sake, Sister Agnes.*

"Let's hear a prayer, Johanna," Sister Agnes said. "Did you learn any new ones at Mass today?"

"Gran would like you, Sister Agnes. She's always teaching me lots of prayers and saying I should go to Mass all the time."

Oh, for Christ sake, Jo, Marian thought. Johanna laughed. Marian watched the look on Sister Agnes' blowfish face.

Jo quickly bowed her head. "Pray our family gets on, Sister. Pray that the turmoil in the North goes away. And for all the turmoil and fighting to end," she said, peeking over her folded hands at Sister Agnes for signs of her approval.

Violence begets violence, Marian thought. Sister Agnes must think Jo had heard the word *turmoil* about the house, no doubt. *Don't talk anymore, Jo,* Marian begged silently.

"A nice prayer. And we all need the church. Our Adrian needs as much religion as he can get," Sister Agnes said but Adrian wasn't listening to her. Sister looked at Marian slicing a raspberry tart.

Marian looked back, directly at her. Sister Agnes' dimples were slyly emerging, her face a beacon of light to the devil.

Sister glanced at Ben engaging Father Brennan in a game of table tennis and commented that she'd never seen a family so engaged in sport. "Right here in the house!" A present for Adrian, Marian explained. "And, Mr. Ellis," Sister continued. "You're quite good." Ben blushed, no doubt agreeing with Sister Agnes.

Sister looked back at Marian, and Marian could feel her face was hot and all but perspiring. *Evil wears many faces, ah, but so does goodness, remember that Agnes.* There is no denying that we love Adrian. One couldn't hide a thing such as love. That was clear from their every movement and Sister Agnes should be moved. Apart from all the hopeful energy in the house, Marian worried that Sister Agnes was on the fence. It troubled Marian that she might think Adrian would spend the summer without his prayers, and perhaps without prayer for good. *I will pray more, and we will all say daily prayers, Sister Agnes, if this helps you.* Marian grappled with God now and what He wanted her to do and found mixed thoughts clouding her mind rather than the prayer itself.

17

By the end of June, Sister Agnes had consented to Adrian's release to the Ellises for "a trial run" during the summer. Marian was not grateful. She was irate that Sister Agnes claimed she needed to see how they all fared for at least one summer before taking the next step. The nun would make her final decision after the holidays. "No need to rush these things," she said when she dropped Adrian off.

Rising above Sister Agnes' ever-present shadow, Marian worked to create a happy scenario for them. "We have to change Sister's pathetic mind," she said to Ben. "But I'm keeping the peace. I'm learning from you, Ben," she added.

Ben smiled, impressed. "You're rising above," he told her.

She spent the first month of June bringing Adrian and Johanna to play by the sea at Dollymount. On the weekends, Ben joined them on their walks to Herbert Park. They sat by the lovely artificial lake, fed the geese and swans stale bread and sang "Those Lazy, Hazy, Crazy Days of Summer." Then there was the weeding to do in late afternoons, and in the evening they went twice to the Gaiety Cinema to see James Bond at Jo's request. Rainy days, and there were many that summer, they lingered over their rashers and eggs before Jo and Adrian retired to their attic playroom.

The attic, Ben thought, as he drove home for his dinner at two o'clock this cloudy afternoon. Jo and Adrian were outside with Anna and Rona and a couple of the other kids on their street.

He walked into the garden. Marian looked happy, her overalls covered in dirt. "Roast beef drippings and fried potatoes," she said. "Our own hothouse lettuce and beefsteak tomatoes."

"Any horseradish?"

"On the table," she indicated, then added, "Adrian's filling out, eating us out of house and home," as she washed up. She urged the kids inside.

In the evening, the family played cards and had their tea: a boiled egg for everyone, sliced ham or cold roast beef, and something extra, a side of garlic mash for Ben, who worked hard all day, Marian reminded the children. After tea, Ben tried to write in the library with a small whiskey.

Tonight, he got a little done and then drifted off, though it wasn't long before the kids raced each other down the stairs for their late night snack of cocoa and sliced bread. Better than most nights, he thought. Their play-acting in the attic, the noise up there, and the content of their plays, often disturbed his sleep. He hated to admit it, but a lot about Adrian did not set right with him, though he could barely talk with Marian about this. She would turn blue in the face. Her da's notorious temper must have been something, because she inherited it. Adrian seemed to have a bad temper also, or his bad upbringing was showing. Ben worried that Jo was suffering because of it but that she, too, would never admit this to anyone. Marian was not protecting her. Even some of the looks Adrian gave to *him*! He wondered what he'd been taught in school about the Jewish people. He had given the boy *The Joys of Yiddish* to glance through. Adrian had grimaced and told him that Hebrew letters reminded him of Chinese Takeaway. *Ridiculous.* And his reading skills were appalling. Ben knew that ol' Darby would probably not allow him to continue his research about the poor math and reading levels in the national schools, knowing that Archbishop McQuaid would not approve of the embarrassing facts circulating, nor would the *Times.* Incestuous bedfellows. Marian was right about that. The church had the whole country in a headlock.

"The Jews are the chosen people," Ben had said last night.

"Chosen for what?" Adrian muttered, a suspicious look in his eyes.

"Chosen by God, Adrian," he said.

"Fuck, no. Then why is it only Catholics go to Heaven?" The boy answered.

Too late. Jo had overheard and giggled and took Adrian's hand to play outside again.

Ben realized he would have to take it slow. "Hey kids," he said coming into the kitchen tonight. "Roses are reddish, violets are bluish—"

"I know, I know, Da," Jo said. "If it weren't for Christmas, we'd all be Jewish," she said and rolled her eyes.

"I have to eat, hungry or not, gobble up maggots if I have to!" Adrian said, grabbing Jo's dessert.

Ben slapped his hand.

"Ben!" Marian shouted and Adrian ran to the wall, placed his palms above his head. "It's all right," she said, running to him, rubbing his back.

"Let's go, Adrian. Anna and Rona are waiting," Jo said, moving toward the back door and Adrian quickly followed.

"You're not going out this late, young lady," Marian said. "Now the two of you, play quietly in Jo's room."

They sulked through the kitchen, and Marian shook her head at Ben. He dragged himself upstairs, shut the door to their bedroom. It was after ten o'clock in the evening and he listened to Marian and the kids yakking down the hall. The noise subsided temporarily.

"I've not yet adjusted to the ruckus. I'm knackered," he said to Marian as she entered. "They said I wasn't allowed in the attic, but they'd put on a show for me soon."

"I heard them acting the *Wizard of Oz* again," Marian whispered. Ben grunted. "Ah, they're not so innocent as they pretend. I was listening by the door last night. Adrian's voice was harsh, acting the boss," he said getting into bed. "And it wasn't the *Wizard of Oz* they were playing."

"They play family, sometimes. Sure, it's healthy for them."

"Marian, he threw Johanna across the room, I think. I went up there and yelled at him. Told him he can't be roughhousing, that it's dangerous."

Marian said nothing. *Big surprise.* He guessed it was understandable, her denial, the burden on her to make sure all was beyond reproach and Adrian could come home for good. He got up and stood listening by the attic door and heard them playing teacher, Adrian reminding Johanna not to wet the bed. Calling her a dirty pup. Telling her to grip the bar, whatever that means, and he opened the door to see Johanna's palms clutching the oak wallboards, her knickers on her head.

"Cut it out," Ben yelled. "Both of you, in bed. And never am I to see you two playing like this again." He picked up the tattered McCall's paper dolls that Johanna had treasured since her babyhood. He held out his hands, displaying his ripped present to Johanna, tilting his head.

"I've told you, Adrian, we don't play school, family, nothing up here. And we don't hit," he said, his voice rising. Adrian looked scared. "And we don't rip up expensive toys." He bent and picked up a few more scraps, and then held the door open for them, escorted them back to their rooms.

"He's just a boy. We're not used to it," Marian said when he came back to bed.

"He's too bottled up, Marian. Like a battered dog off a leash. The nuns have done a grand job making him hell on wheels."

"Kids fight. Though it may be ten, not two of them, they're like a shower of savages," she agreed. "I'm exhausted from thinking about it."

"Ah, you're probably right," he conceded, relieved Marian was worried, too.

"Jo sticks up for him, gets mad at me if I reprimand him."

"She does me, too," Ben said.

"I've told them that we will have only good thoughts and deeds in this house. But you should've seen Jo in her black costume, playing the melting wicked witch, Adrian laughing. Sure, they're having good *craic.* "*Craic,* not *raic*—fun, not foul," Gran keeps telling them. I did tell them not to play witch outside anymore. You know that Mrs. O'Rourke gives Adrian stern looks. 'Tis a wonder the guards haven't put her on the force. She's just cut her hair again and it's sitting on her head like a helmet," Marian said.

"Don't let the kids hear you talking like that, for God's sake, Marian. You and we'll only have good thoughts in this house, too."

"I hate her, Ben, sticking her nose into our business. I wish she'd find herself interested in anything other than our kids," Marian said.

"Sure, seeing them come flying down the street in witch costumes doesn't help."

Marian released a happy laugh, which relaxed Ben, made him notice her unzipping her swishy skirt. An abstract black and white pattern slipped from her hips to the floor. "I'll never forget her hand flying to her mouth when Adrian cackled at her," she continued, smiling, bending in a scoop-neck black jersey, the shape of her porcelain legs in shadows underneath a white cotton slip.

"He certainly is more like you than me," Ben answered.

"Never mind, Mr. Goody Two-Shoes," she said.

He squinted, and she meandered over to him, sat gently on top of him, took off her top.

"Are you twistin' hay now yourself?" he said, as he touched her thighs, kissed her, felt her like one feels music.

Ben had made himself clear to Marian two days ago, when Adrian and Johanna had confided in him that they'd stolen nuns' habits from the basement of Sacred Heart Church. It was not just Adrian, Johanna had a wicked side, too. Marian had shouted at him that night. She never would have thought to do it; he'd shouted back. And without saying more, he knew he was not alone: Adrian's strong boyish presence was beginning to make Marian nervous. Ben could see plainly, though she had shared it with no one, that she suspected Adrian was dragging Johanna down. Ben tried to suppress his feelings, simmering dangerously just below the surface. At times, he might even have preferred their previous life without him.

"Adrian won't be the first boy with filthy knickers from a day of playing about," Marian said between kisses.

"Mrs. O'Rourke would give him a good..."

"Never mind Mrs. O'Rourke," Marian said, grabbing his arms, pinning him. He overtook her, and now there was only the quiet of their lovely rhythm.

They lay there, spent.

"There are some ladies who don't take well to the motherhood routine, and go about miserable with the multiple children," she whispered to him. "I haven't been afforded that luxury. I was miserable before I had the two of them together. I'm delighted with all the washing and cleaning and cooking, all the mess."

He thought about the innocence on the kids' faces early this morning, and then last Saturday, how joyful they had been playing catch with him. Because of the shame involved, Marian had kept Adrian's secret from Ben, as did Jo, but Ben knew that Adrian was a bed wetter. He'd told Adrian privately that all would be calm soon and to have no worries. But he was worried. Ben knew Jo was a good sister, too, a loyal person. That had been a great discovery. She'd never once made fun of him, never mentioned the sour smell on his pajamas. And Jo loved the physicality that playing with a sibling close in age provides. And Adrian appreciated everything: every lemonade, every sandwich, every late morning nap, every kiss. And with his every mouthful of cornflakes and milk and sprinkled sugar, day-old bread and dripping, Marian said she felt as though she were nourishing her own body as she watched the two of them share a meal. It was important for Ben that Marian stay happy. *The four of us will eventually get on.* Each day of their missing years was a lot to ask of one summer. Two steps forward, one step backward, but it irked Ben that it seemed the other way around. He would have to stop Adrian from any more antics.

"They'll be putting on some show Friday night. A circus act," Marian whispered. "They've ruined my favorite lipsticks and tried to take your good suits."

"Keep them away from the suits. I have to go up north Friday. And no more freak shows, please. Try to steer them clear of that attic. Keep them with the ball and the kids outside."

"Into the bloody mess you're going? That's grand, Ben," she said, switching on her bedside light.

He looked at her soft, blonde curls in a hodgepodge.

"Where will you be?"

"I'll be staying at the Crown."

"Only the most bombed hotel in the world, Ben."

"Just two nights."

"Never mind," she said, switching off her light.

"I'm off probation, Marian. It's actually a promotion that Mr. Darby picked me to cover the story. I'm interviewing some Unionists who don't support Terence O'Neill as Prime Minister."

"Never mind," she muttered, turning on her side. Ben listened to Jo and Adrian's naughty voices rising again well past their bedtime. "They should marry Jews," Marian said. "Nobody wants to popify them, except Christ, of course, but who listens to God? We're all too busy shouting at each other," she said, switching on her light again and leaving the room to tuck the pair of mischief-makers in bed again.

18

Adrian felt the warmth of his Ma's shin cradled with his own, the cool sheets warming up with their ritual morning hug, the aloe vera plant she'd purchased to soothe his sunburn from yesterday's outing to Dollymount beach sticky on his shoulders.

"I've never seen the sea before this summer, except in pictures."

"Isn't it grand?"

"It is."

"We'll go to Sandymount Strand, if you like."

"Can I bring Peter here someday?" he asked. His mother looked at him, put her fingers through the short growth of fair hair on his head, but responded only with a goofy-looking smile. *God is a dreamer,* Rosemary had told him once. *Never mind what Sister Agnes tells you, that daydreamers don't amount to anything.* "Don't rest your eyes beyond what is your own," was Thunder Thigh's favorite saying. Adrian loved his mother no matter what Sister had warned against daydreamers and laziness, even if she were a bit simple and sleepy sometimes, an ethereal look in her eyes. Sister Agnes would have slapped that stupid look off her face, but he didn't mind. He loved her, as children do their mothers, and forgave everything about her dreaminess that others might have found nonsensical.

"Peter and I, we're thinking about becoming firefighters when we're grown up," he said, touching a clay pot on her night table signed *I Love You, Jo* in scribble with Rickie Tickie flowers stuck all over it.

"You are, are you?"

"I love the idea, Ma. Jo does as well." Marian smiled at him, really listening to his words.

He glanced at the perfume bottles on her dresser, the lace underneath the glass bottles. The room was a warm red color. Large pale green leaves and pink peonies on the long curtains. Colors were everywhere. Wide pink and green stripes on her coverlet. And the thick beige rug under her bed he liked to feel between his toes.

"Once we get you home, you might go on to university. You're still young, and we have lots of time to talk about your future. You might change your mind, love."

He worried that the summer was going by too fast. Ma could soon become the visitor, bringing him sandwiches and licorice sticks, an extra shilling or two for his pocket, toiletries, a transistor radio, all she could stuff into a tote bag. He took a deep breath, calmed himself. Weren't all mothers relegated to the position of visitor soon enough, he thought. Sons either in a foreign land, or absorbed in their work, like Da, or in their wives' homes, growing close with somebody else. This was not the life she dreamed for him, a life apart from her, he felt this. And his silly talk of becoming a firefighter! But what kind of child ever follows the dreams of their parents, he wondered. Certainly such a child would not have been taught to think on his own, like his ma always said. Certainly she would listen to his dreams.

"There are worse fates, I suppose." She sighed, lingering beside him on her bed. "And true callings. Not many locate their true calling; it could be a lot worse," she said, reaching over to tickle him, "than becoming Fireman Ellis. You'll have to be the highest rank, though." He had a strange sensation suddenly of being unmoored, a strange racing of the heart which he'd experienced only once before at Silverbridge, with this unsettling thought of putting out fires. The fear of danger to his body, of his dying, attacked him. "I'd better stay right here with you," he said, the thought of another separation from her impossible to bear.

"Why did you give me up then, Ma?" he suddenly asked, startling her. She had hoped he would never verbalize that painful question. A sad smile played on her face, the dimple he loved emerged briefly and then disappeared.

"You know that I love you, Adrian," she said soft as the Shirelles melody floating from the radio.

"Yeah," he said. He could feel her love; this was true, even in their short time together. And he could see how her face changed when he asked his question, which confirmed to him that something bad had happened to her. And although Nurse had been as useless as tits on a bull most of the time, she hadn't lied all those years ago when she'd comforted him, told him that he had a Ma who loved him. "Never mind, it's okay. You don't have to answer," he said.

"No, it's not okay, my love," Ma said. "We're going to get you home for good. Don't worry," she said.

Adrian sniffed her Camay soap smell as he nestled closer and let his head fall into her soft, billowy pillow, a grainy lavender sachet inside the pillowcase exhaled its perfume as if taking its last breath.

"I'm afraid of the dark," he said. She'd left his light on last night, and he hoped it would help him overcome his fear and not wet his bed. She'd been worse at his age, would scream bloody murder if the closet door was left ajar, seeing visions of arms and legs, like skeletons, growing out of her hanging smocks. She told him this as she kissed him goodnight, to comfort him. "I used to wedge my little black shoe under my bedroom door so that it couldn't shut, and I could see down the hall. But then the shadows would scare me, and I'd cry out anyway, or go running into my parent's room" Ma said. "'We pay for the good day with the good night,' your Granda used to say, tucking me back in, laughing at me, really."

Adrian chuckled the way kids do out of politeness. He didn't understand what his ma meant with that one, and she must have read his confusion. "Your Granda had some quirky ideas, sure, though you would have loved him, and he would have loved you."

He glanced at the bottle of Old Spice, out of place on her dresser, and he wanted to lather some on himself and see how nice it felt to be a worthy man, like his da. "How long will Da be on a business trip?" he asked casually then, even though there really wasn't a genuine concern in his asking.

Johanna turned the doorknob slowly and entered the room in her flannel nightgown, tiny rosebuds and sea green stripes down the front, and climbed onto the bed, ready to join the conversation.

"Da'll be back tonight," Ma answered him, and left for the toilet.

Blast it, he muttered, thinking what a dolt he was for bringing up Da, which changed the whole blissful mood in the room.

"What are you two going on about? Did you sleep in here last night?" Johanna asked him.

"I've only just come in," he said, but she didn't believe him. She rubbed her crusty eyelashes. She could tell from the feel in the room that they'd been talking intimately for some time about something that didn't concern her. She'd stood outside the door yesterday morning and listened to their lollygagging about, their private conversation about nothing and had complained to him later that Ma slept too much. Adrian wished only that these early morning moments would last forever. He'd said that sleeping was not a sin, like he'd been told in Silverbridge that it was. Johanna looked jealous. Left out again, her timing was off. Ma became busy once she entered the room.

"What shall we do today, Ma?" Jo shouted toward the shut bathroom door.

"Why don't you show Adrian the balloon shop this afternoon? I'll grill the black pudding for you now," she said, coming out dressed in her light blue smock dress, perfect for indoor rainy days and muddy gardens, she always said. "Would you like that?" Ma said, looking always at Adrian. Johanna noticed and breathed loudly out of her nose.

"Go on, both of you, get dressed now and come down for your breakfast," Marian said, and they left. Adrian gazed back at his ma and watched her pick up Jo's clay pot to place it in the closet.

In the spare room in the attic, they played baby, one of their favorites, until they were summoned downstairs. "I don't want to play the baby this time," Johanna said, rummaging for the nappies they used for this game. "You put these on this time."

"No," Adrian said, trying on the white sheet with the head cut out that they'd painted black and grabbing a thin branch of whittled wood, his make-believe pointer. "No talking, baby bollocks."

Johanna laughed crazily at this. "All right, then," she said.

"Get into the playground, baby. Say goodbye to Nurse."

"I can't talk, you dolt," she whispered.

"Yes, you can, or we can't play."

He waited for her to pretend she was on the splintered round-about, surrounded on all sides by high walls cutting off the sky.

"I don't want to go to the Silverbridge," she said like clockwork.

"You wait here with these nice boys and girls."

"I don't want to. I don't like it here, Nurse. I want to stay with you," she cried. Johanna stood there, looking very weak, as hungry eyes watched her. He had described for her the gray school building, which had the biggest windows she'd ever see, too far up for her to look into the rooms inside.

"This is how Sister Agnes walks. I'm as tall as she is, old Thunder Thighs." He walked like a rodeo man, inducing Johanna to cover her mouth to keep from breaking into hysterics.

"Be the good girl and settle down."

"I don't want to go to the Silverbridge!" she shouted.

Adrian grabbed her from behind. She tried to break free, but he held her shirtdress tight and pulled her up off her feet. She wiggled hard, and he felt her getting away. He pulled her up by her hair again, and she was stunned by a smack he planted against her head. She looked dizzily around at him, but he continued to pull her around the room.

"Another one for Dormo One," he said, taking off his sheet and rummaging through their costume box for an old blue skirt. "Bow to your teacher," he said, concentrating on pinning the skirt around him. "I watch you and the rest of the four- to eight-year-old girls. You'll do as you're told." He took a sack to the far side of the room and flung it down.

"You've had your tea by now," he whispered to Jo. "It's time for bed. Put these on." He pulled pajamas from the costume box.

Johanna had recovered and was back in character, standing by a pretend bed in an outgrown nightie.

"You're number Four Seventy-Six. Four Seventy-Six, don't forget it. All your clothes will have this number, and when you're called, you'll stand at attention."

Johanna played her part okay, though she no longer pretended to be scared of him, and he felt silly walking around in a long skirt. She had been curious about the orphanage, but he worried that he was taking this game too far and if he hit her again she was going to quit.

"She looks like she's had a good scrub before she came," he said to the air. "No nits. Get into your bed. I'll go get the other girls from their tea."

"I want my ma to come for me now," she said. "I want to go to the circus," she giggled.

"Are you stupid or something? Why do you think you're here? Your ma doesn't want you. She's not coming."

"Yes, Nurse said she'd come for me."

"Nurse lied. Now what's your number?"

Jo tried to play along and let out a laugh.

Adrian slapped her. "What did you say, you dirty pup?"

"Nothing."

A harder slap against her legs with the pointer. "Tell me, girl, before I give you a beating you'll never forget, you stupid pup. What did you say?"

"I said Nurse lied?"

"Kneel by your cot."

Johanna looked like she might laugh or cry now, he didn't know which.

"Here's your wash bag with your number on it. It hangs from here." He hung the prop from a hook in the wall.

"My ma's coming for me, you dolt," she laughed.

Teacher Adrian slapped her.

"She didn't say she's not coming," she said under her breath.

Adrian slapped her again. "What did you say, you little shite?"

"Nothing."

Adrian turned on the pretend big brown radio on a shelf across the room and began imitating a man speaking almost in a whisper.

"Now, what's your number?"

Johanna startled as he changed his voice again to that of a bad-tempered teacher, and she burst out in tears.

"None of your beeswax," she shouted. "I want to talk about Peter now."

"We're not through. Who are you?"

"A smart girl who wants to talk about Peter rather than play this stupid game."

"Face the wall, you stupid pup. You sleep facing the wall. Everybody up and face the wall."

"Yes, Sister," she mocked.

He pulled her hair until his face came within an inch of hers. "I'm a lay person. You call me teacher, do you understand?"

"Stop, I said!" Jo screamed, and kicked him in his groin. She grabbed the pointer, and slapped him hard on his behind. "You, stupid pup, you!" she said and started laughing.

He turned red and he rubbed his bottom from the sting of her attack. "You're just a dumb, rich girl. You're the stupid one," he said.

"I'm not the one Ma and Da gave away," she countered, an adult's footsteps coming quick. Adrian sat down in the corner as the attic door opened.

"What is going on in here?" Ma said.

"We're talking," Johanna said.

"Give me that stick. That's dangerous," Ma said, grabbing the prop out of Jo's hand, noticing blue-red blotches on her legs and Adrian rubbing his bottom.

"No roughhousing in this house. We've told you. Don't you ever hit each other again," she warned, pointing the stick at them.

Whenever he heard angry talk from a grown-up, the world began to move in slow motion for Adrian. He concentrated on each syllable and let the words float away somewhere above his head.

"We were just playing, Ma," he said, feeling guilty.

"Be careful up here when you play. Both of you. And keep the noise down."

He looked at his mother, and Jo motioned with her head for him to come with her downstairs. They sat on her bed stock-still.

"I'm sorry, Adrian. I didn't mean what I said. I really didn't."

"I know," he said. "Neither did I."

"Let's make a pact or something," Jo said. "A secret signal so we'll know when one of us wants to stop the game, when one of us truly wants to stop. We'll put our fists together when we're dead serious about anything."

He smiled at her.

"Do you really think I'm a dumb, rich girl?" she asked, holding out her fist.

"No," he said, and they touched fists.

Ma walked past Johanna's room. They were sitting on her bed, staring into space. "I don't think I want to go to the balloon shop today," Jo announced.

"Sure, think of something else interesting to do," Marian said.

"I'm not the nanny, you know. I'm in this family, too."

"Of course you are, Johanna," Ma said, coming in and sitting next to her on the bed. Johanna propped up some pillows for them and grabbed her *Little Women* cut-out dolls to show Ma how she'd colored their faces purple and green. She and her ma could lounge around on the bed, too, talking about any old thing. But Adrian began jumping up and down on the bed. He felt Ma's happiness at the three of them playing together. Jo offered to read tales about the ever-popular fairy queen in the most recent edition of her *Jack and Jill* magazine, but he interrupted with talk of his orphan friend named Rosemary who looked like the cartoon poster of Betty Boop that hung on Jo's wall. Ma had the breakfast to make, she said, laughing now. Would he like white or black pudding, she wanted to know.

Rona had told them that she'd overheard her own ma on the telephone wailing that she'd been plopped down into the wrong family.

"That's because your da is never at home for his tea," Jo told Rona and she'd agreed. But now, Jo said that she knew that wasn't all the way true, because her own da was always home with Ma for his tea and, somehow, she felt that Ma was rarely *really* there. Jo said she suddenly understood exactly what Mrs. O'Rourke meant because she, too, felt like she'd been plopped down into the wrong family, and she wondered how much her ma would miss her if something were to happen to her.

19

It was Ben's jocular personality that got him into trouble up North. His wide grin, his laugh; when he got going, he sounded like a chimpanzee. On top of that, he was trusting to a fault. He gave everybody the benefit of the doubt, even those who looked dubious, even in unstable circumstances. He didn't sense trouble in the air, the way most people did, didn't have his guard up. Once, during his last year at Trinity, he allowed a needy student to sleep in his dorm room only to find his wallet and all his belongings gone before sunup, along with the thief. Outraged, Ben ran through the campus in the long johns he'd worn to bed looking for the swindler, his clothes gone from the wardrobe. This time, his youthful sincerity landed him in the hospital.

It was the twenty-seventh of July, Marian would never forget it, a Thursday afternoon. Jo and Adrian were washing and salting beefsteak tomatoes straight from the garden when the telephone rang with the news. She imagined him in front of a television crew on a street corner in Belfast, his raised voice pouring out of him, forgetting completely the dangers of the situation, the dreadful mood of the city. *It wasn't a party you were at,* Marian wanted to say over the phone. *You weren't thinking of your own welfare,* she wanted to rant. *You had no protection and you were covering a controversial political figure, a terribly heated news story.*

"Which hospital are you in?" she said instead.

"I'm at City Hospital, Belfast, in the emergency area. Still waiting to see a doctor. I'm all right."

"You're not all right, then. What do you mean *still?*"

"It's been hours, the queue."

"What happened?"

"They shot at me. A bullet landed in my arm."

"They what? For God's sake, Ben! Jesus, Mary, and Saint Joseph! What have the nurses said?"

"They've wrapped my arm. It took a bloody long time getting out of the rioting and over to the hospital, you know."

"You've got to see a doctor immediately."

"Ah, true enough. I've lost a bit of blood." Whenever he started in with the *ahs* before a sentence, he was either half-asleep or downplaying something, the second instance the more common.

"Not serious?" she screamed. Adrian flinched and Johanna turned off the tap.

"It was a Catholic who'd done it. He threw a couple of rocks at the Prod I was interviewing, and then all hell broke loose soon afterwards."

"And did the bowsie think you were taking sides?"

"I suppose," he mumbled, lighting a cigarette. "It's raving mad at the moment. I was just interviewing him," he said, blowing smoke.

"Ben. Were you wearing your *Irish Times* news badge round your neck?" she asked, but immediately felt sorry for her sharpness, knowing he'd already realized his miscalculations and was in great pain, physically and otherwise. "You were a sitting duck out there, Ben. I'm sorry," she added.

He exhaled and in the background she heard the emergency room chaos.

"I'm coming home tomorrow, just a one night check. Apparently they're making a search for the bastards who started firing."

They both knew that finding any individuals responsible for the damage was unlikely, and he was lucky to be alive.

"Which arm, Ben?"

He exhaled loudly.

"Have you spoken to Mr. Darby?"

"No," he said, sounding cross now. "I rang the *Times* and left a message that I'm in hospital, but Mr. Darby is in a meeting."

"Sure, you'll be a hero at work. Should I come up there?"

"Are you mad, Marian? I'm coming out of this mess tomorrow, I said."

"I'll ring your ma," she offered, shrinking at the thought, wishing she hadn't offered.

"All right," he said. "I'm to go to Mater Hospital in Dublin 7 for observation after this, as procedure. Two nights." He sounded calmer now that she was to call his mother, though she suddenly realized that if she had not made the offer, he would probably have called the Mammy himself.

She told the kids to go out to the garden for the garlic.

"Sure, you'll learn how to tap dance with your left hand soon enough," she said, trying to bring out his humor.

"All right, then. I'll see you tomorrow," is all he said.

She flipped on the telly, fiddled with the rabbit ear antennae, the damn static snow. Fourteen civil rights demonstrators were shot dead by British paratroopers. Twenty-two explosions by the provisional IRA left nineteen people killed by noon. Direct rule from London had been imposed. There had been demonstrations from Coalesland to Dungannon in County Tyrone. Belfast, especially, was a divided city.

An hour later, Ben called back to report that the doctor who treated his arm explained to him that there had been a significant loss of blood. A shame it took so long to get the ambulance to the scene. He might suffer from partial paralysis of the arm as a result, might suffer some depression related to the shootings, the bombings, and the devastation he'd witnessed. He could return to work as soon as he felt able. Would he be able to use his right arm? Marian asked. The doctor said only time would tell and put the injured limb in a sling. No physical activity, not even typing, for at least six weeks.

When the kids reappeared through the door, they held out their hands filled with dirty garlic bunches. Marian handed them children's scissors and asked them to deadhead the lavender rose bushes. She put a cold towel to the back of her neck. It took a tragedy for her to reach for the black rotary phone to ring up Beva Ellis.

20

"Hullo?"

"Hullo, Beva. This is your daughter-in-law," Marian said, unable to keep the tension from her voice.

"Hello," Beva said, brightening a bit.

There was a part of Marian that felt sorry for Beva's losses. Ben once mentioned that for weeks after his father's heart attack she had been bedridden. She wondered again if Beva had blamed her for her husband's demise, though her voice now seemed eager without a hint of resentment. "I'm calling you because Ben's been hurt up North."

"Benjamin hurt? What happened?" she said, the melodic tone of the old Beva voice triggering Marian's memory.

How many times had she replayed Beva's words in her head, "Grovkofskys do not intermarry!" She had bellowed those words during their meeting, when Beva was starring in a melodrama that would finally tear apart the family. "Come in the kitchen, Benjamin so I can put my head in the oven," she had said in all seriousness.

Sam had fallen into his chair holding his stomach. "Bring me a glass of milk, Beva."

And Marian looked at the size of the stone on Beva's finger as she left the dining room with her son. There's a reason the word *Jew* is in *jewelery,* the nuns used to say. Marian picked up her plate, the food spread around the sides as if she had been fingerpainting, and she looked into the kitchen where Beva was scolding her son. "Benjamin, listen to me. We gave you a full childhood. A star tennis player for the Maccabi association, now a star journalist, an educated member of Jewish society. I am proud of you. But you are so brazen in your ignorance. You are about to assimilate, water down your essence."

"It is not my essence," Ben argued. "My essence is human."

"You're a Jew. You don't belong with her."

Marian walked into the old kosher kitchen: the two sinks, the two cutting boards, the two of everything she'd dare not ask Beva about.

She handed the leftover plates to Ben. He placed them with the others on the far countertop. She felt Beva's displeasure with her presence and Ben held out his hand.

"What's all this, Beva?" Tatte said, coming into the kitchen. "You're ruining the Sabbath, Beva."

"Grovkofsys do not intermarry," she repeated. "I have my faith to protect, Sam. My Judaism. You didn't lose your mother. You didn't lose your brothers to Hitler. And I won't lose my son."

"Who said anything about losing your son? Benjamin knows what he's—"

"Benjamin has intellectualized his Judaism. It's not coming from here." Marian remembered how Beva had thumped her heart as she walked back into the dining room. Marian's heart thumping now, she put her hand on the back of her neck. "Beva, Ben was shot by a political fanatic, in Belfast."

An inchore, *a curse over his house, is Beva thinking that?* Marian wondered. No reaction, just silence on her end of the phone. "No need to worry, he's grand," she continued. "He's lost some blood. You know Ben. He was right in the center of things. They couldn't get the ambulance in right away, but he's grand." Marian could almost see the woman on the other end of the line shaking her head, the muscles in her neck tight like stilts. "He hasn't lost a limb, Beva, but he could have." Her words rushed out of her to fill the silence. "He's being transferred from Belfast to Mater Hospital tomorrow for two nights and the doctors expect we can take him home on the Sunday. Will we have tea this Sunday, then? We can all visit him in hospital and then bring him home."

"All right," Beva said hesitantly.

"I'll come with the car at noon. My mother would like to join us," she added. There was other news as well, Marian wanted to add, but not over the phone. She'd introduce her to Adrian on Sunday. Her own ma had not asked too many questions. In fact, she hadn't asked any questions when she'd learned through Father Brennan about the addition to the family. Funny, really, and not so funny at all, how easily her mother accepted Adrian now, how her community had accepted him. Of course, Father Brennan would have explained, there'd been no other option at the time. But with Beva, Marian had no idea what her response would be, had no idea if time's passing had softened her.

21

Beva heard the engine of Benjamin's spiffy automobile and watched from the living room window as Marian parked the car smack on the street in front of her pale yellow door. She watched Johanna get out of the car, skinny and small-boned, the living spit of herself, or so she thought but would never say so to Marian. Her arthritic shoulder and neck pain had worsened in the days since Marian's phone call.

She glanced at the dining table, which she had taken extra time to set, the white lace tablecloth new for this occasion. Time had slowed for her, living on her own. The girl Patsy only came on Mondays and Thursdays to straighten up. Sabbath dinners were now less of a production, sometimes taken alone. But there was the occasional bingo outing at the Adelaide Road Synagogue on Tuesday nights, Estelle and Rita, from the Board of Guardians, still checked on her bi-monthly.

Enough time *had* passed, Beva thought as Marian stood before her with a surprisingly docile look. She could tell from her daughter-in-law's expression that she noted how Beva had aged. Her face was leathery now, and her posture had worsened. Marian stalled by the door, gathering her thoughts, no doubt, as Johanna bustled into the living room. Marian's mother, Mrs. McKeever, stood holding the hand of a sturdy-looking young man while Marian herself seemed gobsmacked that her ma had actually come to the Jewish district.

Mrs. McKeever held her nose from the atrocious smells coming from the Canal, introduced herself, then peered inside the house. Beva watched Mrs. McKeever standing there in her wool coat worn to the bone, the wrinkles around her squinting blue eyes, as she examined the *mezuzah* affixed to the front door. She began to babble about something or other when Beva gestured for them to enter. Mrs. McKeever shoved a soda bread into her hands, an Irish housewarming.

"And who's this little person?" Beva asked, touching the boy's shoulder, hoping she wasn't wearing the condescending smile adults offer children.

"He's someone special," Mrs. McKeever said. "Go on in." She gave him a push and he walked toward Johanna into the living room. Beva looked at the platter of meat kasha on the server. Catholics only eat fish on a Friday, Beva knew, but this was Sunday, so Mrs. McKeever should let the kids try a little.

Everyone crowding inside the narrow foyer made her aware of how much smaller it seemed since the last time Ben's girlfriend had stood there, and she was glad for the homey smell of latkes wafting by. All that was needed were the bowls of applesauce and sour cream from the Frigidaire.

"We should be going," Marian said, not moving from the doorway.

"What? You just got here. You said we'd sit for tea!" Beva said, watching Johanna show the boy the photographs of Benjamin. "We'd have a nosh before we get Benjamin, you said." Disappointment was apparent in her voice.

"I hope you haven't gone to too much trouble," Marian said and reluctantly entered. The dining table was set for four. The same black radio projected a din of Yiddish music. "Come in, Ma," Marian urged. "Take that troubled look off your face. You're not in China, for God's sake," she muttered under her breath.

Patsy took their coats, and Marian led her mother over to the bookshelf where they studied the display of photographs as if they were an exhibit in a museum.

"At least, let's sit down for a *minute*," Beva pleaded, and set an extra plate, all her extended pleasantries unexpected, even to herself. She looked at the homemade *challah* and gefilte fish on the table, the same fish Marian had refused to eat on the night she kicked them out of her life for good. The kids rushed to the table.

"I can tell Johanna's friend here is a good eater, isn't he," she said, scooping some applesauce and latkes onto his plate.

Mrs. McKeever stood by her chair with a genteel smile, and then offered an awkward laugh as Beva pulled out her chair and motioned for her to sit down. "We passed a Jewish synagogue on our way here," Mrs. McKeever blurted.

Beva gave her a quizzical look as she placed latkes on her plate.

"These pancakes look delicious," Mrs. McKeever said rather loudly, looking at the boy.

Beva could see the tension on Marian's face, and in her movements, and she felt a sword fight coming on.

"We'd better tell her," Johanna whispered.

"Eat, Jo," Marian said and opened her eyes wide. "There are bigger things, though, for us to discuss than this meal, as lovely as it is," Marian began.

"We have news, Bubbe," Johanna said, her impish face in full bloom.

She plopped down. "I don't have any energy left for this. I'm *verklempt*. Is there more bad news?"

"We have good news, Bubbe," Johanna said. Beva reached over and pinched her pretty little cheek.

"We have, have we? A *mitzvah*, I hope?"

"This is Adrian, my eleven-year-old brother," Johanna announced between bites.

"What? What do you mean?" Beva suddenly felt confused.

"What did I tell you, Johanna? Run out back and play, both of you," Marian ordered.

"But—"

"You heard your mother," Mrs. McKeever said, taking Adrian and Johanna's hands, and escorting the two of them outside.

They stood still, looking at each other across the table.

"Ben and I had a son, Beva. Our son has been in a Home all this time, Beva. An orphanage."

She stood and came closer, grabbed the back of a chair. "You know I often thought about you, how you must have felt. But I had no idea of any of this, Marian."

"Nothing would have changed—had you known." She unclasped her hands. "Certainly, we wouldn't have been married with your consent."

"How dare you." Beva's hand went rigid as if to slap Marian across the face.

Marian looked startled. "Excuse me?"

"Do you think you're the only one who has suffered all these years? You're the only one who has a right to be angry?"

"That hellatious night was the cause—"

"Do you think I would rather live like this, without a family around me?" She put her hands on her hips.

"You insisted our relationship would never work," Marian said, her voice getting loud. "'What about the *kinder*?' You said. Did you think—"

"Yes, I said that, but I didn't know you were pregnant!" Beva shouted.

They both heard the back door bang. Marian's ma stood there for a moment and then slammed it shut and walked in.

"We can hear you outside," Mrs. McKeever said.

"Here he is in my backyard. My grandson. He doesn't know me."

"You wanted me gone. Let's be honest here."

"Don't continue to do to Benjamin and Johanna and now my grandson what you've been doing all these years, blaming me for everything."

"Why did you hate me so much without giving us a chance?"

"Why haven't you come round to see me, Marian? Why did you keep my Johanna from me all those years?" She shot back. She noticed that Marian's hands were shaking.

"You wouldn't budge. Just like the rest of the world."

"Marian, I'm an old lady. You're young and strong. It's not always the parent that should make amends. Honor thy mother and father," she said. "That's what both our religions believe."

"So you know, I've asked Ben about you," Marian said, more softly this time.

"And I've asked Benjamin about you. Some middle man he turned out to be, my Benjamin. When did he know? What does Benjamin think about all this?"

Marian shook her head and took a sip of water.

She threw her hands up in the air. "You know, I had a funny feeling the minute I saw him." She paused and looked at Marian. "Don't tell me anymore. I'll die of grief."

"Please," Marian said. "Let's not talk about it ever again."

"My daughter's right," Mrs. McKeever chimed in. "You have different ways, but let me tell you. Some things are better left unsaid, Mrs. Ellis."

"I can see in your eyes you're as strong as ever," Marian said.

She arched her eyebrows and looked at her daughter-in-law, who was still a beauty. Could it be that Marian just gave her a small compliment?

"I didn't know you were pregnant. I'm not a Catholic," Beva muttered. "I don't know what I would have done had I known, and neither do you."

"I've had enough," Mrs. McKeever said and huffed over to the closet. Grabbed her coat. "I am a Catholic and so is Marian," she blurted. She tied her scarf in a proud manner and turned to Marian. "I followed you. Went to buy you cold tablets—you looked knackered—but I followed you instead. My daughter paced back and forth over St. Stephen's Green with a handkerchief covering her mouth, shoving herself into the telephone box every ten minutes."

"Your phone rang and rang, off the hook," Marian said. "I'd changed my mind. I wanted to tell Ben I was pregnant. We would have married right away, with or without your consent, Beva. Why didn't you answer the phone?" Marian said.

"Sam died that night, do you understand? He died." Beva sat quietly for a moment. "Right after you left, Benjamin came in, terribly upset at me. I sent him to get Dr. Eisen. It was over so fast."

"Listen, you. Marian didn't kill your husband," Mrs. McKeever said.

"I never said–"

"I don't want another word. Adrian can hear, you know," Mrs. Mc-Keever hissed.

Marian put an arm around her ma, awkwardly, before Mrs. McKeever grabbed the kids' coats and made for the back door.

"Well," Marian sighed, obviously exhausted and no doubt worried sick, too, about Benjamin. "We all have to move on. A united front is what we need now. Any dissonance could hurt Adrian's chances of coming home to us for good."

Beva shook her head again in her way, in slight short movements, and tasted the coral lipstick creasing across her tight lips.

"You don't need to accept me. You need to accept him," Marian said.

"I will," Beva conceded.

"Not *Adrian*, although you must do that, too. I'm talking about your own son," Marian said.

Beva's eyes felt dry.

"Don't say Jews stick together, or anything like that, either, please," Marian said. "We all stick together now."

"I don't remember saying anything like that," she said, a bit defensively. "I think I just said that, as Jews, we integrate; we don't assimilate."

"Memory is selective, Beva. You said too much, but we only seem to remember our own best selves," Marian said and let out a huge sigh.

Beva sat. They looked at each other for a moment longer. "I have a grandson," she said, nodding, incapable of saying anything about her past actions, incapable of asking for forgiveness. But she could see there was a calmer expression on Marian's face, the tightness around her mouth and eyes seemed to have relaxed. An unmistakable shift had taken place in these few minutes since her son's family had stood on her doorstep. Although there was no denying that the tension had not completely lifted, there was no mistake that Marian felt relief that this meeting had finally happened.

And Marian knew that Beva would not try to stop her efforts to bring Adrian home.

22

"After all these years—now almost thirty working here—I've not a shilling to my name," Nurse confided to Officer Dolan in the dark shed, only a small green candle for light, the faint smell of evergreens in the room from the scented wax. "Maybe just three shillings saved from the Ellises, you know. Not a stamp to write to anyone, though I'm not allowed to, anyway."

Officer Dolan rummaged in his back pocket, produced a brown leather wallet, his picture identification card in a plastic flap, and handed her five stamps.

"Don't give me–"

"Go on. What harm? Take the stamps, my God."

She put the stamps in her shoe and felt giddy enough to emit a giggle. She saw paper bills stuffed inside his wallet, too, and asked how much savings he might have. He looked taken aback, the way men do when they think you might be wanting something from them. "No, no," she said, changing the subject. "I'm just hoping they don't put me out to pasture now that I'm old and gray," she said, knowing by his ruddy cheeks and veiny nose he was at least her age, likely older, and would understand her fears of aging alone.

"Ah, you're still young, Nurse. You can't be near my age, fifty this December coming."

"I stopped counting, one day going into the next, you know. Around fifty though, I am, too." She giggled again. "A lot older than the lot of them around here." Nurse hadn't been given a birthday in the orphanage and truly didn't know her exact age.

"Well, you don't look over forty," he said, chuckling in his odd way, like coughing, at her obvious flirtation and at his attempt at a compliment.

"No, Officer Dolan, you wouldn't want to trade places with the likes of them. No, no—regardless of their age. Some of the new girls are unbelievable. Have you noticed? The place is changing entirely.

One got me into bad trouble with Sister Paulinas," she said, feeling his interest in her as he moved closer.

"Would you call me Dan?"

"If Sister Paulinas heard me in here, calling you Dan, what would she think? I wouldn't dare."

He chuckled again, moved closer still, put his hands clumsily around her waist, and she noticed the Brylcreem in his pale thin hair. She withdrew from his arms and began talking fast. "I couldn't keep a new one from talking last night. Sister Paulinas came in, and heard me coaxing this brassy one to stop gabbing with the others. Sister said I was a useless old lady."

"Go on. Sister respects you," he said. And then blushing, he asked, "And what's your real name? Don't want to be calling you Nurse, either."

She ignored him. "You know how young people are. Or maybe you don't know. No children?"

He choked up a laugh. "Never married myself," he said.

She watched his face and neck turn the color of wild cranberries, his breath dense with mints and tobacco.

"I never married, either," she said, and quickly changed the subject. "I was a behaver, mind you. I wouldn't have dared speak up like the new girl. There were some bold ones a while back, but none so bad as now. The one who stood up to me frightened me, and in front of Sister Paulinas. 'Nurse, what are you, listening to this little runt of a child?' Sister Paulinas asked me. That shut the girl up. Shut her right up. 'Get back into the bed,' I said, and the girl obeyed."

Then Sister Paulinas had said, "One runt of a child to another," staring at her. "I thought you'd be able to master your own, but you're as much work as they are," she'd added. Nurse left that last part out. Still, she felt surprise at her candor with Officer Dolan.

But Sister Paulinas's words had troubled her. She knew none of the girls would respect her now, and with all Sister Paulinas and she had been through together, the truth finally hit her: Sister Paulinas would sooner help a cow get milk than she would help her.

"I'd hoped Sister Paulinas would respect me one day. But she despises the sight of me. Sins would sooner be forgiven by our Lord Jesus Christ than by her."

"You have her respect; I see that. You needn't worry so."

Nurse thought about Marian and how Marian knew how to get what she wanted. Marian had once told her that Sister Paulinas kept the girls down by scaring the wits off them. "Have you seen some of them wearing nylons and hair ribbons, as if they're going somewhere when they come in," Nurse said and then giggled. "No, no—one even talked back to Sister Paulinas, telling her not to touch her baby, that she'd do the picking up of her, and Sister Paulinas just looked at her and then walked out of the nursery. I never thought I'd see the day."

"With all the new music they have going now, it's no surprise," he said with another cough and a small move toward her.

"The girl must have figured that there was no more punishment they could do to her than take her baby. They couldn't hurt her; her mother had paid the headage. Some things never change. Money still talks," she said.

"True, that."

"Sister is meaner, her job's getting harder. With the attitudes some of them come in here wearing, Sister's gone mad. But she'll never change. No, no—she's a bitch," she whispered, and then looked round, sorry she'd said such a horrible thing, and in front of her man. "I'll be going," she said.

Nurse ran to her room, took out her penknife and slit quickly and deeply into her thigh. All the girls knew, because of Sister Paulinas, that she'd been a fallen woman, too. Though Sister promised Nurse's deceased sister Anne and Sister's Superior to be silent on the matter. Thirty-odd years or so on the job, and no respect. No change. She thought about Adrian, worried about him. She lay down on her cot letting her blood seep into her underclothes, not trying anymore to hold back her memories.

She cut herself deeply on the same thigh. *Blood is good. It makes babies.* She lay there, thinking about Officer Dolan, and she imagined that he was going to ask her to be his wife. He certainly respected her, like Marian did. Tomorrow, she'd just go about her business. If the girls asked her any questions, she'd tell them to shut it. Her life was none of their business. She'd show Sister Paulinas that these girls respected her.

Sister Paulinas. Bitch. Unhappy, old nun.

Ah, the hell with her! She wrote Marian a missive that said simply, *Help me, need a visit.* And the next morning before nursery duty, she hurried down to the front of the property and dropped a stamped envelope into the letterbox.

23

With Benjamin's arm in a cast, Marian took the driver's seat on the way home from the hospital. The rest jockeyed for positions by the other doors. Beva had not had a chance to chat with her grandson but accepted the middle seat between her daughter-in-law and Benjamin in the front without a word as Gran made a big to-do about everything with the kids in the back.

Where were Jo's hair bows? Gran asked Marian. Where was Adrian's sun hat? And on and on she chattered. "Stop your clowning, now." Gran tapped Johanna's wrist. Adrian retaliated a poke from Johanna and received his own tap on the knee.

Obviously Gran and Marian had been unable to teach these young people manners, Beva thought.

"You won't, either of you, be having the chocs in this box on my lap after tea, I can tell you," Gran said.

Beva suddenly felt badly about the way she treated Marian. She thought about the young woman that Marian was when she first met her, barely out of school. Perhaps Marian had been hoping that they might even be thrilled to have a little one running around the table. Beva understood a tad more now. Marian had been nervous. The nervous Beva herself had been rude, heartless even. With Marian's pregnancy in the picture, it all made sense. She wondered where the boy had been born and how different it would have been if Marian had never gone away, if she had told Benjamin the truth.

"Children, cut it out," Benjamin called.

Raising an eyebrow, Beva turned around. The *kinder* immediately stopped jumping around in the car. She patted her son on his knee. The muggy day proceeded, the sky's gray clouds bunched together. A sudden downpour, replete with thunderous noise, ensued, and they were stuck in an awful traffic jam. Squawking horns from miserable motorists exacerbated the discomfort. Marian took the opportunity to point out Da's office building, or at least the direction of *The Irish Times* and the green further down, with the Shelbourne Hotel on the right, where the Irish Constitution was signed. "A favorite of your ma and da's, this area in general," she said. "Isn't it," she said to Benjamin.

"Ah, it is. Open the windows back there," Benjamin said. "I'm roasting."

"It's raining, Da," Jo answered back, laughing at him.

"That's where your da and I celebrated our wedding day," Marian pointed, looking straight ahead.

Benjamin had told his mother it was a filthy day, with rain slashing the windows of the Registrar's Office. Marian and Benjamin stood in the queue to be married by a Justice of the Peace. Except for Mr. Robert Thompson, their witness, they were alone. They sipped a bottle of G. H. Mumm Grand Cru at the Shelbourne. "May you know nothing but happiness from this day forward," he whispered to his bride. Had thoughts of Adrian crowded her mind? Had she not foreseen the depths of maternal feelings? Or was she surprised by them, as she herself had been? It might have been raining, but it was only weather, after all. There's food, and there's weather, Marian said to Benjamin, who made an apelike face. They kissed and laughed and finished their champagne.

"Ah, we're bloody married," Benjamin had declared. They sat for a moment, looking out the window at the darkening clouds. There was no denying the heat and swelling humidity before the coming rain. "Come on. Let's go to my place before another onslaught." He threw ten pence on the table and put on his overcoat and hat. "It's about to come down hard."

"In more ways than one," Marian said as he took her hand and led her away from the crowds, against furious winds through St. Stephen's Green, and past the usual cut-off to Mercer Street and her home. "Christ!" she shouted as she bolted, his newspaper covering her stiff curls, all the pent-up nerves flying about.

"Marian!" Benjamin called after her and she stopped.

Heads of passersby turned, and she suddenly felt self-conscious.

"Let them stare if that's all they have on their minds to do. I don't care." He tipped his hat and faced them. "I love her!" he shouted, throwing his arms out wide. Shocked, Marian turned toward him, and they both began to laugh. Everything would turn out fine, he told her.

The slashing mist thickening into a sudden downpour, the two continued south like kids in a three-legged race, until the door of his flat on Martin Street shut behind them. She'd only been here that one other time. And it had felt nothing like sin. Marian took in as much of the room as she could: the crumpled brown hat and beige mackintosh dripping on the hall stand, the typewriter and newspapers and cigarette packs splayed across his wooden desk, the pea green couch and glass coffee table, soiled sneakers on the oval tweed mat, the smell of dirty socks. She watched him study her as he slipped off her raincoat.

"My ma's going to think—"

"It only matters what I think," Benjamin said. She held him tightly. "We have a couple of hours," he said, and gave her that squint she loved as he slowly unzipped her dress. She felt it slip to the floor. "Stop shaking," he whispered and kissed her all over and then held her face in his hands. "Everything will be okay, Marian. I just know it."

She did feel safe here. She could let her worries fall away. Whenever they were together, it was as if she had left dreary Dublin behind. She loved the rush. They moved together as if to a slow song until the urgency overtook her. "I have never been so hot and bothered in my life."

"I have never been so happy in mine," he said and moved his own trembling hands underneath her slip. Her stockings slid down her thighs, and they entered their private world of lovers, as they had when she had let things go too far. They were in this together now, though, there was no doubt.

Benjamin lit a cigarette and handed it to her. "Max Berger at the *Times* says people took bets about our wedding," he said. They sat quietly together smoking. Marian let out a chuckle and went to pull on her taupe nylons, picturing her Catholic ma's horror that she'd fallen in love and had married a Jewish boy. They had been giddy enough afterwards to flag a cab; ready for the onslaught they would receive when they announced to Marian's mother that they were the genuine article.

Benjamin squinted at Marian now, and lit a cigarette. She fanned the smoke away with her hand. Marian glanced at Beva's shriveled hand on Benjamin's knee, and then gave Benjamin a look. Her son could feel Marian's uneasiness, but Beva was determined to ignore her daughter-in-law's discomfort, as well as her own.

"That's all of us at the beach, in Dollymount," Marian said, pointing to the photograph she'd taped to the dashboard.

Beva nodded and craned her neck around to smile at Adrian. "Do we have photographs! I'll show you photographs of your father with Reb Leventhal," she said and then clapped Benjamin's thigh gently. Benjamin took the Mammy's hand in his for a moment.

"Would you like to see your father's photographs?" Beva said to Adrian, who simply nodded. "We'll introduce him to the Reb soon, won't we, Benjamin?"

"Oh, Jesus," Gran McKeever mumbled into Adrian's ear.

"You'd like that? And you'd like to meet some of Johanna's new friends from the neighborhood, am I right?" Beva asked.

"I heard that silence," Benjamin said, turning around to point a finger at him and Johanna. "Ah, don't be embarrassed of who you are," he said.

"I'm not, Da," Johanna said, as Adrian cowered in his seat. At Beva's he had peered at the white candles burning in brass candlesticks, casting a glow onto the silver veggie platters, linen tablecloth drooping to the floor. Adrian told Johanna that he knew that the Jews ate well and lived well. He'd heard that they owned all of Grafton Street. Peddlers and leeches, moneylenders who'd charge you outrageous interest—that's what Sister Agnes once told him.

"Why are you hiding down there, Adrian?" Beva said.

Mrs. McKeever popped a chocolate in the boy's mouth.

"I'm going to get the article I completed in the hospital published, even if I do it freelance at *The New World*. It's all about catechism classes in orphanages," Benjamin said. "And the misinformation these kids are learning about other religions."

"*Please.* Don't be doing anything that'll upset Sister Agnes," Marian scolded. "Everything's going to be all right," Marian added quickly, looking at Adrian through her rearview mirror. "The world will come round, the hard times will pass away," Marian sighed, as she spoke into Adrian's ear.

When they finally crawled out of the city and onto Mount Merrion Road toward Black Rock, the expanse of sea to their left, Marian's sigh of contentment seemed to have an effect on the entire party. There was no more banter. Each member of the family settled down into their own thoughts, the children's countenances peaceful. But suddenly they poked each other awake, gawked out the car window at a beehive of activity—the circus had come to the town of Sandymount. A Ferris wheel and other rides could be seen. A blur of busy workers set up the big main tent while others tended to jungle animals. Adrian and Johanna, jumping up and down in the back seat, shouted to their mother that they had to go. *Please could they go!* Marian looked at Benjamin, who frowned, and she conceded that he was right. Everyone turned around in their seats to get a last look as they sped by.

24

Before Ben's morning meeting, he removed his sling. He lied to his coworkers, told them that he wasn't in any pain, and swore to Mr. Darby that he'd be typing quicker than any of them in no time. It was by that afternoon, though, that he realized his promotion as first reporter covering the North for the *Irish Times* had been quietly dismissed. He spoke late in the day about his career concerns with Mr. Darby, who denied this demotion. "You're our best columnist, stick with that," he said.

Since the ban on interviewing eyewitnesses at scenes of violence, most journalists had felt the chill factor and would steer clear of the troubles. Ben knew this, and knew that he should be grateful for his old column. Along with a medal for his bravery up North, Mr. Darby had approved Ben's request for a new column, entitled "Dublin's Little Domain," that catered to the small Jewish community. He should create his own spin on local news stories, particularly Irish Jewish stories. That was the emphasis they wanted, Mr. Darby agreed. "And you'll have complete freedom as well," he'd added.

"Stories about Jewish twins born in the city, interviews with prominent Jewish members of society, a visit with the Jewish Lord Mayor of Dublin," Ben told Marian the next morning, rubbing his upper right arm, thinking the real excitement in the journalism career he'd dreamed about was all but over. "It's the best Mr. Darby can offer, I'm afraid," Ben said.

"You'll have more time at home with me," Marian told him, but he knew she was preoccupied with saving Adrian, not with spending time with him.

Ben felt his nerves fraying and wondered if Jo and Adrian realized something about him was amiss. It upset him that Marian was snapping at Jo yet treated Adrian with kindness because of his fragile predicament. Johanna's brow tightened, her lips fell open in disbelief at what she believed to be her mother's favoritism. All this attention given to Adrian, Adrian, Adrian, all the time. Even *before* the summer began, Johanna had muttered to him in the garden.

Ben took Marian to the Gaiety Theatre, the Wednesday matinee, to see a Marlon Brando picture. The previous night Marian rang Father Brennan to ask if he could watch the children. The priest said he'd be happy to play table tennis with the kids, and inquired again after Ben's sore arm. Ben and Marian agreed: Father was good to baby-sit. And they'd feel refreshed after a little time to themselves.

Little did they know that as they were making their way home after cake and coffee at Quinlan's, Father Brennan sat enthralled in front of the television, disgusted by some heretic talking about contraception, while the children played unsupervised upstairs. As the couple approached the house, they heard Mrs. O'Rourke's muffled cries and saw her hands cover her mouth. They looked up at the third story of their townhouse to find Adrian, his face covered in clown makeup, dangling Johanna by her ankles out of the attic dormer window.

"My fucking God!" Ben ran into the house, petrified that if Adrian dropped Jo from the window, he would be incapable of catching her with only one good arm.

"Don't shout at them! Don't scare them, Ben!" Marian yelled up after him as he climbed the stairs two at a time. "Don't startle them!" she warned. He leapt up the narrow third floor stairway, practically flew into the attic to grab Johanna before Adrian could lose his hold. Ben's good arm gripped her thigh as he snaked the other arm around her waist and coaxed her skinny body back into the attic playroom.

"What in God's name were you doing?" he yelled, wanting to slap Adrian hard. Instead he pushed the boy out of the way. Adrian fled to the corner wall. Ben hugged Johanna tightly as the two collapsed to the floor.

Marian, looking completely drained, pulled Adrian down with her in the corner of the room. Ben kept his arms tight around Johanna. The girl wore a black Halloween cat costume and her Mickey Mouse Club ears. Early evening's cold air rushed in through the window, cooling the family as they sought to catch their breath and collect their wits.

"Let's have a proper answer, young man. You're not getting off so easily anymore. What the hell were you thinking, holding your sister out the bloody window?"

Suddenly Adrian stood, dropped his trousers, and gripped the wall.

Ben knew that it was during a child's first year at Silverbridge that they learned to hold the bar and wait for a thrashing. For Adrian, the flogging must have started when he was around four or five years old. The waiting was as hard to endure as the leather belt itself, Ben imagined.

"Don't make things worse, Ben!" Marian shouted at him.

"Things couldn't be worse, Marian. Wake up! And you. Pull up your trousers, Adrian."

"How the hell could you even try to come to his defense over this one?" Ben said to Marian. He rubbed Jo's back. "No one's going to give you a good larruping, Adrian. Though you bloody well deserve one," he said. "Now, tell me, for God's sake. What you were doing to your sister?"

"It's our fault, Ben. We're the ones bought them the costumes," Marian interjected.

"Lots of children have costumes, Marian! They don't hold their sisters out the goddamn window!"

"It's my fault, Da. It was my idea," Jo said, watching Adrian pull up his trousers.

"Ah, bloody hell, the two of you! Johanna, you know better. What in God's name were you thinking? Don't you ever let anyone harm you, in any way again. God damn it!"

Marian and Adrian stood up as Ben helped Jo to her feet.

"The two of you have no sense. You're both going to bed without your tea."

He lit a cigarette, relaxed a bit, grateful that no one was hurt.

"We have to be extra good these days, you know that, Jo. Adrian, not again," he said, exhaling a tunnel of smoke in his direction. "Not ever."

Later that evening, at Ben's tender prodding, Jo explained how they put on their circus costumes, and then they no longer wanted to be silly old clowns but acrobats on a trapeze. Yes, she was jealous of her mother's attentions to Adrian. That was true, but they were playing a game of pretend. That was all, she said. It was *her* idea to hang from the window. She had begged Adrian to do it, just for the thrill and fun of it. At first, Adrian refused, but when she threatened him with expulsion from their family, he complied. And because it had been her idea all along, she got to go first.

"Johanna, I know you. I can tell that the second half of your story is made up. You never threatened Adrian that he'd be sent away if he didn't go along with your plan."

Johanna shrugged. "I don't want you to blame Adrian. I would have held him out the window next."

"What has gotten into you? You know what you did was extremely dangerous?"

She looked down, touched her stuffed animal.

"Come on, Jo. Use your brains," Ben said. He kissed her goodnight and closed her bedroom door. "Thank God you're safe."

Ben trudged down the stairs. Marian and Father Brennan were sitting on the couch. He opened the lower cabinet of the dining room cupboard, retrieved three tumblers and the Black and White.

"Marian. I think we have to consider what's best."

Marian sighed as she followed Father Brennan and took a seat at the table. Ben poured them all whiskey and took a long sip of his, grateful for the warmth sliding down his throat. She stared at the dusty wood floor. She was somewhere far away from him and he didn't know how to bring her back.

"Marian?"

"What are you saying? I'm sorry," she said.

"I think we may be in over our heads," Ben said.

"It seems a lot to take on in a short time," Father Brennan said.

Marian opened her eyes in that incredulous way she had when she was annoyed. "Why weren't you watching them?" she asked Father Brennan. "Who are you, really?"

Father Brennan stood. "I didn't realize that their games were dangerous, Marian. I didn't know I had to watch them that carefully."

"Well, of course not! Not while the telly's on."

Father Brennan made a grimace. "I suppose I should have been more attentive."

"Well, I guess that's it then," she said. "That's quite unequivocal, don't you think? Certainly, don't feel you need to apologize more profusely, Father."

Father put on his overcoat and hat and went toward the door. "I'll leave you two alone."

"Thank you, Father Brennan. It certainly was not your fault, and we appreciate your coming over," Ben said, looking at Marian. Ben was grateful that Marian stood as well to see him out.

"You know, Ben," she said, coming back to sit with him. "I don't think you ever wanted Adrian."

"Ah, go on outta that one already. He's my son, too," he whispered. "You've always a major bee in your bonnet, and you can't keep bringing up the past and your—"

"Don't bullshit me," she said. "I'm not living in the past. You are. And your apron strings. I know what you're really thinking when you're not up to your eyeballs with yourself and your poor old ma. You think Adrian's too much for me to handle."

"Marian, think for yourself."

"And what would you have me to think?"

"Something terrible could have happened, you know that. Or don't you? I don't know if he's right in the mind, and you're acting as if nothing's wrong. I want him here but he's been damaged. I don't want Johanna damaged along with him."

Ben heard something and got up to look out the bay window. In the dreary light from a battered street lamp, some of the neighbors stood near Mrs. O'Rourke's gate, talking in hushed tones. A group of hags in their housecoats. Curlers in their hair, cigarettes hanging from their mouths. He could plainly see Mrs. O'Rourke shaking her head at her twin girls, and the young girls, mimicking their mother, shook their heads, too.

He didn't notice Marian behind him until she jerked open the front door.

Leaning against the doorway, Marian gaped at the cluster of women, all looking in haphazard directions, none directly at her. "Well, ladies of the night!" she shouted and watched them all gasp. "'Tis better to be the cause of all your concerns than to be subjected—thank God—to even one nighttime's dose of your insipid company."

She curtsied at them before she slammed the front door.

She walked back to the dining room table and sat down, her head in her hands.

"Marian." Ben sat next to her. "You're losing your mind." He suddenly thought of Tatte and was ashamed about how his father would feel with the way their lives had turned out.

Marian took a sip of whiskey. She was overwhelmed, fighting to believe that everything was going to be all right.

"Bringing Adrian back, draining our finances. The whole burden on Jo, the memories dragging around. I don't know if it's right."

"Is Father Brennan the influence?"

"He's talked with me, but no. I'm trying to start over with you. I'm not saying no. I'm saying I'm worried that bringing Adrian into our home won't make our family better. Sometimes that's just the way it is. Just because someone comes back into your life doesn't automatically change everything into roses."

"You sound like Father Brennan."

"No, Marian. I sound like me. Let's work on this together, okay? I want things to work out. But only, and I mean only, if it's right."

"I need some sleep," she said and went up to bed.

Ben put away the liquor and washed out the tumblers. Sitting up sipping whiskey with his wife used to be romantic, now it was a headache coming on. Though she was right about needing sleep. He felt his temples squeezing in the sides of his head. He shut out all the lights, peeked out the window at the neighbor's house, and saw their kitchen light still on. Mrs. O'Rourke's head was resting on the kitchen table, a small cup of steaming milk in her hand. Then he noticed Johanna standing at their front door with an empty picture frame she made in art class, tapping lightly on the O'Rourke's knocker. "I made this for you," he heard her say as Mrs. O'Rourke, in her tattered blue bathrobe, wiped her cheeks.

"I'd ask you in for cocoa but it's late. You should be home in bed."

"Just wanted to let you know," Johanna said, glancing over at their house, "that even though Ma says you don't give a rat's ass about us and that you don't like Adrian in particular, I know Adrian would give his eye teeth to be adopted and live with you any day."

Ben opened the front door and called Johanna inside. He waved to Mrs. O'Rourke, and she waved back as his *maidelah* ran into his arms.

25

"I'd like to say Mass regularly, Sister Agnes," Father Brennan said after his disturbing babysitting day.

"That would give Father Neely a break," Sister told him. "He'd love someone filling his shoes now and again. I'll tell him. You'll do Sunday noon, then?"

"I'd like to do the Mass for the children," Father Brennan said.

"They attend every day at seven."

Every day at seven, he thought. Before they've had their breakfast? (One didn't eat an hour before Mass.) No wonder he had seen a poor little girl strapped into the pew. Not a morsel in her, she must have nearly fainted.

It was through his visits to Silverbridge that Father Brennan began to see the truth and error of his own ways. Here he stands—a priest talking in Latin with his back to the wee ones. He saw this as reprehensible now. He turns his back on those who are most in need. Be charitable. Suffer the little children come unto me—could the Bible reading he had done for over a decade finally have some real meaning? Could he find a way to make a difference? In *these* children's lives? Seeing first-hand the conditions of the refectory. the chaos, the cold, the vacant stares... Adrian...

Last Sunday, the children stopped talking when he entered the dining hall. An unfamiliar teacher walked by and punched a girl on her head. The girl gazed into her bowl of spuds, a line of oleo, like a diluted yellow stroke from a thin paintbrush, dripped down one of the gray potatoes. *You're not one of the favorites, then?* He said this gently to her, wanting to smooth her short, unevenly cut hair. She looked at him. Empty eyes. Empty stomach. And then the blasted bell rang. Adrian hadn't noticed him as he lined up to leave the refectory.

But here is an appropriate metaphor, Father Brennan thought.

Their line and his are divided, and he is on the side of the nuns and teachers who thought of the orphans as lesser people.

He walked home, certain that he was more aware of his surroundings, of the poverty, of the people he passed. Was that not his calling? To take notice? To show compassion? Be a comfort? He knew he was no comfort. It was he who had been comforted by them, the lay people always showing their respect. He had allowed this, even enjoyed this, all these years. That was the great shame.

Jew, Greek, all one in God's eyes. Father Brennan tried to see Ben through a different lens, and when he did, he thought highly of the man. Ben seemed open to their philosophical conversations and wanted to learn as much as he could. They had decided to begin reading Thomas Merton, and Father Brennan looked forward to discussing his ideas. Tonight he would go home, sit in his easy chair with his brandy, and finish *The Screwtape Letters.* A bit radical, Father Brennan thought, this C. S. Lewis fantasy. But Ben had urged him; he thought he might like it, so Father Brennan gave it a go.

26

"Where is everybody, Jo?" Adrian asked, as they mulled around the neighborhood. "It's too quiet. No one hanging about. No street ball. Just you."

"Ha," she said.

"No girls, either. In groups, you know? Lots of girls in the orphanage."

"I'll take you to the Muckross playground. There's always kids hanging around."

They walked along and Adrian wondered why everything was so hidden. "Where are they hiding?"

"They're not hiding, silly. They have their own big yards to play in."

"Peter's ma lives on the North side. Crowded and cramped, sure, but there's lots of kids everywhere."

"We should go one day," Jo said, always game. "Why, the right bastard," she whispered now.

Adrian looked over to the basketball court on the playground. There were two boys about his age taunting a third, smaller kid. He suddenly missed Peter and hoped he was okay.

When the bullies saw them coming closer, they stopped but did not run. Adrian looked around and snapped a long branch off a chestnut tree.

As brother and sister reached about six feet away, all three kids stood stock-still. The older kids glared at Jo.

"That bully is Jeannie Jelly's faggot brother," Jo said. "Hiya Jack," she said to him.

"I'd call him Jackie. Looks like he fights like a girl," Adrian said. He hit the branch against his thigh. "Are you a sissy boy? You like to pick on younger kids?"

"Hump off, would ya," Jack said. He leaned to his friend. "She's off her nut. Completely dingle berries."

"You should see his beast of a sister in the flesh. Looks like he's going in the same direction. He's no oil painting either," Jo said.

"She is, is she?" Adrian said, moving closer. "Shite flies high when it's hit with a stick."

Jackie's bully-friend looked at his mate, then bolted. The little boy looked relieved as Adrian nodded at him.

"Fuck off," the Jelly kid said. "You sicken my pish. Your da's nothing but a slime bucket. Him and all the slimy Jews who killed our Lord."

"What did you say, you boiled shite?" Adrian approached him with his stick. Jackie froze. He had his prey. Adrian knew what the bully was feeling, unable to move from the shock of a sudden attack. No pain, just fear and disbelief that settled the kid right into his hands.

Adrian ran at him and got him in on the ground in a half nelson. He held him there, watching him squirm and sweat.

"You want up?" Adrian asked and shook him. The bully nodded. Adrian let him up, told him to apologize to the young boy.

"I'm sorry," Jackie mumbled.

"Now, in your scivvies," Adrian said.

The bully didn't move.

"Are you looking at me or chewing a brick? Why are you staring at me with your mouth wide open? Get 'em down, I said!" Adrian grabbed the lad and threw him against the school wall. "Face the wall."

Jackie did as told.

"We'll make an example of you." He pulled down Jackie's trousers. No one dared move. Adrian hit him soft against the bottom with his stick, but the boy shouted out in pain. "Why, you little liar. Stop lying!" Adrian shouted.

He hit him harder.

"You shout when you feel something. You won't be a faker anymore! Will you, boy?"

"No," Jackie whimpered.

Adrian hit him across his bottom for the third time, softer, and the boy still cried out. Anger exploded from Adrian. "Are you playing games with me?"

"No, please. It hurts. Please stop."

"What a pansy we have here, boys and girls! And this is the one who'll have you believe he's the tough guy." He hit him hard. "Four! You'll get ten of the best, my boy."

The boy screamed. Adrian slammed the branch, shouting out the numbers until he came to ten. Adrenaline and anger flooded through him.

"You'll stop your wisecracking now." He slapped the tree limb against his thigh and made the boy crawl on all fours. "Is this your sack?"

"Yes," the boy whimpered.

Adrian took out a plastic bag filled with Topps baseball cards and stuck them in his pants. "Now stand, boy. You and you and you," Adrian said to the lot of them. "All stand in a row."

They all did.

"You turn to them, Jackie boy, and then to me, with a full 'I'm sorry that I said those things against the Jews,' yeah?"

The boy did.

Adrian told him to run home in his underwear, and they watched him scuttle away. Jo and Adrian said goodbye to the young boy. He recognized the bewilderment in the boy's eyes. *Sometimes we get lucky,* Adrian thought. *This was his day.*

27

Ben just settled himself into the library when he heard a knock at the front door.

A police officer glowered on the stoop. "Do you have a son and a daughter, Adrian and Johanna Ellis?"

"I do."

"Apparently, your son, Mr. Ellis, has beaten up young Jack Johnson. Principal Hinckley happened to be in his office and witnessed the attack, so there's no doubt that it happened."

"Adrian?"

Adrian came into the foyer looking like an innocent lamb. "Is this true?"

"He was hitting a boy a lot younger than him. And his sister has been calling Jo names. I just put him in his place, that was all."

"He ran home naked, in tears, according to his father."

Adrian shrugged.

"He's also said you've stolen his baseball cards," the officer continued.

"He's a liar," Adrian said.

"You don't have his cards, Adrian?"

"No, Da."

"No one ever knows the full story out of kids' mouths," the officer said.

The officer didn't care all that much, Ben thought. "Children can be the most cruel, officer, particularly with the name calling," Ben said. "A shame."

The officer wrote on his pad and simply stated that if Adrian was seen on or near the Johnson's property, he would be arrested.

"Adrian?"

"I won't be going. I don't even know where he lives, and I don't care to."

"Okay, you've been warned, young man. Do you understand?" the officer said.

"Yes, sir."

Ben felt an urge to scream at this street urchin—his own son! Adrian walked toward the wall as if he knew he was in for it. Ben felt he somehow had to break through to him.

"Everything doesn't have to end in violence, Adrian," he said. Ben collapsed on the couch. "Come and sit."

Once Adrian sat next to him, he pulled himself together.

"It's true that children can be the most cruel. I'm sure part of you was trying to defend your little sister. She's had a rough time with the name calling."

Adrian nodded. "I'm not Jewish, but he called you a slime bucket."

"Don't be embarrassed or ashamed of who you are, Adrian." He put his arm around the back of the couch. "I want us to get to know one another better. I want to teach you a bit about traditions."

Adrian seemed to be in another world, but Ben reached over and gave him an awkward hug.

"It's okay, whatever happened. You're not punished," he whispered, his arm still around his shoulder.

Adrian held on tight. Ben looked over at the dining table. Perhaps tonight he'd teach Jo and Adrian about the four questions. Tell them a bit more about *Sukkot* and *Yom Kippur*, too, and what the Day of Atonement means, if he could hold their attention.

"You know. The Jews have always been persecuted, but we're strong. You ought to be proud to be part of the faith."

"Yeah?" Adrian said. "Are the Jews part of the one true faith?"

Ben sighed. "Never mind. It's the Sabbath. We'll eat now. I bought some white fish, some *rugelach* for dessert, hmm? You'll try a little?" he said and rubbed Adrian's back gently.

Adrian smiled as they rose. "Sure, Da. And I'll keep studying. Thanks, Da," he said.

Ben touched the top of his head, closed his eyes in a moment of prayer.

"Come on, let's break bread." He offered Adrian the platter of *matzoh*, ladled some fish on the cracker.

"I'll try a tiny bit. Smells like arse weed, though."

Ben put the platter down and sat, his head in his hands.

Adrian took the chair next to him. "Come on, Jo and Ma! You Maggies!" Adrian shouted. "Let's have ourselves a good feed."

Ben looked at him. "No, Adrian. No shouting. And no talking slang in your home. This is not a place for bad behavior. Come on."

Adrian's head went down, and Ben was the cruel one now, as his son's face and neck turned the color beets in a bowl of *borscht*. He felt helpless—there was too much to teach—and he was at a loss for words. He dropped his head back into his hands, his temples pulsating.

28

Ten days left with his new family, Adrian realized they had melded into a unit, no longer awkward and formal as they were their first month together. Full of promise, he chose to ignore his own all-consuming worries. Instead, he thought proudly of how natural it was for him to jockey into his role as big brother. It had been his idea to make a pledge with Jo to be more careful, more cautious, about their play. Jo agreed, but tried to make light of it. She shook her head at him, called him a worrywart.

On the last Sunday in August, enjoying the evocative smell, Adrian swept the stray, dry needles and the fallen red berries that decorated the Christmas tree Ma bought (since he would not be back again for good until Sister Agnes signed away her rights). He listened to the record *Music for the Sabbath* and found the Hebrew soothing, almost like the Gregorian chants he loved so well. Recently, to please his da and out of his own curiosity, he'd been stealing time in the library to try to read from *The Joys of Yiddish*. That afternoon, when his da returned home for tea, Adrian greeted him with a wide smile and the Hebrew word *shalom*.

Da put his arm around him and told him that the next time Gran and Father Brennan came to take Adrian to the Church of the Sacred Heart for Mass he would come, too, to show him the altar where the word *shalom* was carved into the lectern. "We're all praying to the same God," Da added, handing him a ten pence for ice creams at Quinlan's with Johanna.

Adrian grabbed Jo and they ran off to get their sundaes. Afterward, licking their fingers, they meandered to the Church of the Sacred Heart to see if they could please their da and find the *shalom* themselves. They peeked through the window beside the great wooden double doors and marveled at its marble pillars, mosaics, and especially the three stained glass windows sitting directly above the hand-carved, wooden confessional box.

They had come to see the lectern and were disappointed to find the front doors locked. Noting that it was well before the seven o'clock evening Mass, they sneaked behind the church and found that they could easily scale the outside of the building and climb up unnoticed to the second-tier window ledges. There they could get a close look at the altar and touch the brightly colored stained glass windows, to boot.

They peered inside but did not notice Mrs. O'Rourke entering through an open side door. She sat in a pew, pressing her rosary beads, a full hour before the service began.

Once situated above ground on the wide ledge, it didn't take much to go from pretending to balance on a tight rope to attempting other acrobatic routines they had wanted desperately to see at the circus. There was still a chance their da would change his mind, Adrian thought.

After a few successful handstands performed by Adrian, Johanna tried to outdo him with a longer handstand than his. Because of her enthusiasm, her hard black shoes smacked into the stained glass depiction of Saint Peter. In a backbend, Jo fell through the window and onto the wooden confessional.

Adrian stared dumbstruck through the cracked window at his stunned sister, lying on the roof of the confessional, the breath knocked out of her.

He was through the window, crawling onto the confessional roof when an alarmed Mrs. O'Rourke came running toward them. Somehow she found a way up onto the confessional and pulled Johanna into her arms. A bit of blood speckled on Mrs. O'Rourke's dress.

"Get help!" she shouted at Adrian, who was still staring at his dazed sister.

He climbed back out through the broken window and jumped down to the grassy ground. He ran fast down the Donnybrook Road, past the Sisters of Charity, and into the graveyard. Frantic, having lost all sense of direction, wanting to find his way home where his mother would ring a doctor for Jo, Adrian ran haphazardly ahead.

Jo, for the moment, was more surprised than hurt. Mrs. O'Rourke called after Adrian, screamed. She sped out the front door to phone for an ambulance from the corner newsagent.

Adrian kept running.

When Adrian arrived breathlessly at the house, Da was waiting for him and he could tell from the exasperated expression on his face that he already knew about the accident.

Within six minutes, an ambulance arrived at the church, but Johanna was nowhere to be found. Flustered by the fall and afraid of the consequences, she had disobeyed Mrs. O'Rourke's orders to wait until her return and, instead, went chasing after Adrian. That's what Ben heard.

With Johanna gone, Mrs. O'Rourke pointed the ambulance in the direction of Mount Eden Road, assuming the children were well on their way home. That's what the medical men said upon arrival at the house. Mrs. O'Rourke and one of the medical assistants went to the Donnybrook Garda Station across the way. The woman explained about the broken church windows and the possibility of broken bones as well, they told Ben.

Da grabbed Jo when she came through the door and lay her down on the oak wood floor, a towel underneath her. Ben put his hand on her forehead. Ma joined him there to attend to her with a wet towel.

"You're all right," Ma whispered, dabbing her sweaty face. When the ambulance workers left, Marian stood to escort them, but the sound of a siren brought her quickly outside.

As the neighbors gathered in the Ellises' driveway, Mrs. O'Rourke emerged from the back seat of a police car. Adrian ran into Ma's arms and she held him, calmed him down before looking around for Mrs. O'Rourke, who stood by her own front door.

"Why didn't you just ring us?" Marian shouted, not intent on an answer.

"I thought I was helping," Adrian heard Mrs. O'Rourke plead as Ma turned her back. Marian pulled him away from the still-growing crowd.

"Don't be worrying yourself about Mrs. O'Rourke," Ben told her. "Stay still on this towel, Jo. Get me another wet cloth, Marian," he said.

"I'm fine, Da, you can see that. It's just dried blood. All I have are some scratches."

Marian ran for some clean towels and wiped Jo's arms clean.

"I'm all right, Ma," Jo said and looked up at Adrian. "How are you?"

"I'm all right, too, Jo. Thanks," he said. Marian took him straight through to the kitchen and wet a washrag to clean his face. His knickers were dirty but intact. He was frightened but he didn't have a scratch on him.

"Your Granda's watching over you," Ma whispered into his ear as Da came into the kitchen with that strained look of compassion one sees at funeral gatherings.

"The guards want to talk to you, Adrian," Ben said.

Marian rubbed Adrian's back hard, as he began to shake. Adrian could feel the tension in the kitchen and started to cry, knowing what they'd done would have dire consequences for him.

Da put a hand on his shoulder. "Jo's fine," he said quietly to him. "That's the biggest concern right now, the biggest relief. That Jo has not been seriously hurt, or worse," he added.

"We'll be right out. You can tell them," Ma countered, shooing Ben away. She dabbed a wet rag on Adrian's eyelids and the back of his neck, took him by the hand into the drawing room.

Adrian didn't dare speak. He could feel the solemnity in the room as Johanna explained to the police about her acrobatics and the damage to the stained glass windows. According to the police, they had smashed an antique mosaic commemorating the Dunn family from Rathgar, and a Eugene Dunn would be notified. Adrian said that he was guilty of doing handstands but that he hadn't been running away. He was trying to find his way home; he was trying to get help, and got lost.

Ma and Da sat next to each other on the sofa. Although a warm breeze could be felt wafting through the open window, they may well have been carved in ice. About this new situation, there was nothing more his parents could say to each other or to the guards.

Sister Agnes was notified immediately.

29

The afternoon Sister Agnes arrived to escort Adrian back to Silverbridge, Mrs. O'Rourke was sitting on her stoop pruning begonias in the pots by the door. After the ordeal with Johanna, it would come as no surprise to Marian that Sister Agnes might not relinquish rights to Adrian. For a while.

No time for tea, Sister Agnes informed Marian. She took Adrian by the hand.

Obedient and careful, especially since Sister had agreed to collect him after Johanna's school was back in session, Marian kissed Adrian on the forehead and opened the front door. "You be a good boy for the nuns, now," she whispered loud enough for Sister to hear, and Adrian grinned on cue. They'd practiced this bit, to make a good impression.

Sister Agnes smiled at Marian, and she felt a rush of hope as she watched the two walk through the gate.

Then Marian noticed Mrs. O'Rourke, the dried string bean, stand up, bow and lower her head as Sister Agnes and Adrian walked by. Although Adrian waved good-bye to Mrs. O'Rourke, she didn't so much as glance at the boy. Marian shut the door and forced herself to take a seat on the couch, repressing a powerful urge to open the door and shout obscenities at the woman. Marian suspected that Mrs. O'Rourke was so displeased and even disturbed by Adrian's presence around her girls that now, with this appalling late summer scene, she had just the excuse she needed to speak ill of the Ellis family. Gossip about the circus incident was sure to spread, and Mrs. O'Rourke would certainly take the opportunity to let everyone know that Adrian was the Ellises' wild, bastard son. She got up and squeaked the back kitchen door open, tiptoed through the garden and crouched by the fence.

Mrs. O'Rourke pulled the Sister aside and talked to her of Adrian and Johanna's friendships with her daughters, how she'd seen them playing chalked hopscotch and other childlike games. They were all just decent, normal children, she went on. They all managed quite well together. Yes, there was the mitching of apples and some unruly incidents, but she wanted Sister to know that there'd been no real harm done.

Jesus, shut it! Marian wanted to scream. She knew this would pique Sister's interest. Boys will be boys, she said to the fat-ass nun. *Bloody keep out of our business.*

The Sister took her leave, and as Marian watched Adrian being dragged off to the orphanage, she thought about Anna and Rona. Didn't Mrs. O'Rourke realize that what was happening to Adrian could easily have been her own nieces' fates, had she not chosen to come live here with her brother-in-law, *as his wife?* Why was she such a blabbermouth?

Later that night Adrian no doubt would be flogged for his deeds. Once, he'd told Marian that after a beating in Sister Agnes' private quarters (he'd never been invited into her room previously), his awe competed with the pain from her hand. He had told Peter, too, about all the whiteness, the prettiness of Sister's bureau: a mirror and fine brushes atop a lace doily, just like his own ma's at home. The night of one of his beatings, he lay in bed, sore, but happy in his own, dreamy world, the chaos of harsh words tucked away. He imagined Rosemary, his other orphan friend, as his wife, he'd told Marian. Rosemary, his cherry-cheeked girl, an apron around her waist, the smell of bread and apples baking, just like in their kitchen. Happiness was there inside him when he daydreamed of her. Along with the love he felt for his newfound family.

Feel protected, Adrian.

30

Even with Adrian gone and the house sterile again, Johanna still suffered from feelings of neglect. She rose early to chat in her parent's bedroom, though couldn't help but notice that the intimacy her ma shared with Adrian was not there for her. The more Jo wanted to talk with her, the more Ma's expression became vague.

"What I really want is to visit my brother. *My* brother," Jo said louder. Ma was washing dishes at the sink, smiling oddly—that same smile reserved for Adrian—as if she were remembering something.

"You're not the only one misses him. I don't want to have to wait for Christmas. *I* miss him. And we all know you do, too, Ma. And we're all sorry for you," she said. She left the kitchen and fell into a dining room chair, her fingers smoothing the scratches etched into the table. Probably etched by Adrian, by the boy wonder himself. God knows Ma wouldn't care that he used to cut into it with his fork.

Ma came into the dining room to put wine glasses in the cupboard.

"I know you love him more than you love me."

"Johanna!"

"It's true. I can tell."

Marian wrapped her arms around her, but Jo did not return the hug, and so Ma squeezed Jo's shoulders. Jo wondered if her mother felt guilty about what she'd done, about giving Adrian away in the first place. Come to think of it, she wondered if Da did, too. Here Da was, starting talks with her about reserving herself for marriage! What a joke. She wondered if they would try to make up for their guilt forever. They were not the brightest of people.

"Ma. Listen to me. I feel so jealous of him sometimes. I want to hate him. The way you talk about him, it's almost as if you're gloating."

"Gloating?"

"I never hear anything about my birth, my anything. Let's face it. Adrian's the only one on your mind."

"That's not true, Johanna. Do you not remember seeing all the photographs taken of you in hospital, the pink bow the doctor put in your hair, the prettiest girl in the nursery? What about that?" Ma said.

"You mean the one framed photograph on the mantel you removed before Adrian arrived?"

"I didn't want him jealous. There are no baby pictures for him to see, Jo."

"You go on and on. Poor Adrian lives in an orphanage. I know he doesn't have enough to eat; I know how this and that was terrible for him. I feel shamefaced just eating, for the love of Christ!"

"All children want to be only children," is all Ma quietly said.

"Not me."

"I don't think there's an adult alive, is what I mean, that had a perfect childhood," Ma said, wiping the wooden cupboard.

Pointless. Jo could see that her mother wasn't really listening.

"I didn't realize you felt this ignored," Ma said. "All your life."

God. Bravo. You're awake. She'd begun to hike up her skirt when she got to school, and had many times borrowed her Ma's lipstick. *I'll get my own love one day. One way or another,* Jo thought. "Forget it. I just feel you're somewhere else, like you aren't home really," she said, giving her an exaggerated smile.

"I want both of you," Ma said, dim and unaccustomed to speaking with her, or maybe anybody, about emotions.

"You do? Listen, I know you love him more, Ma," Jo ventured again. "I see the way you look at him. I didn't come up the Liffey on a bicycle."

"I feel sorry for him," Ma said in a slightly sing-song way, in a voice raised as if she were getting annoyed with her. Marian made Jo's own problems and feelings pale in comparison again, making her feel belittled and ashamed of herself at the same time.

"So do I." Jo started to cry. "I don't know what's got into me. I know I'm the selfish one, the bad one."

"No, dear," Ma said, attempting to hold her. This time the girl allowed her mother's embrace.

"I want my guilt to go away," Johanna whispered.

"You'll be grand," Ma said. Did she really think this tired expression would help?

"Oh, and Ma. Just in case you remembered, I don't want a birthday party this year." She had had enough discussions with her friends about who could come and who couldn't, and she was sick of it.

"Sure?"

"This will be my present. Please. If we could see Adrian, it would help me, I think, without it being a big deal. Just a regular family, like, with you paying attention to both of us," she said with an awkward smile.

"What a grand idea," Ma said. She placed a telephone call to Sister Agnes.

Bravo. Grand. Jesus.

31

Adrian had not been lying on his cot for long before Sister Agnes was standing over him. Her hand was held out to escort him downstairs to his ma and sister. As usual, Peter trailed behind them, watched from the top of the wide front stairs as Adrian was given a common coat from the front hall closet.

"Can we bring Peter," Adrian begged, putting his palms in the prayer position, looking up at Peter's briny eyes and then at Sister Agnes.

"I don't see the harm," Sister Agnes said, sounding a bit put off for his asking.

Peter ran down the stairs, and Jo immediately thought he looked like Archie from the American comic books and said so, squeezing the hard candies she always carried in her coat pocket.

"I don't know about your comics, Miss Ellis, but he's a good lad, and these two are thick as thieves," Sister Agnes commented.

"Wait quietly in the corner for a minute, children," Ma said. She took Sister Agnes by her elbow and began whispering, as grownups do. She took out a five-pound note from her purse. Ma said she worried that the additional ten pounds she had recently given to Sister Agnes for Adrian's care would not be enough to curry favor, nor in any other way help his release. Adrian worried that it might be cause to keep him, as he was proving to be a financial benefit for Silverbridge. More money would be forthcoming is what Sister Agnes might be thinking, more funds for all the children. And better food and accommodations for the nuns over at the convent as well.

"A Christmas offering—a few weeks early," Ma said, touching Sister's hand. Sister smiled at her, grateful, no doubt, for all her generosity, as she indicated and babbled on about the orphanage.

Jo tiptoed around the bend and through the parlor, Adrian and Peter alongside her, and they climbed the narrow back stairwell to the low baby's dormo.

"This is Rosemary, Jo." Jo looked at the teenager, and Adrian could tell that Jo agreed that Rosemary was indeed worthy of his attention. "I've been telling her we're going to marry someday," Adrian said and began laughing.

Jo laughed wildly at this, too, hopped up on the stool and picked up an infant. Sister Adela helped her. Another beautiful teenager, Adrian thought, Sister's shy expression and warm skin almost close enough to touch Jo's, her smile revealing buck teeth. Shiny brown hair, Adrian imagined, hid underneath her wimple.

"I'm going to marry Peter, then," Jo dared to announce, fancying herself a bit like Veronica, a good match for an Archie. The older girls laughed.

Adrian and Peter shrugged off the crazy comment. "Let's go, Jo," Adrian said, noticing Sister Adela's smile disappear as Ma and Sister Thunder Thighs entered the room.

"Would you like a job here yourself, Miss Ellis?" Sister Agnes said. Jo put the baby down.

"Isn't he the cute one," Ma said, studying the baby, taking Jo's hand in hers. "We'll just see your room, boys, and then we'll go," Ma said.

Adrian could tell that Sister Agnes did not like her assertiveness, but he took in a quiet breath and let this pass.

"The others are in the school rooms, so I guess it's all right," Sister Agnes said. "Sister Adela." Agnes gestured with her hand for her to lead the group.

Down the hall, Jo slid out a *Beano* comic from inside her coat, which Adrian quickly put under the rungs of his cot. Two long rows of empty cots left little walking room. With no fireplace, the chill in the air was terrible. A lay teacher stood with a pointer by the lavatory. Ma approached her.

"Use that pointer on my son Adrian—"

"Number Four Seventy-Six?" the teacher interrupted.

"Adrian Ellis, teacher. Use that pointer on him, and I promise you," Ma said in her ear. "I will run that thing so far up your ass it will come out your throat. Did you hear what I said?"

Teacher nodded.

"You must know Father Brennan."

She nodded again.

He's Adrian's grand uncle, did you know that?"

"No, madam."

"He's watching you," she hissed in her ear and then put a finger to her lips.

Adrian raised one eyebrow at the teacher as Sister Adela hurried them back down to the front hall. Sister Agnes, her hands behind her back, seemed to be anxious for the disruption to end.

"I was just telling the teacher about Adrian's grand uncle, Father Brennan," Marian said, coming down the stairs.

It was true, Father Brennan said Mass Sunday mornings, bi-monthly now, and demanded that all children have a hot cocoa in the refectory before Mass, before any chores. *Breaking rules, it must run in the family,* Adrian thought proudly. Jo traipsed loudly down the front stairs. Rosemary, idling just out of sight, waved to him.

After saying their goodbyes, Adrian and Jo and Peter walked with Ma to the Inchicore Sandwich Shop.

"Why hasn't Da come?" Adrian asked Ma as they waited for a table.

"He had to work," she said.

Ben had told her that he had to work downtown. "You mean your old haunts again?" She'd said, nonchalantly.

"I have to drop something off at the Zion School, some papers about the Maria Dulce Society. They're spreading rumors that Jews are Communists. And I have a lunch date with Max Berger and Principal Rosenberg." Marian put on her coat and briskly took Johanna's hand.

"I'll take the car, then," she said. "And Ben? *Our* lunch is more important, Mr. Reporter." She slammed the front door. Once in Inchicore, Marian called her ma and asked if she could watch Jo later this afternoon. If Ben was really working he should be at the Zion School, and one way or another she was going to find out.

An rud anmanh is iontach. What is strange is wonderful. *Ha!* It was strange indeed, all this mistrust. Now their differences no longer made her feel exotic.

"Say my name aloud again," Adrian suddenly asked Ma, as they slid into the corner booth.

"Don't go running your mouth off, or they won't let your ma come back to see you," Peter advised. "Never forget you are number Four Seventy-Six."

"When can you take me home with you?" Adrian ignored his friend.

"After Christmas, that'll be the end of it. Come on now. There's hot tea getting cold," Marian said.

Adrian's gutted eyes welled up. He took a slow sip, and decided he shouldn't discuss any of this now, for Peter's sake. "Get up the yard, I don't believe you," Adrian said suddenly, testing her, acting the man in front of his friend, but Ma ignored him. "Great talk, little action," he muttered.

Just past twelve years old, he'd changed in the four months since he spent the summer with them. He'd toughened up.

"Look at the two of you, getting bigger than your boots." Marian took *Jungle Animals* from her bag. Adrian moved to her side of the table and touched the cardboard book. "Try to read it to me," she urged, shifting her weight.

He shook his head, embarrassed in front of the others.

"Give it a go."

"I'm too tired."

"See the colorful birds flying in the forest," she read, pointing at the words with her finger. "See the funny monkey in the forest?"

He put his head on the table. "I'm terrified of monkeys," he said. "Sister Agnes says she's gonna put us in the cage with her pet monkey if we're mean to him."

Peter laughed along with Jo at fat Sister Agnes' preposterous threat, but Ma quickly put the book away. Adrian put his head in her lap, and she rested her hand on his shaven head. All his soft strawberry curls growing this past summer gone. He hated having his head shaved. She sipped her tea, and he concentrated on the lovely warmth in her lap, his calm breathing restored, his anxiety at bay.

"Come on," Ma gently shook him awake. "Your food's here."

They had all ordered the turkey platters. Ma had asked for an extra helping of garlic mash and cranberry sauce for the lads, and refrained from correcting their horrendous table manners the way Da always would. "Sister Agnes said you boys can't miss your tea, so we don't have much time."

They settled down and ate in silence. After their warm apple pie and another round of tea, Ma got up to pay the check. Jo reached into her coat pocket and pulled out two samples of Tinkerbell perfume and handed each of them a vial.

"What in God's name..." Adrian laughed with Peter and threw the tiny bottles back at her.

"I'll remind you of home," she said, insisting they keep them.

"*You'll* remind me of home, or the smell of the perfume will?" Adrian said, and Jo realized her mistake.

"The smell of the perfume will. You know what I meant," she said, feigning annoyance. "Here, some hard candies as well."

"The big arse eats the candies the minute you chuck me."

Jo looked down.

"The teachers ate the toffee bar you bought me when you dumped me back there, right in front of me."

Adrian watched Jo's face and was pleased to see she was unnerved. She had grown up a bit, too. "Sure, the teachers are worse than the nuns," he continued.

"They're lay people, yeah. Not much in them, I suppose," she said. Adrian lifted his shirt as Ma sat back down. "I wanted to show you the strap marks on my back."

Ma gasped.

"Sister Agnes has taken to wetting the belt before she flogs us. We hate that fart of a nun, don't we Peter?"

"She has a face'd stop a clock," Peter said and laughed.

"Does the bollocks even know how hungry we are? She sat Peter at a table of bigger boys. I want to squeeze the fat rat's muscles until she bursts like a water balloon. Before this lunch, he hasn't had a potato in days, and he'd have his teeth knocked out if he said anything or tried to grab one." Adrian looked at Jo, quiet and repentant now. He gripped Ma's hand as she hurried him from the table, out the door and across the street.

"You'll be home soon," Jo said, running with Peter to catch up to them.

Adrian looked into Jo's eyes and then kept walking. He wanted to tell her about the hollowness in his stomach with every breath, the damp air teasing his throat. He wanted to lick the water off the air and put it in his belly. He couldn't bear the swift tapping of mice feet against the wooden plank floor in the dark. One night, he'd dreamed that a mouse had crawled into his stomach and was eating away his insides. His skin felt tight. His eyes burned. All he could think about was food.

He turned to his mother. She bent down and hugged him there on the street for a long while. He could feel her nervous body. "You're probably afraid you'll get me in trouble if you don't get me back on time," he said to her.

"It won't be much longer, Adrian. And I'm not afraid of anything, except maybe Sister Agnes sitting on top of me," Ma said. She smiled.

"Sister Thunder Thighs, yeah. She'd surely kill you then."

They all laughed, and Jo skipped ahead and put her hand into Peter's as they hurried back to Silverbridge.

32

After their short visit with Adrian, Marian dropped Jo with her gran and drove to the outskirts of Little Jerusalem. She parked and walked into the crowded streets, heading toward the Zion School. Early on, she sometimes felt more like a schoolgirl than a teacher when she played with her youngest charges. She could have chosen St. Mary's or St. Gregory's School for Boys over on the North side, but the pay was better here and she wanted a community of children she was un-accustomed to. She longed to travel, and in her innocence, she thought the Zion School was an experience, almost like leaving Ireland behind. She remembered whispering into Ben's ear that she wanted to explore England or France, that these Zion School rendezvous were getting complicated. Whatever she wanted was what he wanted, he responded. Ben made her feel free, and at the time, this freedom was everything to her.

Look where all this freedom had gotten her. It had gotten her into hell, into a life of secrets, however sacrificial.

Into a life in which she damaged her son.

It was well past four o'clock, and Ben could already be making his way home. Empty pails lining the darkening streets droned out a metallic hum as droplets of rain began to fall. She heard a lonely, soulless sound reverberating inside her like the ding of a ping-pong ball clattering against concrete walls. She walked to the left, down Bloomfield Avenue. She thought about her da. With regret, she knew that if he had been alive, she would not be in this position; he would have found a way to keep her from making a hames of it. A couple of kids spun bottle caps in the playground of the Zion School. It had been so many years since she'd been here. She walked through the familiar front doors and breathed in the smell of potter's clay, looked at the watercolors covering the walls of Principal Rosenberg's office.

Ben had not stopped by today, she was told.

She hurried down the South Circular Road, anxious to get back to her car before the downpour. She passed Ehrlich's and then made a left off the busy street. As she stepped off the curb, she happened to look into the deli window and couldn't believe her eyes.

I'll be damned.

She watched Ben. A giggling girl sat too close beside him. No food on the table, they sipped their drinks. Little demons raced around Marian's chest. The heat of her anger nearly cut off her breath, and she began to hyperventilate. Ben was having more than a lunch date, all right, and Max Berger was nowhere to be found. Alarm hissed through her like an overheated radiator. She continued to stare, unnoticed by Ben. Across from him sat a young man and two young women. And they were all laughing now, something Marian hadn't seen Ben do since...she couldn't remember when.

And were their knees touching?

And was that him reaching over to tickle the girl's waist?

Marian marched in, the bell on the door signaling her arrival. Steam rose out of her. She looked straight ahead and went to the deli counter, wondering if her husband had noticed her yet. She ordered a bagel with extra cream cheese. She was shaking, and she could see from the corner of her eye that Ben had gotten out of his seat and was moving toward her.

The deli man handed her the bagel, and she walked out onto the street. Ben followed her, and she unwrapped the bagel, staring again through the storefront window at the table of *friends.* No one was laughing anymore.

"It's nothing, Marian," Ben began, but she didn't believe him.

"You're sitting here with these people, laughing, while I'm with your *son,* seeing all that he's suffering. Who are *they,* you bastard? You're so full of *shit.*"

"Marian. I just bumped into them and sat down for a second. I was on my way home."

"Don't you ever think about coming home. You are home. You and your apron strings."

She had a sudden urge to spit in his face and took one half of the bagel with cream cheese and crammed and twisted it into his mouth. She made sure that the white cream was everywhere, dripping off his suit, and wished she had ordered a soft egg.

"I mean it," she said. "Don't bother coming home." She walked away.

And he didn't.

33

How grand! The lay teacher had chosen him to retrieve her scarf from the dormo. Could that be Rosemary's lovely voice drifting from Sister Agnes's room? Adrian tiptoed up the front hall steps, peeked through a tiny opening. His forefinger pulled the wooden door wide enough for his right eye.

Yes, it was the lovely Rosemary in the forbidden room, her head straight like a soldier, Sister Agnes circling her.

"Do you like the painters, number Two Seventy-Eight?"

Rosemary looked mortified. She shook her head no.

"Is that why you flaunt yourself at them?" Fat as a bishop, Sister Agnes leered closer, and Adrian wondered if Rosemary could smell what she'd had for her lunch.

He wanted to shout out, to tell Sister Agnes to feck off, to leave the poor girl alone.

"Do you think the painters came here to paint the building today, or to see the likes of you?"

Rosemary said nothing.

"Are you wearing one of those padded bras?"

"No, Sister. I wouldn't."

Sister Agnes suddenly lifted Rosemary's white blouse in a fury. She examined the inside of the girl's bra. Rosemary moved her head slightly to the side, catching Adrian's eye. She quickly moved her head back to Sister Agnes as if to protect him from the nun's attention.

"You need a proper bra. This won't do." She undid Rosemary's shirt and bra, and then went to her wardrobe, returning with a long beige bandage.

Adrian had never seen a bare bosom before, although he'd heard some of the boys talking about them.

Sister Agnes began wrapping Rosemary's breasts in the bandage. "No breasts were meant to be so large. These are simply the product of an unhealthy union. Your mother made you in sin. Where's your mother now?"

"In hell, Sister." Rosemary sniffled.

Adrian wanted to choke Sister Agnes until her blubber face spurt like a zit, and he creaked opened the door.

Before he knew what was happening, Sister Agnes grabbed him and threw him into her room. Landing across the floor, he got to his feet quickly, shocked at how nice the room smelled, like gardenias. The dresser with the oval lace doily held a can of Faberge deodorant and some talc next to the perfume bottle.

"What can be done for a sneaky one such as you?" Her cane slapped the backs of his knees. She caned Rosemary across her bottom as well. Foam spewed from Sister's mouth when Rosemary's bandage unraveled under her white shirt.

"Stop, Sister!" Adrian screamed as she attacked Rosemary, which turned Sister's wrath back to him, landing him on the floor with a blow to his neck.

Rosemary pressed her body on top of him, and he felt her bosom over his face, warm and buoyant, like a floating heaven. He lay beneath her, protected from Sister by Rosemary's body. Her palms cupped his ears. Too soon, she was dragged off him and told to go and clean herself up.

Adrian felt the cane again, and then he was dragged to his feet, ordered to stand at attention. He held in his need to pee, but the more he tried, the more he couldn't get his mind off his bladder. He focused his thoughts on Rosemary. She had saved him, and if he hadn't been bold, standing in Sister's doorway, she would have gotten off easier. There was a burning ache in his groin.

Sister Agnes screwed up her nose at him, like the old fat rat she was. "You're a defect in this society. Now, go to the bath and try to scrub off some of your awful freckles. Do you know why you have so many, my dirty pup? Because God gives the dirtiest among us the most freckles, each freckle representing a sin we've committed. You've collected quite a lot of those dirty little spots."

He ran to the toilets, and the relief was enormous.

Sweating and exhausted, Sister Agnes repositioned the straw rugs by her wardrobe. She took off her wimple and shook out her chin-length dark hair, as if shaking filth out of a feather duster. She undid the rope belt of her habit and put on a bit of talc. Flapping her arms about, she felt dismayed that there were no baths for the nuns in the orphanage and wished she'd been placed at the convent like Sister Joseph had three years ago.

Why didn't Mother Superior choose me to change positions? Why Sister Joseph?

So many years ago, in her innocence, the senior nuns had told Sister Agnes that orphanage duty was just a starter. She should have known better than to broach the subject, she reflected, pulling on her heavy robes again. With her background, she was lucky not to be scrubbing pots in the kitchen with the other poor nuns; Mother Superior had let her know this more than once. Besides, wasn't she pleased with her position of authority? Those were Mother Superior's last words to her on the subject, over two years ago.

But the bigger girls had become too much for her to handle. Especially the overgrown ones. Especially Rosemary. Too pretty for her own good. Too proud. She remembered the first time she met the big girl, ten years ago, and even then as a young thing she had been too pretty. How she wailed when Sister Agnes put the bowl on top of her head and cut off her long black curls. She gave her a funny look, too. An evil look, as if she hated the nun. Most of the young ones wouldn't have been so wayward as to look at her that way. And Rosemary hadn't changed; even after so many years under Sister Agnes's care, the same spirit was in her today. Almost sixteen now, she still had that devious look and unruly mass of short curls. Sister couldn't imagine having the cheek to bounce around like *that one* did in front of men. Her own dead parents, God rest their souls, may have been dirt poor, but they didn't spare the rod to teach her right from wrong.

She rubbed her burning eyes, pulled the habit's tight sleeves down by the cuffs. This was her cross to bear. She was picked to teach the lowlifes manners and morals. An almost impossible task. And for what possible good to society? she thought. Half of them would end up little more than eejits, creating more eejits, which Ireland certainly didn't need.

Most of them simply needed more control and discipline than she was able to give. She had so many to look after. Sure, she'd have to put a few of those beyond help into the Magdalene laundries, last year she'd put in for two transfers. With Rosemary's mother recently deceased, Sister Agnes felt the girl had become a severe case, too emotionally needy to tend to any longer. She would take action at once. For Rosemary's own good, and for the good of the group, she would make an emergency call to St. Vincent's sanatorium in North Dublin.

Agnes crossed herself, took in a deep breath, and braced herself for refectory duty. She wondered what number Four Seventy-Six was thinking now, after seeing that devil of a girl in the flesh. A bit young, wasn't he, to be interested in girls?

But who could judge the animal in a man? How old was he? Eleven? Twelve? At any rate, she knew it was time for him to get away from the girls' shameful temptations, troublemaker that he already was.

She crossed herself again, thinking about Marian, and sighed. The poor mother had no idea how to cope, either. Still, Sister Agnes had seen the grief on her face. No matter how gentle the delivery, any suggestion of an alternative for her Adrian would devastate Marian, and the sorry expression on her face would torment Sister Agnes as well.

Although Agnes would have to reflect on what was best for Adrian. She did know that there was little chance that she would relinquish her rights—she was certain that the boy needed other influences than the ones awaiting him in that unsettled home in Donnybrook.

~ 34 ~

The next morning a ruckus coming from St. Peter's dormitory slammed Adrian's ears, and he flew out of bed. He was too small to fight the men removing Rosemary, his voice his only weapon. Rosemary's cries were not as loud as his own. Hers were helpless, a gasping. She spent her energy trying to free herself from the men's arms. Adrian shouted for help, for Sister Agnes to come, but only a few boys were roused. Rosemary was lifted by her arms and legs down the planks of the staircase. Adrian clung to one of the doctors by the ankle, or one of the assistants; they seemed too gruff to be doctors, the men draped in white cotton coats. A sharp kick to the chest knocked Adrian to the floor. The room moved around in slow motion. From the slats, Adrian watched her struggle. He managed to grab the banister and raised himself to his feet. He coughed and croaked at the bastards as Sister Agnes barreled down the hall. She wrapped her arm tight around his neck and covered his mouth shut with her pudgy hand. He could not stop the double doors opening and shutting in the hall downstairs. He shut his eyes, listening to the clanging of the iron gate, muffled men's voices on the rain-soaked street, car doors clanking.

Three days passed and Marian started to worry. Maybe Ben was telling the truth. Maybe they were all just friends.

Despite everything she missed Ben. "I want to stride right over and bloody well show both Mammys our rings," Ben had said when she returned from *her sabbatical.*

"Amen," she agreed.

"I want a boatload of kids," he whispered.

"Yes," she whispered back.

That will relieve the overwhelming sadness, she thought. She wouldn't think about the stories she had heard, about the inmates scarred for life. It would be different for them.

"I have to go," she said, massaging his shoulders.

"Never."

"No really, I told Ma I'd be home straightaway."

"God, I can't wait until we're married. Let's do it tomorrow."

"Tomorrow?" She waved him off, retrieved her coat and hat.

"Ah, okay. Today, then."

He tackled her to the floor, their arms and legs locking together like Legos. She loved his body. Only a couple of inches taller, she always just felt so right in his arms

"The Central Registry Office," he whispered between kisses. "Let's go tomorrow, start the paperwork. And after our wedding, we'll take off for a weekend."

She kissed him long in reply. Then he pulled off whatever clothes remained, and they made love one more time —like they could ever be kids again.

Marian walked an unsteady burden up the quiet lane now to their red-brick home. The persistent clouds heightened the yellow center of the asters by the iron gate and reminded her of the colors she'd picked for their cozy kitchen. Two large potted camellias perched in her borrowed wheelbarrow. She'd redirect the variegated ivy on the trellis earlier this afternoon, put the camellias by the sidewalls. She carried the heavy plants up the short steps to their blue front door, the only bright colors used to ornament the outside of Irish homes. Whoever made blue the national color of Ireland was colorblind. Ben ought to write about *that* in the paper and wake up the dead, she thought. She looked at Mrs. O'Rourke's lot. Now, that would get the tongues wagging.

She put the pots down with a thud and was greeted by the sound of her mother's voice.

"Are you back home then?"

"Ma." She closed her eyes.

"I just come by. I thought you might need some help. Are you keeping well?"

"Not a bother, thanks," she said, opening the front door.

"What were you carrying those for? Aren't they too—"

"No," Marian snapped.

"Well, you don't have to bite off my head. *Ba mhaith liom cupán tae,*" Mrs. McKeever huffed. "I want some tea."

"Of course. Come in, Ma," Marian sighed as her mother headed with her own packages to the kitchen to boil water for tea.

"Look at you. You look like something the cat dragged in. Maybe Ben doesn't care about those things, I don't know..."

"That's enough, Ma."

Ma McKeever examined the three small acrylic paintings of fruit and bowls, captured in identical thick bronze picture frames gracing the small but elegant kitchen entry, and then nonchalantly placed a change of Mass schedule for Donnybrook Church next to the telephone. "Would you smell the air out here? Not like the city at all. So fresh. You landed well on your feet. Ben makes a good salary, I suppose," she said, "although the *Irish Times* never took a hapenny from me or your da. We wouldn't read their pagan dribble."

"His reporting on the troubles has been first rate. Mr. Darby's said so. And Ben's been able to keep his job—that's the most important thing."

"Well, they're known for wanting the money, regardless."

"What?"

"Nothing."

"Ma." Marian let out a huge sigh. "Let's have that cup of tea." She had no desire for more banter, the one-upmanship, the mother-daughter game they played. Ma McKeever set out the mugs, an apple crisp, and her homemade rhubarb tart warming in the blue Stanley cooker.

Ma made an awkward laugh. There was a pretentious gaiety that challenged genuine delight about Marian's mother. Always an arm's distance away from authentic expression; Marian had always felt that distance. Somewhere in childhood there was a lost connection with her ma that was very real. Marian could never pinpoint any actual event. Sure, there were a few moments of tenderness and closeness when her ma shared her disappointments with life—her parent's poverty stymied her—but these were the only moments of intimate disclosure. What had once been a cause of embarrassment to Mrs. McKeever was now only an unemotional reflection. A relief to be past all the youthful angst. For the most part, though, a pretense of joy commingled with biting humor, and Marian learned to keep her own feelings private. Their love stunted.

"No word, still?" Ma asked.

"He's probably keeping very busy at work." Marian turned on the telly.

"Is that what Jo thinks as well?"

"I've told her that he's on a business trip."

"Well, he must have a face on him as long as today and tomorrow without you. He'll come round," Ma said, but Marian felt uncomfortable talking about it with her ma.

"Adrian should be home for good soon," Marian said.

"I'll be wanting to take him to my house and to my church. He'll love it."

"We're also going to teach him the Jewish faith. Ben and I want Adrian to know about everything."

"Everything? Have you lost your good sense. You have a boy, not a university professor."

"You know what I mean."

"Do what you like. I'll be teaching him what he'll get for Christmas. A ball, a drum, a kick in the bum, and a chase around the table," she said, and let out one of her giggles.

Ma was getting silly on her. *Soon she'll be nailing crosses throughout the house.*

"You look banjaxed. Let me straighten up in here, put on the kettle."

"Thanks, Ma. I'll have a lie down," she said and settled herself on the library couch.

Ma McKeever busied herself unloading groceries. After a bit of tea, Marian felt relaxed and she smiled at her ma, now knitting yet another huge sweater for Adrian. Marian looked into the garden and imagined spending next summer outside with Johanna and, no doubt, her ma and hopefully Adrian, deadheading the six peach and antique white rose bushes. She loved the tomato plants and fresh herb garden they had planted as well, with rows of marigolds down the middle. What a delight it was to have fresh vegetables with their meals. And then there was the lilac bush Ben had planted to commemorate the birth of Johanna. And she'd plant another one when Adrian came home.

She wondered about Ben's wounds of separation from his family and everything he had grown up with. Perhaps he felt like an orphan.

"You must be very proud," Ma said, observing their new ginger velvet couch with matching club chairs that they'd recently purchased at a furniture sale in Ballsbridge, then touching an heirloom on the mahogany bookshelf. There was tension in Ma's movements, pretense always a drain on the system. And yet, over the years, Marian considered that she had grown closer with Ma. After Da's death, Ma showed more compassion, compassion she thought once was only for her father. Together, silently, they shared their loss.

"It's just a silver jar handed down from Ben's grandparents, no religious significance."

"Don't be acting the maggot, Marian," Ma said, leaving the library, opening up the living room curtains. "I'm having my cake now. And turn that bloody television off," she said.

Ma sat at the dining room table now with that genteel smile and began cutting her homemade tart. Brown sugar caramelized on top, a whipped cream in a bowl.

Marian dutifully turned off the television. "Ah, Telefís Éireann, you've saved my life," she sighed.

Ma grimaced, passed a warm cake plate.

"No harm to have television debates, Ma," Marian said, opening the window, her voice rising better than the Dublin transmitter. "Bishop Flanagan, last night on *The Late, Late Show,* said that there'd been 'no sex in Ireland until the introduction of television.' I had a good laugh at that one," she said, sitting down for her pie. "How would he know; that's the real scandal," she muttered.

"Marian," Ma said quietly. "Because he and all the other bishops speak to the people and educate people, they know what's on the minds of their people," she said. "All you ever want to do is shock people with dirty comments. You're a real McKeever."

" We seem to be living in the Dark Ages, that's all, Ma." She wanted to add that the Church and State behave as incestuous bedfellows, keeping the whole of Ireland in a guilt-ridden headlock, but she held herself back.

"Maybe so, but smut on the television day and night is not the answer," Ma said. "Look, let's remember the Russians could blow up the world any minute. And the rate we're going up North, we'll blow each other up right here on our own soil. No more talk."

They were silent then.

"Why didn't you have more children yourself, Ma?"

Ma chose her words. "We couldn't afford more. We wanted to do it right." She stood to go abruptly and put away her knitting in its tote bag. "And anyhow, Da—one of fourteen. Down the country, living with the animals in the house and all the noise, he didn't want his own house crammed up and shite everywhere. No, the one was enough for him. Goodbye for now."

Ma McKeever left Marian to wonder as she got her worn woolen coat. How many times had Ma said, "As long as I don't know about it, I can handle it." A faint shadow crossed Ma's face when her guard was down, when she thought no one was watching. Her blue eyes crinkled at the menorah in the library. She probably thought it was some kind of antique.

Ma stood there for a moment, confused, and then walked outside and toward the bus stop. Marian went into the kitchen and stared out the window at the brown tomato stalks shaking in the wind.

36

Ben knew he looked horrible. Unshaven. A wreck. Another five days passed before she opened the door a slit, and he saw that Marian was exhausted, too. They gazed at each other. No words. And then she opened the door wide, and he felt an enormous sense of relief.

He walked into the foyer. She was wearing a pink dress, her soft hair falling out of place. He leaned and whispered, "I'm sorry," into her ear. He loved her smell. He loved the lightness of her touch against his skin. He knew he was going to fall in love with her the first time they met, couldn't wait to interview her for his article to commemorate the Zion School's fiftieth anniversary, couldn't stop watching the gorgeous girl by the garden, doing a cute American West skit with her little students.

Cowgirl, your turn for a photograph, he'd said, and he'd lightly touched her soft cheek with his when they both reached down for the school's camera. She laughed, removed the cowboy hat she wore for the skit, and tried to fluff up her frizzy hair. The tykes ran toward her. She caught her heel on the box garden's rubber edging and tripped into rows of white and blue daisies. Ben took a snapshot before helping her to her feet

"Well, thank ye, Mr. Reporter," she said, brushing off moist dirt from her hands and dress.

"Journalist, Cowgirl," he corrected her.

"I ain't no ordinary cowgirl, ye hear," she said, walking away as gracefully as she could and ordering her students back to the classroom. Ben caught up to her and held the school door open.

"You come to your alma mater to do a story, but you get a hot and sticky Annie Oakley instead," she chuckled as she dipped into her classroom leaving him outside.

"How's my favorite cowgirl?" he said quietly now.

"Missing my favorite journalist," she answered, and attempted a smile.

They held each other as they walked up the stairs and lay down together. They made love with the tenderness of two ailing people.

"It wasn't going to help Adrian to have me, his Jewish father, show up in Sister Agnes's face. I don't want to be the cause of any more upset."

"Whisht," she said.

"Nothing happened, just so you know."

"I know. Where have you been staying?"

"You know where."

She laughed.

"I can barely look at my son when I think about my part in this," Ben mumbled. "It's like taking your biggest mistake and having it stare at you, sitting with you at the table every day until you can't bear the guilt and the reminder anymore."

As he talked, her face seemed to relax, though she did not speak.

After a smoke, Ben got up and looked out the window. He wanted to reach down and rip a clump of grass, recalling the pregnant girls he saw at Castleboro Mother Baby Home on all fours ripping the grass with their bare hands, shoving it into their apron pockets, a sight he couldn't get over. A hand on her lower back, a big girl had wiped sweat off her forehead, a streak of dirt remaining there, and he wondered if Marian had been subjected to this humiliation during her stay. He couldn't think about it anymore. He reached down and touched Marian's cheek. She began to cry. He buried his face into her neck and held her.

"Don't let the tormentors win," he whispered. "You have to get over what happened. We both do. We have to move forward."

She wiped her cheeks.

"I'm not thinking about that hellatious time anymore—"

"Not thinking about it doesn't help, Marian. You're just doing what you have all along. You can't bury it. You have to confront it."

"Listen to me. I'm thinking about Adrian, that's it, and you should bloody well be, too. I am only concerned with making things right."

He lay down beside her and said, "Maybe the mistakes we made, maybe they can't be undone."

She looked at him, narrowed her eyes.

"It's one thing to imagine, Marian, but it's another to face reality."

"That sounds like Father Brennan. Here we go," she said, getting up.

"Hey, I'm committed to having this family in one piece again, Marian. But we have to think about Johanna, too. We have to move on, one way or another. You're obsessed with the past, and you're harboring guilt more than anything else, and it's hurting all of us. We're a family already and we—"

"Listen up, Ben, for the last time. Nothing you can say will make me give up on Adrian if that's what you're getting at. I gave him away once, and I want him back. God damn it! Why don't you feel the same way? I need to bring him home. You're wearing me thin. You're either with me or you're not, but I'm never going to turn my back on our son again. Never."

She was red in the face as she slipped on her dress. There was no talking to her.

"Marian, calm down. We need peace around here."

"I'm going to do what needs to be done," she said loudly.

"I'm going to mow the lawn," he mumbled. "The grass needs cutting."

37

Ever since Sister Agnes decided Adrian needed more discipline before he was to be ready to reenter society, Marian felt everything in sluggish waves.

Marian pleaded with Sister Agnes to give them one more chance, to let him try the Muckross School in their neighborhood. But after this last incident, Sister Agnes explained, Johanna's school would not be willing to accept Adrian. She was sorry, but Sister Agnes believed that they had rushed Adrian, and she worried he'd become a threat to himself and society. This was not a punishment but a protective step along the way, that was all. Over the Christmas holidays, she had already transferred some of his friends from Silverbridge to the Surtane Industrial School for Boys, so he wouldn't be alone. His closest friend Peter was one of the transfers. He'd learn a musical instrument there as well, and be in the band. He'd be well looked after, and most of all, he'd receive the discipline he desperately required. Sister Agnes handed her the stuff—comics, baseball cards, hard candies—she'd found hidden under his cot, told Marian to keep them at home. They wouldn't be allowed at his new school. If all went well, after a year at the school, she'd be only too glad to relinquish her rights and send Adrian on to the Ellises.

At a special hearing, with Adrian present, Judge Moran agreed with Sister Agnes that at least one year at Surtane would be best for everyone. Marian stood in the court, protested that he was her child, that he belonged at home. The judge sentenced Adrian despite her pleas. He ordered Marian and Ben into his private chambers. There he told them that he had been advised to place the girl in a correctional school as well.

"The girl? What girl?"

"Your daughter, it appears, would benefit."

Ben said, "We understand, but—"

"We understand? What? Ben! What do we understand?" Marian yelled.

"Let's hear what Judge Moran has to say before we rush to any conclusions," he snapped at her. He was fearful, the kind of fear that paralyzes, she knew this. He needed to listen thoroughly before replying. He needed the judge to know, too, that he was not a loose cannon; he was certain it was their only hope of saving Johanna.

"She's made quite a few disturbing comments to her teacher, her principal, and to Sister Agnes," Judge Moran said.

"Johanna?" Marian said in disbelief. "I don't bloody understand what you're saying."

"Let's listen to the judge, Marian," Ben insisted.

Judge Moran looked down at his papers. "Apparently, last year or so, when interviewed, Johanna claimed your wife hit you over the head with a heavy object."

"Hit my husband!" She turned to him for help. "It was the newspaper— tell him! I tapped you on the head with it! She's just turned eleven, for heaven's sake."

"Calm down, Mrs. Ellis, or this conversation will end."

"Quiet, Marian. Now," Ben said.

Marian gave him a disgusted look.

"I understand you're upset, but your daughter Johanna doesn't understand all that's happened in your past, and we wouldn't want her harmed, so I would be willing to place her, as well, Mrs. Ellis, is what I am telling you," Judge Moran repeated, with decreasing patience. "St. Mary's for Girls down in Galway has available spots. She damaged church property and ran from the law."

"They both ran home!"

"Let me make this perfectly clear. Johanna Ellis could have a record now, too."

"They were both terribly sorry, and they've apologized."

"The guards are owed thanks, and you have an outstanding bill for the property damage, Mr. Ellis."

"We've paid the debt, sir," Ben said.

The Donnybrook Citizen News had posted the incident as well as mentioning the miserable sum of sixty pounds, which would be owed the Donnybrook Church. Ben showed the newspaper article to Mr. Darby, explained his son's setback, and asked if he could pre-emptively investigate the goings on at industrial schools, but was told no. This is not the time to stir up trouble, Mr. Darby said. Lay low, he advised.

"We understand, Judge Moran, and thank you for your time with this. We'll look after Johanna, and we're grateful to you for your consideration," Ben said.

Judge Moran closed the folder, looked at the two of them.

"No more talk, then."

Ben nodded. "Can we visit Adrian?" Ben glanced at Marian. She returned the look with a glare; she was appalled at the relative ease in which he handled all of this.

But she should be grateful, too, she thought, they had been able to keep Johanna safe.

"Of course, there are visiting days. You'd have to arrange that with the Christian Brothers."

38

The police escorted Adrian from Silverbridge Orphanage to the Surtane Industrial School for Boys on January 22, 1969, two months after his twelfth birthday. The car drove up a long avenue to a cluster of massive stone buildings. Men in long black cassocks strolled about the grounds. Nurse had told Adrian about the men wearing the black robes, the Christian Brothers, and her report was not good.

"Well, you'll be minding your manners in Surtane, I'm sure," the guard said, jerking him out of his thoughts. "A place to keep your head down, so."

Yes, they would probably kill him here; he was certain he would end up dead. Perhaps, though, he'd have a bit of luck and they'd hit him hard, just hard enough to be taken to hospital where the nurses were grand and the food better than the slop they were sure to serve in this place.

He gazed at a sea of boys on the playing fields, and to the left, the bluestone chapel. The car wound its way to the concrete front entrance of the institution, steel doors on the far left and right led up stairs to what must be the vast dormitories. Like a bunch of half-starved coyotes, the tykes crowded around the car, their greasy palms pawing the hood, their hobnail boots stomping. Brothers in black robes shouted at them. Adrian tensed, feeling as if he might piss himself.

Gawking paupers attempted to pull him out of the car, but he was engrossed, a huge grin coming over him at the sight of Peter, who was standing against the cement wall of the school.

"It's a rap in the snot locker I'll be giving you if you don't get your arse out of the car."

A large boy named O'Connor, also known as Monitor One, opened the car door. "I'll take him to Brother Ryder."

Brother Mack, co-headmaster with Brother Ryder of the school, shook Adrian's hand. "Good day, young man," he said. "He's all right, then," he indicated to the men in the car. He waved goodbye, and the police car drove off. Brother Mack was a middle-aged man with solid shoulders, a square jaw and a broad smile, a gap between his two front teeth gave him a youthful quality. He reminded Adrian of Mickey Dolnz from the Monkees band, except his slick black hair was cropped short.

"March!" Monitor One ordered him. "Left, right, left, right. Stand tall or face the wall. Left, right..."

Adrian followed Monitor One, and some of the boys followed him, pulling at his clothes.

"Well, isn't he the fancy one? Did your Mama buy you that jacket?" they teased.

Adrian turned and gave them a dirty look. They all laughed.

"That's number Four Seventy-Six from the orphanage," a tall, thin boy shouted from the playing field, his shirt too small for his long arms. "He's okay."

Monitor One pushed Adrian against the wall. "He's a big shot, is he? Follow what I'm doing. Left, right..."

"Leave him alone, O'Connor," Brother Mack said.

A whistle blew, and all the boys lined up in size order and began to march in place. Adrian looked for Peter in the crowd, spotted him near the front, and they shared a brief smile.

"What's your bleedin' name?" the monitor asked.

"Adrian Ellis."

"You'd *better* be okay," O'Connor said, marching to the left down the hallway, passing an industrial dining hall on the right where a couple of boys were setting up tin cups and tin bowls. Adrian marched behind O'Connor, enjoying the feeling of his body in motion, figuring his leg muscles would grow stronger with the effort of marching as well. O'Connor knocked on a door and kept marching until the door opened.

"Sir!"

"Yes, O'Connor?" Brother Ryder said.

"Ellis has arrived, sir."

"I see that, O'Connor. Go back to the fields."

39

Brother Ryder, also known as Brother Driver in Surtane, because of his liberal use of a wooden Spalding on the boys, walked back across the makeshift office to his desk and sat down, looking Adrian over. *He's going to teach me the ropes,* Adrian told himself, examining the military expression on the man's face, with its pockmarks and jutting cheeks that seemed sculpted in his cement complexion.

"Come in, boy. Shut the door behind you."

Adrian stepped into the middle of the room, looked at the closed gray blinds, but heard distant hobnail boots marching, the smell of alcohol, pungent despite the draft from open windows. *I repent* was written in faintly noticeable cursive on the chalkboard.

"Take a few steps closer and stand there," Brother Ryder said, reading a document in a manila folder.

"You're to be called 'Ellis,' is it?"

"Yes, sir."

"But you're really a McKeever?"

Adrian shrugged.

"You're a strange one, wanting to be called Ellis."

"That's my family name, sir."

"You're part of our family while you're in here. Our private club. Charter member," Brother Ryder said and chuckled. "We work as a team here. Keep your eyes to yourself, Ellis," he said, reading Sister Agnes's report. "Just answer yes or no. Do you understand, Ellis?"

He said his words slowly, evidently thoroughly engaged in his reading. Adrian peered over the file and upside down deciphered her bloody words. *Episodes of sexual arousal and/or misconduct. Occasional mischievous thoughts and deeds.*

"I want no other words from you."

"Yes, sir." *Overly attached to members of the opposite sex. I expect. Discipline at Surtane will correct this.*

"Any more words out of you and you'll have your knickers round your ankles, and you'll be holding on to that chair for dear life," he said, gesturing with his club. It had a large ivorine golf ball handle.

Adrian dared not look up.

"Are you a nosy boy, Ellis?"

"No, sir."

"I told you, you bloody eejit, nothing but yes or no. Pull down your bloody trousers, and stand there in your knickers."

Stunned by this, Adrian gawked at him.

"Go on now, as I tell you."

Adrian fumbled, feeling his fingers getting clammy as he let his woolen trousers down.

"Not a word from you, just yes or no."

Brother Ryder was staring at him. Adrian heard a humming from the electricity in the eerie silence.

"Are you nosy, Ellis?"

"No."

"Are you curious about what goes on in this room?"

"Yes."

"You are nosy, then. Why are you looking at the cabinets, boy? Look at me."

Adrian looked directly into the man's eyes, black peas, like a pigeon's.

Brother Ryder raised his wooden club, reached out with it, and touched Adrian between the thighs.

"One move from you and you'll feel this Sabbath stick across your back. You'd like that, wouldn't you?" He slowly diddled him with the golf ball grip.

"Do you masturbate, Ellis?"

"No."

"Do you play with these? Look at me, and no lies."

Adrian stared into his face, holding back tears. "No."

"I think you're lying, Ellis."

"No," he said again, louder.

"Yes, you do, Ellis. I've heard about you."

"No."

"Do you like girls, Adrian?"

"No."

"Do you like *boys,* then? Are you a fairy?"

"No."

"Then which, girls or boys? Do you like girls?"

"Yes."

"Aha! Now at least you're being honest. Have you ever done it with a girl, mister big stuff?"

"No."

"Not even at night, diddling yourself?"

"No."

"Let me tell you, boy. Don't diddle yourself. It's not healthy. It'll tempt you. And temptation leads right to the Devil's door. Well," he said and closed the folder. He walked around the desk and stood behind Adrian. He smacked the boy hard in the back.

"Don't," Ryder declared, "let me catch you getting into trouble here. We keep Surtaners free from the Devil, Ellis. I'll knock the shit out of you if I have to. Do you understand?"

"Yes."

"Good."

Adrian felt the shaft of the club stick his backside and then, slide up, and strike his privates. Adrian gasped and let out a scream.

"You have bad blood, Adrian. You'll come to nothing. Pull up your trousers and go into the chapel. Say three Our Fathers. I won't have much use for the shaft if you keep clean, now will I, Ellis?"

"No."

"After you go to chapel, go up to the fitting room and get outfitted."

"Yes."

"Ellis?"

"Yes?"

"Welcome to the Whipping Club."

40

It was two weeks since Adrian's arrival. He dared not ask to write to his sister, but he lay awake thinking about her before the six o'clock morning bell. He fell easily into the morning wash line first because of lack of sleep. This morning Brother Mack along with Monitor Two yanked on Peter's thin arm, placed his belongings beside Adrian's cot.

"You'll be in Adrian's dormo now. It'll be okay," Brother Mack whispered to Peter and then left.

Adrian and Peter found themselves walking toward the chapel after classes that afternoon, no interest in watching the annual hurling game—the Brothers against the monitors and outside teachers. The rest of campus was deserted. No monitor was seen for what felt like hours.

"Any free moment away from the monitors makes ya giddy," Peter said. "I've something to show you," he added. Strands of his hair, the color of corn, stuck straight up like alfalfa. "Brother Mack took me behind the altar to the sacristy. My eyes almost fell out."

Peter brought Adrian to the large white closets, in which hung the embroidered robes worn by the Brothers, all the vestments, extra sets of big red and white candles, boxes of incense. The small back room exuded mysterious smells. Unlike Brother Ryder, who somehow fell through the cracks, Adrian believed Brother Mack indeed rose above his personal frustrations and had empathy for the boys, especially those with parents, funny enough, who knew what they were missing.

Adrian opened a tall cabinet by the side door and saw the storage spot for the host, all those circular piles of toasted bread in rectangular white boxes, and he felt his ravenousness wash over him. He was starving; hunger pains were always his downfall.

"I could eat a child's arse through the rungs of a cot, Peter."

"You can't be thinking what–"

"Just one or two. What would be the harm to have more of Jesus inside us?" He looked around the solemn room, hearing shouts from the playing field.

"If we did it quickly? Make up your mind, will you," Adrian said. "Before we're bloody caught. I swear, Peter, you're such a wanker sometimes."

"Feck off. I wouldn't bother me arse about it."

"Look at this, Peter."

Adrian took one of the boxes off the shelf. It had been days since he'd had a piece of bread. He wondered when he'd be allowed tea with a bit of pandy. A gray moldy mush of mashed potatoes would be better than the grass he'd considered eating yesterday. Rice tapioca would taste delicious. He grabbed a bunch of the crackers and quickly gave Peter a handful. He reached for another batch before he fumbled the box closed and ran outside toward the woodlands, Peter right behind him, their pants pockets filled. And there in the woods, underneath a beech tree, they crunched the dry crackers until all were gone, leaving not a crumb, they thought.

"That wasn't so bad," Adrian said, kicking an acorn across to Peter. Peter sat quietly.

"At least our stomachs are full," he added, noticing red robins feeding on germinating seeds, as if they expected a famine.

Peter tugged at the grass.

"For the love of Mike, would you say something? You look like a boiled shite."

"Have you heard from anyone?"

"Not a word. Although Ryder delighted in discussing the eggs Nurse sent me, rubbing his big belly."

"Sorry about that."

"You?" Adrian asked.

Peter shook his head. "My ma's not feeling well. She won't be visiting this year, she said."

"You'll sit with my family at the Easter picnic, then. Wouldn't we murder for an orange. They'll bring plenty."

"We'd better get back," Peter said. While Peter had a sickly mother, and only make-believe stories about other relatives, somehow this seemed better than the rejection that accompanied Adrian's separation from his real family. Even Brother Mack had explained that he, too, knew the pain of loneliness. So the make-believe stories gave Peter a sense of hope in a make-believe future.

"Yeah, and when we get to the fields, walk away from me, will you?" Adrian kept his voice low. "Monitor Two's been spreading talk that we're faggots, and you know Brother Ryder would beat us black and blue if—"

"Ryder is after me, Adrian."

"You're not alone. He's after everybody. The smell on him, he'd drink out of a whore's boot."

Peter wiped sweat from his fair eyebrows, the faint hairs on his cheeks bleached white, his pale, fine-boned face blanched and moist as the inside of a fresh potato.

"He told me, 'You ought to be very good to me.' He said that to me." Peter puffed his chest and turned down his face to give the impression the words were coming from an older, gruffer man.

"The day Molloy went clattering?"

Ryder had held the boy Molloy by the collar, up to the front of the class. The room hushed. Molloy began to weep and moan and beg for relief as the leather strap came hard against his buttocks.

"I saw Molloy's skin ripping off!"

"Did you have to faint, Peter? For feck's sake, I tried to help you, but Ryder threw me back in my chair. Told me I don't need Catechism. 'I've got a job for you to do when I teach this class,' he says. 'Be in the chapel mopping floors, Cracker Jack.' The bastard. I heard him dismiss the rest so he could attend to you, sleeping on the floor."

"Yeah, well he took me to the showers."

A darkness inched over Adrian. "But it wasn't Saturday."

"What choice did I have? How would I have been able to make a run for it?" Peter confided that he had trailed behind Ryder into the last stall of the concrete shower room. Brother Ryder picked up

Peter's shirt to examine his soft, bruised back, sharing with him that his father had knocked him in the head, much worse than this, with a shoe on several occasions. Once, with a good-sized rock. "Told me I don't have much in the way of parents, but parents hit, too, you know. I finished lathering up. The water changed from cold to freezing."

Adrian picked at the grass, lowered his eyes.

"Ryder reached for the towel and rubbed me down." Peter hesitated. "I tried to fight him, backed away. Ryder leaned all his weight on me, pushed me onto the cement."

"Shh," Adrian looked around.

"Dropped the towel, grabbed me, put a hand over my mouth. Keep still, just keep still." Peter wiped his nose, covered his face. "I faced the wall, repeating to myself the nine ways of being accessory to another's sin. By counsel, by command, by consent, by provocation, by praise or flattery, by concealment, by partaking, by silence, by defense of the ill done."

"Why didn't you scream?"

He *had* screamed, but no one came. The cold water lashed out in fury. He lay on the cement floor, listening to Brother Ryder buckle his belt and march away. Peter dragged himself to his feet, stood under the numbing water. As he dressed, he listened to the distant bells coming from the chapel, the quickened steps of bodies bracing themselves against the bitterness, heavy rain pounding against the old gutters.

"One day, I'm gonna kill that *bastard*," Adrian said.

Peter bit his lip, drawing blood. Adrian reached over to wipe it.

"Don't tell anyone."

Adrian offered Peter his hand now and pulled him to his feet. "You won't be here much longer, think of that." Release from Surtane was assured on a boy's sixteenth birthday. Adrian didn't know Peter's exact birthday nor would he embarrass him by asking, in case he didn't know himself.

"Come on."

They walked silently from the dirt road, and as they neared the chapel, Brother Ryder bellowed to them. Adrian saw the box of hosts in the man's hand. "Come here, you dirty queers."

They walked to him slowly, their heads down, no time for Adrian to make up a story about where they'd been.

"You left a trail of crumbs behind," he said, grabbing Adrian and Peter by their necks and dragging them into the sacristy. The cabinet door was slightly open; a few cracked hosts were on the floor. "I'm putting in for a full stay for you, Ellis. You'll not be leaving until I get through with ya."

Adrian wet himself and felt ashamed, afraid, certain he would spend eternity in damnation.

"You like studying your times table, do you, Cracker Jack?" Brother Ryder asked Adrian.

"I do, sir. I like studying forests, too." Adrian had noticed the favoritism given to the strongest boys that worked past the open field, cutting logs in the nearby woods, felling old chestnut trees.

"Do you?" Brother Ryder seemed interested.

"I think I'm strong enough to work the timber trade, build my arms and legs for my future career."

"Have you big plans, Cracker Jack?" Adrian noticed the mockery but kept on.

"Yes, sir. A firefighter, sir."

"Well, we'll teach you a bit of humility, won't we lads?" he shouted toward the ended hurling game. A shame it was that many of the Christian Brothers were already turning inside, unaware of the scene Ryder was drawing. Some of them would surely have put a stop to his taunts, but the game was over. Adrian saw the Brothers walking together toward the road.

"You'll not learn to be bigger than your boots in here. You'll not be getting an instrument. You'll work in the kitchen with Brother Tyrone, and let the Peter Pansy work felling the trees with yours truly. Come with me."

Amidst cheers, they were marched to the playing field, and with the generous help of monitors, were tied to the main post. Each monitor was allowed to spit on them, their slobber making Peter cry.

"I don't think these two are fit to play in our band. As sure as there's a hole in your arse, tell the boys here what you did, Peter Pansy." Brother Ryder took off his thick leather belt, metal bits sewn into the leather. "Remove their shoes."

Peter struggled, but Monitor O'Neill pulled off his boots and socks.

"Lift 'em."

"Please, sir. I'm sorry. Please, don't do—"

"He's a bit of a molly, isn't he? I knew it the minute I laid eyes on him." The monitor slapped him in the face.

"Keep 'em up," Brother Ryder shouted. Two monitors grabbed his legs and held them straight out.

"Tell us, you wanker. What did you do? We're waiting," Brother Ryder said.

"I stole the host from the chapel. I'm sorry."

Brother Ryder slashed his belt across the bottom of Peter's feet. Peter went crazy from pain.

"Don't cry, Peter," Adrian urged.

"His name's not *Peter*," Brother Ryder said, punching Peter hard in the stomach. "He's to be called *Biscuits* from now on."

"Babby Biscuits!" a monitor roared. Laughter and spittle swirled as Peter was kicked by the monitors.

"He's a little fart of a fella."

"A sparrow fart, he is. Cute as the dickens, isn't he?"

"Leave him alone, you fucking shites!" Adrian screamed.

"You want some of what he's getting, you tough Cracker?"

Brother Ryder nodded to two monitors, who rushed over to pull off Adrian's boots.

"Go ahead, you bastards!"

"It's your own fault, Crackers."

Adrian flailed, kicking anyone he could. It was all over now; he didn't care what happened. He felt punch after punch in the stomach until they got hold of his legs and held him up for Brother Ryder.

Brother Ryder shook his head. "You're a miserable article, Cracker Jack. Not fit for the boots we give ya. Imagine, stealing from Our Lord." He landed his belt right across Adrian's face, the sting and the bleeding powerful. "You try living through the worst war in history and having barely enough food."

Getting the okay, a monitor punched Adrian in the face.

"We hand food to you every damn day of your wasteful lives without so much as a thank you, you spoiled bastards. Work for our Lord—don't steal from Him, for God's sake. We'll learn ya."

The flogging felt like electrical shocks from his feet to his head. Distant screams from seagulls circling overhead cried out to him, and he called back like a madman.

"That'll do," Brother Ryder said. "Untie them." Both boys collapsed to the ground and lay there, unable to rise.

"Both of you queers go to bed without tea."

After the others had headed for the refectory, Adrian helped Peter to his feet, and they climbed the stairs slowly to get into their beds.

"I'm sorry, Peter. It was my fault. Here." Adrian managed to reach under his bed for his chamber pot before he lay himself down and listened to his poor friend heave.

Adrian fell into a hazy sleep, listening to Peter shaking and whimpering. He felt frozen and pulled his knees high into his chest, wrapped his blanket tight over his head, wishing he could crawl into Peter's bed for warmth. He was in the midst of a pleasant daydream about lying beside his ma, when Peter let out another near silent scream. Cracking an eye open, Adrian could see the desperate look on Peter's face, and he reached over and tightened the blanket around Peter's shoulders, whispering that they were brothers, would stick together, no matter what.

The next morning, he swore to himself, he would go to the head superior and rat on the monitors and Brother Ryder. He would stop the sickness in Surtane and get them out of there for good.

41

After breakfast, Adrian walked to the main building, slowly climbed the two flights of stairs and stood for a reluctant moment at the Head Superior's chambers. The Head Superior leaned back into his chair and, listening to Adrian's creaking shoes, urged him to enter the large converted classroom. There was no furniture other than the man's messy desk and some file cabinets behind where he sat, with large windows overlooking the playing fields.

"What is it, my child? Speak up."

"Yesterday, sir, I thought you would like to know, some of the older boys—monitors—sir, harassed and hit Peter and me at Brother Ryder's request, sir. As he has on several occasions, sir."

The Head Superior put down his pen, took off his glasses and studied him. He got up and walked around his desk.

"That's it?"

"That's it, sir, I suppose."

The Head Superior hit Adrian in the jaw.

Stunned, Adrian held his face as the Head Superior bent to look at the damage he'd done and then walked back around to his chair.

"Thanks for tattling to me. Feel free to come back and tell me anything. Anytime."

"Yes, sir," Adrian said, and marched down the stairs, wondering if he, too, should try to become one of Brother Ryder's monitors, though he knew his chances of Brother Ryder's favor were slim.

"What happened to you?" mocked an older jerk, O'Reilly from Dormo Six, as he came out the door.

Adrian felt desperate, knowing O'Reilly and his friends could smell fear. He spit a dangling tooth onto the cement playground. He tried to be strong but was close to tears. The older gang began circling around him. He looked over at Brother Mack who was too far away to see what was happening.

"Buzz off," Adrian managed.

O'Reilly pushed him to the ground, and the crowd grew. "Get up, you little maggot."

Adrian rose but felt faint.

"The little babby needs his bottle," another taunted, kicking him. He was pushed back to the ground, his hands covering his head, waiting for the hobnail boots to slam into his stomach, his neck, his back. It was always worse anticipating the thing to come, not half as bad once the boots dug into him, once he began drifting away.

"Break it up, lads." He heard Brother Mack's voice at last. "Move off to classes." The Brother lifted him up with his strong arms and led him off to the toilet. Janey Mack! The infirmary toilet, the place he'd been dying to get into since his arrival. Brother Mack wiped him off with a cold, wet towel, clearing his head. The room was sparse and old, a faded beige color on the walls, not at all as white and clean as he'd pictured.

"Are there nurses about?"

"There's the one that comes on the odd occasion. You must have seen her."

"I thought she worked with the bakers."

"We all pitch in here. You have to keep to yourself, Ellis."

"I know, sir." He felt like crying. He wanted like hell to tell Brother Mack all that happened during the previous day, and also about this morning with the Head Superior, but there was no trusting any of them now.

Brother Mack cupped Adrian's chin in his hand and examined his jaw. "God love you," he whispered.

"Thank you, sir." Adrian bowed, which seemed to please Brother Mack.

"You're good with numbers, I've been told. What about reading?"

"My sister would read to me, sir."

"Ah." Brother Mack smiled at him. "We'll have to hear more about your family. They'll be coming for the Easter picnic?"

"Of course, sir."

Just the mention of his sister, and knowing he'd have to wait an endless eight more days until Easter and until he'd see Jo, made him cry in front of Brother Mack.

"Would you like to read with me?" Brother Mack pretended not to notice Adrian's tears as he wiped his eyes.

"Yes, sir. Very much, sir." *I'm ashamed when I read with my sister,* he wanted to say.

"You know, Adrian," Brother Mack said, wiping his brow with a fresh, wet washrag. "Is it all right to call you Adrian?"

Adrian nodded.

"Like anyone else, there are good Christian Brothers and bad Christian Brothers, good nuns, bad nuns, good parents, bad parents, good kids, bad kids. We can't judge, really, can we?"

"No, sir."

"There's a reason. There's a reason, yes. Do you know why you're here?"

"I'm being punished."

Brother Mack straightened out the cotton pads that he placed on the medicine chest. "Ah, no. The stronger the wind, the stronger the tree—all right now, you'll be," he said, and then chuckled.

Adrian nodded, as if to acknowledge Brother Mack's wisdom.

42

Father Brennan and Gran were on their way over to check on the family, as they often did on a temperate Sunday after Mass. Marian was in the kitchen preparing a steak and kidney pie for their dinner. Johanna was complaining. And Ben was hung over, bored out of his mind writing an article about Jewish triplets born to a famous singer in Dublin. He read the newspaper and sipped his coffee, bit the eraser off the top of his pencil.

He seemed less committed to his causes, and Marian had to admit, less physically attractive to her. His intensity now, more often than not, took the form of brooding. His leg, constantly shaking, let her know when he was worrying. She wondered if he was thinking about his mother's welfare, or about his family's pressures.

She studied Ben, dazed as he was. Since February, he had kept his distance from her, his mind and emotions elsewhere. She noticed that his shoulders were slightly rounded, perhaps to shield himself from the pain he still felt in his arm. Certainly, they both noticed the weight gain.

She came out of the kitchen and walked over to him, put her hand on his jerking knee. "What is the matter with you, bouncing up and down like that?"

"Just stress," he said, taking off his glasses, "common for men in their early thirties. The *Times* ran a story about it. The kids, the wife, the job, the money." She knew he was alluding to the fact that they recently had to sell their car to cover solicitor costs.

"The bicycle will keep you fit, and Adrian's worth every penny."

"Ah, he is, of course. Did I say he wasn't? Jo's worth every penny, too, and it's she should be riding a bicycle." He was angry now; she could hear in his strident tone.

"Sure, why don't we buy Jo another something?" Marian retorted.

"Look, I'm tired," he responded, taking little note of her dusting the photograph of Jo she'd put back on the mantel.

"So am I," she said, emptying an ashtray brimming with butts. She went back into the kitchen, to halve the beef and freeze the second portion for another meal, to compensate with more cucumbers from the garden, a small hot potato salad as well. Ben brought most of the garlic she grew to a homeless shelter; the remaining garlic and scallions she froze. The bread and butter would be saved for their late evening cocoa.

Marian stared out the back window at the brown bush that desperately needed a trim. She wondered for a brief moment if Ben were having an affair. She knew from her reading of *Ladies Home Journal* that often, in pursuit of the children's happiness, a couple can lose each other and the marriage suffers. And of course the one thing can lead to the other. She opened the junk drawer she had filled with bags of penny candy. "Need something to sink your teeth into?" she called to him.

Thinking about that girl with the bulbous eyes, she grabbed bunches of the shit from the drawer and marched into the library. "Did you hear me or are you lost in your daydreaming?" she said, and raised her hands in the air and watched the hard candies rain all over his paperwork. "Want some *penny* sweets, dear?" She gave him the evil eye.

"What's all this?" he said.

"Oh, don't bullshit me, Ben. You're not the only one who can do a bit of research, Mr. Reporter. I found out her name. It wasn't hard. I just asked your mother to describe your 'friends,'" she said. Her fingers drew the quotation marks in the air.

He shook his head and began sweeping penny candy into the trash.

Marian began to calm down as she watched him tidy her mess. "You have a choice to make, Ben. I've made mine. I'm getting Adrian back, and you're either with me or you're not."

He stood and began to laugh at her, put his arms around her waist.

"I'm with you. I'm not going anywhere, Marian. Not when I have you," he said, but with effort. "Marian the librarian, you're not," he whispered and kissed her neck.

"Not funny."

Ben laughed and sat back down.

She leaned over his desk and threw the remaining pieces of candy into his trash bin and then stared at him until she felt she had his attention. "I will tell you this, Ben. I'm not kidding. If you're fooling around, if you ever leave again, that's it. The door won't be opened for you to return. That's my word," she said.

"You're mad," he said as she left for the kitchen.

Communication is everything, that's what she read in her *Ladies Home Journal.* They never had it out about that girl and the time he stayed away, and because of it a quiet anger seethed inside her, and a fear that he might at any time walk away and abandon her and the children. She did, though, believe that nothing happened with that Penny character, *though the Journal did say that the wife is often too gullible.* What Ben didn't realize was that he was not alone in his misery. She'd been so preoccupied with getting Adrian back home that she'd lost her amorous feelings, or her wifely duties as Father Brennan would have called them. But she dared not talk with Father Brennan of such matters. He'd always been a sad man. Never been easy to talk with, God no. Yet interestingly, he and Ben spent more and more hours talking together. During Father's last visit, she observed an anguished look on the priest's face, as well as Ben's. They talked about God knows what until the wee hours. God—yes, that was the subject of their conversation. Before she excused herself and went to bed, the two of them wondered aloud if God ever wanted faith to circumvent love.

43

Easter came, and the boys were thrilled. They shined their shoes in the outfitting room. The whole place was alive. The boys had only to complete morning chores with the proviso to appear content and clean and well fed.

Brother Ryder, as much as anyone, looked forward to this event. All year, in fact, he thought about this festive picnic, the only all-school social gathering. Careful not to mess his gelled hair, he lowered a thick wooden crucifix around his neck, then belted his black missal with an embroidered gold rope his mother had given him. With his parents both gone and his sister married in Pittsburgh there were no family visits, no one to fawn over him, but there would be others there that afternoon who would revere him. Many fine women among them.

Manipulated as a boy into becoming a Christian Brother, he winced now at the memory of the Monkstown Seminary beside Dun Laoghaire Harbor. He always wanted to be married and have a family, so felt utter confusion when his mother sent him to seminary along with their neighbor Christopher Mack. *You'll keep each other company,* she said, and his father agreed that Christopher was a good example for their boy. They said their goodbyes at the side of the road. Unaware of the hardships to come, he placed his bag on a pony trap and walked with the other newcomers the nine miles to their new school. Countrymen lined the roads, and waved Irish flags at them, handing them jam sandwiches for the journey, as if they were heroes on parade. His mother hadn't told him that he'd remain there, without any visits at all, for four years. He was a different person by the time he came back home. He became awkward around the girls, and Mary, the girl of his dreams, had married a Jack Ryan, a farmer from Kildare. Barely eighteen, his brains, his achievement, and his closeness to the Lord's work, positioned Eddie Ryder with Christopher Mack for Surtane before he could have any say in the matter.

Brother Mack, unlike himself, was mercifully unaware that something was lacking in his life and took his lot the way an old maid might. Once, when he'd asked Christopher why he was so content at Surtane, Mack told him that his eyes and thoughts fell on the beauty in life, and in any life there was beauty: the scent of lingering ash from a woodbine enjoyed in the garden, the rain bathing the ivy leaves on the gate lodge, honeysuckle smells in spring. Ryder guffawed.

Now that their parents were gone, he thought about calling his sister in Pittsburgh, but he hadn't yet worked up the nerve to ask her husband to pay his way. Although he kept his claustrophobic room immaculate except for a dirty rag draped over an open jar of boot polish by the trash bin, he felt like an animal in a cage. There was barely space to walk around his cot. Smells of brylcreem and smoke and Old Spice choked the space. He took out a stylo and his worn leather journal from the nightstand drawer, marked the date of this special Easter event. There was a flask on the old dresser, a couple of black belts and crosses hanging from a nail on the wall, a magazine article taped to the mirror: "England ties US in the Ryder Cup match after five consecutive defeats," the caption read. He whistled at the thought of leaving the country, slapped some Aramis aftershave on his cheeks as shouts exploded from down the hall. He eyed his wooden golf club, erect against the bedside table, ran his fingers over the MacGregor insignia, and then along the lettering in black ink scrawled unsteadily along the shaft.

Ryder marched toward the noise. He was, he believed, a role model for the real boys. He wasn't for the faggots and maggots, he said. Cream rises to the top, he told them, and in this world it is the survival of the fittest. He himself kept trim and fit all these years, working the timber, lifting logs with the best of the lot in here, his monitors.

He detected noise was coming straight from Dormo Three. As his boots trailed close, the noise vanished.

"All right, everybody downstairs. On your best behavior or there'll be consequences."

He noticed from the dorm window the morning sky was a steely turquoise. Several people were already mulling about the playing fields. Ellis and Pansy were greeting Ellis's mother, father, and sister, a pretty thing, budding slightly, a cardigan swinging off her shoulders. She fawned over her brother and perhaps even Pansy. It was their time, he supposed, for girls in kitten heels and boyhood crushes.

Brother Ryder felt an insinuating lust come over him whenever he would see Brother Mack making his way to speak with Adrian. He'd never have taken Adrian to be the type, although he was sure Brother Mack had more on his brain than conversation. He looked at Brother Mack for a moment and couldn't help recalling him as a pudgy, unpopular schoolboy, not one for sports like him, not one the girls took a shine to. He was in every way then as he was now different, a bit of a molly. And it was no wonder he wanted to become a Brother. He didn't seem to like doing much except sitting quietly in his room reading. Some relief was there inside Brother Ryder at times like this, a bit of his guilt removed for the abuse he caused some of the boys over the years. At least he wasn't outwardly having relationships with them, setting up house as it were, he thought. He had peered at the two of them last week as they sat in the chapel "reading the Bible and talking."

"Talking, is it," he said, lingering for a moment. "About what?"

"We just thought we'd ask if Peter might join Adrian as a Kitchener. They work well together. Brother Tyrone could use another set of hands as well."

Ryder immediately thought the transfer might incite others to start requesting favors and fights would break out. Also, Ellis and Pansy, they would be distracted from their work. And Brother Tyrone, along with the outside baker, Mr. Donnelly, would have to pick up the slack, to boot. He remembered Peter hurt himself cutting logs. "No," he muttered and meandered over to the infirmary.

He hadn't given it another thought until this moment, when he knew it would be wrong, and left for the party, couldn't wait to be part of all the fun.

The Ellis family spread their red-checked cloth in the far corner of the refectory. He watched Adrian for a moment, his muscles growing strong with the extra work he'd been assigned—mopping the chapel floors and cleaning the windows in lieu of confirmation classes, which Ryder felt he didn't need. He looked at Mr. Ellis and wondered about the man. He felt the familiar urge come over him when he saw Peter and knew he would have to continue keeping him company when he was alone in the infirmary.

The queer Nurse finally arrived, on her own: the request from Father Brennan made to the Reverend Mother of Castleboro, for Adrian's sake, had been granted.

"I received your letter. Are you not all right?" Ma inquired upon seeing Nurse. She told her to sit with them on the picnic spread, between the lemon tart and the egg salad. Nurse appeared more agitated than usual.

"Just wanted to see our Adrian here. Did you enjoy the eggs I sent?" she asked him.

He looked around, shook his head yes, but his eyes lowered with the lies he was forced into. I never saw one, he wanted to say. Hadn't she grown up in an orphanage herself? *Doesn't she know what is going on here? Tell someone, tell my ma, you blasted eejit.* Distressed by the casual tone of her comment, he wanted to scream, but he knew she was not well, and never had been. She reminded him of a donkey, dumb and lost.

"How is Sister Paulinas?" Ma asked Nurse.

"Reverend Mother chose Sister Theresa to replace her. She's retiring, too old now. The job's getting harder for Sister Paulinas—she's getting on, too. And the new girls seem to get younger and bolder. A different girl these days."

"Harder for you, too, no doubt."

"'Tis," she said.

"What's he staring at," Ma whispered, looking worriedly at Brother Ryder, his hands clasped behind his back. A second phone call she'd made requesting special visitation rights before Easter the right bastard had denied. Adrian, his back turned away from the man, grimaced at her, wild with fear that his mother might be heard.

"Ah, the beginning of the adolescent years," Da said, trying to underplay the anxiety on his face.

Johanna peeled an orange and handed it to him.

"Adrian, do you remember Rosemary? She's asked after you," Nurse blurted.

"What?"

"Sister Adela told me. She's been released for good behavior and is working at the Jolly Roger Inn near Ringsend, she wanted you to know."

"Ringsend," he murmured. "That's grand."

"He used to call her Betty Boop," Johanna said, giggling, eyeing Peter.

"Sure, go on," Ma said, laughing too loudly. "Although I call Johanna Annette Funicello."

Johanna turned coy, looked away from Peter. Peter also looked away, embarrassed, probably not knowing who Annette Funicello is.

"We're thrilled you're all here. Aren't we, Peter?" Adrian said.

"Yes, sir. Thrilled to bits," Peter said, recovering from Johanna's attentions.

"I have something for you, Adrian." Nurse pulled out a bracelet from her black handbag.

"Why would a bracelet be for me? No gifts allowed, Nurse," he said.

"I'm off to London, maybe, and I wanted you to have this to remember me by," she said.

"London?" Ma exclaimed.

Nurse had heard the girls whispering that there were some investigations going on into past Irish adoptions. She overheard the location, near South Kensington, of a private tracing agency and she was determined now to look for her Beth.

"Have you told Sister Paulinas?"

"I wouldn't dare," Nurse said, reddening. "It's the girls' talking all the time about London. It just popped into my mind, but I said maybe, if I have the nerve."

"Sure, I think you would have the nerve," Ma said, squeezing her arm. Adrian noticed Nurse did not repel the touch.

"Pawn the bracelet," Adrian said. "Keep the money for London."

If Nurse could be thinking of escape, if she could get up the nerve, Adrian thought that he, too, could hatch an escape plan, and if she had the courage to escape Sister Paulinas, surely he and Peter could flee Brother Ryder. Figuring out an escape route would keep him sane while he was in there as well.

"Listen to you, telling her to sell it. It might not be hers to sell," Ma said.

"Ma, sometimes you can be a maggot," Adrian said, studying his ma's glamorous face, all made up for the picnic and wearing a blue dress with brass buttons. He couldn't help but notice Johanna's pretty dress, too, and Da in his smart brown tweed suit.

"Never mind, you. A maggot out of your mouth," Ma said. "I don't like the language you're picking up. That looks as if it could have been an important confirmation gift."

"And we all know how much your confirmation meant to you," Johanna said, giving Ma a wry smile. "Gran told me all you cared about was the dress."

"That's not true, young lady. I loved church for a while there. I used to sing the melody of the 'Ave Maria' in my room, practicing my walk toward Father Riordan, my white puffy veil growing out of my head like a calla lily. Sure I remember loving that communion."

"It was the dress you loved. That's all you talked about, Gran said."

Ma protested. "Everything had turned white in my mind on my communion morning. I felt no longer of this world, as if I was floating among angels." She hesitated, and then she said softly, "I've never told anybody, not even my da, about this inexplicable feeling. Kept it a secret all these years, never enjoying it again. But I loved church for awhile," she said.

"Indeed. Love thy neighbor, that sort of thing," Ben added. He and Johanna both snickered with that comment. "Be kind, now."

"Have you never heard of a work in progress? Sure, Rome wasn't built in a day," Ma said with an Italian accent and her fingertips twirling in the air.

"Lucille Ball herself, right here in the flesh," Da said.

"I should say not. Lucille Ball'd give her right arm to look like me."

Da made a face at her like a chimpanzee and scratched under his armpit with his good arm.

"How is Gran?" Adrian asked.

"She sends you her love, and this." She reached for her bag.

"We're not allowed gifts, Ma, for the love of God! I'm begging you to follow the rules." He turned his head around at Brother Ryder and felt a deep panic seeing him staring at their party. Ma put the wrapped package down.

"Bubbe sends her love, too," Ben said.

"She does?"

"She doesn't come round much, but–"

"I go to see her," Johanna said. "Have sleepovers, go to *shul* with her and Da–"

"You look too thin, Adrian. Have another piece of chicken, please," Marian said. "You, too, Peter. Come on boys, eat up." The two of them ate in a frenzy. "He's missing a tooth, Ben," Ma said.

"Can you keep your voice down, Ma?" Adrian said, looking behind him at Brother Ryder for the umpteenth time.

Ben took his son's chin in his hand.

"It fell out playing ball, Da."

"You like sport, Mr. Ellis?" Peter quickly asked. "You enjoy rugby, sir?" Adrian noticed a few of the boys tossing a ball around outside with their fathers.

"Of course, son. The games are good, Peter. I should have brought a ball but with the bad arm."

Adrian could tell Da regretted that he hadn't thought to plan an activity for father-son time.

"With the bad arm, even writing's a struggle, so ball is out of the question," Da said.

"The arm's getting better, though, isn't it?" Ma said.

Da shrugged. "I guess so," he answered, seeming a bit annoyed by her diagnosis.

"I've brought you a cap, Adrian," she said, putting it on him. "You can use it to bat away these flies," she added, waving her hands around to keep the insects off the food.

Adrian eyeballed her underneath the hat and could only hope that she understood that he was worried about what would happen to him and Peter in Surtane. And then he stared into the drive, and then back at her, hoping that she understood he wanted out.

45

Brother Mack startled Adrian, who was atop an old ladder washing the highest windows of the stone chapel.

"Those windows look clean enough, I'd say. Wouldn't you?"

Adrian came down off the unsteady rungs. "I'd say so myself as well, sir. I'll give the floor a proper scrub."

"You can scrub, and I'll sit and read my Bible. We'll have our own private confirmation class," he added, a smile crossing his face.

Brother Mack wished Adrian had been sent to the O'Brien Institute, which catered to the upper middle class, or to St. Vincent Orphanage for boys from middle-class families. He knew from his file that his parents were not working class poor. As it was, he would learn no trade but kitchener here, thanks to Ryder. A right bastard Brother Ryder had been when Adrian had asked for the timber trade. It was Brother Mack's opinion that Eddie Ryder desperately needed to put in for a transfer.

"If you remember one thing from this Bible, remember all things come to good for those who love the Lord," he said. "Now, you might think differently. You might think you don't care a hoot about studying or thinking or listening, and scrubbing these floors is bad enough without listening to me go on. You might be thinking that. It's all in the way you're looking at a thing."

Adrian gave him another nod.

"There's good in everything; even if you can't find it, it's there. God will make something good from it. You have to have the right attitude, I suppose is what this is saying here. Many roads, but they're all going to the same place."

Adrian didn't seem to know what he was talking about. Mack wondered if Adrian thought about what possible good could come from what was being done to Peter. Each day his friend was growing weaker, quieter, keeping more to himself. Adrian left the dirty bucket in the aisle by the third row and accepted the Brother's invitation to sit beside him.

"You probably don't want to read this, so we'll just sit and talk. Tell me about your sister."

"I don't mind; I love reading. Johanna has a pink room, a tall bookshelf painted pink, too. Stuffed animals and loads of books. Listening to her reading aloud *Blyton's First Term at Malory Towers* and the "Teddy and Cuddly" magazine stories is great. Just thinking about her smooth talking leaves me embarrassed."

"The pen is mightier than the sword," Brother Mack continued. "You may not understand the logic of such a thought or what relevance it has."

"A gifted thought it is," Adrian said. "Brother Tyrone says this all the time. A gifted thought, he says, when we talk about life. And I'll not play the judge, another gifted thought you've taught me."

"And how is it in the kitchen? How is Brother Tyrone treating you?"

"He's lovely. A good man. Very smart, too. Kitchen work is grand. I'm never hungry."

He was stealing hot baked loaves for him and Peter, slipping them up his sleeves since the first day. Brother Mack knew but did not say.

"Brother Mack, do you think you might try again to transfer Peter into the bakery, sir?"

"And what do you think might happen if the two of you are always together?" He rested his arm around the back of the pew.

"I'd be glad to switch with him and work the timber trade, and have him work in the bakery. I'm worried, sir, for Peter. He's in poor health, sir," he added.

"We'll see what can be done."

Adrian's nerves skidded as the heavy chapel door swung open and Brother Ryder marched in. He jumped up, went for his mop.

"Have you not finished the floor?"

"Leave him alone. You could eat off these floors. We've just been talking."

Brother Ryder peered at the two of them. "Talking again, is it," he said, lingering for a moment. "About what?"

"We just thought we'd ask once again if Peter might join Brother Tyrone's crew as a Kitchener."

Brother Ryder shook his head.

"Well, I better go," Brother Mack sighed, closing his Bible. "I'm on duty at the playing fields."

After Mack left, Brother Ryder felt the familiar urge come over him and he remembered Peter was alone in his bed. No way to put the brakes on, he'd once heard a drunk use that phrase, and he understood what that meant. He knew the pattern: the guilty act, exhaustion, sleep. Sometimes, after an incident, he awoke with a heaviness in the head and unsure of what exactly had taken place.

"I'll go and have a word with Peter," he muttered to himself and left.

46

Johanna ran the tap over the dishes still in the sink. Ma was throwing her a party, she'd announced last week, for no reason. Because. Jo knew the party was intended to fix their family.

"Da will be here any minute with Bubbe and those Jewish children. And the twins, too—Ma! Look at me," Jo cried suddenly. "Ma, you never look at me!"

"What are you going on about, Johanna," Ma said, squeezing her shoulders. "You look grand altogether. And, oh, here comes Gran." Marian left the kitchen to answer the door.

"What about the plates sitting everywhere?" Johanna called after her. "The place is like Johnny foxes," she muttered.

But she couldn't blame Adrian, nor would she want to. She was confused lately, she told herself. Five months past her eleventh year she experienced "the change into womanhood." Her mother explained all about it, and about the "roller-coaster feelings" that accompany it. All without much sympathy, Johanna thought. She tied an apron around her waist and continued the relentless kitchen clean up.

Can't Ma give me a break? This one day, my "party" day? Why was Ma always such a big mess, she wondered. She hated her. Ma looked forward to her next visit to Surtane, she told Da last night, so her mind could rest. All she ever wanted to do was rest. Rest from nothing, Johanna thought, emptying bits of rashers and scrambled eggs into the trash and all Da's damn cigarette butts smelling up the place.

"Could you please take out the bins, Ma? Hello, Gran."

"*Conas ata tu?*" The old woman hefted a whole turkey in her arms. "How are you?"

Typical Gran, she walked right into the kitchen with an enormous bird she brought with her and opened the cooker to keep the turkey warm.

"I'm grand."

Johanna watched her ma dutifully lift the dustbin, watched her through the kitchen window putting the garbage in the bin. After the slashing rain, everything looked speckled in mud; a late-planted morning glory added a lovely blue.

She wondered whatever happened to Ma's blather just a couple of weeks ago, gushing over all the fancy table settings in her *Woman's Week* magazine, ranting that she could make her a party every bit as chic as an American housewife. She was like the barber's cat. Full of wind and piss. Talk, talk, talk—about the garden, garden books everywhere, about ritzy garden parties that were not to be.

And Ma going on about how they'd buy a color television soon, and Watusi and funky chicken dance records, too. American mammies would not outdo her. Not Ma. We'll keep up with the best of them, she said. *She's become a dunderhead,* Johanna thought.

"Don't be glum," Ma said. "I'll finish up in here. Go on with Gran into the living room. Put on the Beatles. Enjoy your party."

"*My party?* What are you talking about, Ma?"

Johanna slipped out back and clipped some yellow roses for the hall table. She wondered sometimes what Da had seen in her ma, he being so different. Even with his arm, he found time to watch her tennis lessons and listen to her schoolyard antics, so caring and interested in everything she did.

"The door knocker," Gran said.

Johanna touched her dark wilting curls as she opened the door to see her pals Anna and Rona standing there. They gaped at each other and then at her. Here she was, wearing velvet-striped bell-bottoms. Paul McCartney himself would have been impressed. They jumped up and down in delight, and Johanna straightened her black velvet choker with the gold peace emblem sewn into the middle.

Just then Da and Bubbe pulled up and out of the car came three boys and three girls, all dressed in fancy clothes.

"Hullo," Johanna said and smiled at the ones she recognized. She never before saw such big ribbons stuck like paper airplanes into girls' hair. All of them in puffy dresses, too. They looked like a confirmation class, except for the two boys sporting the spiffy Davy Crocket raccoon hats.

"Come in," Johanna said, making designs on the doorknob.

She watched them cross the foyer, their eyes on her hoola hoop.

"Is this a *kholem* of a house or what, *kinder*?" Beva said. "A gorgeous home, children. Go on, Johanna. Introduce yourself. Look at my granddaughter. Looks a little like young Leonard over there doesn't she? They could be related."

"Listen, Johanna," she continued, calling her over to the coat closet, taking her hands in hers. "Do you know, during the War, if you had just one grandparent who was Jewish, you would have been taken. *Kaputt*, like the rest of us. So why should I not think of you as—"

"Mammy," Da said.

"What? You married out. She may marry in," Beva said, motioning with her eyes at the new kid, Leonard. Johanna gave her Bubbe the look. "All right! All right, no matchmaking."

Da marched out of the foyer.

"What? What did I say?" Bubbe muttered as she found preparations to attend.

Thank God Da turned on *Sgt. Pepper's Lonely Hearts Club Band*.

"The *oul wans* will be drowned out now," Jo joked to her friends, turning up the phonograph's volume. "Come on. Let's do the monkey."

Bubbe helped Ma lay out a white tablecloth, placed honey-dipped apples on a silver platter she brought with her. Johanna noticed her ma's momentary vitality as she began filling the table with goodies, and wondered how much energy Adrian would have siphoned from her if he was home. She felt a jealousy that she detested rise for her ma's attention, and then she thought of Adrian and how much she wanted him home for good, too, and her envy fell away.

"*Oy*, there's a lot of *tuml* coming from that thing, Johanna. A lot of noise. Turn the music down before we all have headaches."

"Ma, did you remember the orange soda?" Jo asked, running into the crowded kitchen.

"I'll bring it out," Da answered.

"Come over here." Bubbe squeezed her hard on the cheeks. "Ah, *shayna punim*. What a pretty face on you!"

Ma nodded awkwardly. God would strike her down, Johanna supposed, if she dared boast about her daughter. How many times had she heard her tell Da that he'd have to be careful or else she might get a swelled head.

"I love your pants—I think," Gran said, now giving her the look. "But pants to a party? Is this another thing you've seen on television, some hippie-dippie thing?"

Johanna rolled her eyes.

"Wait'll you see these kids eat my chopped liver like they've never tasted anything before," Bubbe said, leaving for the drawing room with a bowl of the pâté surrounded with Jacob's cream crackers.

Gran waved her hand in front of her nose, said the kosher stuff was stinking up all the other food in the fridge.

"Gran, quiet," Jo said.

"How do you understand anything she says?" Gran mumbled.

"I'm bilingual, Gran," Jo said, rolling her eyes and leaving the kitchen.

"Johanna's a real Grovkofsy. Looks like my father," Bubbe said, kissing Da, saying something about looking forward to a sleepover in her home next Sabbath. Soon, Jo would share the Sabbath with Da and Bubbe in Bubbe's warm home—with all the photographs of Tatte, and Da as Bubbe's *kaddishel,* saying the prayers for the dead. Her wee son. He'd talk with his hands, too, and laugh at Bubbe's Yiddish jokes. During the dinner conversation, they would relive the celebration over the Six-Day War. They would all be at ease to argue about this or that. Da and Bubbe would dispute the student riots in Paris, riots against the Vietnam War in America, black power conferences. Jo'd argue for free speech via rock 'n' roll. And Bubbe would say, "*Got tsu danken.* She's not afraid to talk." And with that, she'd do her rendition of "Born Free," until she'd get a klop on the head from Bubbe.

"We said the *Kiddush* last night," Johanna said to Bubbe.

"You said a blessing over the wine. Do me a favor, Johanna. Once in a blue moon, say a blessing over the bread, too. A couple of blessings are not enough for Johanna, Benjamin. She'll know nothing about Judaism."

Da shrugged.

"Doesn't she go to Hebrew lessons, Benjamin?" Bubbe asked.

"No catechist classes either, Beva," Ma said. A heavy silence followed.

"I'm not saying another word," Bubbe said, moving closer to the young guests. "Watch these kids dance. Forget the Pappa. Joy you only get from grandchildren."

Ma studied Da as he busied himself playing deejay, and then she downed her Bloody Mary. She leaned against the drawing room wall, watched the kids dance and then went back into the kitchen.

After a while Jo entered the kitchen and saw Ma's dirty apron on the counter, but her ma nowhere in sight.

"Ma?" Jo yelled as she went upstairs to check on her.

Ma lay across the bed on her stomach, both arms hanging off the edge, her wrists limp. The rotary phone was off the hook, the monotonous, loud dial tone reminded Jo of vital signs gone dead.

"Our request has been denied," Ma informed her. "Adrian will not be coming home after his first year." It would be six weeks until they could see Adrian again.

Johanna picked up the receiver and placed it back on the hook. She looked down at Ma, strands of hair from her outdated bouffant tangled into a bird's nest at the nape of her neck. She felt a familiar discomfort in the stomach. If it weren't for her insisting they perform hand-stands on the Donnybrook Church stained-glass windows, Adrian would not have been sent away.

"I'm to blame for getting Adrian sent to Surtane," she managed. "You think it's my fault."

"Johanna, no, dear, it's not your fault. Sister Agnes said she made

up her mind after an incident at the orphanage. Nothing to do with
you at all. I'm tired now, Jo. Tell everyone to go home."

"You're always tired. Tell me, Ma, why did you keep me?"

"What are you talking–"

"To help do the washing? Put on the tea?"

"Johanna!"

"How can you go around like a slug and hurt all of us with your
silent treatment?"

"I'm trying, Jo. I really–"

"No, I'm the throw away child, not him. Face it."

By the time Ma looked up at her, she was walking out of the room.
Jo slammed the door behind her. She sat down on the couch. Bubbe
tapped her head, to knock some sense into it. Always physical with
Bubbe. Like a prisoner, she felt she was in her own lonely world.

"Don't bother, Da," she said, as he mounted the stairs. "She asks
that everyone go."

Da came over and sat down with her and Bubbe.

"Ma needs a breather," she sighed. A breather from what? From
her own daughter? Johanna wished she could be more of a girly-girl,
less tomboyish, but there's the way the thing goes, as Gran would say.
Too much trouble for Ma, she was. *Too much work.*

Over the following weeks, Marian made concerted efforts to focus on Johanna. Ben, for one, felt relieved. He was confident Marian listened and respected him when he voiced his concerns, which had grown more frequent. Marian even surprised Johanna two Saturdays this May and took her shopping and to lunch. Twice Marian told Ben they were having a "mother-daughter." He was pleased; his *maidelah* was elated.

By the second Saturday in June, the three of them made their way to the Surtane graduation day picnic in good spirits, carting bags of goodies. No personal gifts for Adrian this time, they brought oranges and pomegranates, a meat and potato pie, boiled eggs, warm Bourneville cocoa in two thermos bottles, and toffee apples for dessert, a ten pound note Ben would thrust into the pocket of Adrian's knickers.

Johanna had been corresponding with Peter, having sent two letters to Brother Mack in hopes he'd pass them on. She seemed particularly glad to see him. She wore a brand new outfit: a raspberry maxi coat, white go-go boots, a pink mini skirt, and pink fishnet stockings. Her hair was different, too, recently cut to the shoulder with bangs.

"All a bit much," Ben mumbled to Marian on their way out the door.

As the taxi drove up the long drive, Adrian and Peter stood outside, waiting. Johanna got out of the car and sauntered over to them. Marian pointed out distant oak trees already budding, a lime canopy of new apple leaves protected their perfect picnic spot, yellow ferns and wildflowers, in untidy beds bloomed near the outer buildings. The group ventured under the trees. Peter reddened as Jo lay her long coat down and patted the skirt of it to indicate that he should sit down with her.

"Come on, kids. Help your ma lay out the blanket," Ben called, as Brother Mack approached. The two shook hands and Ben invited him to join them, but the Brother refused, saying he had to pull up his socks and make sure everything went well.

"Your son," he added in a low voice before he left, "is a fine young man. I've gotten reports from Brother Tyrone and Mr. Bernard Donnelly in the bakery that Adrian has never once been late to work. Up at three-thirty every morning, he has the building open and ready for business. A fine boy you have there, a smart boy," Brother Mack said.

"Look after him," Ben begged him, noting to himself from the first that Brother Mack seemed a decent sort. "Adrian should be home, you must know that. He was originally only to be here for the one year."

"I know," Brother Mack answered before moving along, saying he was sorry, too, for Brother Ryder's recommendation to Judge Moran that Adrian be detained for a full stay.

Peter sat next to Johanna, trying to stop his thin face blushing, but he could not. He seemed nervous sitting on the Ellises' blanket, under the seemingly casual eye of Brother Ryder. Marian offered the basket of fruit, and Peter followed Adrian's lead and groped for an orange. Marian, too, looked ill at ease as she sat there, but Ben supposed it was the setting, the muffled mirth of orphans sitting together at industrial picnic tables, pent-up boys bursting with high spirits, the array of Christian Brothers littering the lawn. Ben assumed, too, that Marian was aware of the growing flirtation between Peter and Jo, and that he did not particularly like it.

Neither, it appeared, did Brother Ryder, who stood too close to their party, his hands behind his back. He watched as Johanna and Peter and Adrian engaged in a game of tag around the apple tree, leaving the grown-ups on their own. Ben noticed during the game Johanna pushed a leaf of notepaper into Peter's hand that the boy accepted and stuffed down his knickers.

"What's he always staring at us for?" Marian wondered aloud to Ben.

"Ah, he's a cool half, isn't he," Ben said to her.

"Would you give us a few minutes, Brother Ryder?" Marian asked, rising to her feet.

Adrian's face twisted with fear with this more-than-likely punishable request coming from his own mother's lips.

"I'd like to have a walk with my son, alone. You don't mind, do you?"

Holding the bark of the tree, Adrian looked at her. "No, Ma. That's not allowed. I don't want to break the rules," he managed, glancing up into Brother Ryder's face where a faint smile turned up.

Brother Ryder sauntered casually over to Peter and held out his hand. Ben noticed Peter's body slouch and Adrian's extreme discomfort. His head lowered, Peter handed over Johanna's note, the handwritten lyrics to "Puppy Love" with little red hearts drawn all over the paper.

"Would you like a toffee apple, Brother Ryder?" Ben offered the plate of sticky apples for Brother Ryder. "May I see the note?"

"I suppose I will," Brother Ryder said. "Seeing everyone's partaking." Brother Ryder handed Ben the paper, and Ben leisurely walked over to their blanket and exposed the note while the Brother negotiated the candy apple.

"Surely there's no harm in the lyrics to 'Puppy Love,'" Ben said to him, reading the note. "Surely you must have had puppy love yourself?"

Johanna giggled at this and the three teenagers hid together behind the apple tree.

"I have an idea," Marian offered.

Besmirched by everyone's glee at his expense, nonetheless Brother Ryder listened to Marian's spontaneous idea of a summer dance for the boys before Ryder nodded his leave, and lurked for another group.

"No worries, children. Come now and eat," she called out.

"Which one is the bakery building," Marian asked Adrian. "Da tells me Brother Mack mentioned that you're doing a fine job."

"He is," Peter said. "I can attest to that," he whispered, and the boys chortled.

"It's the third gray building from the back gates, Ma," Adrian said, considering another time the details of his possible escape.

The visit was long, a paradise for the boys. But after everyone was gone, the boys discussed the earlier tension with Brother Ryder and prayed for a miracle. They hoped Ben managed to smooth things over. Peter was already dreaming of Johanna's next visit, he confessed. Hope filled his days now, he told Adrian.

"Hope," Adrian laughed, throwing his arm around him, a quick light jab to his jaw. "We'll be eating those eggs and drinking hot tea every day soon enough." Adrian and Peter tumbled down in playful punches at one another under the shade of the apple tree.

"We'll be building boats soon enough as well," Adrian said, "the smelly taste of minnows on our breath." This was their new plan for their futures. They'd build boats rather than put out forest fires.

"Yeah," Peter allowed, and then a quiet grin spread across his face likely sparked by the thought of Johanna's appealing, adorable, impish face. Peter said that he was daydreaming of a possible future career together, when their faces would be reflected in Dublin bay, the black salty water healing their limbs, the two of them working the docks.

Adrian lay down in the grass close to Peter, each boy allowing the other a moment alone to bask in his private reveries. Adrian thought about his Gran, the way she set the perfect tea tray, pansies sketched into her ancient supper plates, her thin, aged hands preparing scones, butter melting on the biscuits, clotted cream scooped into a matching cream bowl rimmed in violet. The gray film on the lace curtains before she took the duster to them, the cobwebs he pointed out to her in the corners of the guest room, the room that was now his, she told him. He was her *stór*, her darling, she said often, wiping a smudge or simply touching his cheek. The statue of Mary she placed inside his room. Kneeling in prayer together, he in cotton pajamas, soft against his clean skin, she fragrant with the smell of Nivea just applied. Clear, strong memories that grew in power as he imagined their most minute details until he was feeling more pleasure than pain.

Their reverie was interrupted before too long by taunts from O'Connor and O'Reilly. Soon, Brother Ryder himself came over, told O'Connor to give Peter a little time up in the timber trade to teach Adrian that we don't go off privately to tell tales out of school.

"Peter's the real mama's boy, but he don't have no mama," the monitors teased.

"He does, too," Adrian shouted at them. He had his fists in the air as they led Peter off to the woods to cut tree stumps.

"It's all right, Adrian," Peter said, as the sun began to sink behind the woodlands. Anything to be away from Brother Ryder, he must have meant.

"Every time you ask for special favors, Peter'll get his," the monitors called back.

Adrian looked to Brother Ryder.

"I'll learn ya, ya cabbage. We'll scour the grounds for litter. There's always work to be done," Brother Ryder said. "And the two of you don't have a brain between you, breaking rules under my nose." He laughed aloud and continued. "I remember my own dirty thoughts at your age." He hadn't been so stupid around girls, though, he said, picking up ant infested apple cores, throwing them into an aluminum trash bin.

Adrian stumbled upon a wrapped flake bar and two pence just sitting there in the gravel. He looked toward the fields for another glance of Peter, far away now. He bent down to pick up trash and stuffed the goodies into his pocket.

48

As regular as ever, at three-thirty the following morning, especially invigorated after the picnic, Adrian opened his bleary eyes in the still blackness. He put his arm out to ruffle Peter awake before going off to the bakery.

Peter's cot was empty. In a trancelike state, Adrian meandered past the long parade of cots into the hall. He might be using the downstairs loo, he thought, but halfway down the stairs, he gasped.

Leaning over the railing, he spied Peter lying motionless on the cold stone floor below.

"Somebody, help!" Adrian tried to scream but little came out of his mouth.

He hurried down the stairs and knelt by his friend's side. Blood oozed from Peter's mouth. His frame was stiff. Dried blood and smears of dirt covered his colorless face.

Boys gathered on the stairs and in the hall.

"Call the ambulance! Get him to hospital!" Adrian shrieked.

Brother Mack roused and emerged from his room. He left immediately to call for help.

"He must have jumped from the landing," one boy whispered.

"He was always a bit delicate. Maybe went soft in the head. Poor fella."

"He committed suicide, the ultimate sin."

Waking boys shook their hallowed heads.

"He was murdered," Adrian shouted. "Who pushed him?" He screamed up at the onlookers. "You motherfuckers! You killed him!" he cried as Brother Mack approached, and Adrian broke down in his arms.

The timber traders said he'd taken the saw, cut his own arm, and would have lain bleeding to death if they hadn't been there to carry him home. They'd no idea how he landed on the floor.

Adrian didn't believe the bastards. The very ones who buggered

Peter up there in the woods. From the mad look in his friend's eyes, the exhaustion in his defeated body each night, the rage on his small, fair face each morning—Adrian knew. Brother Ryder had given the bigger lads free rein over Peter. Everyone knew it. No one supervised the goings on in the woods.

The following morning, dark vengeance crowded Adrian's mind during the simple burial service held for Peter. Past the woodlands, in a fallow field, a small, crooked cross marked his friend's coffin in the boys' cemetery.

49

This was only the third time since May that Nurse dared kiss Officer Dolan, his arms snug around her. Silver mints on his breath glossed over the drink he took. She continued to be careful, meeting him in the shed only after her work day had long ended. In the pitch black. The babies bathed and asleep, the girls' maternity ward lights out for at least two hours. Sister Paulinas more than likely asleep.

But for some reason tonight, Nurse and Officer Dolan heard Sister's heels clicking closer to the maternity ward.

Sister Paulinas whisked open the door to the shed, a torchlight shining in Nurse's eyes.

"Suffering ducks," Sister Paulinas said. "I wondered about this."

Officer Dolan removed his arms from Nurse's waist. Sister Paulinas slammed the shed door behind her.

"You have to help me," Nurse whispered to Officer Dolan. "I have to leave or there'll be trouble now."

"Shh!"

"I'll go up to Marian's."

"Shh! Go collect your things, I'll tell her it was my–"

"Mention Father Brennan, and please wait for me. Don't leave–"

He put his finger to his lips to quiet her, promised he would stay right there in front of the shed until she returned, and urged her to hurry up.

Nurse felt terrified as they opened the shed, thought about Marian and Father Brennan, and managed to look Sister Paulinas square in the eye.

The nun scowled at the two emerging from the shed, her arms crossed, a long crucifix gracing her white robe like silverware on a tablecloth.

"That one surely will rot in hell," Sister said to Officer Dolan, pointing at Nurse as if smelling something rotten.

"And you, Officer Dolan—I'm appalled. You ought to be ashamed, taking advantage of the poor creature."

Nurse twitched at her, gave a little curtsy, and tiptoed toward the maternity ward door.

"Where do you think you're going, sneaky one?" Sister hollered after Nurse. "I always knew you'd never be any good to anybody. You've become a hindrance to all of us. Is that clear?"

Nurse stopped. "Yes, Sister," she said.

"You're good for nothing. A dirty whore and nothing more. I knew one day you'd cause trouble. Too stupid to be saved. Get back inside that ward now."

"Yes, Sister," Nurse said, and shuffled to the door. Sister followed close behind. Nurse sneaked a look back at Officer Dolan, who fingered the set of keys dangling from his belt.

No, no—it was clear, Sister, that you never liked me, Nurse thought, as she raced to her room, Sister Paulinas making a racket behind her, switching on the light in the hall to her office, ranting about what a whore Nurse was. *You'll not be going back to work for her, Nurse. You'll not be going back to the laundry, either, to live out your years behind bars no, no.*

She'd never forgotten what Sister Paulinas had told her, that she could remain as long as she was a help and not a hindrance, and she entered the scullery, putting her forefinger through an apple tart that she'd baked for the convent nuns. The last supper, she thought, still brave somewhere inside her from Officer Dolan's kisses. She poked the pie again then hurried along to her room.

Dear Jesus, forgive me for I have shamed the world. She breathed out one long sigh, glad for the inhalation of air that followed. From her night table, she grabbed her Bible and diary, her little penknife and her rosary beads and packed her second uniform and extra shoes and boxed memories of Beth, and then ran through the empty scullery.

Sister Paulinas stood by the large staircase, her arms still crossed. Many of the girls peered from behind the day room door, others at the window.

"You're nothing but a dumb ox," Sister Paulinas bellowed, looking at Nurse's packed suitcase. "You know that, don't you." Her wild eyes glowed, and Nurse thought of her own sweet sister Anne. This nun was not fit to clean her boots, and Nurse walked right past her down the long hall to the back door.

"Get back here. Nurse!" Sister Paulinas roared.

"Nurse *this!* Nurse *that!* The hell with you," Nurse cried back.

"Start praying to Saint Jude, hopeless case that *you* are." She managed out the door and fled to Officer Dolan standing with a torchlight by the shed.

50

Officer Dolan called and told Marian to expect Nurse. Marian greeted the haggard woman with a hug upon her arrival.

"You're looking round like you're to be arrested. You didn't do anything illegal, Nurse, for heaven's sake. You've got us."

"No, no," Nurse said. "I won't stay. I just thought I might be able to borrow a few shillings," she said.

Marian went for her handbag on the foyer table. "Now sit awhile."

Ben could be heard upstairs in the shower. Trickling water and his occasional *humpf* as he chuckled with comedian Jimmy Clitheroe on Radio 2. A good thing he was in good spirits before another meeting with Nurse.

"Sure, you'll need a bath yourself," Marian said and handed her the money.

"Thanks."

"And you've got Officer Dolan now as well, haven't you?"

"He took me to the train station. He's a kind fellow," she said, unable to contain a self-conscious smile at the thought of him.

"And?"

"I thought I might write a letter, see if he would want to join me."

After Marian calmed Nurse down with tea, they wrote a letter to Officer Dolan in care of the Castleboro Garda station so that Sister Paulinas could not seize the mail.

"You'll wait here now until his response. We could use the company," Marian said, listening to the tick tock of the big brass ship's clock on the mantelpiece.

Nurse accepted Marian's invitation to stay with them until she heard a reply from Officer Dolan. For the entire weekend, when Ben should have been free from work, he spent most of his time other than meals out of the house interviewing Jewish alumni from Trinity College at the Gresham Hotel. When he was at home he was reading the paper in the drawing room or typing at the library desk.

Most recently, Ben worked on a rare and welcome assignment, an international news brief dedicated to D. A. Glaser, the Nobel Prize winner for physics, a story Ben found to be a relief from local news. Mainly he spent his time wherever Nurse was not. Her presence made him edgy, reminded him of what Marian had done, she supposed. In the evenings, or if it was spilling rain, Marian and Johanna played gin or old maid at the dining table with Nurse. Otherwise they were cooking cabbage and potatoes or walking about the garden, all three of them amazed that several white camellias had already bloomed. They were especially thrilled to notice the recent purchase of a large chrysanthemum was also flowering, the scent of pale pink buds especially fragrant this cool July.

It was nearly one week later when the return letter arrived from Officer Dolan, and it was no surprise to Nurse that he did not accept her offer, that his job was too important to risk losing.

The letter, though, brought a surprise of a different nature. Nurse's loss of the man she loved appealed to Ben's empathetic side; the savior in him responded to her rejection, and for a moment, Marian found herself thinking of Beva. If there was one thing the two women agreed upon it was Ben's sensitivity to the plights of the underdog.

"May I read Officer Dolan's letter?" Ben inquired.

Nurse nodded. She tried to appear strong as she uncreased the folded stationery and left the missive floating on the dining room table.

Ben took his time with every word. Dolan's writing was practically illegible. Why do men (large men) tend to create such tiny, stilted marks? Ben folded the letter and placed it gently in front of Nurse. He walked over to the cabinet and placed the whiskey and three port glasses on the table. He sat down next to Nurse. Still without speaking he poured generously and handed one to each woman.

"*Sláinte*," Ben said. To Marian's surprise, he attempted an awkward clinking of their glasses.

"Cheers," Nurse giggled.

Ben's kindness was already working; Marian could see it on Nurse's face. Marian took a chair and raised her glass.

"I admire that Officer Dolan, that friend of yours," Ben said. "It's not every man who would have the strength to turn you away."

Nurse looked across the room, reddened, tried to keep from another bout of giggles. She finished her glass, as did Ben, and he poured them another round.

"No, no. It's fine," Ben said.

No, no. It's fine? Did Ben feel talking like Nurse was the best way to get through to her? The only way? Rather endearing of him, Marian thought.

"I respect a man who respects his job, don't you?" Ben turned to Marian who nodded in agreement.

"Things will change, though. I'm guessing we haven't seen the last of him. He's smitten with you, Nurse," Ben said.

"Ah, go on—no, no."

"He is. I can tell from the tone of his letter. He'll be back, you'll see."

Ben topped off all three glasses.

"Ah, I'm off to bed," he said. "You women have my head reeling."

Ben grinned and downed his drink as did Nurse. When he stood, Nurse stood with him. They chatted gaily, and Marian was delighted to see Ben's playful nature peek out from its shadowy regions.

Late that evening, close to midnight, she lay beside him and massaged his damaged right arm.

"She's going in the morning?" Ben asked.

Marian smiled. "You've been good, though you've had more than a pint to get you through it."

"Ah, you know she's like your mother. She'd come for the wedding, and stay for the christening," he said. "I've done my best."

"Johanna'll miss the company, no doubt. There's no flies on that Jo. She hasn't lost a card game since Nurse got here."

"The ever whippersnapper Jo."

Marian inched a bit closer to him, his red plaid nightshirt she'd taken to wearing hung off her left shoulder.

"Let's have more kids, Marian McKeever Ellis," he whispered, capturing the moment. "We thought we would by now. Twenty of them."

Massaging his arm, Marian recoiled when Ben suddenly jerked from the pain.

"I'm past my prime, Romeo. And look at you," she said, as he held his injured forearm, "you'll be forty this year."

"We're not too old, Marian."

"You just want things to be different," she said as a matter of fact, wondering if he was using his arm as a crutch. She couldn't believe the pain could still be so severe.

"Ah, I want things to be better," he said, his voice rising. "Yeah, I want things to be different."

"Ben," she sighed. They'd had this exchange before. "Let's get your arm better, let's get Adrian home, let's deal with what's on our plate before we start thinking about adding more to it."

Sensuality left the room like an embarrassed eavesdropper.

Ben turned, lit a cigarette, and lay quietly looking up at chipped pale paint.

"Why the cold shoulder?" Marian asked, trying to make light.

He didn't like the condescension in her voice, Ben said.

"I'm worried about Adrian more than ever now, after Peter's death," she whispered, looking toward their closed door. They'd agreed not to tell Johanna about Peter's gruesome death. They both felt she was too young to cope with such a trauma. "Please, for Adrian's sake, try to help him through this," she said, turning off her night table lamp.

"For his sake. For all our sakes, Marian. It's awful."

If only she knew how guilty he felt about the fate of his son. He pitched Mr. Darby another slant about industrial schools just last week and was told categorically no. Stick to his profile of the Briscoe family and their upcoming trip to New York, and a memorable march in the St. Patrick's Day Parade for our first Jewish Lord Mayor of Dublin. He felt a powerful urge and ethical obligation to report on these hidden atrocities, even if they hadn't been personal, but he was denied. He wasn't sure if he didn't fight his boss and stayed silent out of fear of losing his job or of being blacklisted. Or was it deeper and more hideous: the selfish fear of losing his reputation.

He put out his fag and got up to find an old box of photographs he stored in the closet. Sorting through them for good ones of Tatte he planned to give Adrian one day, he came across an old school award from 1949. Voted unanimously by his peers, "Most likely to succeed." He tossed the box aside and noticed a piece of pottery made by his *pistoy*, his plucky girl. Wiping it off, Ben brought it out of the far reaches of the closet. He watched Marian as she slept, wondering if she were faking to avoid sex.

Marian rubbed her eyes, glanced at Jo's vase in Ben's hand. "I've been looking for that," she said, smiling like a dream. "I'm pleased you found it."

He stared at her for a moment and then returned Jo's handiwork to its rightful place on her night table as he left the bedroom for a nightcap downstairs.

51

Three months passed since Peter's death. Adrian trudged to the bakery building by four o'clock each morning, very much alone. At this hour, when the madmen slept in their pious cells, he slowly grew to love the hum of silence in the bleak darkness surrounding him and found that he now craved the quiet, whose mysteries made him feel small, and then his problems somehow became smaller as well.

He turned on the bakery lights. Squinting, with a large horse brush in hand, he shoved the squirming rats caught on the sticky board into the boiler. Chores that once made him cringe now were done by rote.

Although Peter was gone, although much of his appetite had left him, Adrian continued to steal hot crusty ends of loaves, not ready to relinquish the routine that he and his friend treasured. As his sleepiness wore off, as daylight began, thoughts of Peter flooded him: Peter's pale face, his beaten down body, his murder. Adrian's clear memory of Peter's dreadful end was like a leaking water tap that could not be turned off. Peter had come back from the woods bruised countless times. They killed him, all of the monitors. That night his shirt was torn and bloody. Nothing was said about rape or murder, but Adrian was certain he was killed. Bullied he was that night. God knows the monitors learned from the hardchaw Ryder how to torment.

As he entered the kitchen, his thoughts turned to Brother Mack. A kind man, like a father would be, bringing him Urney's Regal Chocolate bars on Fridays, complimenting his cooking skills. Adrian enjoyed sharing Brother Tyrone's baker's lessons with Brother Mack and cooking the flavorful hash he created from a variety of leftover ingredients. And then he thought of his own father, and guessed Da would likely been glad to have him in Surtane, the uncultivated arse he'd been at home. How could he blame him?

Adrian never mentioned Peter's death to Brother Mack and wondered if he should, wondered if he knew details about the incident. His loneliness grew worse daily, his mind filled with murderous thoughts, and he wondered if he'd end up a killer himself. It became harder to hold back his anger and his growing desire to take Peter's murderers a hot crusty loaf, a couple of sharp knives hidden up his sleeves. If he didn't plan a successful escape, he'd end up doing something that would get him dragged off and locked away forever.

52

Nurse set off from the Ellises' wearing Marian's long, navy wool skirt, a simple white blouse, and a multi-colored wool sweater, which came down past her waist and hid the tightness of the unbuttoned waist. Marian's tan overcoat and an umbrella hung over her arm.

Six o'clock on a Saturday morning, one wouldn't think that the Irish Ferries terminal would be so jammed, but it was late August, the tourist season. A group of children in gray dress knickers ran about the terminal in circles, their guardians opening their luggage for the guards. Loud noises and crowds of people in twos and threes shouting over the competing noise of the children in the terminal made Nurse dizzy.

"What is your occupation?" a customs officer half her age inquired. "Would you be stating your address in London for us," he barked at her.

A nurse, she replied, letting out a small giggle for no apparent reason, nodding at the strangers around her, making others in line uncomfortable. The young man, obviously new in his position, peered at her, giving her the jitters when he asked in what town was she employed. "Dublin," she said, her eyes blinking.

Do you plan to visit relatives in London, and if so, may we have their whereabouts? May we have a look in your suitcase?

To this final question, she said, no, no—she forgot some business and would be back. She had no intention of letting an officer see her personal items, her penknife and the rest of it. A small vacation in a hotel by the sea would be lovely for a few days, and she wondered if the twenty-five pounds Ben had given her would do. She hurried along by foot from the North Wall Terminal to the Heuston train station. She worried that the custom officer might have called the guards as two police officers stood on the next corner, observing her. She averted her eyes and pulled down her kerchief as if she were on the way to church. Why did she torment herself? She wished she knew. But there she was in the heart of Dublin, passing by the familiar blue and cream buildings, and then Mr. Tubs Launderette, imagining being dragged into a Magdalene laundry, door shut, gate locked, an officer patrolling the grounds. She imagined Sister Paulinas's face and then Castleboro, and suddenly, dots swam before her eyes. She took a deep breath and revived herself from the feeling of faintness. She found herself saluting the officers the way she automatically saluted a priest, and they nodded at her as she passed by.

As Adrian had suggested and Marian insisted, she stopped at a shop just outside the train station and pawned Marian's bracelet, receiving enough for a good lunch and a weekend stay at any fine boarding house in Portrush, the pawnbroker assured her. Off-season rates still applied in some establishments; in any event, she'd have no trouble finding a room.

Immediately upon the train's arrival in Portrush, she relaxed, took in the refreshing smell of the sea. She found herself sitting down on the street curb of an intersection about a ten-minute walk to the main attraction: the sea views and a littering of lively pubs at the pier. While eating an apple, she was approached by a tiny, wrinkled Sister with vibrant, gray-blue eyes, who warned her about the motorcars cranking by. "Are you lost?" the nun wondered.

"No, no—I have relatives in the area," Nurse lied. But if she could find Sister Paulinas's relatives, and then surprise her with updated news from Sister's hometown...but—no, no—she'd do no such thing. Or would she?

No, no—don't be a mentaller, she told herself, looking up at the wee nun's lively face. The only thing she'd like to remember from that place is her sister Anne and Officer Dolan. "No, no—I don't have relatives here. I'm only making a stopover on my way to London." Nurse rose suddenly, but confused, a fuzziness coming over her eyes, a tingling on her tongue, she sat back down and blurted that she was out of a job.

The old nun introduced herself as Sister Cecilia and offered her a room for the night. "You're knackered is all, just like me, you old goat," Sister Cecilia said. She laughed, and picked up Nurse's case.

Nurse stayed on with the small order of Dominican nuns, the Convent of Our Lady of Compassion, at their generous invitation in the neighboring seaside town of Portstewart. The Convent House overlooked the Irish Sea and no doubt had a positive effect on these fortunate nuns. Their views were spectacular and so were their world-views. They were open-minded, energetic and fun-loving, especially Sister Cecilia, who enjoyed a good game of gin rummy with her nightly gin aperitif. Around the fire one night, Nurse confided to Sister Cecilia about her relationship with Officer Dolan and told her about her daughter Beth, as well.

Throughout the remainder of August, Nurse sat on a green deck chair most days making rosary beads for the African poor. Noble work, Sister Cecilia complimented her often. Nurse hated making them as a child, the long tedious process and the wire cutting into her fingertips, but now looking out at the sea, she found the precision work engrossing. An antidote to her headaches and to the stress and confusion of trying to figure out how to spend the rest of her life.

"What to do with the rest of your life?" Sister Cecilia admonished Nurse one afternoon. "Get off your fanny. What is your name, your real name, for God's sake?"

"Ava."

"Ava what? Let's have it."

"McDonald."

"All right, then. Stop the malarkey. Use your name, for God's sake. You're a person first not a nurse, are you not?"

Sister Cecilia's words came out harsh, but her eyes, their shiny quality, said she was trying to help and was speaking out of loving kindness. The other nuns who laughed with Sister Cecilia, confirmed this, and sometimes Nurse would join in. They would all laugh at Sister Cecilia's rambunctious tone.

"You want to know my advice, Miss Ava McDonald?" she said now.

Ava nodded.

"It would do nobody any harm to write to this Officer Dolan. Perhaps he could track down Beth, you never know. He is an officer, after all. And he fancies you." She rose, hands on her hips, waiting for Nurse's reply.

"No harm, I suppose. I have his address."

53

On a late July afternoon, it was Officer Dolan himself who reached into the brass letterbox at the Garda Station and retrieved the envelope from the Convent of Our Lady of Compassion in Portstewart. Sister Cecilia's name was handwritten in black ink above the return address. Inside was a faded photograph—*Beth, 1948,* inscribed on the back. A letter asking outright if he could search for her file, they were kept in the metal cabinet in Sister Paulinas's office. She would await his reply. *Ava McDonald, sister of former headmistress Sister Anne McDonald* scribbled at the bottom, enclosed with a light blue rosary.

Besides feeling stunned that Nurse had a child, Officer Dolan, to his own surprise, missed the time spent with Nurse in the shed. He often wondered about her. So he saw this favor as an opportunity to see her again. Tickled he was, too, that she ended up in so lovely a spot.

The following Tuesday, at four o'clock sharp, while Sister Paulinas had her regular check-in with the Reverend Mother, Officer Dolan entered her office. With the help of Nurse's note, he found the file quickly and left with detailed information on the McDonalds' history. Most of the girls' files were nearly empty, but there was some general information about Anne, and about Nurse and her child, perhaps maintained by the late Sister herself. Officer Dolan used his skills in the field and tracked Beth down at University College Dublin. He found his way to her dormitory address and rang her, requesting a meeting about "a distant relative in trouble" and they set a time to meet.

Meanwhile, back at Castleboro, the missing file went unnoticed. A few days before he was to depart for a week's vacation in Dublin, Officer Dolan slipped the manila folder back into Sister Paulinas's metal cabinet, and left her office as quietly as he came.

With great anticipation and curiosity Officer Dolan set out for his meeting with Beth. Sitting at the last table at Brewbaker's, a small coffee shop across from University College, he ordered black coffee but didn't bother to look at the menu. Not yet eleven o'clock, the place was nearly empty and serving food was on no one's mind as the young waiters bustled to set up their stations. There was another group of three young people at a table in the window, and he wondered how he would recognize the young lady he was here to meet. Dolan had found Beth enthusiastic on the phone and was on the lookout for an eager type. And there, yes. He could guess that this rather large-boned young woman with a fashionable black handbag peering through the restaurant's door before she entered was Beth. Officer Dolan put up his hand and she waved, came bustling over.

"Sorry. I'm a bit late," she breathed, her cheeks flushed from the cold. She appeared to have been running, a bit out of sorts as she anchored herself in the wooden chair. He took a sip of his coffee to give her a minute to collect herself. She had all the qualities of the young and healthy about her: rushed, apologetic, a large appetite for drama in her manner. He wasn't really sure how to talk with her. She was so different from the inmates at Castleboro. She breezed out a bunch of words he didn't quite catch.

"Shall we have a coffee?" he asked as a waiter stood by their table.

"I'm grand," Beth said. "Nothing for me right now." Beth said hello to the fellow; apparently this was a familiar place for her.

She had a big, round face and a ready smile. "I'm sorry if I'm staring, but I haven't seen a uniform up close." She seemed fixated with the police cap on the table.

"Go on. Have a look," Dolan said, handing her the cap.

As she took the police cap in her hands, she began to talk quite naturally, and already he had the feeling this meeting, this discussion about Nurse, would be easier than he had imagined.

"May I, really?" She laughed.

"Go on," he said.

Beth had thin brown hair, not unlike her mother's, but worn pulled back. They talked of her school and her family and about the fact that she had made no decisions about her future, although she knew she was interested in police work. Officer Dolan told her about her birth mother and Beth seemed almost intoxicated with the idea of meeting her.

"I'm excited and interested and honestly grateful to you for finding me out, Officer Dolan. Do you think..."

"I know for a fact she wants to see you, Beth. Shall I make the call?" He pulled the phone number from his wallet.

"I'm so nervous, but, yes, how exciting!"

"I'll not be a minute," Officer Dolan said and went to the telephone box on the corner.

He reached Sister Cecilia with the news that he hoped to bring Beth to meet Nurse.

"Ava," Sister corrected him over the phone. "Call her Ava, always," she said. And then, warm but still brusque, Sister Cecilia none too politely advised them to get their bums up there, so the two boarded the train at Connolly Station for Colcraine, just four miles from Portstewart and the Convent that very afternoon.

Not three and one-half hours later, "No, no," Nurse said. Sister Cecilia hustled down the sloping lawns of the convent grounds waving her wrinkled hands wildly at her.

"You have visitors, Ava."

Nurse touched her hair. "I'm not prepared for any visitors, you can plain well see that."

"It was to be a surprise for you, you ninny. Since when is anyone prepared for a surprise?" Sister Cecilia said. "Save us your melodrama, Ava. You've been sitting on your fanny for weeks, for God's sake. Up, up, for God's sake. Greet your guests!"

Nurse blushed as Sister Cecilia pointed toward the open convent doors by the terrace. Officer Dolan waved, popped a mint into his mouth. She stared and saw clearly the girl by his side.

"Ah, my God!" she whispered.

Beth made the first move. She strode down the slope, smiling, her arms swinging, giving Ava pause. Not at all what she expected. She could barely budge. Officer Dolan followed behind Beth.

"No, no—I'm not myself today." She almost giggled, as Beth approached too closely. Then, Beth bear-hugged her.

"I won't stay long," Beth reassured her, still holding her.

"No, no—you should have told me. I would have–"

"You would have done nothing different," Sister Cecilia said.

Officer Dolan sauntered down and greeted Nurse with a wet, offhand kiss to her cheek, his tobacco and minty smells still delighting her.

"Ava, your daughter's a pistol," he said, and Beth laughed. "It's our little officer joke," he explained. Beth reprimanded him with a wave of her plump hand.

"I'll put on the tea," Sister Cecilia said. "Likely I'll put out the bottle of gin for Officer Dolan as well." The three of them managed a slow stroll across the hilly expanse of lawn, and Ava regained herself, just barely.

"Every time you feel nervous," Officer Dolan said, "think about Sister Paulinas and say 'to hell with you' to her again in your mind. You'll be all right."

The three spent the afternoon in conversation. Mostly Beth talking about this and that, about university and the future. She told Ava about her contented life with her adopted family and, at the same time, how she always wanted to know her real mother and often fantasized about meeting her.

"I'm thrilled to bits and grateful to Officer Dolan," Beth said.

"I've never stopped thinking of you," Ava answered quietly. "Thrilled to bits, as well," she blurted, thinking suddenly and with shame about her penknife as the blood was rushing to her head. She wondered aloud if maybe the visit should end, but Officer Dolan seemed to have another plan.

"You'll not keep us from the seashore. What do you say, Ava? Will you join us?" Officer Dolan coughed slightly. "I've decided to leave Castleboro behind now, Ava." He paused as Nurse blinked at him. "I'll be looking for work in Dublin, so we'll want a good rest before all that."

Nurse giggled, thought about Sister Paulinas' reaction when she learned that Officer Dolan had left, too. And by all appearances, to her surprise, he seemed to be telling her that he thought she might join him in Dublin.

"No, no," Ava answered, her eyes darting about, Sister Cecilia fussing about the room. "I have a letter you can bring to Marian for me. No, no—she'd be happy to meet you. And Father Brennan, he'd help you if you need a place while you're looking for work."

Officer Dolan nodded at her, and she turned away.

"Seriously," Beth whispered. "If you don't want—"

"No, no," Ava said, giggling again. Officer Dolan seemed to want to wipe the distress off her face. "You can't leave me here with Sister Cecilia and the others after I've seen the likes of the pair of you," she said in her mixed up way. Her attempt at humor brought an apprehensive smile to Beth's face and a scoff from Sister Cecilia.

"We can go hunting around for a B-and-B. I can afford a few days off before the job search begins," Officer Dolan said.

"You and I could share a room," Beth suggested. "And Officer Dolan could—"

"Beth. Call me Dan for now, would you?"

"He's off duty, so he is, Beth," Sister Cecilia interjected. "We all use our first names here."

"I'll go and get my case. If it's all right, Sister, I'll leave for a day or two."

"Go on, Ava. You can do as you like. I'll find someone else to torture with gin rummy for a few days," she said with a wink.

54

Adrian stuffed his pockets with day-old bread and escaped through the scullery door in the early morning. Never to be heard from again, he hoped. *And who is the eejit now, Brother Ryder?* Whenever they could steal the chance, he and Peter were smart to play on the outskirts of Surtane. He learned his way through the woods and through the fallow fields to Malahide Road. No more stuffing his pockets full of chestnuts with his friend. No more Peter at all.

After a full day in hiding and a sleepless night of terror stuffed inside an empty trash bin in Phoenix Park, Adrian spent another half day riding around Dublin on a city bus so he could get some safe sleep. He'd have his payback one day, he told himself as he stepped out of the bus past the hordes of people carousing up and down O'Connell Street. Adrian knew his escape would have had punishing repercussions for all of the boys at Surtane, and some would want to kill him. There would be no movies for months now, letters withheld, food further rationed. But maybe the Brothers would just as soon let him go, he thought, lowering his blue woolen cap. No doubt they'd be better off without bad blood. Let him starve, they might think, though he was sure he wouldn't starve. He ate the last crabapple he mitched from an orchard and stood silently in front of the Custom House with the lion and the unicorn carved in Portland stone on the roof and marveled at the beauty of it.

He set off for the dank cobblestone streets behind the quays, his feet frozen from wet puddles he walked into, the smell of urine in the air obscene. He watched a group of lorry truckers loading boxes of artificial manure from the Wicklow Manure Co., no doubt for farmers down the country. He'd gone to Dollymount beach once and seen the big ocean liners on the horizon and dreamt about Dublin's seaport with Peter, but this rat infested loading dock was no sandy beach and there were no picture book blue skies.

He'd be off to the big sea himself and a new life away from this rat's nest, he hoped, trying hard to locate the Jolly Roger Inn by the docklands near Ringsend. Small, rundown cottages littered the lanes, smells coming off the River Liffey of sewage violated his senses. He kept his head down past prowlers and pawnbroker shops, disheveled mothers pulling their prams and snotty nosed kids through the back alleys as the noise of the traffic and the dense smog polluted his thoughts of Rosemary. He hurried along, the darkening day giving him some relief from the strain of trying to look normal.

Past three o'clock this Friday, it was payday for dockers who started in the early morning hours before sun up. Weary men filled their pints at the bars, their shots of cheap whiskey lined the bars as well. It wasn't much longer before he'd found the scummy sign for the Jolly Roger Inn. The G hung crooked like a hapless drunk.

He opened the hotel door and saw a bustling crowd hanging off the bar, and there stood a thin girl in her twenties, lifting a tray of drinks to take to crowded tables of hungry men.

Sweet Jesus, be thou my love. He wouldn't have recognized her without staring hard, but sweet Jesus. There was her black hair, much longer now down her back. Three hundred days off his purgatory sentence for pure thoughts, Brother Mack had once told him. *Indulge me this one day, sweet Jesus,* he begged, looking at her curly hair, her weary face. Her once creamy complexion and wide-eyed expression gone.

She didn't see him and trotted off toward the hollering men.

Instantly he knew he'd have to find himself a job, get some money to help her. He took fifty pence from the money he taped inside his shoe, bought his first ale, and waited for her to return to the service end of the bar.

"Would you know who I could talk to about getting work?" he asked a mucky man beside him.

"What kind of a job you looking for?"

"On a ship."

"On a ship, he says!" The man patted his pal on the back. "He's looking for a job on a ship, he says," repeating the joke.

"A closed shop," a grubby man mumbled, sucking off the bones of his portion of ray, a few chips left on the plate. "Go on back where you come from."

"I'm a Surtaner, sir."

"What?"

"I've been living in Surtane," Adrian said.

"And what have you done to be put in Surtane?"

"What do you mean, sir?"

"What crime have you committed? Nothing too serious, I hope."

"I suppose my crime was being born, sir," he said, sipping his ale.

"Better than most, then. And your training," the first man continued, "or do you have any family connections?"

"None, sir, but I–"

"None! Oh, Jaysus." He couldn't contain himself from laughing.

"You're not going to walk down to the pier and start shoveling without a connection to you. You're going for a long walk if you do."

Adrian wiped his nose, lowered his eyes.

"There's been more than one murder on the docks," the man grumbled.

"Murders?"

"Ah, you can believe it now," the man said, taking a long swig of Harp's. "There's been a bit of back biting, you know what I mean, a lot of jealousies going round with some of them waiting for years for a bit of work, and then these young buggers with no background in it..." He guzzled his glass.

"Go and join the union and come back. We'll see you unloading soon."

"Thank you, sir." Rain slapping the windowpanes felt like stings on Adrian's cheeks.

"Come on, are you fond of drink? We'll buy you a few scoops."

"Sure, he looks like he'd lick it off a scabby leg," said another laborer who'd joined in to laugh at him.

"Leave the lad alone, he's only trying. Sure, you could be a casual—
if you get picked—but you wouldn't be getting your pin now," the
mumbler said. "You wouldn't want to try, hear?"

"Sure, he can go and talk to the foreman. He might be picked
every now and again for work, or at least you could rob yourself a
bit of coal for your poor old mother," the man said, pointing to his
own head in tribute to his intelligence.

The smell of dead fish stuck to the men, and Adrian turned away,
taking a sip of his ale. He found himself looking straight at Rosemary who had reappeared.

"She's a good one. I'll have her one day," the man said. "I'll have her,
I will." He nodded in her direction and nudged Adrian's arm.

"Over my dead body you'll have me," she retorted. "I'll have you
kicked out if you don't mind yourself, mister."

Like a dark angel Rosemary stood there, tightening the belt on
her loosely fitting dress. Adrian stared at her, a waif of a thing now,
the loveliest small face he'd ever seen. Big eyes looked at him. The ale
tasted bitter and woozy.

"Go on. Go over and introduce yourself like a man. You look as if
you could use a poke."

The men's breath smelled of whiskey and reminded him of Brother
Ryder. The waitress's eyes softened as she sauntered over to him. Men
lingered about her like mongrel dogs before a meal.

"Jesus Christ, I'm off," Rosemary said, untying her apron and
pulling Adrian out of the bar with the touch of her hand. "You're
not for real," she said, her voice hoarse. "Is it you, then?"

He nodded, felt a bit ashamed of his crew cut. Rosemary told
Adrian not to worry about the cackling calls from the men. She
flipped the finger at them and started up the street. He watched her
strut in black stiletto heels and a short dress and felt the man growing inside him. He followed her up three flights of narrow stairs and
watched her take out her key, looking over at him, her eyes trusting,
just the way he remembered.

There was a cot and a nightstand in the room. The stale smell of cigarettes and aerosol spray fused to the faded olive wallpaper, one chair by the window and a hot plate on a crate. Textbooks and notebooks and pencils were stored under the cot. He followed her over to the window and she put her hands on his shoulders, lowering him into the wooden chair. He fingered her gypsy-gold nylons, the buckle of her garter belt, looked into her heart-shaped face and told himself, *Don't believe what they've fed you all these years. You're a man now. It is the madmen that don't fit in, or why would they be locked up in there?*

"What are you doing here?" Rosemary asked, and he wanted to ask her the same thing.

"I was looking for you, Rosemary."

She turned away from the sound of her name as if reminded of someone else, and then she turned back smiling. Adrian grinned at the sight of her childlike mouth, with those Chiclet teeth he loved. Little crossed lovers missing the mark.

"I've come to marry you," he said.

"You're still such a boy, Adrian," she said, her dimples emerging.

"I'm a sad boy without you, Rosemary."

"You look sad." He turned away, but she pulled on his chin, touched his cheek, and he stared at her beauty, this girl who could show him what love is.

She flipped on the transistor radio on the windowsill. He turned it off.

"I can't bear the silence," she said.

"Say something, then."

"You look filthy."

He dared touch her breasts and she slapped his hand away.

"Watch yourself, young man."

"Talk to me, then."

"You can stay," she said, "but mind your manners, Adrian."

She flipped on the radio again.

Rosemary finally told him that she was no hooker, that she'd been with a man only twice, the boyfriend whom she'd met a few months back and who cherished her. The young gentleman she adored spent his nights studying to be an accountant. He promised that he loved her, that they would marry when they got on their feet. They'd see to their future.

Her beauty and womanly ways titillated Adrian. He wanted her comfort in a different way. She was still fairly innocent, and she knew the boy from the orphanage would not hurt her. They would not hurt each other. Despite all her recent headway, she must have been glad to see Adrian and knew that she herself could use some comfort.

He kissed her softly on the cheek and pulled off his work shirt. He moved his hands up her torso, grabbed her neck, rubbed her tense muscles until she gently untwined his grasp.

She leaned her body into his like a baby curling up to sleep, nestled her little head into his neck. He wondered where Sister Agnes had sent her, why she was all alone. No roommate. He looked around. There was the single ratty chair that had sat too many one-nighters. An ice box doubled as a stained counter, plastic plates on top. A clumsily closed box of Cheerios, a small bag of crisps. There could have been another easy chair or perhaps a table lamp but that would have blocked the ajar wooden door of the grim closet space. The loneliness was everywhere.

He stood, lifting her in his arms, and placed her on the bed, his limp rag doll, tossed and tired now. He lay beside her. He took off her stockings and laid his head on her stomach. "I love you," he said.

"No, Adrian. Just lie here next to me, wrap your arms around me if you need to and fall asleep with me. That's all."

He grabbed her wrists and pushed himself on top of her, but she shook her head no and he released his grip. She smiled up at him, and he smiled back at her, kissed her cheek and neck. She lightly rubbed his back and they lay there, their bodies close, the rise and fall of their breathing in sync.

The early morning light brought a thick, garbage smell from the docks and cast into view the grimy alleyways out the back of the seedy motel.

When Rosemary rose and began to dress, Adrian felt like ripping her clothes off her body.

"What about me?" he demanded suddenly, afraid she would run away, never to be seen again, never to be held by him again.

He grabbed her around the waist and she stopped, stared straight at him, and then laughed and played with his knobby head. He sensed her desperation. Lonely people can read each other's thoughts.

"What are you doing to yourself here, Rosemary? This isn't for you."

"I'm moving back into a hostel run by the Sisters of Charity, a lot better place than this dump. They've found me a receptionist job. I've been studying during the day and on my nights off from that rat hole. I'm going to complete my Leaving Certificate next spring," she said.

"That's grand, Rosemary. Fair play to you."

I love you! He wanted to scream it at her. But then he looked at her and wondered if she or anyone could love him.

"Talk to me awhile." He sounded pathetic clinging to her. "Where did you go when you left?"

"To a sanatorium." She lit a cigarette.

"I'm sorry, Rosemary. I never should have—"

"For God's sake, Adrian, it's nothing to do with you. Sister Agnes was looking to put me away. I knew it, and it's a miracle I'm not in there still." She put an arm around herself and took a deep, comforting drag off her smoke. "My aunt, she would have come for me within the year, but she died. Tuberculosis. I was almost sixteen, about to get out, but that put an end to it all. I had no one to stop that Viking. I'd like to strangle her. She had no call to that."

She took another drag. "I'll have to go back there, but I'm saving up the nerve."

"Why would you ever?"

She stamped the cigarette as if she were stamping on Sister Agnes. "Retribution. They nearly killed me in that half-wit place."

Smoke swirled around the single overhead light bulb.

"Yeah well, I've just escaped out of Surtane and am on the run." He sat up, started buttoning his dirty shirt.

She flipped the radio on loud.

"Turn that blasted thing off. I've spent years listening to military drills."

"You used to love that brown radio, remember?"

He grinned at her. "You saved me in there, you know that."

"Go on."

"And you saved me in Surtane. I thought about you all the time."

"I had no one in that loony bin. I would have gone mad without the people talking on the radio. Silence is unbearable."

"Rosemary, it is amazing what you can hear in the silence. A bit of solitude, it's the only way to survive."

"What about love, you big fool?"

"It is love. For me, it is the only true love."

He pulled up his pants, fiddled with the shillings in his shoe, looked at her willowy shape by the window.

"Go on, you haven't changed. It's still love you're after," she said.

"Yeah well, there's some things that don't change," he said, hoping to get another kiss out of her before he left, but he did not.

"We'll see you again," he said, lingering by the door.

She smiled at him. "My virgin lover. My young Adrian." And there was a feeling, somewhere floating between them in their counterfeit smiles, that this was more than likely goodbye.

55

Adrian rubbed traces of cyclamen lipstick off his collar and tried to clear his mind. A Saturday afternoon bus to Donnybrook to get more money, say goodbye to his family, hide out at Gran's for awhile, and then he'd begin to look for work.

It was after five o'clock. He knew he'd have to find food soon. The shops were closing and a gloomy fog rolled in as the bus stopped in front of Hansen's Sweet Shop. Newspaper boys younger than him were on every corner, shouting at the top of their lungs, shillings pouring into their black aprons as men in brown tweed suits descended with him from the crowded bus.

Jamming his cap low over his eyes, he kicked a can down the gutter of a side street, trying to look tougher than the boys in finer clothes clustered together down a cobblestone alley. He pulled his collar up around his ears, feeling out of place amongst the rushing crowds. Over one year since his summer visit, he still remembered the way to 5 Mount Eden Road. He watched the people coming and going, imagining fires warming their city flats. Never had he seen so many lighting adverts high above the shops. Two pigs playing ball with a sausage. A cat fishing for pinkeen. The adverts alone made him feel his hunger.

He thought of Rosemary and wished he were back with her in her dingy room, all warm and smoky. Odd and grand he felt today, though. Worth it all to have spent a night with her.

His mind was jumpy as he rushed through the back roads, and he reminded himself that he needn't worry so. *Someday I'll fit in.*

Adrian arrived at the house, scrambled up the drainpipe, and tapped on Johanna's window.

"Jesus, Mary and holy Saint Joseph!" she gasped. He put his forefinger to his mouth, and, like a tugboat, she pulled him through the window.

"Well if it isn't the flying nun herself!" she whispered.

"Peter's been murdered, Jo."

Adrian sat next to Johanna on her cushiony bed. Her eyes questioning, she let out a wrenching skepticism.

"They're calling it a suicide, but I know he was murdered. I have to get out of here. I don't have much time. Just needed to let you know. Tell Ma, I'm a runaway now. I'll be hiding out at Gran's until I can get away."

The beam of a torchlight shot through the window. Adrian ducked as Johanna crept over and glanced out.

"I don't see anything," she whispered. "Oh, wait. There's Mrs. O'Rourke."

"I have to go," he said and rushed down the stairs. Johanna followed him into the kitchen. "Tell Ma I could use a union card, that I'm heading to the docks to try and get work. I'll contact her somehow, but I've got to get out of Dublin or they'll hunt me down. Tell her I'm sorry for the trouble."

"Can I come?"

"Don't be daft, Jo," he said as they tiptoed around the kitchen. Scavenging a plate of cheese and some Walker's biscuits, he reached for an open tin of Heinz baked beans and it clattered to the floor.

"Shit!"

"Go," Johanna said. She looked into the living room and outside the bay window she could see two guards with batons. "Go! The police are here."

There was loud banging on their front door, and Marian hurried downstairs to see what was wrong.

"What's all this?" she said opening the front door, appalled to see the two officers.

"We've had an emergency call about an escapee from Surtane. You better tell the boy to come out," one barked at her and they pushed themselves into the foyer. They ran through the living room into the kitchen.

Adrian grabbed a heavy metal pot soaking in the sink. With a grunt, he threw the pot toward them. Jeyes fluid soap splashed everywhere.

He scrambled out the back kitchen door, crashing through the hedgerows when the guards seized him. They pulled him to the ground.

Marian screamed.

Ben suddenly appeared as Marian, using all her strength, tried to pull the men off Adrian.

"Shove off! Let him alone!" Ben shouted, kicking open the back door.

In the commotion, Adrian clambered to his feet and ducked around the front of the house where the guards chased him down and wrestled him to the ground again. With a strong knee in his neck holding him still, he was cuffed. As he kicked wildly to free himself, one guard raised his stick and beat him on his back.

Ben grabbed hold of the abusive police officer and delivered a swift, hard punch to the man's jaw.

Within seconds the other guard had Ben handcuffed. The one turned to his partner and the two jerked Adrian to his feet.

His eyes gritty with dirt, Adrian stood blinking at the guards.

"Leave him alone!" Ben shouted as the officers dragged Adrian toward a police car.

"They'll kill me in there," Adrian screamed. "I'd be better off dead than going back. I don't care anymore. I'd just as soon be dead."

Marian and Jo watched as a guard shoved Adrian into the police car. Ben was pushed out of the way.

Glassy-eyed, Adrian glared out the car window. Visions of Brother Ryder and Mountjoy prison filled his head. The terror of being locked away without ever being found again overwhelmed him.

"Please don't let me die, Ma. Please don't lose sight of me. Please don't..." he wailed, his cheek pressed up against the window. Marian knelt with her hand against the police car window as Jo stood by helpless.

"I just want to be small again so I can start over with you. I want

to be born again, begin at the beginning," he cried. Ignoring his an-
guish, a guard pulled a roll of tape out of the car and leaned inside to
tape his mouth shut.

"Take him out of that car! Untape him," Ben demanded as the
neighbors began to gather on the sidewalk.

"You're coming down to the station, Mr. Ellis."

"Take him out of the car! Take that tape off his mouth, for God's
sake. Look at the way you're treating him. He hasn't done anything!"

"Your boy has broken the law on two counts, Mr. Ellis. We don't
make the laws, but we do have to enforce them."

"What laws?" Ben bellowed.

"He's a runaway, charged with breaking and entering. He left Surtane illegally."

"We'll no longer abide by laws that are unjust," Ben shouted at the
officer as he was escorted to another police vehicle.

Adrian stared at his ma and his da, at Jo and all the neighbors as
the police car drove him away from his family.

56

Marian stayed behind, an inconsolable heap on the stoop. Johanna, too, hadn't the energy to move and stayed by her side. "Ring Father Brennan," Marian muttered. "Although God knows what good that will do."

Johanna left for the kitchen and made the call. Then Marian could hear her mopping the mess of beans from the pot on the linoleum floor. Marian knew Jo felt determined to put the pieces together, but she imagined the news of Peter's death must be overwhelming her. She could hear the heaves and the uncontainable tears coming from the kitchen. The mop streamed across the floor.

Mrs. O'Rourke walked over to Marian with Anna and Rona, a soda bread, jumping jacks, and a packet of pink gum cigarettes for Johanna in the girls' hands.

Looking up with squinting eyes at the faded mother, Marian said, "You don't give a tinker's ass about my son. Go on home."

"Take that inside, girls."

Marian brushed Mrs. O'Rourke away with her hand.

"Not true. I care about them all."

"You're nothing but a mole. Do you know," Marian began, and then broke down as if she were trying to remember what her mind could barely grasp. "He won't be allowed out of there," she mumbled. "Tell me, Mrs. O'Rourke. Why the hell did you ring the police that time? Why didn't you just ring me, tell me to come get my kids from the Donnybrook Church?" she said.

Mrs. O'Rourke looked stunned.

"I rang the ambulance. You know that," she said. "It was the medical people who took me to police because Johanna ran away. I tell her to wait while I call an ambulance for her. She was bleeding a lot. When I get back, she was gone. The medical men took me to police to help find her."

"We're neighbors," Marian said. "I wished you had just rang us, not an ambulance."

Mrs. O'Rourke nodded almost imperceptibly, saying nothing to defend herself. Marian glanced up at her. She looked drained by the whole ordeal, too. *Guilt will do that to a person,* Marian thought.

"I try to do a good deed, what a neighbor would do," Mrs. O'Rourke said.

"I don't need a meddling neighbor, Mrs. O'Rourke. What I need are friends."

Marian focused on several housewives loitering by her front gate. "I want to say to the lot of you, that I know you don't give a hoot. And that you're all a lot of tinkers." She paused, watching the reaction to her words. The ladies shook their heads no. "Though I see you're not tinkers exactly," she continued, a fit of defensive laughter coming out of her.

"Go on home, Mrs. O'Rourke. What more can we say?"

As usual Mrs. O'Rourke's facial expression was hard to read. Maybe there was nothing to read. Maybe her life was stunted for good.

Marian sighed and pulled what was left of herself together, and slowly made her way up the steps and through the front door.

57

During the seven-block ride to the Donnybrook Station, Ben continued his long rant against the system. What seemed like hours later to the bedeviled policemen, Ben was delivered to a cell, hoarse from the shouting. His final words echoed against the walls of the small station.

Officer George Conrad who was charged with guarding the prisoner made a grimace that told Ben he agreed with him.

"The children in those institutions," Ben shouted, insisting on being heard, "the laws don't protect any of them, not a single one."

Within the hour, Father Brennan arrived at the police station. Officer George Conrad took him aside and Ben overheard him confide to the Father that Ben's cellmate was potentially violent. Hoping this disclosure would encourage Ben's signature on the bail bond so he could be released, Father Brennan relayed the message and quickly discovered his niece's husband had no intention of cooperating with the authorities.

Ben would do nothing until his son was released from his "prison term" at Surtane, he declared.

Once again Conrad tried to reason with him, reminding him that the boy had been court ordered to put in a full stay until the age of sixteen, insisting that there was nothing anybody could do to change the outcome.

Ben roared. "Then I'll stay in this bloody hell until he's sixteen."

"Ben, there's no sense sitting in a jail," Father Brennan mumbled. "Don't you think you'll be more useful on the outside, Ben?" But Father Brennan's efforts were half-hearted. It was more than obvious that Ben was not about to back down, and although Father Brennan would not admit it, he admired Ben for his fortitude.

"Father, you know what we've been through. You know what Marian has suffered. You've seen Johanna's confusion," Ben said, and wiped sweat from his forehead. "I won't eat or drink until I free my son." He pounded the bar, shouting into the air after Father Brennan's retreating figure.

Throughout the gloomy night, Ben's guilt overwhelmed him. He admonished himself for asking only once, and meekly at that, to publish his comprehensive story about abuse behind the walls of industrial schools. When Mr. Darby had turned him down, calling his idea rubbish, he was embarrassed and never brought it up again.

Marian had been right all along. He had spent too many years backing down.

How had they justified the unthinkable: turning their backs on their first born?

58

Early the next morning, Marian and Father Brennan arrived at the police station.

"Where's my *maidelah*?" Ben asked Marian. He missed Jo and worried about how she was holding up.

"At home with the neighbors," Marian answered with a sigh, walking toward Officer Conrad and the front desk. Father Brennan followed her.

"He won't leave," Father Brennan whispered to Marian, looking over at Ben who was hanging on their every word.

"Would you be willing to help us with the Brothers at Surtane?" Marian said.

Conrad did not give Father Brennan a chance to respond. "I don't think a visit to Surtane is the answer," he said. "Better do some of our own digging first."

"That's right," Ben called from across the small room. "Let's check into the breaking and entering charge at the Ringsend hotel. That doesn't sound like my son."

"I agree," said Father Brennan, walking over to Ben. "We should stay away from Surtane for now."

Marian stood with her back to Ben at the officer's desk, talking quietly to Officer Conrad. Again, Ben's voiced boomed out at them. "Breaking and entering, my ass. Has anyone talked to the manager at the Jolly Roger? Who exactly has pressed charges against him?"

"Officer Conrad, you look like you know something. Is Brother Ryder involved?"

Conrad didn't answer. "I remember my own son at Adrian's age, caught shoplifting along with other indiscretions. Lord knows the trouble he might have found himself in or what godforsaken institution my son might have been sent to if I was not a police officer," he said to Father Brennan.

"Adrian has a friend staying there," Marian told Officer Conrad. "Nurse mentioned her."

Officer Conrad left his paperwork and joined Father Brennan in front of Ben's cell.

"Your wife is right. I made some inquiries late last night. There seems to be no one who knows the facts. Except a Rosemary, who indeed claims to be Adrian's friend and says he did not break into her room."

"All the lies," Ben answered angrily. "No doubt Ryder's involved in this. We've got to get into Surtane, Marian. We know they're hiding something." Ben turned to Conrad. "What about Peter Twombly's death? What I told you last night."

"I'll go to Surtane, ask some questions," Conrad responded.

"Marian, let's get Robert Thompson from the *Times* on the phone," Ben shouted.

She looked over at him, gripping the bars.

"Would we do that, Officer? Would we ring the *Times*?" Marian said.

"Tell him I'm here," Ben said. "And that I want to talk. Tell them I refuse to eat until justice is done."

"What are you saying, Ben? You'll lose your job," she said.

"I don't give a shit about my bloody job, Marian! Get him on the phone."

Marian heard her husband sound like the young man she'd married and sighed. She dialed, and held the phone receiver in the air.

"Get down here, Thompson!" Ben shouted at the phone. "I'm at the Donnybrook jail, being held for trying to protect my son. Tell Darby I will not sign any bond unless the guards get my son released from Surtane. God knows they'll kill him. They've killed enough souls already." He thought about Johanna again, no doubt sullen, home alone, panic-stricken.

"I have a right to protect my own son!" Ben shouted. He shook the prison bars with all the violence he could.

Marian put her ear back to the receiver briefly, then hung up.

"Thompson's coming down to the station, Ben," Marian said. She came to him and put a hand through the bars. He took it in his. Officer Conrad looked ragged to Ben after such a long night. The man spent hours trying to get some sleep but couldn't with all Ben's ruckus about Adrian.

"Johanna spoke to Adrian, and he mentioned a union card, Father," Marian whispered to her uncle, touching his arm.

Father Brennan looked into his niece's desperate face and found himself saying to Officer Conrad, "The Customs House could most likely get him a union card, couldn't they?"

"Yes, go see Mickey down there," Officer Conrad murmured into Father Brennan's ear. "Tell him George suggested it. He'll sort it out." Father Brennan glanced at the officer's cheek still swollen from Ben's blow and then at Ben.

"If you can help, Father, but if not, we'll manage," Marian said.

Father Brennan left the jailhouse. Ben was not sure the Father would be willing to break the law, to lie to a Customs Officer to obtain a union card for Adrian.

59

A band of undeterred wives from the neighborhood were milling in the Ellises' kitchen on Sunday afternoon, preparing a roast beef with drippings they would later serve with tea. There was an egg collection, sliced ham and cold meats. Whatever was left over would be taken home for their husbands.

At eight o'clock in the evening, Mrs. Brady arrived to prepare a light repast; the neighbors worked in shifts. The house had taken on the character of mourning, pettiness was put aside and people tended to the necessities.

Marian spent the previous night awake. Stomach or intestinal or posterior pains, she didn't know which kept her from sleep. She wondered if she'd ever be able to forgive herself for the pain she caused her child. *And Johanna,* she thought, *what of her?* Finally, she had no choice but to succumb to her faith, the little of it that remained. She had to trust in humanity, however harsh, and in a God she hoped existed. Rather than have the life sucked out of Adrian for another three and a half more years, she would have to bear the unbearable and come up with a plan to free him.

If Adrian were to be safe, he would need his freedom.

Marian sat on the stoop that Sunday with a strange serenity, a detachment, and a dull peace she could only attribute to exhaustion. The physical pains were gone and in their place was emptiness. She felt nothing. Marian accepted this for the moment and found a bit of relief in it. She could not expect to find peace if she forever blamed the State, or the Church, or God, or herself, or the times in which she lived.

The paradox taking seed inside her didn't come with an explanation. She needed to look at the situation in a different way. Her entire focus had to be on how to get Adrian out of Surtane.

Mrs. O'Rourke came to Marian's door, even after the previous insults, a barmbrack cake in her arms, and invited Marian over to her own house for tea.

Marian shook her head in disbelief. "A bit too late for any of that now. This time, tell the truth. You rang the guards?"

"I did no thing. I thought it was a burglar, yes, but I rang nobody," she said, her English deteriorating under the duress. "The guards were here. They came, yes. Somebody else must have rang them. Not me."

Marian grappled with the sequence of events, and for the first time she considered what Mrs. O'Rourke was saying as if it might well be true; the guards had said so themselves. They'd said that Adrian, for reasons unbeknownst to anyone at the time, had gone to Ringsend. A barman rung Surrane, and Brother Ryder rung the guards.

"Why do you hate me, Mrs. O'Rourke? I don't understand."

"I don't understand. It's me that don't understand."

Mrs. O'Rourke started to walk away. Marian took a moment to consider the possible reasons why the two of them had never liked one another. The most she could muster was a painful disconnect that disguised something similar in each of them. Perhaps Mrs. O'Rourke would have wanted to be invited for tea. Perhaps there was something essential missing from Mrs. O'Rourke's life, something that Marian couldn't have known. Marian had not taken on the mothering of a relative's kids, and she had no idea what a loveless marriage was like.

"Please don't go," Marian said quietly.

Mrs. O'Rourke turned, and they looked at each other. Marian began whistling on the stoop and looked at the ground, but it was clear when she looked back at Mrs. O'Rourke that their shared expression was one of relief.

"I never rang the guards. I always liked Adrian. He knows."

Marian shrugged as Mrs. O'Rourke walked back toward her, clutching the cake.

"Can I make tea? Let me explain myself, please. Johanna told me about this union card. Come. To my house, please. I tell you something, you'll see."

As Marian walked with Mrs. O'Rourke into the O'Rourke living room, she noticed a homemade picture frame. Mrs. O'Rourke smiled as Marian reached for the frame. This was the first time she saw Mrs. O'Rourke smile, and she looked with her at the photo. It was a picture of the four of them: Anna, Adrian, Jo, and Rona holding hands in swim caps, the O'Rourke's sprinkler in the background.

Marian let out a sad smile and put the picture down. For the rest of the evening, she sat at her neighbor's oak kitchen table. It had been before seven o'clock on Saturday night that Mrs. O'Rourke saw a figure climbing up their drainpipe, but she did not call the guards, she explained to Marian once again.

"The one thing that would kill me is not being able to protect my kids," Marian said to Mrs. O'Rourke.

They shared a smile this time, though neither of them felt any happiness. It was then that Mrs. O'Rourke told her own story, how she married her sister's husband to take care of her sister's kids, how this act had not been completely voluntary, that there had been family pressures as well.

Late that Sunday evening, Mrs. O'Rourke asked Marian to call her Barbara. She explained as best she could that she had two brothers, and a father before them, who worked the coalmines and that eventually, until World War II, the family managed to own Koliknova Coal Company. Now under the same company name the brothers held permanent positions in the largest state-run coal company in Poland.

Mr. O'Rourke briefly joined in the discussion. "Your boy seems he's got no other way," he said, "but that she make a call back home. They'll look after him for a while anyway," he advised. They agreed it was worth pursuing.

60

On Monday morning, Ben again refused his breakfast and the pen to sign the bail bond for his release.

Adhering to the law, Officer Conrad had no choice but to bring him into Dublin to the Four Courts Building for sentencing. Marian alerted Robert Thompson of this development, who told every newsman he knew. As the police car pulled up to the famous architectural landmark with its large green dome and stately entrance along the Liffey, a great crowd of reporters and pedestrians were gathered, pushing to get inside the building.

Ben sat in High Court for hours until he was brought before a judge. He, Father Brennan, and Officer Conrad spoke as Thompson and others jotted notes. Father Brennan came forward with some of what he knew about the Surtane School from giving Masses there: the unsanitary conditions of the heinous place, the nonexistent visits by the Health Board, the children's hunger. Officer Conrad talked of the charge of breaking and entering brought against Adrian by a bartender in Ringsend, who made the false accusation after a bribe from Brother Ryder. And then there was alleged abuse described by an unnamed source, including the inexplicable death of a young orphan named Peter.

The Ellis story spread quickly because of impressive media coverage, not to mention the growing public outcry.

With emotions running high, the judge ordered Ben to sign the bail bond for his release. Ben again declined, stating that he had principles and the law had to make provisions for cases like his. He was not the only one, he stated with force. There were thousands of cases yet to be heard, thousands of Adrians, he shouted. The judge warned him that if he did not sign, he would be held in contempt; if he did not sign, he would be sent to Mountjoy Prison indefinitely.

Still, Ben refused.

So it was in front of an increasing number of spectators that Ben was handcuffed and brought to the infamous Dublin jail.

Father Brennan sat in his easy chair, a glass of brandy in one hand, a prayer book in his lap, deliberating about how much he should disclose, whether he should help secure an illegal union card for Adrian. What he'd been asked to do was unlawful and, if discovered, he would be excommunicated or worse. No pressure if he couldn't get Adrian the card, Marian had indicated as they left the Four Courts Building Monday afternoon. "I'll get him out myself—no way that I won't. Just let me know by the morning," she said.

There came a shameful time in Father Brennan's life seven years ago when he experienced a spiritual crisis and sought help from his mentor, Father Flanagan. Father Flanagan tried to reassure him that no one knows the condition of another's heart, as he listened kindly and without judgment to Father Brennan's confession. The more Father Brennan focused and prayed, and willed God's peace to enrich his homilies, the more incompetent and alone he felt and the more frustrated he became with God.

It had been years since he had felt the joy of simply being in the presence of God, and he missed the peace it brought. Instead he was filled with an intense self-loathing brought on by what he perceived as his lack of depth, and this torment drove him further from the truth he'd once known. Over the years, the time he spent with Ben had been thought-provoking and fruitful. Although Ben's God was an intellectual one, these philosophical discussions somehow brought Father Brennan closer to his faith. But now this.

He felt yanked out of his ambiguous state to take some action to help Adrian. He was once again besieged by the terror of the unanswered question of whether he was a Pharisee or a Christian. The drama of the situation and particularly Ben's reaction to the predicament with Adrian, the pureness of his devotion, provoked new doubt within Father Brennan. Perhaps he didn't have enough compassion or desire or passion to be a priest.

Early Tuesday morning, during a confidential visit at the Mountjoy Prison, Father Brennan told Ben and Marian it would take twenty-four hours to process the union card. Men everywhere were clamoring for union pins; they'd get no work anywhere without one, and procuring one had become more than a dangerous business. Marian shared with Ben and Father Brennan her discussion with Barbara Koliknova O'Rourke. Trembling, Marian said that even if it meant sending Adrian far away, perhaps forever, she felt they must, for his own well-being. It was time to take matters into their own hands, she added. Everyone agreed.

Marian whispered the details as she huddled next to Ben. Barbara had notified her brother Jakub that Adrian would be on the Koliknova steamer from Dublin before dawn this Wednesday. Jakub would be there when Adrian got off the boat and would make arrangements for work: To load coal boats in Poland or be sent to the mountains to work in the coalmines.

Jakub Koliknova might impound his union pin, Father Brennan warned. Once Adrian reached Gdansk Port, he'd be at the man's mercy, and Father Brennan prayed aloud that he wouldn't be bringing him to Upper Silesia to work underground for free. He knew from the talk, too, how dangerous the coalmines were in Poland; diseases of the lungs befell many a Dubliner who was lucky enough to get work. Emphysema was a killer among the dockers. The living were losing their eyesight in droves. He kept to himself the stories he heard firsthand from priests administering last rites down the back alleys.

"I have other news," Father Brennan said, hoping to lighten their load. "The barman at the Jolly Roger Inn has dropped the charges. Officer Conrad rang me this morning. After all the press, there is hope," he added. "Inside of a year, you'll likely receive custody of Adrian."

"An Officer Dolan, Nurse's friend, paid me a visit as well," Ben whispered to him, but looked at Marian.

She rang Nurse last night, Marian explained, offering her congratulations on her reunion with Beth and asking for Dolan's help in their emergency.

Father Brennan brought Tuesday's *Irish Times* and showed them Ben's statement printed boldly on the second page of the newspaper. "Justice has her back turned on the people of Ireland," Ben quoted words written on a famous Dublin monument. Marian said the words brought her back to the beginning of their life together when the two of them were standing in Ben's mother's kitchen as Beva walked in like a general with leg wounds. The nervous woman had grabbed Ben's arm, touched the gold band on her son's hand. She stared at him, her eyes burning, but he didn't budge. He looked calmly back at his mother and firmly took Marian's hand in his, willing to take a risk on love.

63

Brother Mack placed a damp hand towel on Adrian's forehead as he lay in the infirmary recuperating from his Saturday night beating. He suffered serious wounds to his jaw and more than likely broken ribs. Three days ago when the Garda pulled up to the playing fields of Surtane, Adrian's mouth still taped shut, Brother Ryder took his usual stance in front of the eager, waiting crowd: dignified, his hands behind his back, he watched as the officers uncuffed the boy and the car pulled away. Crooning, jumping up and down, singing "A Nation Once Again," the boys cheered for the return of one of their own, his attempted escape an indictment of their odd brotherhood. Then, en masse, the lads pinned Adrian's kicking arms and legs as one of them punched him in his right eye. O'Connor and a few others hogtied his feet to his wrists and Brother Ryder raised his golf club in the air and slammed it down hard on Adrian's exposed feet. Another whack of the club against his back, and he fell into a stupor. Brother Mack appeared out of nowhere and stopped the attack.

Brother Ryder had laughed at Brother Mack's plea to put an end to the torture, his insistence that Adrian would not run again. "He won't walk again when I get through with him," Brother Ryder said. "Called us pigs. Thinks we're the ones need the Devil lifted out of us. I'll teach him to call me a pig." Ryder commanded the boys to strip him.

"You should never have gone to Ringsend," Brother Mack said now. "You should have come to me."

"I was trying to help a friend," Adrian said.

Brother Mack frowned.

"Isn't that what we're supposed to do, Brother Mack?"

"If we can."

"They'll make a murderer out of me yet," Adrian muttered, thinking about the knives in the bakery.

"What did you say?"

"I'll end up in Mountjoy."

"And to what end, Adrian? To who's good? Certainly not yours."

"How's my father?" he asked.

"He's there himself doing good work for you. You may yet be released from here; there's been talk of that now. They want to end your father's rants." He looked around, then pulled an *Irish Times* newspaper clipping hidden in his pocket. "Father Brennan's been here to talk with me about you," he whispered.

Adrian glanced at a picture of his da with his fist raised in the air. A bold caption stated, "This father won't eat unless justice is served." Adrian tried to picture his da in prison. "Might he forgive me, do you think, for messing up his life?"

"Your da loves you. Put away the talk of revenge, Adrian," he said, stuffing the article back into his pocket. "'Forgive them, Father, for they know not what they do.' Forgive me, too, for not protecting you from them," he said softly. Brother Mack would never forget the whiteness of Adrian's exposed neck, as the lads charged toward him with a thick rope, and he had felt the boy's desperate eyes follow the back of his black cassock as he walked away, resigned, seeking refuge in the chapel.

"You've been like a father to me," Adrian whispered back

"You'll be soon gone."

Adrian closed his eyes.

Brother Mack laid his head on top of Adrian's chest. Adrian put his arms around him and, with timidity at first, began to pat his back. Brother Mack stroked Adrian's bald head, kissed his brow.

For a few moments, they lay there quietly. Then Brother Mack whispered Father Brennan's plan. "Half an hour earlier than your normal rising. It's perfectly arranged, you need not worry," he whispered. "I'll make sure you're up and you'll go to the bakery as usual. Turn on the lights and wait for your mother by the back door."

Adrian stared into the Christian Brother's face.

Brother Mack unclasped a gold cross from around his neck and placed it around Adrian's.

"My father's, now yours."

Adrian didn't know how to respond. He said he couldn't believe that such a gift would be given to him and protested shyly.

"I want you to have it," Brother Mack said, urgency in his tone.

Adrian touched the cross.

"That's right, go ahead and hold it. Don't be afraid, you'll know what to do."

64

It was two o'clock in the morning when Johanna, who had been up all night, emerged from her room.

They sat, mother and daughter, in the back seat of Officer Dolan's new police car, the City of Ballsbridge embossed in gold lettering on the door. Marian put her arm around Jo's shoulder, looked unswervingly into her face, and told her that she was sorry, that things would get better. "I promise," she whispered, laying her head on Jo's shoulder and then they held each other for the forty-minute ride to Surtane.

They pulled up behind the school. Officer Dolan dropped Marian in the alley, turned off his car lights, and he and Jo waited silently in the dark for her return.

Inside, Brother Mack hurriedly made his way to the security guard station, an unusual look of desperation on his face. "I heard something outside. Quick, go check for vandals at the front entrance," he ordered the man on duty. Marian hunched low, heard their voices, and like a ghost, stepped quietly to the back gate. As soon as the guard left, Brother Mack let her in and she waited behind the bakery building until she heard footsteps and a light flashed on. It was Adrian, frail, one eye half open, blotches of purple and red covering his round face.

Without speaking, she grabbed his hand and hurried with him to the back entrance.

Behind the back buildings, she tripped on a piece of bark and fell into mossy grass. Adrian lifted her under her arms, and she scrambled to her feet, ignoring the throbbing pain in her lower back.

They made it out the gate and to the waiting car. She opened its doors for Adrian, motioned him inside, and handed him a change of clothes from a bag.

"What have they done to you?" Marian said in a voice below a whisper. She reached out and lightly touched his cheeks. His pitted

skin reminded her of a crushed grape. Her remorse over the botched
attempts to get him home reared up again.

He stared hard at her before he spoke. "Hogtied me to the pole,
Ma. Ran screaming for the shaving cream, nicked my head, beat me
senseless with a wooden golf club," he said, looking into her mourn-
ful eyes. "There was cheering and singing. They were singing 'A Nation
Once Again' before I passed out."

She touched his tender face, and she wondered about those boys
who watched the beating from the sidelines, those who left him there
naked, the rain bucketing. The blessed drops had soothed his
parched mouth, and when the harsh light coming from the high
walls of Dormo Three was switched off, he said he dared to loosen
the rope around his wrists. He slid down the pole, lay there in the
drowning grass, and watched the darkness descend. He wondered if
there were any amongst them who were aware that their silence at
his torture would surely kill them.

Marian angled her way into the middle of the seat and held
Johanna and Adrian close to her, despair and clarity entwined as she
felt their arms around her.

"Things will be better now." She whispered her words softly into
Adrian's ear, and then told him the details of the escape plan.

But Brother Ryder had noticed Brother Mack's light and then
heard the rustle of footsteps. From his window, he glimpsed a woman
and a boy limping behind the buildings and he himself fled to the
back gates. He ran to the infirmary, and there was Adrian's bed,
empty. Brother Mack was mulling about.

"You better not be in on this, Mack."

"No more than you are, Driver," Mack countered. "You might
need your golf club where you'll be going. You'll have no more use for
it here."

Down to the bakery Brother Ryder went, and the baker Bernard
Donnelly told him that he hadn't seen Adrian but that the light was
on when he arrived.

Enraged, Brother Ryder ordered all guards, both in the front of the school and the back, to scan the grounds for evidence of an escape. The police were phoned and a cab called. Ryder would go to Donnybrook, he raged, to retrieve the bastard himself.

Traveling at high speeds through the silent night, Ryder arrived at the Ellis residence. There he found a nun, dressed in her full habit and wimple. Ryder bowed respectfully to the Sister before launching into his tirade and asked to speak at once with Mrs. Ellis.

"Sister" Barbara explained politely that Marian and her daughter had gone to see the *Fairy Queen*.

Ryder's face momentarily confused and contorted at the comic book reference that was designed to infuriate him. Barely four o'clock in the morning, could it be any more obvious that this lying, stone-faced woman was there just to taunt him? Filled with poisonous venom, Ryder left for the police station, hoping like hell that the security guards or police had news of the missing boy's capture.

At the appointed morning hour of three o'clock, a security guard and personal friend of Officer George Conrad's retrieved Father Brennan from a hiding place inside the prison refectory and led him to Ben's cell. There they would wait for the bail bondsman, who lived in a cottage just outside the prison gates. Privately, without any publicity, Ben would sign the bail bond.

This time, there could be no leaks. There could be no press following them to the docks.

One slip up, one lazy link. A faulty alarm clock. Simple human error, and their plan would go awry. Where was the bondsman? No one wanted to show their apprehension, but as the minutes passed, and the hour of four approached, Father Brennan broke out in sweat.

"Fuck it all," Officer Conrad said, all formalities aside. "We have no more time. Get us out of here. I'm releasing you on your own recognizance."

The guard escorted them through a maze of underground tunnels to the ground level parking lot of the prison. There, Mr. O'Rourke waited in a friend's taxicab to take them to Dun Laoghaire Harbor.

"We've missed our mark," Ben said. "We took too long. We should have—"

"No worries, we're on our way," Father Brennan interrupted him. But he, too, had his doubts about whether they would make it.

"Speed it up, would you," Ben said, and O'Rourke nodded. He threw his cigarette out the window and sped through the foggy streets.

As they sat quietly waiting for Ben in the dark, Marian lightly moved her fingers up and down Adrian's arm and Jo's shoulder in soothing, circular motions.

There was only blackness now. Out the hazy window of the cab, Marian became acutely aware of the buzz of silence in the air. She no longer worried if Adrian was to be set free. Her eyes were trying to shut and she began to drift into a semi-sleep, her son's arm stretched around her.

She awoke from the murkiness to the *chjj, chjj* sounds of barn swallows and searched through the dark for the source of their song. Listening to their music, Marian nestled her face into Adrian's neck, aware of the synchronicity of the birds' voices and her own breath. She looked beyond the plate glass window through the gauzy gray and made out the sensual outlines of hedgerow bushes, watched the ghostly light ascend from the darkness. As the minutes crept on, a nameless calm descended upon them.

Marian escorted her two children from the car. She held tightly onto their hands, whispering to find courage, assuring them that the pain would pass away. Marian looked at her watch, looked up and down the empty streets along the harbor. Ben and Father Brennan had still not arrived.

"We have to get you on board," she said, and they began to walk toward the docks. There was no time or energy left for sentiment. Adrian had been filled in on the plan, and she promised him that custody would be granted or, well before a year was out, she herself would come and get him.

Marian handed Adrian a bag of sandwiches and a container of raspberry lemonade. She stuffed into his shirt pocket a photograph of them at Dollymount Beach. Johanna's arms were around his neck. She pushed a wad of bills forward. "Find a safe place for this," she said. "We'll send more."

Ben and Father Brennan's cab finally arrived at the docks. They shot out of the car and rushed toward the three shadowy figures in the distance. Ben sprinted ahead but knew not to call out to them.

Adrian stopped and turned. He watched his father rush toward them, his great-uncle gasping behind.

Finally Ben stood awkwardly next to his son. They eyed each other tentatively. Marian couldn't help but notice how gaunt and exhausted her husband looked. Adrian put the cross dangling around his neck under his shirt.

"I'm sorry, Da," Adrian said, but his da hugged him.

"Shush." Ben kissed him softly on the temple. "I've always wanted you, Adrian. Always wanted you, you must remember that. Go on. The boat won't wait." His voice was hoarse.

Father Brennan handed Marian the union card for Adrian and a union pin that would give him legitimacy if there was trouble on the ship. The priest made the sign of the cross and left.

Crews of rough boys from the Ringsend gang were already working on the docks, emptying coal boats, two and three thousand toners, up to their eyes in coal. Their young features were buried beneath the grime. On the stern of a large steel vessel, Koliknova Coal was engraved in onyx block letters.

Adrian walked to the end of the concrete pier, twelve-and-one-half years of age, and jumped aboard the Koliknova Coal Company's steamer. The ache in Marian's chest as she watched him was familiar and would never completely go away, but she was not the same woman she had been thirteen years ago. Crushed grapes turn into God's wine, Father Brennan used to say. She would never again allow herself to be cowed into doing something she knew was wrong. Let them come and get her if they dare. This time she was doing right. And this time she would permit herself the feelings of loss and sorrow, grief that she had been previously denied.

She knew, too, that there was no gain in continuing to blame herself. She had been young and confused, manipulated and selfish. She hadn't stood up and been the mother her baby needed. She hoped with all her heart that as her son grew up, he would find a way to forgive her. She yearned for forgiveness but understood that she had to muster compassion for the guilt-ridden young lady she had been. No point burying her before making peace, before saying farewell.

"He'll be throwing up in no time if he isn't water-oriented. Are you water-oriented, boy?" a shipmate jeered.

"Don't call me boy," Marian heard Adrian tell the crew cronies, unafraid of this lot, Marian was sure. He'd seen his share, at least he had that. He took his lemonade and sandwich out of the bag and threw them whatever was left. He watched as they greedily grabbed at the food. He stood on the deck and looked out at his ma, his da, and at Jo.

Marian watched her young son from their place on the granite steps and remembered with regret that in the scurry to get Adrian aboard, he had no time to hug his sister goodbye. She glanced at Ben and Jo beside her, a trinity of sorts, as Adrian's figure grew smaller and the ship slipped away.

Noticing the rags and other garbage the low tide brought in, Marian waved to the son who had been ripped out of her arms long ago. Watching him disappear from her life yet again, she felt the pit of mourning and let out a silent scream.

She needed someone to touch. She took Ben and Johanna's hands in hers. It was a cold, fall morning. A cloud of coal dust and smoke swept the shore. Marian no longer believed in God as she'd been taught, but she did believe in love. She knew this fight was not over, and she would protect her children as fiercely as she must in the months and years ahead. There were the sins of the past and the future, a certain sadness would always remain, but she would never allow her newly found convictions to desert her. Her private shame and resentment were dying, leaving her open and searching and without hate.

Foghorns blew from a distant lighthouse, its beam blinking in the hazy dawn. A rising mist of light along the waterway would guide Adrian's journey.

A READING GROUP GUIDE for THE WHIPPING CLUB

1. Can you understand why Marian chose to conceal her pregnancy from Ben? Why did Ben go keep up the pretense of not knowing?

2. What role did Father Brennan play in all of this? Is he the voice of the Catholic church?

3. What role does "Nurse" play in the book? What were her intentions in revealing to Marian that Adrian was still at the orphanage in Dublin?

4. Why was Jo so quick to protect Adrian?

5. Why do Johanna and Adrian play so roughly together? Is this normal play for any brother and sister, or is it heightened somehow by their unusual situation?

6. What specific themes did the author emphasize throughout the novel? What do you think she is trying to get across to the reader?

7. How did Marian and Ben's marriage evolve over the course of the book? How did Adrian influence their relationship?

8. Was it fair for Sister Agnes to yield so much power over the Ellis Family?

9. How did Adrian's upbringing at the orphanage affect his personality? In what ways did the abuse he underwent manifest itself?

10. Did certain parts of the book make you uncomfortable? Although this book takes place in the 1960's, in your life, do you see some of the same painful issues still resonating?

ACKNOWLEDGEMENTS

This novel benefitted from the generous support and expertise of people from all walks of life and on both sides of the Atlantic. It gives me particular pleasure to thank Da Chen, Donnybrook Garda Station, Paddy Doyle, Bernadette Fahy, Fairfield University MFA colleagues and friends, Joan Cusack Handler, Tom Jenks, Pamela Malpas, Mike Milotte, Mary O'Connor, the late Mary Raftery, Scott Snyder, The Briscoe Family, The Fairfield Public Library, The Pequot Library, Pauline Turley, Rob Weisbach, Michael White, May Wuthrich.

To my editor, David K. Wheeler, my deepest gratitude for your poetic sensibility and nurturing spirit and to Laura Barkat, the publisher who first believed and then shepherded this labor of love into the novel you hold in your hands, my heartfelt gratitude.

CPSIA information can be obtained at www.ICGtesting.com
Printed in the USA
BVOW021658070312

284658BV00002B/1/P